Promise of Pleasure

CHERYL HOLT

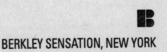

BERKLEY SENSATION, NEW YORK

THE BERKLEY PUBLISHING GROUP
Published by the Penguin Group
Penguin Group (USA) Inc.
375 Hudson Street, New York, New York 10014, USA

Penguin Group (Canada), 90 Eglinton Avenue East, Suite 700, Toronto, Ontario M4P 2Y3, Canada
(a division of Pearson Penguin Canada Inc.)
Penguin Books Ltd., 80 Strand, London WC2R 0RL, England
Penguin Group Ireland, 25 St. Stephen's Green, Dublin 2, Ireland (a division of Penguin Books Ltd.)
Penguin Group (Australia), 250 Camberwell Road, Camberwell, Victoria 3124, Australia
(a division of Pearson Australia Group Pty. Ltd.)
Penguin Books India Pvt. Ltd., 11 Community Centre, Panchsheel Park, New Delhi—110 017, India
Penguin Group (NZ), 67 Apollo Drive, Rosedale, North Shore 0632, New Zealand
(a division of Pearson New Zealand Ltd.)
Penguin Books (South Africa) (Pty.) Ltd., 24 Sturdee Avenue, Rosebank, Johannesburg 2196,
South Africa

Penguin Books Ltd., Registered Offices: 80 Strand, London WC2R 0RL, England

PROMISE OF PLEASURE

A Berkley Sensation Book / published by arrangement with the author

PRINTING HISTORY
Berkley Sensation mass-market edition / April 2010

ISBN: 978-0-425-23508-9

BERKLEY® SENSATION
Berkley Sensation Books are published by The Berkley Publishing Group,
a division of Penguin Group (USA) Inc.,
375 Hudson Street, New York, New York 10014.
BERKLEY® SENSATION and the "B" design are trademarks of Penguin Group (USA) Inc.

PRINTED IN THE UNITED STATES OF AMERICA

10   9   8   7   6   5   4   3   2   1

To Karen and Cindy for taking a chance on me—
when I needed it most.

. . . MONSIEUR PHILIPPE DUBOIS . . .

offering only the finest in female restoratives!

Love Potions!

Invigorating Tonics!

The Latest Therapies Known to Man & Science!

A Woman's Daily Remedy
for Improved Contentment!

Curses Foiled!

Romances Found!

Broken Hearts Mended!

SPINSTERS CURED!

Chapter 1

BARNES MANOR, RURAL ENGLAND,
JUNE 1814

"FETCH my blue dress."

Mary Barnes glared at her half sister, Felicity, and asked, "Which one?"

"The blue one! The blue one!" Felicity snapped. "Which one do you suppose?"

"You have *eight* blue dresses," Mary said. "Could you be a tad more specific?"

Felicity spun toward the mirror and primped her blond ringlets, dimples creasing her rosy cheeks. "Bring me the one that sets off the color of my eyes."

Felicity's eyes were a lovely sapphire that any fabric would enhance, but no gown could disguise the fact that she was spoiled and horrid. Mary seemed to be the only person who had noted Felicity's fickle temperament, but then, Felicity was very rich, so many sins could be overlooked.

With each passing month, as Felicity was courted by various gentlemen who hoped to marry her, she grew more vain and impossible. As a wealthy heiress, she had swains fawning over her, and she could be very choosey. So far, she'd found none of them to be acceptable.

Jordan Winthrop, Viscount Redvers, was the next candidate scheduled to visit, so the stakes were very high. Felicity would probably insult and snub him as she had the others. Mary yearned to inquire as to why Felicity bothered with any of them, but she wisely kept her mouth shut.

Early on, Mary had learned that it was useless to speak with Felicity about any topic of import. The eighteen-year-old girl was so conceited, her sense of entitlement so vast, that normal conversation was a waste of breath.

Mary went to Felicity's dressing room and retrieved an enticing gown suitable for Felicity's introduction to Lord Redvers. The material would hug Felicity's plump figure, which was a shape men were said to enjoy. Not that Mary had had any experience in masculine preferences.

At age twenty-five, she'd had scant male attention. Her own figure was slender and willowy, the exact opposite of Felicity's, but Mary was also poor and plain, so it was difficult to assess why men never noticed her.

As her stepmother, Victoria, constantly harangued, there were a myriad of reasons for Mary's lack of suitors, but she valiantly strove to ignore them.

Why feel sorry for herself? With no dowry and no prospects, she couldn't alter her fate.

She returned to Felicity's boudoir and draped the gown across the bed. On seeing it, Felicity grumbled, "Oh, for pity's sake, that's not the one I wanted."

"It's fine, Felicity."

"The shade is completely wrong for me. Can't you do anything right?"

Several bitter replies coursed through Mary's head.

Had any woman in all of history ever suffered so egregiously? Had any woman ever been so unappreciated? Surely even Cinderella's lot hadn't been as bad as Mary's!

She whirled away, planning to stomp off in a huff, when Felicity complained, "Where are you going?"

"I have better things to do than stand here and let you scold me."

"But what about Viscount Redvers? I'm not ready to greet him."

"I don't care. Call for your maid."

Mary stormed out, so angry she felt as if she might explode. In the past, she had calmly tolerated Felicity's vitriol and spite. But lately, Mary was changing.

She was questioning her plight, her lowly status.

Her father had been a prosperous merchant, her mother a gentleman's daughter who'd died when Mary was born. Victoria was his second wife. She'd birthed him two more daughters—Felicity and her older sister, Cassandra—then he'd passed away, leaving Mary alone and unprotected.

Mary had endured unending torment at the hands of her malicious relatives, and she was beginning to rebel. Why had Felicity and Cassandra been given so much and she been given nothing at all?

Mary longed to marry, to have a home and family of her own, but their neighbor, Harold Talbot, was the only suitor who'd evinced any interest in her.

He was forty and still lived with his widowed mother. Supposedly, she'd refused his request to wed Mary, and he kept dangling the idea of a betrothal someday *soon*, after his mother was deceased, but that day never seemed to arrive.

Mary had waited through a decade of his broken promises, and her patience was exhausted. She was anxious for something—anything!—to happen that would improve her condition.

She slowed her pace and continued to the other wing of the house, to the grand suite where Viscount Redvers would reside for the next month.

She'd supervised the servants who'd prepared his rooms,

and while she didn't give two figs about Felicity or her marital schemes, Mary hoped he'd be impressed.

The space was magnificently appointed, fit for a king, and she tiptoed about, smoothing a quilt, rearranging the flowers in a vase, then she entered his dressing room.

It contained an ornate mirror, and she studied her reflection, critically evaluating herself. She hated her looks. As Victoria bluntly reminded her, she was too short, too thin, too dark, too ordinary.

In a world where nearly everyone was blond and blue-eyed, her hair and eyes were brown. Her skin was unblemished, her teeth straight, her cheekbones high, but with her hair pulled back in a tight chignon, and swathed from chin to toe in an unflattering gray dress, she might have been a dowdy nanny or an irritable governess.

For a brief instant, she wished she was pretty and rich like Felicity and Cassandra, but she tamped down the notion. She'd never wanted to be *like* them.

"What would I do with a fortune anyway?" She sighed.

"Why would you consider wealth to be cumbersome?" a male mused from behind her. "I've always been able to devise numerous uses for large amounts of money. It's really not that difficult. You'd be surprised at how quickly you adapt."

Mary whipped around, coming face to face with a man who had to be thirty-year-old Jordan Winthrop, Viscount Redvers, the only son and heir of the Earl of Sunderland.

He was very tall—six foot at least—and very handsome, his features masculine and perfect: high forehead, strong nose, generous mouth. His hair was black as night, his eyes a deep indigo, like the sky at sunset. His legs were impossibly long, his waist narrow, his chest and shoulders broad and muscled—which she could clearly see because he wasn't wearing a shirt.

She didn't think she'd ever viewed a man's naked chest before, so she hadn't understood that it would be covered with hair. It was dark as the hair on his head, thick across the top, then tapering down his stomach to disappear inside his trousers.

Though she couldn't fathom why, the sight was exciting and disturbing.

Why hadn't she been notified that he was on the premises? How would she explain her lurking in his private quarters?

Gulping with dismay, she made an awkward curtsy. "I apologize, milord. I wasn't told that you'd arrived."

"I was just about to wash. I asked the footman to send someone to assist me, but I didn't realize he'd be so accommodating. I'll have to convey my gratitude."

She blanched, eager to rush out, but he was blocking the door, her sole route of escape.

They were in an isolated part of the mansion, and he was renowned as the most infamous rake in the kingdom. His dastardly repute was built on amorous peccadilloes, duels, debts, and deceits.

He might do anything to her.

He took a step forward, and she took one back, until she was at the wall and could go no farther.

Evidently, he presumed that she would bathe him. Did the housemaids attend guests in such an outrageous fashion? Was it common?

How could Mary not be aware of such illicit behavior? She spent enough time with the servants; she should have had an inkling of what went on behind closed doors.

What might a woman do for a man like Redvers? She wished she knew. A more brazen female would probably have poured water in a bowl, dipped a cloth, and swabbed it all over him, but she never would.

In her entire life, she'd never committed a single daring act, and she wasn't about to start now.

"Would you . . . you . . . excuse me?" The quaver in her voice apprised him of how he'd unnerved her.

"No."

"I'm not about to help you wash."

"You're not?"

"No."

He chuckled, a low, seductive baritone that tickled her innards and made her knees weak.

"You don't have to pretend," he said.

"Pretend what?"

"You don't have to play the shy maiden with me—unless you enjoy a good fantasy? I don't usually care for games, but I'm happy to oblige you."

He took her hand and placed it on his trousers, as if he expected her to unbutton them. Her knuckles brushed his flat belly, and she yanked away and huddled against the plaster, feeling like a canary that had been cornered by a very large, very hungry cat.

He drew her to him until her torso was crushed to his, and the intimate positioning had a peculiar effect on her anatomy. Her skin prickled, her breasts ached, and the mysterious woman's spot between her legs grew relaxed and wet.

"I demand that you let me leave," she said.

"No."

"Please?"

"No."

"You've made a mistake."

"Have I?"

"Yes. I'm not here to . . . to . . ."

"To what? To *fornicate*?"

"That word"—she scowled—"what does it mean?"

"What do you suppose? It means every wicked deed you can imagine—and even some you can't."

She had no idea what he was describing, and she wasn't in any mood to find out. Especially from a notorious libertine who had come to Barnes Manor to discuss marriage with Felicity.

"If you continue," she threatened, "you'll be sorry."

"I doubt it. I've never been *sorry* about anything. Ever."

"But you don't know who I am."

"I don't care who you are. You're very pretty, which is all that matters to me."

At his remark, she was frozen with surprise. No one had ever told her she was pretty. In fact, her stepmother insisted she wasn't, as did her tepid beau, Harold.

The odd compliment distracted her, so she was unprepared for him to bend down and nuzzle at her nape. His bold advance was so shocking—and so delightful—that she was paralyzed, unable to fight or flee as she ought.

He nibbled away, his crafty fingers sneaking up, caressing her thigh, her hip, rising till he audaciously stroked her breast.

She hadn't realized the mound was so sensitive, and she became so agitated that she might have swooned, but his strong arm kept her from falling to the floor in a stunned heap.

"Please . . . stop," she breathlessly murmured.

Her plaintive supplication registered, and he pulled away and frowned.

"Aren't you carrying your maidenly protests a tad too far?" he asked. "You're too old for all this virginal umbrage."

"Old! I'm only twenty-five."

"Then quit acting like a debutante. I don't like it."

Just then, the door to the outer chamber opened, and a female called, "Redvers, are you in here?"

Mary didn't know who had arrived, but if she was caught with the viscount, there'd be hell to pay. She squealed with alarm and tried to draw away, but he wouldn't release her.

"Who's out there?" she whispered.

"It's my special friend, Mrs. Bainbridge." He appeared humored by Mary's panic. "She won't like finding you with me."

"Let me go!" she begged.

"No."

"Redvers," Mrs. Bainbridge called again, as she marched toward the dressing room.

Mary pushed at him with all her might, but Redvers merely

laughed and turned them so that he was leaned against the wall, with Mary snuggled to him, her back to his front. His arm was draped across her abdomen, holding her in place.

A voluptuous beauty entered. She had auburn hair and big green eyes, and she was attired in a stylish maroon gown that accented her striking features. She oozed a sophistication and polish that Mary couldn't have managed in a thousand years.

"Who is *that*?" Mrs. Bainbridge inquired, nodding at Mary, her displeasure clear.

"The footman sent me a valet," Redvers explained, "but she's the wrong sex and she's terribly prim and boring. May I keep her anyway?"

Mrs. Bainbridge's gaze was lethal, and she assessed Mary as if Mary were a pet dog. "No, you can't *keep* her, darling. I won't have you trifling with the servants."

"She was about to wash me," he claimed.

"I was not!" Mary seethed, but they ignored her.

"If you need washing," Mrs. Bainbridge declared, "*I* shall tend you. Don't pester the hired help." She glared at Mary. "Be gone, you filthy harlot, and if I catch you sniffing around the viscount again, I'll have you whipped."

"I'm going, I'm going," Mary muttered, stumbling away from Redvers.

She skirted Bainbridge and hurried into the adjoining bedchamber.

Cheeks burning with mortification, she slowed, trying to regroup and ease the rapid pounding of her heart. What had just happened? And what should she do about it?

Would Redvers tattle to Victoria? Should Mary, herself, confess what had transpired? What would she say? That she'd been groped and maligned by a reprobate?

Gad! Mrs. Bainbridge had to be Redvers's mistress, yet he'd brought her to Barnes Manor with no thought to Felicity.

How could Felicity marry him? He was depraved in a manner beyond comprehension.

While Victoria had first crowed over Redvers's visit, she'd

been brutally frank about his scandalous character. But had she been informed as to the extent of his corruption?

Victoria was a baronet's daughter, who'd married down by accepting Mary's father. She'd never forgiven him for her plunge in status, and she was determined to rectify her mistake by arranging a lofty union for Felicity. Victoria was set on the match with Redvers—as was Felicity herself.

Dare Mary enlighten them as to the true state of his degeneracy? Would they be concerned about it?

As Victoria often counseled, a woman could overlook many faults in order to become a countess.

Feeling conflicted but more calm, Mary was about to tiptoe away when she noticed the door to the dressing chamber hadn't shut all the way; she could peek through the crack and spy on Redvers. And though she was positive she'd be damned for all eternity, she did exactly that.

Mrs. Bainbridge was standing very close to him, stroking a wet cloth across his chest and stomach.

"Better?" she asked as she tossed the cloth on the floor.

"Much."

"I can't believe you let that drab little maid assist you."

"She was convenient."

"If I hadn't walked in, I suppose you'd have had her skirt up over her head."

"Most likely."

Mrs. Bainbridge leveled a glance that was meant to both chastise and seduce.

"You know I detest it when you dabble with slatterns."

"And you know that it's none of your business. Don't presume to scold me."

She scowled as if she might quarrel, but on seeing his stony expression, her pout changed to a smile.

"You are the worst libertine in the world," she charged.

"I've never denied it."

"Let me remind you of why you don't need anyone but me."

"Yes, why don't you? My encounter with that little *drab*—as you call her—has left me out of sorts. Why don't you do something interesting to earn your keep?"

"You don't pay me any longer, remember? Not since your father snipped the financial cord."

"Then do it for free—and get on with it."

"Ooh, you are such a wretch! Why do I put up with you?"

"Because you're mad about me, and you know it."

"I know nothing of the kind."

"Give over, Lauretta," he chided, using her Christian name. "You're a mercenary, and you've cast your lot with me. Your claws will be dug in till I've inherited and spent my old man's last farthing."

"Yes, they will, and Felicity be damned."

"Yes," he concurred. "Felicity be damned."

Their cold words cut Mary to the quick. She wanted to sneak out, to escape the evil pair, but despicable as it sounded, she remained rooted to her spot.

Mrs. Bainbridge grabbed the waistband of his trousers, pulled him to her, and initiated a passionate kiss. Their lips were melded, their arms entwined, their hands everywhere, and Mary watched, agog, as they writhed and touched.

Other than a hasty, furtive embrace she'd once witnessed at the harvest fair, she couldn't recollect ever having seen two people kissing. She hadn't understood that it would be so physical, and the spectacle rattled her.

She felt tingly all over. Her nipples hardened and throbbed; her heart started pounding again.

Mrs. Bainbridge pushed him out of sight, which irritated Mary enormously. She couldn't see them, but she could hear their groans and sighs, the rustling of fabric. A few minutes later, Mrs. Bainbridge moved back into view. There was scant evidence to clarify what had occurred, but the woman's dress was askew and her hair had fallen from its combs.

She flashed a confident grin at Redvers. "Next time you consider embarrassing yourself with a housemaid, please recall that I'm your mistress. No one can satisfy you as I can, and don't you forget it."

"I'll try not to," he tepidly replied, yawning.

"You are such a rude beast!"

In a snit, her hips swaying to and fro, she sashayed from the room. Mary couldn't make it to the door without Mrs. Bainbridge observing her, so she dashed over and hid behind the drapes until Mrs. Bainbridge exited into the hallway.

As her footsteps receded, Mary was anxious to creep away undetected. She peeked out, but Redvers was over by the dressing room, leaned against the doorjamb, waiting for her to emerge.

She gasped with dismay.

"She's gone, my sly voyeur," he said. "Would you like to continue where we left off?"

He'd seen her? He was aware that she'd been spying?

"Aah!" she shrieked.

"Did you enjoy the show?" he asked, smirking.

She blushed a dozen shades of red. "You are the most disgraceful, disreputable person I've ever met."

"I'm sure that's true."

"I have to tell Victoria what you're really like," she absurdly threatened.

"She already knows."

Mary spun and fled, his contemptuous laughter ringing in her ears.

Chapter 2

MARY dawdled in the dining room and stared out the window across the garden to where Viscount Redvers was strolling with Felicity. With him so tall and dark, and her so shapely and fair, they were a striking couple. It was difficult *not* to watch them.

Redvers was very dashing, very gallant, and he chatted with Felicity as if she was the most unique woman in the world. His behavior was perfect, providing no hint of the depraved character lurking inside, and Felicity appeared to be charmed.

Mrs. Bainbridge pranced along behind them, accompanied by Mr. Paxton Adair, who'd been introduced as Redvers's best friend. He was handsome, too, but with golden blond hair and piercing brown eyes. He seemed of an age with Redvers, and he possessed a similar sophistication and refinement.

He'd bragged about being the illegitimate son of an earl and scraping by on minimal funds—as was Redvers. Both men had exhausted their fathers' generosity. Both had been disavowed. Both were flat broke.

According to gossip, Adair made his living through gambling and vice, and he was purported to be even lazier and more wicked than Redvers.

With Redvers, Adair, and Mrs. Bainbridge as her guests, Victoria had to be hosting the most scandalous trio in the kingdom. Mary understood that Victoria hoped for Felicity to marry into the aristocracy, but honestly! Were there no limits as to what was allowed?

Apparently not.

Victoria was sitting at the table, watching Redvers, too. Her other daughter, twenty-two-year-old Cassandra, sat with her. Mary went over to them.

"I don't like Lord Redvers," Mary said when Victoria glanced up.

"So?"

"He'll make Felicity miserable."

"Every husband makes his wife *miserable*," Cassandra interjected. "It's the way of matrimony."

Cassandra, a widow, was blond and blue-eyed, as pretty as Felicity but not nearly so plump. At age sixteen, Victoria had wed Cassandra to an elderly baron who'd turned out to be a brutal despot. Once, she'd been as haughty and sure of herself as Felicity, but time and cruel experience had smoothed over her more disagreeable tendencies.

She was no longer conceited or confident. She never smiled.

"I've heard," Mary pressed, "that he has no conscience or scruples."

"I've heard the same," Victoria divulged.

"Don't you care?"

"Not particularly."

Victoria shifted on her chair, her heavy weight causing the wood to creak in protest.

As a debutante, Victoria had been a beauty, but at her current age of forty-five, her looks had faded. Her hair was a dull silver, and she had frown lines circling her mouth. She loved to eat, and as a result, was very fat.

Her baronet father had been strapped for cash, so Victoria's dowry was very small. She'd ended up shackled to Mary's prosperous father, but his money hadn't bought her any happiness.

She was selfish and moody and never satisfied. Not with her home. Not with her daughters. Not with her servants. And most especially, not with Mary, whom she'd never liked.

"Why are you so concerned about Felicity?" Victoria queried. "Her marital negotiations are hardly any of your business."

"I think he's wrong for her."

"And who would be more *right*?" Victoria sneered. "He's a viscount; he'll be an earl. Nothing can change those two vital facts." She waved her hand, dismissing Mary. "Go away. You annoy me."

Mary peeked at Cassandra, wishing her half sister would offer a supportive comment, but Cassandra merely shrugged as if to say, *what did you expect?*

Without another word, Mary left them.

She couldn't figure out why she was complaining about Redvers. Felicity could wed whomever she wanted. It just seemed inequitable that, while Mary constantly dreamed about marrying, Felicity would choose Redvers with barely a thought as to the consequences.

Mary had the same Barnes's blood running in her veins, had had the same wealthy father. Why couldn't *she* have a suitor like Lord Redvers?

Previously, she hadn't minded Victoria's obsession with making brilliant matches for Felicity and Cassandra. Mary had deemed it all so much nonsense, but recently, the unfairness had begun to gnaw at her. She didn't even like Redvers, but he'd stirred a pot of restlessness that had her boiling with frustration.

Why couldn't she—just once!—be the girl everyone adored?

She'd intended to go to her room and sulk, but instead, she headed for the woods and the path that led to the house where Harold lived with his mother.

As she moved into the trees, she saw Harold coming toward her, which wasn't surprising. The supper hour was fast approaching, and he had a habit of showing up at Barnes Manor as the meal was about to be served. Victoria always invited him to stay.

He was fussy and bookish and pudgy—the total opposite of masculine, vigorous Lord Redvers.

Normally, she ignored Harold's plain features and persnickety routines, but with Redvers's arrival, she had grown critical. After meeting the viscount, Harold seemed ordinary and . . . and . . . boring.

There! She'd admitted it. He could be positively tedious, and it galled that she'd had to set her sights so low.

"Hello, Harold," she greeted as he neared.

"Mary, I've advised you not to walk through the forest unescorted. Why won't you listen to me?"

It was a recurring argument she couldn't win. "You know I'm not allowed to use the carriage."

"Then you shouldn't visit me."

"But I had to see you. It couldn't wait."

"What is so urgent?"

"I'm tired of keeping our betrothal a secret, and I want to have the banns called at church."

"Call the banns! Are you mad? Mother would never agree."

"Harold, you're forty years old! Inform her that it's going to happen—with or without her blessing. She'll come to accept it."

"What if she doesn't? What if the news sends her into a decline? I won't be responsible for . . . for . . . killing my own mother!"

"I'm not suggesting you *kill* your mother," she snapped. "I simply want to marry you. Is that a crime?"

"We'll have plenty of time to tie the knot after the old girl passes on."

"I want to do it now."

"It's out of the question."

His obstinacy incensed her, and contrary to how she typically acted, she refused to take no for an answer. She stepped in, so close that her skirt brushed his legs. At her bold advance, he looked as if he might faint.

"What are you doing?" he inquired.

"I'd like you to kiss me. You never have, and I'm asking you to."

"What?"

"You heard me. Kiss me. Right here. Right now."

"You *have* gone mad. Mother always said you were too—"

She grabbed his coat and shook him. "Stop talking about your blasted mother! If you don't kiss me—this very second—I can't predict what I'll do."

She yanked him to her and pressed her lips to his, and they stood like two marble statues. It was awkward, it was horrid, it was embarrassing, and it was completely different from the torrid embrace she'd witnessed between Redvers and Mrs. Bainbridge.

Disheartened and dismayed, she released his coat and moved away as he retrieved a kerchief and mopped his brow.

"What's come over you?" he sputtered.

"Nothing. It was a moment of temporary insanity."

"It certainly was, and I must tell you that I didn't care for it."

"I wasn't exactly thrilled myself."

"I'm not a spontaneous person, Mary. Nor am I the sort to appreciate a physical display. I can't believe you'd instigate one."

"Neither can I."

"I'm disturbed by your behavior."

This was the spot where—usually—she'd have profusely apologized, but she couldn't bring herself to grovel. When it became clear that she wouldn't, he bristled.

"I'd intended to join you for supper," he huffed, "but I've changed my mind."

He spun and proceeded for home.

* * *

JORDAN Winthrop, Viscount Redvers, gazed across the park as the little drab from the previous day marched into the trees. She was definitely on a mission, prepared to knock heads together, or perhaps rap a few knuckles with a ruler.

Who was she? *What* was she?

A loafing housemaid? A prickly governess? The preacher's unhappy wife?

Any choice seemed likely.

He couldn't explain why, but she'd caught his notice. In a mansion brimming with blonds, she was a refreshing brunette, though with her hair squeezed into that tight bun, it was difficult to discern that she had hair, let alone the shade.

She was very pretty, with a pert figure and big brown eyes, and he'd been amused by their encounter in his dressing room. He was a cad and a scapegrace who went out of his way to offend, but still, it was shocking that he'd dallied with Lauretta while knowing that an innocent spectator lurked on the opposite side of the door.

Even by his low standards, it was despicable conduct.

"Who is that woman?" he inquired of Victoria, pointing at his prey as she was swallowed up by the forest.

"No one of any account whatsoever," Victoria replied in her usual haughty tone.

He couldn't abide Victoria, and he was already calculating how to ensure that he never saw her again once he and Felicity were wed.

"I didn't ask her status," he retorted. "I asked her identity."

"She's my stepdaughter, Miss Mary Barnes."

"Really? I wasn't aware that your late husband had had another child."

"Why should you have been apprised? She's of no consequence to your situation."

"Too true."

Yet he couldn't keep his attention from wandering to the spot where she'd vanished. What was she up to?

He was positive that—whatever her plans—they would be more intriguing than his. Supper and cards with Victoria, Felicity, and Cassandra would entail hours of dull conversation that not even Paxton could enliven. Jordan would much rather spend his evening teasing and tormenting Mary Barnes.

"Did Mr. Barnes leave her as rich as Felicity and Cassandra?" he asked.

"No, she's poor as a church mouse."

The news was so unfair. Why dower two daughters but not the third?

"So she's never married?"

"No. She's resided here as my ward and benefited from my charity."

"Lucky girl."

"She certainly is."

Jordan was being facetious, but Victoria was too thick to realize it, and his interest in Mary Barnes spiraled. What a horrid life she must have led!

He wouldn't want to be beholden to Victoria for anything. She was too conniving, and if Jordan's father hadn't cut off his allowance, Jordan wouldn't have bothered with her. But desperate times called for desperate measures.

He'd wed Felicity, deposit her fortune in his bank account, and be forever free of his father's domination.

That didn't mean he had to like Felicity—or even be courteous to her. In fact, after the ceremony and consummation, he doubted they'd ever fraternize, unless he bumped into her at an occasional London party.

"And what is your opinion, Felicity?" he queried.

"About what?" she simpered.

"About your sister, Mary Barnes. Is she a *lucky* girl?"

"I hardly consider her to be my sister, Lord Redvers. She's always been little more than a servant."

"Does she brush your shoes and iron your gowns?"

"Of course," she said arrogantly, apparently presuming he would be impressed by snobbery.

He was being facetious again. Felicity didn't notice his sarcasm, but, like mother, like daughter, intellect was not her strong suit.

He ushered the women to the foyer, and they proceeded up the stairs to dress for supper. When he should have followed them, he found himself marching in the other direction, gleefully eager to discover Miss Barnes's purpose.

Within minutes, he was out in the forest, and it didn't take long to locate her. She was down the path, talking to a chubby, balding fellow who—from his prissy attire and demeanor— Jordan knew he would loathe. Neither of them had noted his quiet approach, and he rudely spied on them.

From how they were arguing, it was clear that they were well acquainted, but even so, Jordan was stunned as Miss Barnes suddenly grabbed her hapless companion, pulled him close, and kissed him.

The incident was too humorous for words, and it was all Jordan could do to keep from laughing aloud.

They drew apart, her partner giving her a good scold. Then he huffed away, and Jordan shook his head in dismay.

Lucky girl, indeed.

She looked so sad, so beaten down, and he felt a peculiar stirring of sympathy.

Why had he watched her being humiliated? If she turned and saw him, she'd be mortified. He was disgusted by his crass conduct, just as he was annoyed that he'd suffer any compassion for her.

What was the matter with him? Why was he tagging after her like a besotted swain?

He'd worked to cultivate his image as a wretch, and it wasn't all show. His father's constant and harsh criticisms had molded Jordan into the contemptible reprobate he'd become.

Jordan had been the second and flawed son who'd been unable to replace his perfect older brother, who'd drowned when Jordan was a boy.

Jordan's father was convinced that Jordan was a useless incompetent, and Jordan delighted in proving him right. He'd behaved badly for so long that he'd forgotten how to commiserate or care.

As Miss Barnes spun toward him, prepared to slither home in defeat, he'd recovered his aplomb and any concern for her was vigilantly masked. He was casually leaned against a tree and grinning from ear to ear.

On seeing him, she blanched.

"Hello, Miss Barnes."

"How do you know my name?"

"I made it a point to find out. After our previous meeting, I couldn't bear that we hadn't been properly introduced."

"You are such a liar."

"Don't you want to know my name in return?"

"I already know it—*Lord* Redvers—and I wish I didn't."

"You may call me Jordan when we're alone. May I call you Mary?"

"Never, you bounder. What are you doing out here?"

"Following you."

"Following me! Are you insane?"

"It's often claimed that I am, but mostly I'm just aggravating as the dickens."

He pushed away from the tree and started toward her.

"Hold it right there." Her palm was extended to ward him off.

"No."

"I'm serious. Don't come any closer."

"Women have been ordering me about my entire life, but I never listen."

"How much did you see?" she demanded.

"Enough."

"What does that mean?"

"It means you could benefit from some lessons in kissing, and I'm volunteering to be the one who provides them."

"Ooh!" she fumed. "You are a swine and a bully."

"And those are my good qualities."

A veritable ball of umbrage, her fists were clenched, her body trembling, her brown eyes ablaze with fury.

She was a petite, slender jewel, hidden in a dowdy gray dress and severe hairstyle. Beneath the bland exterior, she was actually quite magnificent. Had any man besides himself ever noticed?

Her face was heart-shaped and lovely, her skin creamy and smooth, her lips red and lush as a ripe cherry. In a fashionable gown, with a low-cut bodice and a tightly-laced corset, she'd definitely be a sight.

He reached out and—quick as a snake—yanked a few combs from her hair. The lengthy tresses, shot through with strands of red and gold, tumbled down her back in a rich, mahogany wave.

She yelped with outrage. "You are the most offensive, ill-mannered cur I have ever—"

"Who was that fellow?" he interrupted.

"What fellow?"

"Your partner—and I use the term loosely—in passion."

"You must be mistaken. I was out here by myself. The whole time."

"You deny that you were kissing a man?"

"To my dying breath," she insisted, and he laughed and laughed.

"Miss Barnes, you certainly know how to brighten up a boring afternoon."

She glowered. "If you ever tell a single soul, I will kill you in your sleep."

"Mrs. Bainbridge would miss me if you did."

"She'd likely be the only one."

"I'm sure you're correct."

She shoved him, hoping to flit by and continue on, but he was too much of a boor to let her go with any grace.

He clasped her wrist and tugged her near, and he could sense that she was terrified as to his intentions, and he wasn't clear, himself, as to what he planned. He wasn't about to become involved with Felicity's spinsterish half sister, so what was he doing?

He hadn't a clue.

"Let me show you something," he said.

"I'd rather you didn't."

"I told you that I never listen to women."

"Couldn't you turn over a new leaf just for me?"

"Why would I want to?"

He drew her even nearer so that her entire front was pressed to his. He could feel her thighs, her mons, her belly, and most of all, he could feel her pert breasts crushed to his chest.

At the naughty contact, his anatomy reacted so vehemently that he frowned, not able to understand her allure. For some reason, she spurred his desire to misbehave. If he lingered too long in her presence, he couldn't guess what transgressions he might commit.

"I'm going to kiss you," he advised.

"You are not."

"I am."

"I forbid it!"

"I don't care. I'm going to do it anyway. Close your eyes."

"No."

"You need this from me."

"I don't."

"It will work wonders for your character."

"My character is fine just the way it is."

"No, it's not. Trust me: You need a thorough kissing like no woman I've ever met."

She appeared firm and adamant, determined to deflect any advance, which was absurd. Why fight the inevitable? It seemed as if fate was carrying them along, and he could no more avoid kissing her than he could will himself to stop breathing.

"Close your eyes," he said again, and he dipped down and touched his mouth to hers.

In the history of kisses, it wasn't much about which to brag. He didn't maul or grope, didn't hug or fondle—though he did stroke a curious hand across her soft, beautiful hair.

Other than that, he simply stood very still, the sweetness of the moment sinking in, and he had to admit that he'd never felt anything like it.

He pulled away and scowled at her, and her expression wasn't much better. They were both surprised; they were both irked. There was an unwonted connection between them, and they were flustered by it.

"That was . . . was . . ." she stammered, struggling to describe what had happened, but she couldn't quite clarify it.

"Let's do it again," he amazed himself by saying, and he bent to her, frantic to initiate another kiss, but craving so much more.

For the merest second, she permitted the embrace, then she lurched away.

"I don't want this from you," she claimed. "I don't want this at all."

She pushed by him and ran, and for a crazed instant, he considered shouting her name, chasing after her, catching up to her, and . . . and . . .

The ludicrousness of the notion astonished him.

What was he thinking? She was a flirtation, a passing fancy. Nothing more. Nothing less.

With her gone, the magic that had fueled the interlude vanished, and what they'd done seemed silly and strange.

Why was he so affected by her? Why had he fallen under her spell?

If the deserted spot could produce such bizarre conduct, perhaps he was standing on bewitched, fairy ground.

He shuddered, then started after her, walking slowly, as if he had all the time in the world.

Chapter 3

"LOVE potions! Medicinal tonics!"

Mary stared down from the curricle at a peddler, who was hawking his wares by the side of the road.

"Love potions! Medicinal tonics!" he cried again. "A cure for every affliction known to man!"

It was market day in the village, and Felicity had asked that Mary accompany her to carry any packages.

Mary usually enjoyed the outing and went along eagerly, but when she'd agreed, she hadn't realized that Felicity had also invited Viscount Redvers. He was driving, and Mary was squished onto the too-small seat, with Redvers in the middle and herself and Felicity on either side.

Her thigh and arm were pressed to his, and though she squirmed and shifted, there was nowhere to move so that he wasn't touching her.

He kept glancing over at Mary, as if they shared a naughty secret—which they did. Once, when Felicity had been looking in the other direction, he'd even winked at Mary.

Every time he opened his mouth, she braced, certain he was about to reveal their shenanigans in the woods. So far, he'd been blessedly silent on the issue, which she deemed a miracle.

He was more obnoxious than anyone she'd ever met, and she couldn't figure out why he hadn't seized the opportunity to humiliate her. No doubt he was waiting for the exact moment when he could inflict the most damage.

She'd never been so uncomfortable, and she was grumpy and exhausted, having lain awake all night, pondering their kiss. She hated to admit that it had been marvelous, and the thrilling episode left her overly depressed.

As Felicity proceeded toward matrimony, Mary seemed further away from it than ever, and she was desperate to change her fate.

"Oh, do stop, Redvers," Felicity gushed when she saw the peddler's brightly painted wagon.

Redvers tugged on the reins, expertly bringing the horse to a halt. "Needing a *love* potion, are you, Felicity? Would you like to climb down and sample his merchandise?"

"I hardly require a potion to make men fall in love with me." She placed a coin in Mary's hand. "Mary, find out if he has any green ribbons for sale."

"And if he doesn't?" Mary queried.

"Buy me some at the milliner's in the village."

"How am I to get home?"

"You'll walk. How would you suppose?"

Mary always walked to the village and back, so she wasn't surprised by Felicity's pronouncement. Nor was she upset by the contemptuous tone in which it was delivered. Felicity didn't understand how awful she sounded, and she'd view her conduct as a means of showing off for the viscount.

Mary had only inquired because if Felicity needed Mary while shopping, or if Mary couldn't be found when Felicity was ready to depart, Felicity would erupt in a rage.

Mary couldn't win, no matter what she did, and she was in no mood for one of Felicity's tantrums.

If Redvers hadn't been with them, Mary would have voiced a caustic retort, but with him watching, she ignored Felicity and slid down from the high perch, declining his offer of assistance. As her feet hit solid ground, he leaned over the rail.

"You're looking a bit peaked, Miss Barnes. Why don't you buy a ribbon for yourself, too? Try a red one. It might put some color in your cheeks."

As if she were a begging pauper, he dangled a coin between finger and thumb, and she gazed up into his blue, blue eyes, wondering why he'd be cruel to her in front of Felicity. Felicity's derision she could tolerate—she was used to it—but his was too much to bear.

She was about to stomp away in an embarrassed huff, when Felicity said, "Honestly, Redvers. Don't spoil her! Next I know, she'll be demanding lace for her petticoat!"

Mary's temper flared, and merely to spite Felicity, she plucked the coin from Redvers's grasp. He laughed, cocky and confident in his ability to induce her to take it. He clicked the reins, and they sped off, dust from the wheels wafting over her as she struggled to calm her fury.

It was pointless to let Redvers's behavior bother her. He was a dandy and a fool, and after he wed Felicity, Mary would likely never see him again. He and Felicity would move to London or wherever it was that he kept a house.

He was insignificant to her future, yet his disdain hurt.

How could he cavort with her one day—as if she was special, as if he relished her company—but treat her like a servant the day after?

She took a deep breath and shook off his condescension. Why dwell on it?

She went to the peddler who, unfortunately, had observed the pitiful scene. He was very handsome in a rugged way, young and dark-haired with olive skin and black eyes that made her assume he was a Gypsy.

"Bonjour, Mademoiselle Barnes."

Mary scowled. "Why do you know my name?"

"The monsieur mentioned it."

"Oh."

"I am Philippe Dubois, and I am so very happy that you have stopped at my humble cart."

"Hello, Mr. Dubois."

He had a charming French accent, and he swept up her hand and gallantly kissed her knuckles. He glanced down the road to where the curricle had disappeared, and he clucked his tongue, his expression sympathetic and concerned.

"The grand gentleman," he said. "He does not love you?"

"No, of course not."

"But you wish he did."

"No, no."

"I can see, *cherie,* that you don't tell me the truth. Will he marry the blond beauty, instead?"

"It's being arranged even as we speak."

"Ma pauvre amie," he mused. "What will become of you when he does? Will your heart break?"

"Definitely not," she scoffed. "I'm here to purchase some ribbons. Have you any?"

"You do not need ribbons. But something else, perhaps?" He led her around the wagon to a rack filled with bottles and jars. "Would you like a potion to change his mind? Or maybe a curse so she grows ugly and old?"

"No, just ribbons."

"How about a tonic that makes you irresistible to him? You slip it into his soup or his brandy, and after he drinks it, he will kill to have you."

Mary chuckled, humored by his aggressive selling. Unsuspecting females often acquired these sorts of fake medicinals—and swore by them—but she was a modern woman and unaffected by superstition or nonsense.

There was no cure for what ailed her.

"I'm not marrying Lord Redvers. I wouldn't *want* to marry Lord Redvers. He would be absolutely wrong for me. So if you have no ribbons, I'll be going."

She might have left, but he clasped her wrist, turned over her hand, and studied her palm. He traced a finger over and over the center as if an imperative message was written there.

After a lengthy assessment, he sighed with dismay.

"What?" she asked, even though she hadn't planned to encourage him. "What do you see?"

"You would like to marry someday, yes? But just not the fancy lord?"

"How did you guess?"

"It is what all women crave."

He evaluated her, and it seemed that he could read her mind, that he comprehended how lonely she was.

"You have hopes for a certain man," he said, "but he has never appreciated you. He has never valued you as he ought. Am I correct?"

Stunned by his perceptive abilities, she gaped, then nodded.

"Well . . . yes."

"*C'est scandaleux!* You've been waiting so long! You've been so patient!"

She nodded again, her discontentment bubbling up. "I suppose I have been."

"I have what you need," he claimed.

"You do?"

"Here."

He opened a small box and retrieved a vial containing what appeared to be red wine. He placed it in her palm, carefully, as if it was priceless and fragile.

"What's in it?"

"It is the Spinster's Cure."

"The what?"

"The Spinster's Cure," he repeated, as if it was a remedy with which everyone was familiar.

"You're joking."

She tried to give it back to him, but he wouldn't take it.

"You laugh now," he advised, "but you do not understand magic."

"Not only do I not *understand* magic, I don't believe in it."

"You will," he vowed. "If you drink this tonic while staring at the man you are destined to wed, you will have him as your husband. Within one month, he will be yours."

"He will not."

"He will! *Je garantie!*"

She peeked in the vial, shook it, sniffed it. "What? No eye of newt? No bat's wing? It looks like wine to me. It doesn't seem very mysterious."

"Pah! I don't need a witch's brew to help you. This is an ancient recipe passed down from my grandmother—and all her grandmothers before her."

Obviously, he'd seen Felicity and Redvers giving her money, and he was hoping to wheedle it out of her. But she wasn't about to be gulled into parting with it for a worthless elixir.

"No, thank you. I don't require any assistance in managing my personal affairs."

He scrutinized her, then threw up his arms in disgust. "You think I cheat you! You think I try to steal your money with false healing! So . . . you will have it for free."

"Have what?"

"The cure! You will have the Spinster's Cure for free. I can't bear that you are so unhappy, so it is my gift to you."

He pressed the vial into her hand and curled her fingers around it, as if sealing the deal.

"I don't want it," she insisted a final time.

"Yes, you do. Just remember: You must drink it while staring at your true love. While staring at him! *Il est tres important!* Do not forget!"

"I won't, I won't," she grouched, deciding it was pointless to argue.

"When it works, and you are blissfully wed, you will return and pay me double what I am owed."

"I'll be sure to," she fibbed, intending that they would never cross paths again.

She hurried off, the tiny vial hot on her skin, and she thought about tossing it in the ditch, but for some reason, she didn't.

She tucked it into her reticule to keep it safe and sound on the long walk home.

PHILLIP Dudley who—when he was running a scam—went by the alias Philippe Dubois, peered down the road, watching Miss Barnes scurry away.

He was a charlatan and confidence artist. His expertise was honing in on a mark's weakest spot, on manipulating it, and he earned his living through deceit and chicanery.

"Did she say her surname was *Barnes*?" his pretty, sensible sister, Clarinda, asked as she climbed down from the wagon.

"Yes." His French accent was suspiciously absent.

"Isn't that the name of the top-lofty family over on the estate?"

"I believe so."

"Is it wise to scam her then? She could bring a load of trouble down on us."

"The rich are the only ones with money for frivolities."

"Money!" she scolded. "I didn't see any coins change hands, and I was spying on you the whole time. You have to stop giving away your concoctions. How are we to eat if everything is free?"

"Consider it an investment. She'll reflect on what I told her, she'll fret over it, then she'll drink the tonic—after which it will fail to work, so she'll come back for other remedies."

"For which she'll pay dearly?"

"Of course. We'll be able to stay in the area for weeks— maybe months—on the cash she'll fork over."

"I don't know, Phillip. She might be a Barnes, but she seemed impoverished to me. You saw her dress. She's nearly a pauper."

"But in affairs of the heart, finances don't matter," he sagely counseled. "She's lonely and alone, and she's desperate to be loved. She'll try potions; she'll try curses; she'll try blessings, and I happen to have them all in ample supply."

"The poor, gullible fool," Clarinda grumbled.

"Isn't she, though?"

"Who'd want a man that badly?"

"You'd be surprised."

"WHERE are my ribbons?"

"What ribbons?"

"The ones I asked you to buy from that peddler," Felicity said.

"Oh . . . ah . . . he didn't have any."

Mary glanced away. After her ludicrous discussion with the smug vendor, how could she be expected to recollect something as silly as hair ribbons?

"Why didn't you get some at the milliner's?"

"I completely forgot. I'm sorry."

Mary looked around the parlor. She was seated on a sofa with Victoria and Cassandra, waiting for the butler to announce supper. Redvers was present, as were his guests, Mrs. Bainbridge and Mr. Adair.

Mary had tried to refuse the invitation to dine, but Victoria had insisted, claiming Redvers had requested it, which made the event all the more wretched.

Why would he care if she attended? Why torment her?

With the group attired in their finery, she was conspicuously out of place. She had two dresses—a brown one and a gray one—with the brown being the newer of the two, so she'd worn it to the meal, but she couldn't bear to appear so frumpy.

Especially in front of Mrs. Bainbridge, who constantly smirked at Mary's plain clothes.

Since Mary hadn't purchased Felicity's ribbons, Felicity would pitch a fit, and Mary hated to have Redvers witness it.

She loathed him yet she was fascinated by him, and she wanted to strut over to Felicity, to stare into her arrogant face and say: *He may be about to propose to you, but would you like to know what he did with me out in the woods yesterday afternoon?*

"Where is my money?" Felicity snapped. "Or are you intending to keep it?"

"Don't be absurd," Mary retorted. "Why would I keep your money?"

"Go get it! This instant!"

Blazing with humiliation, Mary stood and left, her head held high. Over in the corner, she thought Redvers might have flashed her a sympathetic glance, but she was sure it was her imagination.

She trudged up to her room and sat on the bed. Tears flooded her eyes.

She was so unhappy! How much longer could she continue on like this? Why couldn't she alter her plight? She'd always tried to be a good, kind person. Where was her reward? Was there no justice in the world?

She opened her reticule, and as she did, she noticed the vial of Spinster's Cure. She clasped it in her palm, running her thumb over the smooth glass.

Why not? a voice whispered. *Why not try it?*

How could it hurt? Her life was so dreary. Even the tiniest beneficial effect would be better than none.

Clutching the vial, she took Felicity's coin, as well as the one Redvers had given her and stormed back to the parlor.

For once, her civility and reserve had vanished. She was spitting mad, and she felt as if she might do any wild thing.

She went straight to Felicity and flung the coin into her lap.

"What . . . ?" Felicity sputtered. "How dare you!"

"Mary!" Victoria scolded.

"Here's your precious money," Mary seethed. "I hope you choke on it."

"Mary!" Victoria repeated more loudly. "Where are your manners?"

Mary whirled on Redvers, tossing his coin in the same discourteous fashion.

"Here's yours, too," she said. "Why don't you use it to embarrass some other poor, unfortunate girl?"

There was a stunned silence. Mouths dropped in shock. Mrs. Bainbridge snickered.

"We've finally pushed her over the edge," Cassandra mumbled. "I always suspected we might."

Mary spun and marched out, unaware of what an imperious, aggrieved spectacle she presented.

"Where do you think you're going?" Victoria huffed.

"I'm not hungry," Mary replied without slowing, "and even if I was, I wouldn't eat with any of you!"

After two decades of misery, it was the only truly rude behavior she'd ever exhibited toward Victoria, and all in all, she was quite satisfied with herself. On the morrow, she'd have to grovel and apologize, but for now, she was unfettered and unconstrained.

She kept on down the hall, then out to the terrace at the rear of the house. Harold was lumbering down the garden path, eager to arrive in time for supper.

She plopped down on a bench, watching him come, letting him get closer and closer. When she could make out the striped pattern on his vest, she tugged the cork from the vial and raised it to her lips.

Harold waved to her, and she glared at him—hard—then poured the liquid into her mouth. She'd started to swallow, when suddenly, a shadow fell over her.

Harold was blocked from view.

"Hello, Miss Barnes," Lord Redvers said. "Fancy meeting you here."

"Redvers?" she wailed, coughing and sputtering, trying to *un*swallow the elixir, which was impossible.

He was directly in front of her, his wide shoulders taking up her entire line of sight. She lunged from side to side, desperate to peer around him, but she couldn't see Harold anywhere.

There was only Redvers, and no one else.

Chapter 4

CASSANDRA Barnes Stewart shuffled her deck of cards, the noise sounding inordinately loud in the quiet room.

It was very late, everyone abed, yet she sat at a table in the parlor all alone, the light of a single candle keeping her company. She was too wide awake to sleep, and she leaned back in her chair and gulped an unladylike swig of brandy, savoring the burn as it slid to her belly.

She smirked, disgusted by how much she'd changed from the innocent child she'd been.

Once, she'd been as proper and fussy as Felicity. Once, she'd been sixteen and had stupidly supposed that events would turn out exactly as her mother had planned. Cassandra had swallowed Victoria's folderol about husbands and status and making the right marriage.

That is, until Cassandra's wedding night. Leave it to Victoria to send a bride to her marital bed to naively suffer the consequences.

Cassandra's spouse had been cruel and sadistic, but he'd had the good grace to die after two years of despair.

He'd also crassly wasted Cassandra's dowry, so she was twenty-two and penniless and living with her mother again. Her plight was little better than Mary's, whom she'd frequently scorned for no crime other than being impoverished.

Cassandra and Felicity had never been close, but she couldn't stand to observe as Redvers sniffed around Felicity, and before the ceremony, Cassandra would have a private chat with her sister. Felicity deserved to know what was coming, though she wouldn't believe the truth. What girl would?

Footsteps traipsed down the hall, a sign that her solitude was about to be interrupted. When Redvers's friend, Paxton Adair, strode through the door, she frowned.

What was he doing awake? She had to socialize with him during the day. Must he inflict himself on her in the dark of night, too?

"Hello, Mrs. Stewart." He nodded in a lazy, smug way that carried a hint of derision. "May I join you?"

For the briefest instant, she thought about denying his request, but courtesy prevented her from being rude.

"If you wish."

He entered and sauntered over; he walked so gracefully—like an athlete or a dancer—that it was impossible not to watch him. He pulled out a chair and sat across from her, the glow of the candle accenting the planes of his perfect face, his golden hair, and his mesmerizing brown eyes.

He looked angelic, but appearances could be deceiving, and she'd heard stories about him.

As a gambler and drunkard, he prided himself on his low reputation. He exuded devious intent, always scheming to the detriment of others, and she had no desire to add her name to his growing list of victims.

"I've removed my coat," he mentioned. "You won't swoon, will you?"

"I'm hardly the type."

"Good. I can't abide a timid woman." He noted her brandy glass and raised a brow. "Where is the bottle?"

She indicated the sideboard, and he went over and poured himself a glass.

Since he'd arrived with Redvers, she'd avoided him like the plague. They'd scarcely conversed, which was fine by her.

He was tall and lithe, his shoulders wide, his legs long, and he was too handsome, when she didn't like handsome men. They made her nervous; they reminded her of how her life might have gone if she'd chosen a different path, if matrimony hadn't been held out as such an imperative, lofty goal.

"Did you have trouble sleeping?" he asked.

"Yes."

"Is it a common affliction for you?"

"Yes," she said again.

She didn't enlighten him as to the fact that, before her wedding, she'd slept like a baby. It was only afterward that insomnia had become a constant companion.

He gestured to her cards. "Do you like to play?"

"It passes the time."

"It certainly does."

He took the deck and shuffled it as he silently studied her, his probing gaze digging deep, and she didn't like how she was being assessed. He seemed to be calculating the odds or plotting her downfall. He seemed to peer straight to the center of her cold, black heart.

She'd once been a fairly happy, animated person. Now, she didn't feel anything. Not joy. Not anger. Not humor. She was dead inside.

"I'd heard," he said, "that your husband left you broke and miserable. Is it true?"

"How tactless of you to inquire."

"I'm not much for fussy manners. If I want to know something, I ask. Isn't my method better than gossiping about you behind your back?"

He had a point, but she wouldn't concede it to him. "*Man-*

ners are exhibited for a reason, Mr. Adair. Perhaps you should reconsider."

"Or perhaps not." He flashed a roguish grin. "I also heard that he was a perverted ass. Was he?"

"He could be."

"You poor girl."

His sympathy appeared genuine, but with him it was impossible to tell. He was a master at deception, a complete fraud.

She shrugged. "I survived. It's more than some women can say."

"Yes, it is. And now, you've run home to your mum. What is your plan? Will you fritter away the rest of your life, hiding in the country with her? Having met Mrs. Barnes, I offer my condolences."

He gave a mock shudder, which made Cassandra smile.

"It could have been worse," she said. "I could have had nowhere to go at all. At least my mother was willing to take me in."

"And if she'd slammed the door in your face, what then?"

"I don't know."

He relaxed in his chair, pretending to be intrigued by her responses. He seemed to be flirting with her, but then, he flirted with everyone.

London drawing rooms were purportedly littered with inconsolable women whom he'd loved and abandoned. He had a way of looking at a female that made her ponder things she had no business pondering, and Cassandra was perturbed to discover that she wasn't immune to his significant charm.

After the welcomed end to her marriage, she'd told herself that she would never again entertain romantic notions. Yet Adair merely stared at her, and her pulse was fluttering like a debutante's.

"I don't understand," he commented, "how you could leave Town and move back here. Aren't you bored out of your mind?"

"Occasionally."

"What do you do to amuse yourself?"

"I walk. I read. I sew."

"How about if I shoot you and put you out of your misery?"

She chuckled. "It's not that unbearable."

"You're very pretty," he said, the compliment not unusual. She'd always been beautiful.

"Thank you."

"Are you living like a nun? Or have you a dozen secret lovers?"

She'd just taken a sip of brandy, and at his voicing the audacious remark, she swallowed wrong, and she coughed and sputtered.

"You are the most impertinent man I've ever met."

"Have you?" he pressed.

"Have I what?"

"A lover."

"Gad, no."

"Would you like one?"

The conversation was becoming more bizarre by the second. Did adults actually conduct themselves so brazenly? She was a widow but still had scant idea of how grown-ups behaved.

"Are you offering your services?" she asked.

"Yes. Depending on how long Redvers dithers over your sister, I may be here an entire month. It's an eternity for me to go without carnal companionship, and I'd hate to have to start chasing after the housemaids."

"So if I agreed, I'd be doing you a favor?"

"Yes. When I'm without a paramour, I get cranky."

"We wouldn't want that, would we?"

"No. We definitely wouldn't."

He picked up the deck, shuffled it, then dealt them each a card, facedown. "Let's play. High card wins."

"Wins what?"

"Are the stones in your necklace real?"

"Yes."

"Then if I have the high card, I win your necklace."

"You can't have it. And besides, I've heard that you cheat, so why would I gamble with you?"

"Maybe—deep down—you'd like to give me exactly what I want."

"I don't think so."

"Are you sure about that?"

He scooted his chair so that it was right next to hers, and he leaned in, effectively blocking any chance she had of escape.

She probably should have been afraid, but she perceived no danger. He was challenging her, or daring her, and she sensed that she could tell him to desist and he would. To her amazement, a flicker of excitement kindled in her belly.

He was so close, and she suffered from the most insane impression that he was about to kiss her.

Would she let him? Should she let him?

Although she'd been wed and widowed, she'd never been kissed. Her deceased husband had had no amorous tendencies. There had been one thing he'd sought from her, and he'd taken it without seduction or delay.

What would it be like to be kissed by a man who was eager to? By a man who knew how?

"I'm going to win your necklace," he said, "then I'll go after your clothes—until I have them all."

The image of herself being stripped, a garment at a time, was so shocking and so intriguing that she trembled.

"You are mad," she charged.

"Why would you say so?"

"I would never remove my clothes for you."

"We'll see, won't we?"

His hand had been carefully placed on her knee, and he dipped under her chin to nibble at her nape. Goose bumps cascaded down her arms.

She groaned in agony, not knowing what to do. She wanted him to leave her be, but her entire body was ablaze.

"I'll be here a month," he murmured. "A whole month."

It sounded like a promise; it sounded like a threat. It would be heaven; it would be hell. She pushed him away and stood.

"I don't want this from you," she insisted.

"Liar."

He smirked, his wicked smile hinting at the paradise she'd dreamed of as a girl but had never found as a married woman.

She spun and fled.

.

"REDVERS?"

"What?"

Lauretta Bainbridge loitered in the doorway that separated his bedchamber and his dressing room. She'd checked her reflection in the mirror, so she knew she looked fabulous, but he hadn't noticed.

She was wearing a new negligee her seamstress had brought over from Paris. It was made of red silk, cut low in the bodice to bare most of her breasts, yet she couldn't get him to turn around. He was lost in thought, perched by the window and staring out across the park.

"Jordan!" she grumbled, exasperated and trying not to snap at him.

He glanced over his shoulder. "What is it?"

"You're being positively boring." She affected a credible pout.

"Yes, I am. Sorry."

He gazed out the window again, not the least bit repentant, and she couldn't figure out what was wrong with him.

Ever since that frumpy spinster, Mary Barnes, had caused her scene in the parlor, he'd been very glum, which was so unlike him. Usually, he couldn't care less about what other people said or did, but for some reason, Miss Barnes had left him in a state.

Well, Lauretta wasn't about to have her evening spoiled by the likes of Mary Barnes.

She sauntered over and snuggled herself to him, her front

to his back, but he didn't react. He was completely impassive, and his behavior was frightening.

Was he growing weary of her? The notion made her ill.

They were a perfect pair. He was so dissolute, and she was so greedy, eager to give him what he wanted so she could get what *she* wanted. They'd both been happy with their arrangement. She still was, and though Lord Sunderland had cut off Jordan's allowance, the funds would flow soon—either from his father or from Felicity.

For five long years, Lauretta had stood with him through thick and thin, through poverty and plenty, and she'd never once failed to satisfy his every whim. So what the bloody hell was his problem?

She reached around and caressed his stomach, but he stepped away, his arms crossed over his chest as a barrier to her snuggling herself to him again.

"Now that you've met Felicity," he absurdly asked, "do you still believe I should marry her?"

"Absolutely, darling. Why wouldn't you?"

"She's so young, and she's so . . . so . . . stupid. She annoys me with her chatter."

"So? We discussed this. You wed her, you receive her money, you dump her in a house far out in the country, and you never have to see her again."

"It's so calculated."

"Of course it is. It's *marriage*. It's always premeditated for personal gain."

"I'm just . . . just . . ."

He paused, having the strangest look on his face, and his vacillation alarmed her.

Though he had to pick a bride, Lauretta was determined that it be a match without affection or even cordiality so that there would be no threat to Lauretta's position as his mistress. She'd chosen Felicity, had promoted her to him, and she couldn't have him getting cold feet.

"Think how much fun your wedding night will be," she

counseled. "Think how much fun you'll have screwing your rich virgin. I'll even help you if you'd like." She neared and hugged him. "Does the idea excite you? Would you like to see Felicity and me together? I'd do it for you; you know I would."

"The thought of fornicating with her is revolting to me, and should the moment ever come to pass, I would never allow you to participate."

Lauretta sighed. He would have sex with anyone, in any configuration, so his ill humor was very dangerous, indeed.

"You seem terribly fatigued, Jordan. Why don't you lie down and let me relax you?"

She stroked his phallus, stroked it again, then stopped.

The bastard wasn't even hard!

She clutched at his trousers, anxious to slip a hand inside and provide a bit of encouragement, but he grabbed her wrist.

"Not tonight," he said for the first time ever. "I'm not in the mood."

The peculiar phrase raced around the room like the kiss of death. What was bothering him? Was he sick? Exhausted? Insane?

Something had disturbed him, but what was it? He was a disgusting, immoral libertine and always had been. He couldn't go changing on her. She wouldn't permit it, and the sooner she ascertained the cause of his sulk, the better for all concerned.

"HE'LL propose, won't he, Mother?"

"Yes, he will."

Victoria rested against her pillows, watching Felicity braid her hair as they prepared for bed. She'd spent much of the past decade in the same spot, parlaying over marriage with her daughters, and it had become an evening ritual.

"Do you promise?"

"Yes."

"What if you're mistaken?"

"I'm not."

"All the other girls will be so jealous."

"Yes, they will," Victoria smugly agreed.

"In the end, if he cries off, I'll die. I'll just die!"

"Don't worry so much," Victoria advised. "He's desperate. He needs your dowry so badly that I wouldn't be surprised if he got down on his hands and knees and begged me to give it to him."

Felicity had had her debut the previous year, and they'd dawdled through two Seasons, hoping for an aristocrat to come sniffing after her money. She'd had many, many offers—from merchants, from destitute gentlemen, from clergy and soldiers—but she'd refused them all.

With the arrival of Jordan Winthrop, Victoria's prayers had been answered. She, herself, had once dreamed of a noble match, but she'd been sold by her father to a lower societal rung, and she'd never recovered from the shame of it.

As a result, she was determined that her own daughters would never suffer the same fate. She was using the fortune of her loathed, dead, common husband to see them married as they deserved.

After Cassandra's nuptial debacle, Victoria felt driven to ensure that Felicity's union was the ultimate success. With poverty-stricken Jordan Winthrop in her home, her task was incredibly easy.

"How will you make him propose?" Felicity asked.

"I won't have to *make* him do anything. He'll be eager to have you."

"I want to be wed a month from today."

"I'm certain it can be arranged."

"WHAT is the matter with him?"

"How would I know?"

"You're his best friend. You're supposed to know."

Paxton Adair reclined on his bed, staring at Lauretta as she paced across his bedchamber.

"I've been acquainted with Jordan since we were boys, but that doesn't mean we chew over our troubles like a pair of females over tea."

"He's ailing, I tell you."

"Why do you think so?"

"He wouldn't fornicate with me. Me!"

She tossed open her robe, displaying her negligee. With that auburn hair and curvaceous figure, she was sinfully beautiful, every man's sexual fantasy come to life.

If Jordan had declined to frolic with her, he had to be going mad.

"Yes, he must be terribly ill," Paxton concurred. "Perhaps he's dying. Should we summon a doctor?"

"You're making jokes while my world is collapsing around me. Be helpful, or be silent."

"What would you have me say, Lauretta?"

"Is there something wrong with me?" She flung her arms to the sides, like a woman being crucified. "Am I getting fat? Am I looking old? Are my breasts starting to sag? What?"

To his delight, she yanked on the straps of her negligee so that her bosom was bared. He'd seen her naked before, when she'd been in bed with Jordan and too brazen to cover herself, so the sight was nothing new, but it was late, they were alone, and he was still rock hard from his encounter with Cassandra Stewart.

If he wasn't careful, he might wind up copulating with Jordan's mistress.

"You're fine," he claimed. "As always. Jordan is just tired. He's had a few bad days."

"He's about to wed an heiress, for pity's sake. How could his days possibly be *bad*?"

"Yes, but the heiress is *Felicity*, Lauretta. You've met her. The poor fellow needs our support—and our eternal sympathy."

"You men!" she fumed. "It's all about you! You never consider anyone else."

She was mistaken. He actually thought about others—those

others being women. His ruminations centered on how quickly he could either get one into his bed or get her to give him some money. He wasn't fussy; he would accept sex or cash.

In his many peccadilloes, he took after his father, who had impregnated Paxton's mother without benefit of marriage. Since the man had already *been* married, matrimony hadn't been an option, so Paxton tried not to be critical.

His father had been generous, though, had paid for their housing and sent Paxton to school, which was where he'd befriended Jordan. There was even a small trust fund, but it was never enough. Paxton's tastes were too extravagant, his expenses too high.

He was too lazy to work at a job, so he'd perfected the only two means by which he could supplement his income: gambling and womanizing.

He enjoyed both and indulged constantly, and he didn't regret his choices. He simply wished that the endeavors were a tad more lucrative—and his father a tad less miserly.

Lauretta sashayed over and perched a hip on the mattress. She leaned in, her breasts taunting him to misbehave.

"Tell me the truth," she said. "Do you see any flaws?"

He pretended to ponder, his eyes roaming down her body.

"No, I don't see anything, but I should probably assess the condition of your legs. Would you remove your negligee?"

Without hesitation, she stood and let it slither to the floor, and in a thrice, she was naked.

He frowned. She was a mercenary, and she didn't proceed with any venture unless she'd fully calculated the payoff at the end, so he didn't understand her game. Obviously, she was hoping to seduce him. But why?

She didn't dally for pleasure. With her, it was all business. So if she was offering, she'd expect something in return. He didn't have any funds, so what was she after?

"You're magnificent," he said, recognizing it was the comment she'd sought.

"I am," she agreed.

She came back to the bed, and this time, she crawled over his lap so that her thighs were spread, her breasts in his face. His cock pounded with anticipation.

"What the hell do you want?" he asked.

"I want to know what's going on with Jordan."

"I told you: I don't know."

"Then find out for me."

"He and I don't have that kind of relationship."

Their association was forged on vice and carnality. They wagered, they drank, they chased women, but they never discussed their personal lives, and Paxton wouldn't have the slightest idea how to probe for intimate details.

"You could find out if you wanted to," she insisted.

"Maybe I don't want to."

She laid down and stretched out, her lush torso crushed to his all the way down.

"I could make it worth your while," she coaxed.

"I bet you could."

"Haven't you ever wondered what it might be like between us?"

"Yes, I have."

He couldn't deny it. He was a mortal man, not a saint.

He clasped her nipple, squeezing it with light pressure, and she arched her back and moaned in ecstasy, but he was sure the reaction was faked.

She could be fucking him or anybody.

Still, he reveled in licentious play, so he treated himself to a few naughty touches. To his surprise, he caught himself wishing he was with Cassandra Stewart instead of Lauretta. For some reason, Cassandra fascinated him, and before he quitted the estate, he intended to have her as a lover.

She just didn't know it yet.

In an instant, his ardor fled, his erection vanishing.

Lauretta noticed immediately, and she scowled and sat on her haunches.

"What is it?" she snapped.

"I have no desire to spy on Jordan for you, and I'm not too keen on copulating with you, either."

"What are you saying?"

"I'm not in the mood."

"Not in the mood? *Not in the mood?*"

"No," he said. "Sorry."

"You are the second man tonight who's told me the same."

"Then perhaps you should give up and head to your own bed."

"And perhaps you should choke on a crow."

She scooted away, furious, as she yanked on her negligee.

"If I change my mind," he informed her, "about tattling on Jordan, I'll let you know."

"You do that."

She whirled away and left, and he snuggled under the blankets, suddenly overcome by visions of Cassandra losing her clothes to him in a fixed card game where he'd cheat at every hand.

At the prospect, he was thrilled to note that his erection hadn't waned after all. He couldn't wait till *she* would be the one to tend it for him—and if he had his way, the event would occur very, very soon.

"Do you think I made a mistake?"

"At what?"

"By moving home—after my husband died."

Mary frowned at Cassandra.

"Absolutely not. Why would you even ask such a ridiculous question?"

Cassandra shrugged. "It's merely something someone said to me. It had me wondering."

Mary straightened and dropped her scissors into her basket. They were in the rose garden, cutting flowers for the supper table.

The gardener usually saw to it, but he was elderly, and with the recent rainy weather, his arthritis was painful. It was becoming more and more difficult for him to complete his chores, and Mary was terrified that he would neglect an important task and Victoria would fire him.

It didn't matter that he'd worked on the estate for seven decades, that his father had been head gardener before him. Victoria had no loyalty to those who served the Barnes family, and her attitude was troubling to Mary.

She couldn't bear to imagine the dear old fellow losing his job and being tossed out of his cottage, so she assisted him whenever she could.

"Who suggested," she asked, "that you shouldn't have moved home?"

"Mr. Adair."

Mary rolled her eyes. "You listened to him?"

"Not really. I just . . . felt he might have had a point."

"Why on earth would you heed his opinion on any topic? He's an ass."

"Mary!"

"Well, he is."

"Such language!" Cassandra sarcastically scolded. "I'm shocked. Shocked, I tell you!"

They both chuckled, and Cassandra slipped a hand into Mary's arm as Mary grabbed her filled basket and they started toward the manor.

"You were destitute and alone," Mary said. "What else should you have done?"

"That's what I told him, but anymore, I'm so . . . so . . ." Her voice trailed off, and she gazed to the horizon, as if seeing a road through her past. "Don't mind me. I have no idea why I'm being so maudlin."

"It was hard for you to return," Mary empathized. "Of course you'd occasionally have doubts. It's only natural."

"Yes, it is," Cassandra concurred, "but I didn't bother to explain as much to Mr. Adair. If I'd stayed in Town, what would have happened to me?"

"I suppose you could have found employment as a tavern wench."

"Or a doxy."

"You could have trolled for customers in the shadows at Vauxhall Gardens."

"Mary!" Cassandra gasped. "Stop it! You're making me blush."

"You need to remember that Mr. Adair is an idiot. He doesn't know anything about you, yet he has the gall to lecture you over your choices."

"He certainly does."

"You were in a horrendous situation, and you arrived at the only decision you could."

Mary didn't add that, in many ways, Cassandra's matrimonial debacle had been good for her, had rendered constructive changes.

While growing up, Cassandra had never been cruel like Felicity, but she'd definitely been conceited and spoiled, and positive she was exceptional.

Now, she was wiser, shrewder, more willing to question her mother. The vain edges had been softened. She was self-deprecating, not afraid to scoff at her foibles and accept her failings.

Most of all, she was kind to Mary, and in a life where Mary had had few kindnesses bestowed, it was a marvelous development.

"I still wish," Cassandra said, "that I hadn't had to come back, though. I just hate that Adair noticed."

Mary laughed. "Maybe someday, when we're digging in the flower beds, we'll stumble on a buried treasure and you'll have the funds to leave again."

"You can join me. We'll retire to Town and scandalize everyone by living alone and together."

"We'll be society matrons, and we'll surround ourselves with artists and actors. We'll have risqué romances and cultivate disreputable companions."

Cassandra snorted. "You've been out in the sun too long."

They strolled on in a companionable silence, when suddenly, Cassandra halted.

"What is it?" Mary asked.

"Lord Redvers is on the terrace. He's watching us."

Mary glanced up to see him leaned on the balustrade, his pompous smirk clearly visible. She wouldn't be able to get in the house without walking right by him.

"Oh, joy," Mary grumbled.

"He's smug as a king, surveying his minions."

Cassandra drew away and went in the opposite direction.

"Where are you going?" Mary inquired.

"My mood is already extremely foul. I'd rather not exacerbate it by speaking with him. I'll go around to the front."

She hurried away; Mary would have to run to catch up with her. She peered over at Redvers, who continued to watch her.

He raised an imperious brow, indicating that he was aware of why Cassandra had fled. He seemed humored by her dislike and was daring Mary to react in the same rude fashion, but she wasn't scared of him. And she wasn't about to flit off like a coward.

She braced and proceeded toward him, determined to pass by without incident.

"Hello, Mary," he said as she climbed the steps.

"It's Miss Barnes to you."

"You're cutting flowers?"

"Yes."

"Why?"

"Because I enjoy it. Why would you suppose?"

"Your basket looks heavy. Let me help you."

"No, thank you."

Despite her protest, he reached to take it, but she wouldn't release it, and they engaged in a brief tug-of-war. He won, but was gracious about it.

He draped the handle over his arm and gestured to the door.

"Where to?" he queried.

"The kitchen."

"Lead on."

"Don't you have better things to do than harass me?"

"No, actually, I don't."

Hoping to shoo him away, she dawdled, scowling, but it had no effect, so she spun and went inside, keeping on to the rear of the house, then down the stairs. He followed without complaint or snide comment.

As they entered the large room, it was empty and quiet, and she cursed her luck. Usually, the area was bustling with activity. Where was everybody?

He set the basket on the table, and with his task accomplished, she expected him to leave her in peace, but he didn't. He pulled out a chair and sat down.

"What are you doing?" she grouched.

"Entertaining myself."

"At my expense. Why?"

"I'm bored, and you amuse me."

"Couldn't you find someone else to annoy?"

"I could, but it's more fun to pester you. You get so flustered."

Her cheeks reddened. He was flirting with her again, and she didn't know what to make of it. She wanted to order him out, but she was flattered by his attention.

Was she mad?

He'd humiliated her, had caused her to lose her temper and behave like a shrew in front of her family. She was still awaiting Victoria's punishment for the episode, yet she was pathetically eager to fraternize with him as if nothing unpleasant had occurred.

She ignored him and went about her business, quickly snipping the stems on the roses and arranging them in three colorful bouquets. He observed, not speaking, and it was nerve-wracking to have him study her so closely.

Why are you staring? she almost demanded, but she didn't.

She pretended he wasn't there, filling vases, then picking them up to carry upstairs. She could have summoned a footman to do it for her, but they had so many other chores that she hated to bother them.

As she juggled the load, he leapt to his feet and took the vases from her. She frowned, her consternation clear.

"Why are you being courteous to me?"

"Can't I act like a gentleman?"

"I didn't think you knew how."

Her insult rolled off him. He laughed and headed for the door, and he looked ridiculous, such a big man, awkwardly cradling several dozen roses to his chest.

She hastened by him and climbed to the dining room. She grabbed the bouquets and positioned them on the polished table. The servants would be in soon to lay out the china and silverware, and Mary smiled at how pretty the flowers would be in the center of all the finery.

"This place matters to you, doesn't it?" he said. He was casually leaned in a corner, one booted foot crossed over the other.

"It was my father's house before it was anyone else's." Her reply was mildly impolite to Victoria without mentioning her. "My mother planted the rosebushes herself. I'm fond of them because of it."

"I can tell."

An uncomfortable silence descended. He was gazing at her, the typical conceited expression noticeably absent. He appeared younger, approachable, friendly.

"I'm sorry about yesterday," he suddenly murmured. "I'm sorry for how you were treated."

"You are not."

She didn't like to view this side of him, didn't want him to be kind or considerate. If he was charming, it was difficult to loathe him.

"Come here," he commanded. He was standing ten feet away, and he motioned for her to walk nearer.

She didn't move so he came to her instead. In an instant, she was trapped against a chair, and he loomed over her.

What did he intend? Would he kiss her? What if a servant traipsed in? What if they were caught? Her pulse was fluttering like a frightened bird's.

"When we stopped at that peddler's wagon," he said, "I told you to buy yourself a ribbon, but you didn't. You gave me my money back."

She scoffed. "What would I do with a ribbon?"

"Wear it in your hair—so I can see how fetching it is on you."

He reached into his coat, and to her astonishment, pulled out a long strip of red ribbon.

She gaped at it as if it were a venomous snake, as if it were a dirty trick.

She couldn't remember the last time she'd received a gift. It was a lovely gesture, which left her unaccountably distraught. Tears welled into her eyes.

"For . . . for me?" she stammered.

"No, for the fox in the forest. Yes, it's for you." He waved it at her. "Take it."

"I can't."

"Yes, you can."

"It would be wrong."

"Don't be silly. It's just a ribbon. Every girl should have a new one now and then."

She scrutinized him, trying to read his mind, trying to understand what was motivating him.

"I can't," she insisted more forcefully.

He wrapped it around her neck and tied it in a bow at the front.

She was so stunned that she was speechless. She pushed away from him and ran all the way to her bedchamber.

Chapter 5

❦

"I apologize for my behavior," Mary said.

"And?" Victoria asked.

"I'm embarrassed at having made a spectacle of myself in front of Viscount Redvers and his friends."

Mary had finally calmed enough to face Victoria and learn her punishment, but of all the repentance she had to exhibit, being contrite over Redvers was the most galling. She bit her tongue, struggling to appear penitent—which she wasn't—while awaiting Victoria's verdict.

"Your antics shamed me," Victoria stated.

"I know."

"But you shamed Felicity most of all. Apologize to her, as well."

Mary spun toward her half sister. "I apologize."

"Mother, she doesn't look very sincere," Felicity protested.

Victoria studied Mary, then shrugged. "You're aware of how

stubborn she can be. This is as much remorse as we're likely to see. You'll forgive her, and we'll not speak of it again."

"But if she's rude to me in the future," Felicity persisted, "may I demand that she be whipped?"

Mary rolled her eyes.

"There will be no whipping," Victoria declared. "However, since Mary has proven that she can't control herself, she shall not socialize with us during Lord Redvers's stay." She frowned at Mary as if Mary was a lunatic in an asylum. "You'll remain in your room and take your meals there. Keep yourself away from Redvers and his party."

"I will," Mary said, happy for the excuse to avoid him.

"Should you precipitate a second outburst for his lordship to witness, there will be dire consequences. Do you understand me?"

"Yes, ma'am."

"You're excused."

Mary hurried out, relieved to have the meeting over, but more angry on leaving than she'd been on arriving.

Her entire life had been one long string of threats by Victoria. Threats to discipline her. Threats to cast her out. Threats to disown her.

After being terrified so frequently, she was beginning to wish Victoria would follow through just so Mary could cease worrying as to how the slightest misstep might cause her to be evicted.

She went to the far wing of the house and climbed the rear stairs to her small bedchamber on the third floor. The modest space was the complete opposite of the grand boudoirs occupied by Felicity and Cassandra, and thus, it was another insult to Mary.

When she'd been younger, she'd been envious, but not anymore.

She enjoyed being away from the rest of the family, enjoyed the quiet corridors that were a haven from the crazed women to whom she was so closely related.

She was weary of their spite, of their fixation on money and marriage, and she relished having a place to which she could escape.

The evening was waning; as she entered, the shadows had lengthened, and it was difficult to notice what was in plain sight.

"Hello, Mary," a deep, masculine voice said.

She jumped a foot and whipped around. "Lord Redvers! What are you doing in here?"

"I haven't seen you all day. I decided I should check on you."

He was over by the window, lounging in a chair. His coat was off and casually flung over the edge of the bed as if it belonged there. His shirt was unbuttoned, his sleeves rolled back, and he was sipping on a glass of what had to be liquor. There was a half-empty decanter on the windowsill next to him.

Why had he visited? How did he even know where her room was located? Why would he have gone to the trouble of finding out?

Her first and only absurd thought was that that stupid spinster's tonic was working. As she'd swallowed it, Lord Redvers had stepped in the way of Harold. Had it somehow altered the universe? He'd given her the red ribbon, and now, he'd sneaked into her bedchamber.

Was he becoming obsessed?

At the frantic queries, she was extremely aggravated. Was she losing her mind?

She reached for the door as if to yank it open and push him out, even though she was sure he wouldn't depart until he was good and ready.

"You can't stay."

"Of course I can. I'm a viscount. I can act however I please."

"You're so spoiled."

"I don't deny it."

"Have you always been this way?"

"Yes."

"How can people tolerate you?"

"They don't very graciously. I'm renowned for being impossible; I don't have any friends."

"How about Mr. Adair?"

"He just hangs around because I let him cheat me at cards."

The charming, kind man who'd helped her with her flowers had vanished. The arrogant, haughty aristocrat had returned with a vengeance.

He rose and came over to her, and she stood her ground, instinctively realizing that she shouldn't give any indication that she was scared of him—which she wasn't.

Where he was concerned, she had a heightened awareness. He might bluster and bully, but he wouldn't harm her. At least, not deliberately.

"Where have you been?" he inquired.

"If you must know, I was down in the front parlor, apologizing to Victoria for throwing your money in your face."

"Are you sorry?"

"No."

He chuckled, and she snapped, "What do you want?"

He considered her question, but having no answer, he asked one of his own. "Why are you living in this section of the manor?"

"This has always been my room."

"Why don't you reside near the others?"

"Why would I?"

"It seems odd to me. They're rich and you're poor. Didn't your father provide for you?"

"No."

"Why not?"

"How would I know, Lord Redvers? I was a tiny child when he died. I scarcely remember him. Perhaps he didn't like me very much. Perhaps he didn't think I was worth the bother."

She spun away, hating how he'd probed at old wounds. The

subject of her father's disregard was hurtful, and she never discussed it with anyone.

She went to her dresser, toying with her brush, pretending to straighten what didn't need straightening.

"Why don't you go?" she said. "If we're caught together, there'll be a big fuss."

Her back was to him, and she heard him approach. He kept coming until he was directly behind her. He leaned in, trapping her.

"When we're alone, you're to call me Jordan."

"Don't be ridiculous."

He sounded as if he'd be dropping by constantly, and the prospect made her heart pound with excitement and dread.

"Who's being *ridiculous*?" he scolded. "I'll call you Mary, and you'll call me Jordan."

"I will not."

"If we're to be lovers—"

At the preposterous suggestion, she wiggled around. "We're not going to be . . . be . . . lovers or anything else."

"Aren't we?"

He was so close. Too close. Would he try to kiss her again?

He gazed at her with what seemed to be heightened male interest, maybe even a blossoming of affection, and she panicked.

There was no reason for him to pay attention to her. There was no reason for him to have stopped by, and once more, she recollected that idiotic tonic.

"Listen to me, Lord Redvers."

"Jordan."

"No."

"Yes."

He was adamant, and she didn't want to argue. She just wanted him to leave.

She capitulated.

"Listen, Jordan"—at his small victory, he smirked—"I'm not certain why you're here, but you should know something."

"What?"

"I drank a special tonic, and it's provoked a change in our relationship."

"What kind of tonic?" He grinned. "Was it a love potion?"

"Don't be absurd," she scoffed. "Why would I need a love potion?"

He studied her, and when her cheeks flamed bright red, he crowed, "I was right! It *was* a love potion!"

"It wasn't!" she protested, mortified to her very core.

"Are you that enamored of me, Mary?"

"No," she tried to claim. "I can't abide you."

He was in a fine state, chortling and guffawing, making her embarrassment all the worse.

"So let me get this straight: You believe that a . . . a . . . magic elixir is forcing me to fall in love with you? Is that why you suppose I'm here?"

"No! I'm simply afraid that it might have altered things between us."

"Really? Now that I'm ensnared, how will you be shed of me? Will you drink an antidote?"

"I don't know if there is one," she miserably replied, and he laughed and laughed.

"I'm here, Miss Mary Barnes, because I'm intrigued by you."

"You are not."

"I am, and no tonic was necessary."

"But there's no reason for your interest!"

"I'm a libertine, Mary. I don't need a reason. Haven't you heard? I'll chase anything in a skirt." He took hold of her hand. "Come with me."

"To where?"

"I've been pondering our kiss out in the woods."

She gulped with dismay. "You have?"

"Yes, and I want to do it again."

They were walking toward her bed, and she dug in her heels. "What are you planning?"

"I told you: I want to kiss you again."

He tumbled onto the mattress, and she tumbled with him. She landed on her back, and he was hovered over her, an arm and thigh pinning her down.

She understood that she should complain, but a secret part of her was thrilled by his behavior. Still, ingrained habits prevailed, and she thought she should at least try to sound affronted.

"Let me go."

"No."

"You're a bully and a fiend."

"I admit it. What fun would life be if I wasn't?"

He dipped down and kissed her, and immediately, it was apparent that it would be nothing like the embrace they'd shared in the forest. There was an urgency about it, as if they were in a hurry, and she shut her eyes and reveled in the moment. Her foolish pride soared at the recognition that Jordan Winthrop would go to so much trouble merely to dally with her.

His tongue flicked out and slipped inside her mouth, and they engaged in a merry dance that teased and cajoled, and she was astonished at how easily she knew what was required.

When he roamed his hands over her body, she roamed hers over his. When he shifted positions to get more comfortable, she shifted, too. When his torso dropped between her thighs, she spread her legs to give him greater access. He started an unusual flexing, his hips moving with hers, her skirt and petticoat a soft cushion against which he could thrust and push.

He began massaging her breasts, rubbing them in slow circles. The sensation was so titillating that it was painful. His crafty fingers pinched her nipples, squeezing them with just the right amount of pressure so that they ached and throbbed.

"Oh, stop, Redvers. I'm begging you. I must catch my breath."

"No. And it's Jordan to you."

"Please?"

"If you call me Jordan, I'll do as you ask."

She scowled, then gave in. "Please, Jordan?"

He pretended to consider, then shook his head. "I don't think so."

She whacked him on the shoulder. "You are such a beast!"

"Yes, I am. You shouldn't forget it."

He dipped down again, and though she assumed he'd kiss her on the mouth, he descended farther so that he was directly over her chest.

"Have you ever had a lover, Mary?"

"No. How could I have?"

"I'm delighted to hear it. Let me show you something."

"No." She was begging again. "Don't show me anything."

"You'll like it. I promise."

One hand continued to torment her breast, while the other was lifting her skirt, and very quickly, he was sliding his fingers into her drawers. With no hesitation, he tangled them through her womanly hair and glided them into her sheath.

To her surprise, they fit perfectly, and she was stunned by the discovery. As he stroked them back and forth, she was even more stunned. The movement was mesmerizing, as if it was precisely what she'd been craving without even knowing it.

He'd aroused her to a fevered pitch, and of their own accord, her hips bucked against his palm, as if intent on pulling him deeper.

He chuckled. "You are just what I've been needing."

"How could that be? I don't have any idea what's occurring."

"Don't worry. Your body will take you down the proper road."

The tempo increased, and with his thumb, he caressed a spot she'd never noted before. It was extremely sensitive, and she arched up, trying to escape the stimulation.

"What are you doing to me?" she asked, panting and stammering.

"I'm giving you sexual pleasure."

"Well, I don't want it!"

She felt peculiar on the inside, as if she was about to explode. There was a tension building, and she knew there had to be an end point, but at what cost? Would she survive it?

Suddenly, he bent down and nuzzled at her breast, biting her nipple through the fabric of her dress as his thumb flicked out again and again.

She shattered and cried out, being so overwhelmed that she couldn't fret over whether someone might be out in the hall and overhear. She'd never experienced anything remotely similar. In a life that was all drudgery and tedium, he'd opened a door to an entirely new land where exotic conduct was allowed and encouraged.

"What was that?" she queried as her pulse slowed and she could talk coherently.

"The French call it the 'little death.'" He was grinning, looking like the devil himself. "Would you like me to make it happen again?"

"Yes!" she gushed, before she could tamp down the eager word.

"If you're very, very nice to me, I will. But only if you're very nice."

"How *nice* do you mean?"

"You have to agree to do this whenever I ask. Will you?"

"I might."

"I'll be here but a few weeks. I'd like to see how thoroughly I can rattle your staid existence."

He drew away and stretched out as she frowned at the ceiling, terrified over what she'd set in motion.

How was she to go on as plain, humble Mary Barnes, when he'd shown her his magic?

After what they'd just done, she could never tell him to stay away, and she was already calculating how quickly they could arrange another tryst. Questions riveted her: When could they meet? Where? How often? For how long?

The passion with which she yearned for future assignations frightened her. Was she bewitched? Was the carnal behavior addicting—like a dangerous drug?

Would she spend the rest of her life waiting for him to sneak to her room?

The fact that she hoped he would, that she was agog over the prospect, was complete proof that she'd gone mad.

Fatigue crept over her, and she yawned, as he laughed.

"Are you tired?"

"Yes."

Her limbs were all rubbery, and she was glad there was no need to stand, for at that moment, her legs couldn't have supported her.

He tugged a knitted throw over them, then snuggled close, and he wrapped his arms around her as if he actually cherished her.

It was the sweetest, most romantic thing she could imagine, and gradually, her eyelids fluttered down.

She dozed, and when she woke, it was dark, the moon shining in the window. She was all alone. Lying very still, she listened for any sound, and it was so quiet that she wondered if he'd really been there with her.

She rolled onto her side, toward the spot where he'd been, and she smoothed her hand across the pillow and mattress, but none of his bodily heat remained. There was only the very slightest disturbance in the air, and it hovered like a cloud to remind her that nothing would ever be the same.

She shut her eyes again. She slept.

Chapter 6

❦

"YOU want what?"

Phillip Dudley stared at Mary Barnes, then furtively glanced over at his sister, Clarinda. A worried frown marred his hand-some brow.

"You heard me, Mr. Dubois," Miss Barnes said. "I need an antidote for that Spinster's Cure you gave me."

"For the Spinster's Cure?"

"Yes. You shouldn't be allowed to roam the countryside dispensing such dangerous medicine."

Phillip imagined the sheriff descending, a dank cell in the local gaol, a fast trip on a prison ship bound for the penal colonies in Australia.

"I can assure you, mademoiselle"—his French accent was exaggerated—"that I only offer beneficial remedies. They have been developed and tested by the world's preeminent physicians."

"Ha! It's magic, that what it is. You trot around, selling your wares, but you leave a trail of bewitched women in your wake. How can you live with yourself?"

At her injecting the word *magic* into the conversation, he was unnerved. They weren't too far past the time when rural villagers burned people at the stake for dabbling in the dark arts, and he couldn't have her spouting nonsense.

If he wasn't careful, he'd be hounded out of the county by an angry mob wielding tar and feathers.

He assumed his most patronizing, most sympathetic demeanor. "What has happened?"

Miss Barnes blushed. "I drank the tonic."

"And it worked?"

"No. Well, yes."

He scowled. "What do you mean?"

"There is a man I had in mind, whom I'd like to wed, so I . . . I . . . swallowed the tonic while I was looking at him—just as you instructed."

"He wishes to marry you now?"

"No. Another fellow stepped into my path, so I was gazing at the wrong man!"

"So this man—this *wrong* man—is the one you saw?"

"Yes, and he's completely smitten. I don't know what to do."

"Why must you do anything?" Phillip asked. "Is amour not sweet? Is amour not grand?"

"No, it's not grand! There's no reason for his fascination, and if he can't put it aside, it will bring catastrophe down on my head."

Phillip glared at his sister, urging her to chime in with a discerning remark, but as usual, when he wanted her to speak, she had nothing to say.

"Mademoiselle," he cajoled, "of course there is a reason. How could he fail to be enticed? You are very beautiful."

"Cease your drivel, and tell me how to proceed. He can't be besotted with me!"

"Miss Barnes," Clarinda interjected, "the potion Philippe gave you isn't magical."

"Have you ever drunk any yourself?"

"No, but I assist him in combining the ingredients. He uses fortifying herbs and female restoratives. There's nothing mysterious about it."

"Then how could it have rendered such a change in behavior?"

"It couldn't have," Clarinda insisted. "My brother's remedy was devised to . . . to . . . enhance your feminine appearance. You're simply growing more fetching, and this gentleman has noticed."

"No, no"—Miss Barnes seemed very disturbed—"it's much more sinister than that."

"Sinister? No!" Phillip scoffed. "Love is in the air, *ma petite amie*. You should be celebrating."

"He's a great lord!" Miss Barnes wailed. "He's here to marry my sister."

"Oh," Clarinda and Phillip murmured at the same time, a dozen silent messages flitting between them.

"I'm desperate," Miss Barnes said, "to stop whatever it is this tonic has started. Have you an antidote?"

"Yes," Phillip lied.

How could there be an antidote for a potion that was fake? Then again, human beings were very strange. She believed that the Spinster's Cure was real, that it would work, and it had—in her view, at least. So maybe if she believed she had an antidote, that would work, too.

He went to his wagon, opened the door, and sifted through the bottles. Eventually, he took out a huge dollop of sleeping powder and stirred it into some red wine, which he poured into a flask.

He handed it to her.

"What is it?" she asked.

"It is a treatment for love sickness," he said. "I prescribe it to those who have fallen in love, but whose love remains unrequited. It calms the broken heart."

"But how will it help?" Miss Barnes retorted. "*I* am not in love with anyone."

"It is not for you. It is for the man in question. *He* must drink it."

"How am I to make him?"

"How can I know, mademoiselle? I am only a simple peddler. Perhaps you can slip it into his soup?"

"For pity's sake," Miss Barnes grumbled. "Do you promise its potent effect? Will his interest wane?"

"Absolument!"

"How fast?"

"Now *that*, I cannot predict. But it will fade soon. *Je guarantie!*"

"Thank you."

She turned and walked away, the bogus potion tucked under her arm, as he and Clarinda stood, mute, watching till she vanished around the bend in the road.

"Is she the first disgruntled customer you've ever had?" Clarinda inquired.

"No, but I was so sure she'd be an easy mark."

"What did you give her?"

"A sleeping draught, mixed with wine."

"So in the middle of his wooing her, he'll nod off? Is that your plan?"

"Have you a better one?"

"No."

"WILL you marry her?"

"I suppose. Why not?"

Jordan sipped his brandy, staring over the rim of the glass at Paxton. They were alone for once, sequestered in the dining room and enjoying their after-supper liquor, while the women awaited them in the parlor. Jordan was weary of visiting and in no hurry to join them.

Since Mary never ate with the family, he felt no compunction to fraternize. She was the only female in the house whose company he relished. If she wasn't present, then socializing didn't seem worth the bother.

"Felicity is so immature," Paxton mentioned.

"Yes, she is."

"Couldn't you set your sights a tad higher?"

"If I chose somebody else," Jordan explained, "it wouldn't make a bit of difference. I need an heiress, and these rich girls are all the same. They're convinced they're special because of their fortunes, so they put on airs they don't deserve. One is as bad as the next."

"I've never thought a woman should have her own money. It throws the world out of balance."

"But if they were all poor, why would we marry any of them?"

"Why, indeed?"

They both chuckled.

"What will you do with her after the wedding?" Paxton asked.

"I haven't decided."

"You won't let her live in Town, will you?" Paxton was aghast at the prospect.

"I might—if she doesn't pester me too much."

"What if she objects to Lauretta and the others?"

"My relationship with Lauretta isn't any of her business."

"You might think so now," Paxton counseled, "but I'm told that after the ceremony, wives tend to develop the most absurd notions about fidelity."

"Her opinion will never matter. It's ludicrous to presume that she could have any influence over me."

"She might disagree. She might imagine that her wedding ring gives her the right to complain."

"*She* would be wrong."

Paxton sighed, as if he felt sorry for Jordan. "I don't know why you refused that girl your father picked for you. She's a duke's daughter."

"You know why."

"To aggravate him as much as possible?"

"Yes."

Jordan's feud with his father was long-standing and bitter. In Lord Sunderland's eyes, Jordan had never been good enough. Despite what he did, despite how hard he tried, he always came up lacking.

His older brother, James, had been the perfect, adored son, but James had drowned in a boating accident when Jordan was ten. Suddenly, Jordan had found himself to be the heir, a position he'd never anticipated or wanted.

Jordan had been in the boat with his brother, and Sunderland blamed Jordan for James's death. Jordan had fought to save James, but there was no persuading their father. Once, shortly after the tragedy, Jordan had heard Sunderland asking a friend if Jordan might have murdered James!

Why was Jordan the one who survived? Sunderland had moaned.

Looking back from an adult perspective, Jordan understood that Sunderland had been crushed with grief. He probably hadn't meant what he'd said, but his cruel words still stung, and they colored all of Jordan's subsequent interactions with his father.

They bickered constantly, usually over finances.

Jordan actually owned a house and property north of London. It had been James's, so Jordan inherited it when James died. As Jordan had been a minor child, Sunderland had managed the estate for him, but Sunderland had bankrupted it with his inattention. The house was a dilapidated ruin, the fields lying fallow.

In his more morose moments, Jordan wished he could flee to the rural haven, but the place wasn't livable, and he'd never had the resources to make necessary repairs. Nor would Sunderland refurbish what he'd wrecked. He contended that renovation was a waste of expense because Jordan would bungle his ownership through sloth.

Until his father passed on, Jordan didn't have a single farthing to call his own, and Sunderland used his fiscal advantage to extort all sorts of concessions.

When he'd shown up with a signed marriage contract, the bride already selected and a demand that Jordan wed her immediately, Jordan had had enough. He'd tossed the document in Sunderland's face, which had promptly caused the man to cut off all funds.

But Jordan would win in the end. He'd snagged his heiress, and soon, he'd have all her pretty money in his bank account. For the rest of his life, he'd never have to worry about his finances again.

In the process, he'd bind himself to a merchant's daughter—a fact likely to send Sunderland to an early grave.

He went to the window and glanced off across the park, admiring the vibrant hues of the forest, when he noticed Mary returning from a walk.

Instantly, he wondered if she'd been off trying to kiss the buffoon who resided on the adjacent property. At the notion that she might have been, he was extremely irritated.

Was he jealous? Why would he be?

He couldn't figure it out. She claimed she'd drunk a tonic that had stirred his heightened regard, and maybe she had. There was no rational reason for his fascination, so why not accept a supernatural one?

Paxton came over to stare out the window, too, and he saw Mary just as she slipped in the rear door.

"She's an interesting baggage, isn't she?" Paxton said.

"Very," Jordan mused. "I feel sorry for her."

"You do?"

"Yes."

"Gad! Lauretta insisted you were ill. Are you?"

"No."

He had no business dabbling with Mary Barnes—only disaster could result—but his conduct seemed unavoidable, like a bad carriage accident. In a life where he'd had very little joy, she made him laugh, and he was determined to spend more private time with her.

"Have you seduced her?" Paxton asked.

"Not yet."

"But you will?"

Jordan shrugged. "Perhaps."

"Is that wise?"

"Beneath the plain clothes and stern hairstyle, she has the most amazing, erotic allure."

"But to ruin her? That's a tad cold—even for you." Paxton frowned. "If you proceed, and your affair is uncovered, what will become of her? Victoria would throw her out. With you about to wed Felicity, she'd hardly have any other option."

"No, she wouldn't," Jordan agreed.

"So you'd forge ahead anyway?"

"I'm debating."

Paxton looked as if he'd continue his admonishment, but he stopped.

"I was about to scold you," he admitted, shocked.

"How odd."

"Wasn't it, though? I don't know what came over me."

"Maybe you should dabble a bit yourself," Jordan advised. "It will help to pass the time. Have you found any intriguing housemaids?"

"No."

"You can use Lauretta if you'd like. I don't care."

"Actually, she offered herself just the other night."

"She must have wanted something from you. What was it?"

"She's terrified that you're about to toss her over. She begged me to probe your *feelings*."

Jordan snorted. "I have no feelings."

"That's what I told her."

"Did you sleep with her?"

"I'd rather copulate with a scorpion." Paxton shuddered. "Besides, I've set my eye on someone else."

"Who?"

"Mrs. Stewart."

"Cassandra, the purportedly frigid widow?"

"I don't think she's quite as frosty as she's made out to be."

"Really?"

"Yes."

Jordan lifted his brandy in a toast. "May we both succeed in our amorous endeavors."

"May we both get precisely what we deserve," Paxton retorted.

"If we do, we're in a lot of trouble."

Jordan walked to the door that led to the hall and away from the parlor where the ladies awaited him.

"Where are you going?" Paxton inquired.

"I've suddenly remembered a previous engagement."

"Mary Barnes?"

Jordan grinned, but didn't reply. A few hours with Mary would be much more amusing than listening to Felicity drone on and on.

"Make my apologies, will you?"

He left quickly, not giving Paxton the chance to dissuade him.

In a matter of seconds, he was climbing the stairs in the far section of the manor, headed for Mary's small, isolated bedchamber.

"HELLO, Mary," Jordan said, chuckling at how he startled her.

He slipped inside, shut and locked the door. She was sitting on her bed, wearing her nightgown and robe, her hair down and brushed out. A tray of bread and cheese was balanced on her lap.

"Why are you here again?" she asked.

"I missed you at supper."

"You did not."

"I did. Why are you eating bread and cheese? Didn't the cook save you any hot food?"

"I like bread and cheese. I don't need a fancy meal."

He wondered if Victoria had her on reduced rations, like a

convict or a slave, but he wouldn't embarrass her by prying. Nor could he bear to know too many details about her relationship with Victoria.

It was obvious that Victoria abused Mary, and any confirmation of the fact would simply make him feel more compassion for her, when he was already becoming bound to her in ways he didn't like.

"I thought I'd better check on you," he said.

"I'm fine. You can leave now."

He came over and sat next to her. She scowled, but didn't move away, which he regarded as enormous progress. He shifted closer, their arms and thighs touching, and strangely, his body seemed to rejoice at the intimate placement. He forced himself not to heed the sensation, not to revel in it.

"You were out in the woods," he stated.

"Were you following me again?"

"No, but I probably should be. You can't be sneaking out and kissing that . . . that . . . oaf. You didn't try, did you?"

"His name is Harold, and no, I didn't."

Harold! Even his name was tedious.

"Good, because I'm rather vain about my amatory skills, and I've given you sufficient instruction for you to realize that your *Harold* is a lost cause."

"Is there some reason you assume I'm any of your business?"

He was unable to let the matter drop. "What do you see in him anyway?"

"If you must know, he and I are betrothed."

"Betrothed!" He laughed. "You are not."

"We are, and don't you dare tell anyone."

"So it's a grand secret, is it?"

"Yes."

"Isn't he concerned about your penury?"

"No. He's not as greedy as some people I could mention." She glowered, making it clear that she was referring to him. "He'll wed without a fortune being thrown at him."

"How decent of him."

"He doesn't need any money from me. He's set to inherit his mother's house and income when she dies."

"How long have you been waiting for the old girl to go?"

A muscle ticked in her cheek, but she didn't answer, which told him it had been years.

Poor thing! Dithering away, with her hopes pinned on a boor who would never do as he'd promised!

The information tugged at his heartstrings, and he couldn't abide it. He didn't want to care about her!

"Would you like some wine?" she asked as she scooted away and stood.

"Why not?" He'd had plenty of liquor, but he never turned down the offer of more.

Oddly, instead of pouring some from a bottle, she retrieved a leather flask from a dresser drawer. There was an empty glass on her supper tray, and she squeezed the wine into it.

He took a sip, found it to be cheap and sour, and he tried to give it back.

"I'll usually drink anything," he said, "but this is putrid. Thank you, but I believe I'll pass."

"It's all I have."

"Better left alone, then."

"Take another sip. You'll grow accustomed to the taste."

He obliged her, not finding the second attempt any easier than the first, but it seemed important to her so he held his breath and downed the contents.

"Are you happy now?" he teased when he'd finished.

"Yes, very happy."

"I bet you're surprised to learn that I can be so obedient."

She snorted. "You only drank it because you felt like it. I couldn't make you do something if you didn't truly want to."

"You know me well."

She dawdled in front of him, studying his eyes, and after a few moments, she said, "Are you feeling any different?"

"Should I be?"

"No. I was just curious."

"Have you poisoned me?"

"Don't be ridiculous."

She didn't look all that sure, which was unnerving, but he hadn't yet engaged in conduct that might goad her to homicide. In the past, he'd driven various women to incredible frenzies of dislike, so he recognized the signs.

She wasn't anywhere close.

He reached out and clasped her wrist.

"I want to kiss you again."

"You do? You *still* want to?"

"Yes. Let's lie down."

He flopped onto the mattress and pulled her down with him, and she came more willingly than he might have predicted.

He grinned.

"Do you know what I think?" he asked.

"What?"

"I think you like me a bit more than you care to admit."

"And I think that *you* like me a tad more than you should."

"It's entirely possible," he conceded.

At the prospect, she appeared miserable, and he was very annoyed. Didn't she comprehend that females all over the kingdom would give their right arms to be in her shoes?

She ought to be smiling! She ought to be glad!

"Don't look so morose," he complained.

"How should I look?"

"Ecstatic! Delighted!"

"Why should I be?"

"Because you have *me* in your bed."

She chuckled, then sighed. "You're not going to leave me alone, are you?"

"No. I'll be here for a whole month. Would you have me die of boredom?"

"We wouldn't want that, would we?"

"No, *we* wouldn't. I demand that you entertain me whenever you have the opportunity."

She rolled onto her back and stared at the ceiling. "We're courting disaster. What if Victoria catches you? Or Felicity? I'd be in so much trouble."

"I'd protect you," he lied.

During his amorous pursuits, he wasn't in the habit of practicing veracity, and he saw no reason to start.

"You're aware of how Felicity treats me," she mentioned.

"She's a total shrew."

"Yes, she is, and how you could consider marrying her is beyond me."

"If you could see the balance in my bank account, you'd understand."

"There are some things in this world that are more important than money."

"I can't name any."

Their discussion irked him. He wasn't worried about Victoria or Felicity, for he never fretted over consequences. If he stumbled on something he liked, something he wanted, he grabbed for it, and he wouldn't waste time commiserating over every probable catastrophe.

"I won't listen to your predictions of calamity," he said.

"I'm just pointing out the obvious."

"You're being absurd. No one will ever know that we've been involved."

"How can you guarantee such an outcome? Are you a sorcerer?"

"Yes, I am. Let me show you some of my best magic."

He came over her, his body pressing her into the mattress, his lips mere inches from her own. As he gazed at her, his heart did the strangest flip-flop.

She made him wish he didn't have to marry Felicity. She made him wish he was a different sort of person, one who was kind and generous and honest. Gad, she made him wish he could wed *her* instead of her unbearable half sister.

The yearnings were so peculiar—and so foreign to his

character—that he wondered if he wasn't coming down with an ague.

He kissed her, and he was thrilled to find that she joined in with an equal amount of vigor. Despite her maidenly protests, she wasn't immune to his many charms.

He laced his fingers through her hair, the lengthy tresses tumbling over her shoulders. His hands descended to her breasts, and he massaged them until she began to squirm and writhe, but as he eased her skirt up her legs, he realized that he was awfully sleepy.

He slid onto his side and yawned in her face.

Drowsiness was quickly setting in, and it occurred to him that she must have mixed a drug into the wine, after all. Why would she have? And what could it have been?

He certainly hoped it wasn't fatal! He'd hate to perish before he had the chance to have sex with her.

"What's the matter?" she anxiously asked. "Are you ill?"

"No. I'm tired."

"Tired! Why?"

"What did you put in the wine?"

"The wine! Oh no!"

His limbs were heavy as anvils, and he yawned again, his eyes drifting shut.

"Lord Redvers!"

"Hmm . . . ?"

She had the sweetest, most soothing voice. He smiled, feeling as if she was an angel floating over him.

"Jordan! Jordan!"

She shook him, but to no avail. Just then, if she'd offered him a thousand pounds, he couldn't have roused himself to answer her.

As he glided into a quiet, peaceful slumber, he heard her hissing, "Jordan! You can't fall asleep in here. You absolutely can't."

Chapter 7

❦

"REDVERS? Are you in here?"

Lauretta tiptoed into his bedchamber and scanned the empty room.

From the looks of the tidy blankets, he hadn't slept in his own bed, so where was he? In whose bed had he slept instead?

She was his paid consort, so she was in no position to complain about his conduct. He'd made no vows of fidelity, nor would she have demanded any.

Yet she liked to know what he was doing and with whom he was doing it. If she wasn't vigilant, a less scrupulous female could slip in and take her place before she even realized what was happening.

It was important to be cautious.

"Where are you, you bastard?"

She searched his dresser drawers and coat pockets but she found no pertinent clues, so she gave up and headed downstairs to the dining room. Felicity was sitting at the table and gulping down a huge breakfast.

"Have you seen Lord Redvers?" Lauretta asked, hating to admit that she, herself, had no idea where he was.

"No," the snotty girl answered, "have you?"

Lauretta wondered what Felicity had been told as to the true status of Lauretta's relationship with Redvers. Felicity was so provincial that it had probably never occurred to her that her future husband was a philanderer. After she was married to him, and his actual character exposed, how would her vanity survive the revelation?

"If you find him," Felicity fumed, standing, "you may inform him that I'm extremely aggravated."

"What did he do?"

"After supper, he vanished without a minute of socializing. Then, this morning, we were supposed to go riding, but he didn't appear."

"You poor dear," Lauretta falsely commiserated. "I can't imagine what kept him away. Can you?"

"No, but it will take an enormous amount of effort for him to get back in my good graces. I'll expect an apology before noon."

"I'll be sure and tell him."

"You do that."

Felicity flounced out, and Lauretta huffed with disgust. Jordan would never care about Felicity's wounded sensibilities or anything else.

Oh, what a painful awakening the awful child would have when she was thrust into the adult world with the likes of Jordan Winthrop as her spouse!

Lauretta couldn't wait to watch it unfold.

As Felicity's footsteps retreated, Victoria lumbered in and pulled up a chair. A servant presented her with a plate so loaded down with food that it spilled over the edges onto the tablecloth.

Without so much as a greeting to Lauretta, Victoria shoveled down the meal, not speaking until every bite had been ingested.

"Good morning, Mrs. Bainbridge," she finally said.

"Mrs. Barnes," Lauretta returned, nodding. "How are the marital negotiations proceeding? Will wedding bells soon chime?"

"Certainly. Lord Redvers is eager, as are Felicity and myself."

"Really?" Lauretta mused. "I talked to Redvers, and he didn't seem to be in any hurry. Are you sure you haven't misread his intentions?"

Victoria narrowed her gaze, studying Lauretta with a dislike that mirrored Lauretta's own.

"If you're trying to tell me something," Victoria snapped, "don't dilly-dally. Spit it out."

"As a matter of fact, there is a private topic I'd like to address—if you can promise me your complete discretion."

Victoria considered, then gestured to the servant, who slithered out and shut the door, leaving them alone.

"May I be frank?" Lauretta started.

"I hope you will be."

"I'm intimately acquainted with Lord Redvers," Lauretta bragged.

"I know all about you, Mrs. Bainbridge." Victoria's tone wasn't complimentary. "Please spare me any details."

"Since you apparently know *all* about me, then you must be aware that I understand Redvers better than anyone."

"And . . . ?"

"His attention span—when it comes to females—is very short."

"Your point being?"

"He didn't sleep in his own bed last night, he didn't sleep in mine, and I'm positive he wouldn't have slept in Felicity's."

"I'd kill him if he had."

"So where was he? If he's dabbling with a housemaid, you'll never get him to focus long enough to propose."

"He'll propose." Victoria was supremely confident in the power of her money. "He's too desperate not to."

"If that's what you assume, then you're a fool. He hates to

be pushed, and he won't be cornered. If you pressure him, he'll walk away, and I don't care how many bloody pounds your daughter has in the bank."

"Why are you discussing this with me? You can't be in any rush to see him wed Felicity."

"Au contraire. I'm delighted to have him marry Felicity. I recommended her."

Lauretta looked smug, oozing the distinct impression that as easily as she'd persuaded Redvers to accept the match, she could dissuade him just as easily.

"Your enthusiasm seems odd to me," Victoria mentioned.

"Why would it be? He has to pick someone, and I'd like him to select a girl who won't give me any trouble. Felicity is very young, and if she becomes his bride, she'll offer no interference to my own relationship with him."

"You're quite certain of your position."

"He and I are very close."

"If that's true, why are you so worried about where he's spending his evenings?"

Victoria shot such a malevolent glare that Lauretta blanched, and she was more determined than ever to have the stupid wedding concluded so that they could head back to London.

Redvers had promised they would continue on to Scotland, to attend some of the autumn hunting parties, and Lauretta needed funds for a new wardrobe to wear on the trip. At times, she felt as if *she* wanted the blasted dowry more than Redvers, and he had to concentrate on the task at hand.

"We both want the same thing, Mrs. Barnes. We want a quick wedding."

"Yes, we do."

"We must work together to make it happen." Lauretta stood and went to the door. "I'll try to keep him on track, but would it be too much to ask that you keep your servants in line, as well?"

"None of my servants is bedding him. They wouldn't dare."

"Wouldn't they?"

She strolled out, and as she stepped into the hall, she smirked. She'd needled Victoria just enough to have her suspicious of everyone.

If Jordan was fornicating with a maid, Victoria would expose the interloper and send her packing. Lauretta wouldn't have to do anything, at all, except celebrate once the vows were spoken.

MARY sat in a chair by the window, staring out across the park. The sun was fully up, the staff engaged in morning chores, yet Jordan still slumbered in her bed. He'd been out for hours and hadn't moved. Not even when she'd tugged off his boots, unbuttoned his shirt, or covered him with a blanket.

How was she to get him up and returned to his own room undetected?

What had Mr. Dubois put in that draught? What if Jordan never roused? What if he was a male version of Sleeping Beauty, destined to remain unconscious for all eternity?

She'd watched over him all night, and the quiet interval had created an odd intimacy. She felt as if he'd been given to her for a special purpose, as if he was hers to guard and protect.

She was exhausted, her back aching from the hard chair, and she yearned to take a nap. The bed called to her, and she rose and tiptoed over. She untied the sash on her robe and let it fall to the floor, then carefully eased onto the mattress and stretched out on her side, listening to him breathe.

It was the sweetest moment of her life. His skin was so warm, and he smelled so good, and she couldn't resist resting her palm on his stomach. As she touched him, his eyes opened, and his devil's grin was firmly in place.

She couldn't help but smile with relief that he was finally awake.

"What time is it?" he calmly asked as if lying next to her was the most common occurrence in the world.

"It's nine o'clock already."

"I've got a pounding headache, but I didn't drink enough to be hung-over." He frowned, reflecting on his condition, then he accused, "You tried to poison me!"

"I did not."

"Then what was in that wine?"

"I don't know." At his skeptical glower, she said, "I swear! I slipped you a tonic that I hoped would quell your fascination with me."

He studied her, his rapt focus meandering down her torso, taking in the fact that she was wearing a nightgown and naught else.

"I'm going to let you in on a little secret," he murmured.

"What is it?"

"I'm still fascinated, so whatever you gave me, it didn't work." He leaned in and kissed her. "Tell me the truth."

"About what?"

"While I was out, did you have your way with me?"

"I wouldn't have the vaguest idea of how to go about it."

"Are you sure you didn't peek inside my trousers?"

"Gad no!" She blushed.

"I wish you had. I'd have enjoyed it immensely."

She chuckled. "You are the worst."

He dragged her over so that she was on top of him, her loins pressed to his, and the wicked contact made her tummy swirl with butterflies.

"My dearest Mary," he said, "you're scarcely dressed, and you boldly climbed into bed with me."

"I didn't," she contended.

"Then how did you end up next to me? Did you float?"

"No."

"Well, you're here and I'm here, and I'm awfully aroused with morning passion, but my head is hammering so badly that you'll have to take the lead."

"Take the lead on *what*?"

"You know what you want."

He lugged her about so that she was hovered over his lap, kneeling, with her thighs on either side of his.

Once he had her where he wanted her, he yanked off his shirt, and suddenly, she was confronted with too much bare flesh. She yearned to stroke her hands across it, but she was too tentative to proceed, so he took hold of her wrists and laid her palms on his chest.

A blaze of sensation shot through her.

She rubbed in small circles, moving up and down and around, learning the width and breadth of him. His skin was very hot, as if he burned for her, and he was extremely responsive. When she touched him in various spots, he trembled.

He eased her forward and bestowed a lush, stirring kiss, then he rooted to her bosom and suckled her breasts, the fabric of her nightgown providing an extra measure of friction.

Very swiftly, her pulse was racing, her nipples throbbing.

How was it that she'd so rapidly become a wanton? Why was he able to spur her to such licentious conduct?

"Stop, Jordan," she ultimately said, pulling away. "You drive me wild with your caresses."

"Good."

"This is too overwhelming for me. I think you should go."

"In a minute. There's no hurry."

Due to her moral underpinnings, she knew she should demand his departure, but when he'd refused to leave, she was so relieved. She wanted him to stay; she wanted him to stay forever.

"Did you enjoy the passion I showed you the other day?" he asked.

"I won't deny it. Yes, I did."

"Would you like me to do it to you again?"

Her entire body, down to bone and pore, quivered with anticipation.

"If you feel you must."

"Oh, I must, Mary. I definitely must." He clutched the hem of her nightgown and worked it up her torso. "Even though I'm nearly comatose with the headache you've inflicted, I shall martyr myself in the name of your pleasure."

The hem was raised higher and higher. At the last second, she panicked and tried to fight being disrobed, but he was too quick for her, and she was naked.

She was still hovered over his lap, her nude form fully visible, and she wondered if she might ignite from discomfiture.

"You're embarrassing me," she murmured.

"Hush. Let me look at you."

She folded her arms over her breasts, but he gripped her wrists and urged them away so that he had a clear view. He evaluated her, taking his time, as if memorizing every detail, then he drew her to him and kissed her tenderly, sweetly.

"You're very beautiful, Mary."

Secretly, she was thrilled by the pretty compliment, but she didn't know how to reply to it. She burrowed her face into the crook of his neck, wanting to hide, but strangely, wanting to be more brazen for him, too. She was suffering from a peculiar combination of exhilaration and shame.

She was aware of what type of female tickled his fancy—a woman like Mrs. Bainbridge—but Mary had no idea how to go about being so loose. She wished she knew every coquette's trick, and she was depressed by her lack of turpitude.

She'd always been a perfectly behaved daughter, but where had it gotten her? What if she was a little ill-behaved? Would the world cease to spin if she reached out and grabbed for what she craved?

He settled her onto her back, and as he came over her, he was staring at her with an expression of great affection. It made her heart pound, made her eager to do whatever he asked—without hesitation, without regard to the consequences.

He started kissing her again, and as her hips began to respond, he abandoned her mouth to nibble a trail down her bosom, to her belly.

"What are you doing?" she inquired.

"I'm going to kiss you in a special way."

Not able to imagine what he meant, she lifted off the pillow to see that he'd spread her legs and wedged himself between her thighs.

She frowned.

"You're not going to . . . to . . ."

"Yes, I am." He grinned.

"But . . . but . . ."

He laved his tongue across her privates.

"Jordan!"

"What?"

"It's unseemly."

"And tremendously wicked, which makes it just the sort of deed I relish."

He laved her again, and all complaint was silenced. She flopped back onto the pillow and gazed at the ceiling as he kept on with his torment. Very soon, she cried out and soared to the heavens.

As she spiraled down, he was nuzzling up her body, laughing, kissing her. He pulled her into his arms, and he appeared so delighted, his usual air of boredom and arrogance having vanished.

"Why are you smiling?" she asked.

"Because you make me happy."

"I do? Why?"

"You're so different from the women of my acquaintance."

"How am I different?"

"You're just . . . you."

"What a lovely thing to say."

He sighed, holding her sprawled across his chest. "Before I'm through, I intend to thoroughly corrupt you. Do you mind?"

"Will I enjoy it?"

"Absolutely."

"Then, no, I won't mind a bit."

"I'm so glad I'm here," he said. "I'm so glad I met you."

"So am I."

He seemed on the verge of making an important confession, when suddenly, footsteps sounded in the hall.

They froze, his eyes widening in question as to who was approaching, but Mary hadn't a clue. She shrugged.

"Mary," Felicity snapped, banging on the door, "are you in there?"

Felicity hadn't visited Mary's room in months, so what were the chances that she'd arrive when Redvers was in Mary's bed and behaving precisely as he oughtn't?

When Mary had been alone with him, it had been easy to forget why he was at Barnes Manor, but with Felicity on the other side of the door, reality crashed down.

"Mary!" Felicity called again, impatient for an answer.

Mary raised up on her elbow. "Felicity, is that you?"

"Yes. Let me in."

Felicity rattled the knob, and Mary shuddered with relief that Jordan had had the foresight to spin the key in the lock the prior evening.

"I'm not dressed."

"For pity's sake. It's after nine. Get up before I tell Mother."

"What do you want?"

"I'm going for a ride in the carriage. Lord Redvers was supposed to accompany me, but he's nowhere to be found. Will you come with me instead?"

"Yes."

"When, exactly, will you drag yourself downstairs?"

"I'm getting up this very second. I'll be down in the foyer in ten minutes."

"You'd better not keep me waiting any longer than that!"

"I won't. I promise."

She stomped off, and as her strides faded, the intimacy between them had been shattered.

"I should go," he said.

He slid to the floor, seeming unaffected by their near discovery.

He tugged on his shirt, his boots, then he glanced in her

mirror and ran a hand through his hair. With that minimal adjustment, he looked completely put together, providing no discernible evidence that he'd just debauched her.

Coolly, he assessed her, then he leaned over and kissed her hard and fast on the mouth.

"We shouldn't be doing this," Mary advised as he drew away.

"Why not?"

"We'll be caught. You know we will."

"Oh, don't worry about her," he scoffed as if Felicity was of no account whatsoever. "I'll stop by again tonight. After everyone is abed. What time is best?"

"Jordan!" she protested. "Will you listen to me?"

"How about midnight? Don't lock your door. I'd hate to have to kick it down."

He walked over, peeked into the hall, and sneaked away.

Chapter 8

❧

"HELLO, Mrs. Stewart. I thought I might find you here."

Without waiting for an invitation to sit, Paxton pulled up a chair.

"Hello, Mr. Adair."

"Were you suffering from insomnia again? Or were you loitering in the hopes that I'd join you?"

"I couldn't sleep, Mr. Adair. *You* had nothing to do with my decision."

"I'd be delighted if you would call me Paxton."

"If I referred to you by your Christian name, it would indicate a heightened regard."

"Yes, it would. What keeps you up? Bad dreams? Bad memories?" She glared, but didn't answer, and he added, "I've heard all about your husband. If I'd been married to him, I wouldn't be able to sleep, either."

The remark brought a ghost of a smile to her pretty lips. She wasn't immune to his many charms—no woman was—

and eventually, he would seduce her. He was too much of a cad
not to.

She was holding a deck of cards, and he took it from her.
He shuffled, then dealt a single card, facedown, one to her and
one to himself.

"Let's play," he said.

"I'd rather not."

"You wouldn't? You'd rather mope in the quiet and the
dark?"

He went to the sideboard and poured two brandies. She accepted hers without complaint, keeping an eye on him as if he
was a wild animal that might bite.

He extracted a cheroot from his pocket. "Do you mind if I
smoke?"

"No."

He touched it to the flickering candle, and she was particularly focused on the glowing tip. He offered it to her.

"Would you like a taste?"

"You won't be shocked?"

"I'm *un*shockable."

"Thank you."

She reached for it and puffed away, and she appeared so
comfortable that it couldn't have been the first occasion she'd
indulged. He imagined her passing the long hours of the night,
lost in rumination, alone, depressed.

Oddly, he was saddened to think of her being so tormented,
and he actually wished she'd confide in him, that he might
have a chance to ease her woe.

His relationships with women were always fleeting. He had
few attachments, and he viewed life as a grand lark where he
expected—at the end—he'd feel he'd lived extravagantly and
well.

If he behaved despicably toward her, it would be typical
conduct for him. But if he was kind—if he was a friend—now
that would be peculiar.

"Let's play," he said again.

"What are the rules?"

"High card wins."

"Wins what?"

"Whatever you'd like."

"You don't gamble for sport? There must be stakes?"

"Yes."

She assessed his coat, his clothes. "You don't have anything I want."

"You might be surprised."

She snorted. "I suppose you've already picked out what you want from me."

"Yes, I have."

"What would that be?"

"I'll start with your bracelet."

She twirled it on her wrist. "No."

"Partial to it, are you?"

"Not necessarily, but it was quite expensive, and as I'm positive you'll cheat, I have no desire to surrender it to you."

"Cheat?" He placed a palm over his heart. "Mrs. Stewart, you wound me."

"I doubt that's possible."

He turned over her card, then his. Hers was a king; his, a deuce. It was an old trick, a ruse to keep his opponent in the game.

She wasn't fooled, though, and she scrutinized him, trying to figure out how he'd done it.

"I win," she said, dubious over her victory.

"You certainly do."

"Take off your coat."

"Are you claiming it as a prize?"

"No. I'm simply curious to see what you have hidden up your sleeve."

He chuckled and slid out of it, tossing it over to her. She checked the lining and hem for suspicious openings, but finding none, she gave it back. He laid it on a nearby sofa.

There was a companionable intimacy growing between them, which he was happy to exploit. He loosened his cravat and rolled his cuffs, delighted that he could reveal his forearms without sending her into a swoon.

"Do you ever worry," she asked, "that you might be shot?"

"Shot for what? Cheating?"

"Yes."

"Never. But as to illicit fornication, larceny, or various other scams in which I regularly engage, I'm always a tad nervous."

"Have you dueled?"

"Many times." He grinned. "Shall I regale you with tales of my adventures?"

"My maidenly constitution probably couldn't stand it."

"If you fainted, I'd have to carry you to your bed."

She made a sour face. "A fate worse than death, I assure you."

He dealt them both another card. She flipped them over, and they were the exact opposite. *He* had the king, and she had the deuce.

She scowled. "How did you do that?"

"Do what?" He looked as innocent as a cherub painted on a church ceiling.

"Have you ever been caught?"

"No. I'm too good." He pointed to her wrist. "Are the stones in that bracelet real?"

"Real enough."

"Then hand it over."

"You admit to cheating, yet you have the audacity to demand payment?"

"I never said I cheated." He gestured again. "The bracelet—if you please."

Fuming, she removed it and shoved it at him. "I never liked the gaudy thing anyway."

She grabbed the deck and shuffled, then *she* dealt a single card to him and herself.

"If I'm such a swindler," he asked, "is it wise to try again?"

"You have to give me a chance to win it back."

"Be my guest."

He had a ten, and she had a three.

Her eyes narrowed. "Now I know you're cheating."

He held out his palms, as if in surrender. "I didn't even touch the deck."

"I'm not giving you anything else."

"Aren't you?"

He imbued the question with every bit of innuendo he could muster, and he let the moment stretch out so that there could be no doubt as to precisely what he was considering.

His gaze dropped to her bosom, and he kept it there until she grew uncomfortable and began to squirm. She wasn't as cold as she appeared; she simply drifted through life half alive, as if too weary to experience any joy.

She was a very beautiful woman who had been badly used, and she could benefit from some gentle male attention. It would be his great pleasure to seduce her.

In fact, it would be no chore at all.

"What is your wish, Mr. Adair?" She blushed. "What do you request as your prize?"

He raised a brow. "A kiss."

"A . . . kiss."

"Yes."

"No."

"You shouldn't deal before you've hashed out the terms of the wager."

"Really?" she mocked.

"It's the cardinal rule of gambling. It saves one from disagreements later on."

"I'm not kissing you," she insisted.

"But it's the only thing I want. Will you deny me my reward? If you think to, I should advise you that I don't take promissory notes. I expect full imbursement when the game is concluded."

"We can play all night. I'll never pay you."

"Fine, but you'll still owe me. Can you bear to be obligated?"

"No."

"Then wouldn't it be better to get the dastardly deed over with as quickly as possible?" He leaned back, acting as if he hadn't a care in the world, which he didn't. "If you renege, I'll inform everyone you're indebted to me and that the price is a kiss."

"You wouldn't."

"I would. What will your mother say if she learns we're flirting?"

"We are not flirting."

"Aren't we?"

She frowned, her mind racing as she tried to devise a method for wiggling out of the mess. Except she didn't actually want to avoid it.

"All right," she finally grumbled. "I suppose it won't kill me. One kiss. Just one. Then I'm never wagering with you again."

She braced, trembling, as if worried he might wrestle her to the floor. So he didn't move. Casually, he sipped his drink.

Eventually, her trembling turned to an impatient fidget, and she snapped, "Well? Get on with it."

"Are we in a hurry?"

"Yes. I want this over with."

"Oh. Never let it be said that I failed to satisfy a lady."

He stood, unfolding slowly. He took his chair and placed it next to hers, and he dawdled, fussing with it, pretending that he couldn't position it correctly.

As he sat, he eased toward her, just the tiniest bit, but she lurched away, looking terrified, so he held himself very still. She was skittish, like a horse that had been beaten, and it would require an enormous amount of work to tame her.

He rested a palm on her thigh, and she tensed, but when he tried nothing further, she relaxed. He proceeded in the same fashion, shifting nearer, waiting as she acclimated, shifting again.

Ultimately, he brushed his lips to hers, and the experience was so sweet that he sighed with pleasure.

He kept on for a very long time, gradually enhancing the pressure until she could stand no more.

With a great show of effort, she yanked away.

"Enough," she murmured. "That's enough for now."

He drew away, giving her the space she needed to collect herself, but inside he was reeling, and he refused to let her know that he was rattled.

He grinned. "Yes, that's quite enough. For *now*."

"So we're even?" she asked. "You're content with my payment?"

"No, I'm not at all *content*. I'm afraid we'll have to meet tomorrow night."

"Never in a thousand years, you bounder."

"I'm certain we will," he replied. "Would you like to bet on it?"

"I told you: I'm not playing cards with you again."

"We'll see, won't we?"

He rose and left her to her cheroot and brandy.

"LORD Redvers?"

"Yes?"

"I have a marvelous surprise. Your father is here."

Jordan glared at Victoria, who was huffing and puffing from her dash up the stairs to his bedroom suite. Paxton was over in the corner, smoking and drinking, and he coughed down a crude retort.

"My father?"

"He bids you join him in the drawing room at your earliest convenience."

At the realization that Edward Winthrop, Earl of Sunderland, had deigned to visit, she was positively aflutter.

"Thank you, Victoria. Tell him I'll be right down."

"I shall! I shall!" she gushed, but she didn't depart.

"Was there something else?" he asked, eager to spur her along.

"Would you expect—if we agree about your marriage to Felicity—that he might grace us with his presence at the wedding?"

"I'm sure he wouldn't," he curtly responded.

While Jordan loathed Victoria and couldn't abide the prospect of having her as his mother-in-law, he wasn't cruel by nature. She was thrilled to imagine that Sunderland might socialize with her, but he would view Victoria as being thoroughly beneath his station and worthy of no courtesy.

Victoria was still hovering, and he said, "If you'll excuse me, Victoria? I need a moment before I go down."

"Of course, of course."

She waddled out, and he shut the door behind her. As her strides faded, Paxton whistled softly.

"So, dear old Sunderland has tracked you down, has he?"

"Bastard," Jordan muttered.

"How do you suppose he heard that you were here?"

"I can't spit on the ground without someone tattling. You know that."

"What will you say to him?"

"I won't say anything. It's pointless to converse. I'll sit silently, let him rant and rave, then he'll leave and I'll be free to go about my business."

"If he's traveled all this way to stop you, you might not be shed of him so easily."

"He enjoys making a grand entrance and a grand exit. He won't stay long."

"Perhaps he'll become so worked up that his heart will explode from rage."

"Perhaps."

"Would you like me to come down with you?"

"To do what?"

"I love watching you two spar. It's my favorite sport."

"Very funny."

"Seriously, Jordan, I'll come with you, if you'd like."

"I can tell him to bugger off all by myself. I don't need you to hold my hand."

"Just thought I'd offer." Paxton punched the air with his fist. "Get in a good shot for me, will you?"

"I will."

Jordan marched out, braced for battle.

He and Sunderland had never gotten on, had never understood each other. He wanted to blame it all on his brother's death, but they'd been at odds before then. In Jordan's earliest memories, his father had been an ass, and Jordan had never known why.

Previously, Sunderland's contempt had made Jordan angry, but now, he was merely annoyed by it. And tired. He was very, very tired of being treated as if he was an ill-behaved lad who needed a scolding.

He entered the parlor, seeing Sunderland on the far side of the room. He was seated in the largest chair, as if they were in a king's presentation chamber, with himself the monarch.

Though they were father and son, they shared no features. Sunderland was short and stout, with brown eyes and thinning gray hair. He'd put on weight, had slouched a little. He looked worn down and weary and older than his age of fifty-five years.

There'd always been rumors that Jordan's mother had had an affair, that Jordan wasn't Sunderland's child, which would certainly explain Sunderland's dislike. When Jordan was most aggrieved, he told himself that the stories were true, that he and Sunderland weren't related.

"Hello, Sunderland." Jordan used the mode of address Sunderland insisted upon. Heaven forbid Jordan call the man *Father*.

"I would have a private discussion with you," Sunderland said by way of greeting. "Close the door."

At the regal order, Jordan left it wide open and proceeded to the sideboard, where he poured himself a brandy. Then he sat down and made himself comfortable.

"What are you doing here?" Jordan asked.

"The better question is: What are *you* doing here?"

"I'm here to get married."

"You will not marry that—"

Sunderland was about to utter a perfectly horrid remark about Felicity, when he remembered that the door was ajar.

"Dammit!" he cursed.

He glanced around for a bellpull to have a servant shut it, but not seeing any, he had to rise and complete the task himself.

He strutted over, pacing, while Jordan ignored him and sipped his liquor. When Sunderland couldn't seem to begin, Jordan said, "What is it you wished to say?"

"You will not attach yourself to that . . . that . . . low-born gold-digger."

"Actually, *she* is the one with all the money. I believe that makes *me* the gold-digger."

"Don't be smart. You know what I mean."

"And what is that?"

"Victoria Barnes may have a few drops of blue blood from her father, but in Felicity, it's so diluted as to be nonexistent."

"I'm not marrying her for her blood. I'm marrying her for her fortune."

"This is not funny!" Sunderland roared.

"Who's being funny?" Jordan retorted. "I'm serious as an undertaker on funeral day."

Sunderland started to pace again. "I understand that you find it humorous to aggravate me. I also understand that you enjoy tormenting me with your repeated follies, but I will not let you do this."

"If you hope to stop the wedding, you'll have to reinstate my allowance—although I have to advise you that there will be stipulations."

"Stipulations! You would make demands of me?"

"Yes. After your recent antics, you'll have to deposit the funds in a trust account that you can't touch."

"No."

"I won't put myself in a position where you can cut me off again. I'm sick of you treating me like a child."

"If you didn't act like a child, I wouldn't treat you like one. I have no doubt that if I gave you a large amount of cash, you'd fritter it away in a week."

"Then I guess I'm marrying Felicity, aren't I?"

Jordan shrugged and drank as Sunderland paced, then paced some more. Finally, he halted and pulled up a chair, confident in his ability to persuade, but they would never reach a resolution. They had had so many arguments that Jordan knew exactly what was coming next.

Sunderland would try rational conversation, then bribes, then shouting. When he didn't get his way, he'd storm out.

"Jordan," Sunderland coaxed, "be reasonable."

"A huge infusion of money would make me more *reasonable* than you can possibly imagine."

"Think of what you're doing! Think of appearances! Doesn't anything matter to you?"

"Not really."

"Then consider the children you'll have with that girl. Our line goes back hundreds of years. Would you sully it over want of a few measly pounds?"

"I don't care about your lineage. I never have."

"You will wreck your children's futures."

"I suppose I will."

The prospect of his siring offspring with Felicity was so far down on his list of concerns that it was laughable.

If he and Felicity had children—which he deemed unlikely, since he planned to fornicate with her only once, on his wedding night—he would never inflict himself on them as Sunderland had on Jordan. Jordan would hire a sweet, loving nanny, would place them in a house full of servants who were paid to be kind.

"What a cold son of a bitch you are," Sunderland seethed.

"Like father, like son."

Sunderland's expression became cajoling. "You know, I talked to Jessica's father. She's still willing to have you."

"Who is Jessica?"

"The fiancée I picked for you! It was all arranged."

"How could it have been? I wasn't consulted."

"She's a duke's daughter!" Sunderland complained. "Gad, you sneer as if I'm foisting the scullery maid on you."

"If she's so grand, wed her yourself. You're single. Have at it. Be my guest."

His father grew sly. "If you would inform me that you've changed your mind, I'll write you a bank draft—this very second—for five thousand pounds."

"Five thousand?"

Jordan pretended to ponder the offer, but Sunderland would never be able to convince him.

"My carriage is parked out front," Sunderland mentioned. "We can leave immediately and be in London tomorrow. If we apply for a Special License, you'll have Jessica's dowry by the end of the week."

"And all I'd have to do is marry her?"

"Yes. What do you say, hmm? Let's do it!"

Jordan downed his liquor and stood.

"No, thanks."

Sunderland had been expecting the opposite response, and he gaped, then shook his head as if his hearing was blocked.

"No . . . thanks? *No thanks?*"

"I'm weary of your harangue and intimidation."

"If you assume you can best me, you haven't begun to see intimidation, my boy."

"You don't scare me. You're an obnoxious bully, and you can take your bloody fortune to the grave with you. Have them pack it in your coffin if it will make you happy. Your days of using it to coerce me are over. Now, if you'll excuse me, I need to propose to Felicity. Her mother is waiting."

"You will not proceed!" Sunderland shouted. "I will not allow it!"

Jordan was about to reply when the parlor door opened, and Mary peeked in.

"What on earth is going on in here?" she asked, frowning. On seeing Jordan, her eyes widened with surprise. "Lord Redvers, are you all right?"

Jordan never fretted over other people's opinions, but having Mary walk into the middle of the dreadful scene was extremely disconcerting. He was ashamed to have her view the true picture of his life.

He flushed with chagrin.

"I'm fine, Miss Barnes. I appreciate your checking."

"Who the hell is she?" Sunderland snapped.

"May I present Miss Mary Barnes," Jordan said, "the late Mr. Barnes's oldest daughter."

Sunderland was too furious to mind his manners. "Haven't you the good sense to stay out? We're having an important discussion. Be gone, you little tart."

At the insult, Jordan advanced on Sunderland, for the first time ever ready to knock him to the ground. He reached back to throw a punch, when Mary softly begged, "Jordan! Don't do it."

He hesitated, then dropped his hand. Despite how desperately he wanted to land a blow, he couldn't continue when Mary had asked him to stop.

Jordan glanced at her, torn by her pleading look, and Sunderland couldn't help but notice their heightened regard.

"What's this?" Sunderland snickered. "She calls you *Jordan*? Are you courting one while sniffing after the other? Even *you* couldn't be that reprehensible."

"Shut up," Jordan warned.

Mary was undeterred by the slur against her character, and she marched over until she and Sunderland were toe to toe. She appeared regal and tough, and Sunderland was unnerved by her bravado. Some of his bluster waned.

"I don't know who you are," she stated quietly, but imperiously, "and I don't like you, so I won't be civil. Lord Redvers is Mrs. Barnes's special guest. How dare you come into her home and abuse him!"

"I'll speak to him any way I please," Sunderland declared.

"No, you won't. Not here, and not while I'm listening. Get out, or I'll summon the footmen and have you tossed out on the lawn."

Sunderland bristled, but didn't move.

"Go," Jordan urged. "I'm sick of your tirade."

"You haven't heard the last of me," Sunderland threatened.

"Unfortunately, I'm sure that's true."

"I'll be back with . . . with lawyers! I won't let you get away with this."

"You're embarrassing yourself," Jordan said. "And me. Go away."

With a growl of frustration, Sunderland stomped out, and Mary went over and closed the parlor door. Silence descended, and Jordan began to shake, overly affected by the encounter.

"Who was that?" Mary asked.

"My father."

"You poor man. Why is he so angry?"

"He's always in a snit about something."

"But what brought him here today?"

"He doesn't want me to marry Felicity. He thinks it's a mistake."

Mary chuckled. "He's correct. It is a mistake."

Jordan snorted and walked to the window, watching as Sunderland's driver readied the coach, as the outriders prepared to depart. With great fanfare, the vehicle rattled away, the bells on the horses' manes jingling as they trotted off.

Mary came up and laid her hand on the small of his back, touching him tentatively, uncertain as to how they should act outside the confines of her bedchamber. Then, as quickly as the fleeting caress was started, she ended it and stepped away.

"Has he always been so horrid to you?" she inquired.

"Yes, always."

"I'm sorry."

"Don't be. I'm used to it."

He was mortified that Mary had observed their argument, that she'd felt compelled to take his side. No one had ever stood up for him before, and he was deeply moved by her remarks on his behalf.

His little champion was a dynamo, and he was fighting the strongest impulse to pull her into a tight hug, to tell her what his childhood had been like. He yearned to relate every terrible, unfair thing that had ever transpired, and he was afraid to speak for fear of the painful stories that would tumble out.

Behind them, the door opened again, and Victoria entered.

"Is your father gone?" She pretended to be unapprised of his whereabouts, when there couldn't have been a person in the manor who wasn't aware of his exit.

"Yes, he had an appointment in London. He had to get home."

"Did you have a chance to ask him about the ceremony? Will he attend?"

"You oughtn't to plan on it."

He could feel Mary's intent, unwavering gaze.

At Victoria's mentioning the wedding in front of her, he was flustered, and he hated to be so conflicted.

Victoria noticed Mary standing with him, and she demanded, "Mary, why are you in here?"

"I . . . I . . . happened along as Lord Sunderland was saying good-bye. Lord Redvers introduced me."

"You pestered the earl?" Victoria seethed. "How could you? Where are your manners?"

"No, I—"

"Leave her be, Victoria," Jordan scolded. "Just leave her be."

He stormed out, the stares of both women cutting into his back.

Chapter 9

❧

"THE dress looks blue," Felicity gushed, "but it's actually more of a silver color. There are rows and rows of lace, and the prettiest bows along the hem and it . . ."

Her voice trailed off as she and Jordan turned the corner in the garden and vanished from sight.

They were ambling arm in arm, in another of Victoria's attempts for them to get acquainted. At listening to Felicity prattle on, Jordan appeared so pained that he might have been sitting in the barber's chair and about to have a tooth pulled.

Mary lurked on the terrace, and she knew she should go inside, but she couldn't tear herself away. If she'd believed in Mr. DuBois's concoctions, she'd have demanded one to make her blind so she couldn't see what Jordan was doing.

He'd traveled to the estate for the express purpose of proposing to Felicity, and he'd never given any indication that he planned to do anything else, yet she was bonding with him in dangerous and risky ways.

How could he seduce Mary at night then flirt with Felicity

the next morning? How could he flit from one sister to the other with nary a ripple in his conscience?

She was on a fool's errand, with only heartbreak and misery coming down the road. Yet she wouldn't change her path for all the gold in the world.

With great effort, she forced herself away and started toward the door, when she saw that Mrs. Bainbridge had been watching her watch Jordan. She was blocking Mary's retreat into the house and smiling as if Mary were a humorous object.

Since the day they'd met, Mary had made it a point to stay away from her, and in light of Mary's budding romance with Jordan, she was more determined than ever to avoid Mrs. Bainbridge.

Bainbridge was another piece of the puzzle Mary didn't understand. Jordan fraternized with Mary *and* Bainbridge, but how could he? And when he'd proved himself to be such a libertine, why had Mary formed a connection with him?

Had she no pride? No sense?

"Well, well," Bainbridge began as Mary approached, "if it isn't the *other* Barnes sister."

"Good evening, Mrs. Bainbridge."

"You like hiding in the shadows, don't you?"

"I have no idea what you mean."

"You're always around when you shouldn't be. Why are you spying on Lord Redvers and Felicity? You were positively enthralled."

"They're a very handsome couple," Mary said evenly.

"Yes, they are. It must be difficult for you to tarry in the background and silently observe as he woos Felicity."

"Why would it be difficult?"

"Don't you wish his roving eye would fall on you instead? Don't you wish *you* could be the chosen sister for once?"

"Hardly," Mary insisted. "I wouldn't know what to do with a man like Lord Redvers."

"I bet you could figure it out quickly enough. Most women do. He's quite the rake."

"Really? I'm rather sheltered here in the country. I wouldn't have heard any gossip."

Mary wasn't sure what their conversation was actually about. Bainbridge seemed to be probing for information, or perhaps warning Mary away from Jordan—but why would she?

Mary and Jordan had been extremely discreet, and Mary spent so little time around the family that no one could have any suspicions of an affair. Then again, maybe it was Bainbridge's habit to threaten any prospective rivals. With Jordan's philandering so blatant, it had to be frustrating being his mistress.

If Mary hadn't been so jealous, herself, she'd have felt sorry for Bainbridge.

"How about you, Mrs. Bainbridge?" Mary asked, eager to shift the scrutiny away from herself.

"What about me?"

"You like to brag about your special friendship with Lord Redvers. When he marries Felicity, won't it be difficult for *you*?"

"Felicity will never have any effect on my relationship with him."

"You don't mind if they wed?"

"Why would I? I encouraged the match."

"You did?"

"Yes."

Mary's thoughts raced as she struggled to find an explanation for the woman's easy acceptance of the situation. Bainbridge and Redvers were wicked in a way that was beyond Mary's comprehension, yet Mary wasn't convinced that Jordan was truly the scoundrel he appeared on the surface.

She'd seen him during the quarrel with his father, had noted how distressed he was after Lord Sunderland stormed out. He'd been wounded by his father's disdain.

Brutal forces had shaped him into the mocking, infuriating man he'd become. After such an upbringing and such a father, who wouldn't be bitter? Who wouldn't be cynical?

"I don't understand you," Mary murmured.

"What's to understand?"

"I assumed that you and Lord Redvers were . . . involved."

"We are," she answered without hesitation. "We have a business arrangement that works perfectly. I'm indispensable to his happiness, and we both know it. Why would his marriage to Felicity have a bearing on anything?"

"But he'll be *married* to her."

Bainbridge chuckled. "You're so provincial, Miss Barnes."

"I'm surprised you noticed," Mary sarcastically replied.

"Despite what you suppose here in the country, matrimony has nothing to do with love or any of that folderol. This union is about money and naught else."

"She's a vicious, cruel girl," Mary said very quietly, treading on dangerous ground. "If Lord Redvers is your friend, as you claim, why would you urge him to take such an awful step?"

"We are after her dowry, Miss Barnes. We don't care about her."

Bainbridge sauntered off, smirking, having emphasized the word *we* in both sentences, and Mary was more confused than ever about Jordan. Bainbridge made it sound as if she was more than a mistress—as if she was his wife, in fact.

Could it be?

Mary was crushed all over again, hurt by the notion that she was so unimportant to him. She'd never previously participated in an amour, so she hadn't realized the swings of despair and joy that such an endeavor could produce.

She yearned to escape to her room, to be alone with her anguished ruminations, but Jordan and Felicity were headed toward the house, and Mary stood, watching their advance.

Felicity was so pretty, so fashionably turned out, her gloved hand clutching Jordan's arm in a proprietary manner, and Mary's old feelings of injustice rose to the fore.

She was so envious that she was ill with it, and she wanted

to break something, to cry out in fury and pound her fists on the wall. Instead, she dawdled, visually daring Jordan to walk past without some type of acknowledgment.

"Hello, Miss Barnes," he deigned to comment. "How are you this fine evening?"

"Lord Redvers." Mary nodded but refused to curtsy.

"Why are you loitering out here?" Felicity snapped. "I'm about to dress for supper. I need my clothes laid out."

Jordan glared at Felicity and asked, "Isn't Miss Barnes your sister?"

"Only my half sister."

"Then why should she prepare your clothes for you? Surely you have a maid who can see to the task?"

"Mary always does it. Mother assigned her the chore ages ago."

"Well, she's not helping you tonight," he asserted, "and not again while I'm visiting."

"Honestly, Lord Redvers"—Felicity stuck her pert nose up in the air—"I know you're a guest, but I don't believe that gives you license to countermand Mother's orders."

Mary had never been more embarrassed. It was bad enough to have him witness how she was treated, but it was worse to have his pity. He didn't realize how Felicity would retaliate, how Mary would suffer long after he'd departed.

"It's all right, Lord Redvers," Mary said. "I don't mind helping her."

"*I* mind," he insisted. "It's not appropriate. Felicity, your maid will assist you from now on. Come."

He led her inside, and he didn't glance back, and Mary was relieved that he didn't.

She slumped against the wall, and she remained there, listening as their strides faded. Then she went in and climbed the rear stairs to her bedchamber.

For an eternity, she gazed out the window as the sun set, the sky changing from indigo to black. It was so quiet, her wing of the manor so isolated, that she felt as if she was the last person on earth.

. As darkness descended, she lit a candle and got ready for bed.

She undressed, washed, and drew on her robe and her floppy woolen socks, then she stared out the window again. The stars twinkled, inviting her to make a wish, but what would it be? That Redvers would fall in love with her? That they could live happily ever after?

Such a wish would be ludicrous.

Through the woods, she could see a light flickering from Harold's house. She hadn't spoken to him since the day she'd drunk the Spinster's Cure. From that moment on, she'd scarcely thought of him at all, having devoted hour after foolish hour in dreamy speculation about Jordan Winthrop. Her imprudent infatuation had only pitched her further into his sphere of influence, had left her more miserable and restless than ever.

She had to stop fantasizing about him, had to stop yearning for a future that would never occur.

First thing in the morning, she'd call on Harold. She'd remind him of the dance in the village on Saturday night, would ask him to walk her home from church on Sunday as he usually did.

She had to get her life back on track to where it had been before Redvers's arrival, to where it would be after he married Felicity and returned to London.

Off in the distance, she heard someone coming toward her room. She supposed she could have locked her door, but what was the use?

Jordan Winthrop was like a disease in her blood. She couldn't be shed of him. She didn't *want* to be shed of him. She wanted to be wicked and witty and loose like Mrs. Bainbridge, and in an instant, all her good intentions regarding Harold vanished.

She was so pathetic!

He spun the knob and slipped inside, but she didn't look

over at him. She wished he'd go away, but in the same breath, wished he wouldn't. Where he was concerned, she had no fortitude; she couldn't be strong or do what was proper.

"Has it always been like this for you?" he inquired.

"Yes."

"Why is she allowed to treat you that way?"

"I don't know." She peered at him over her shoulder. "Don't marry her."

"I have to."

"You'll regret it forever."

"I'm sure you're correct."

She whirled to face him and boldly announced, "It will hurt me if you go through with it."

"I'm sorry." He shrugged, but added no more.

"I can't bear to imagine you with her," Mary pressed.

"Oh, Mary, don't be upset. I'm not worth it."

He stuffed his hands in his pockets, his back leaned against the door, his beautiful eyes so terribly blue. He hadn't shaved in many hours, and his cheeks were shadowed with his evening beard. He appeared rumpled and magnificent, and she was so dangerously attracted to him.

She would do whatever he asked, would shame or debase herself in any fashion he requested, and the insight stunned and frightened her.

Why was she weak in her need for him?

"Why did you bring Mrs. Bainbridge to Barnes Manor with you?"

"I knew I'd be bored; she entertains me. I saw the two of you conversing. Was she rude to you?"

"Of course she was rude to me! She doesn't have a civil bone in her body."

"I'll speak to her."

"Don't you dare. It would only make matters worse. She'll think you have a heightened interest in me."

"She'll be right."

"Doesn't it bother you to have her here while you're courting Felicity?"

"Why would it? One woman has nothing to do with the other."

"Your conscience is clear?"

"About Mrs. Bainbridge? Yes."

"Will she still be your companion after you're wed?"

"Why wouldn't she be?"

"Are you in love with her?"

"Gad, no."

"But she's your mistress."

He hesitated, then admitted, "Yes."

"Do you do the things with her that you do with me?"

He flinched as if she'd struck him. "Sometimes."

"Will you do the same with Felicity?"

"She'll be my wife, Mary," he gently replied.

"You can dally with anyone, can't you? Without a qualm?"

"I've never claimed to be a saint."

They were silent, neither of them moving or talking, the only noise the tick of the clock down the hall.

Finally, she asked what she was dying to learn. "Do I mean anything to you?"

"What?"

"You heard me."

"It's pointless to hash it out," he said. "Let it go."

"But I want to know what we're doing, where it's leading."

"It's not leading anywhere, Mary. I'm sorry; I thought you understood that."

The comment was soothingly offered, but brutal all the same.

Sighing, she stared out the window again, making the wish she hadn't made earlier. She wished she could snap her fingers and become rich and pretty and beloved. She wished she could wake up in some other, better place where people cared about her, where she belonged.

"Don't be sad," he murmured.

"I'm not," she fibbed.

She turned and gazed at him. "I had assumed I was sophisticated enough to involve myself with you, but I'm not. Why don't you go?"

"I don't want to."

"I'm not like the other women in your life."

"I know you're not. That's why I relish your company."

"You should leave and not come back."

"I can't."

"It wounds me to see you with Felicity. Do you mind that it does?"

"Yes, but I can't stop. I have to marry her—or someone just like her."

"Then let it be someone just like her."

"Wealthy heiresses don't grow on trees, and I need to wed as fast as I can. My financial straits are very dire; I don't have time to pick another girl."

"Could you travel to Barnes Manor for Christmas dinner— as her husband—after how it's been between you and me? Could you spend a summer holiday and chat with me as if we're old friends?"

"Yes."

She scoffed. "You pretend it would be so easy, but I can't stand to consider it."

It was too painful to look at him, and she wrenched away and studied the floor, praying he would save her from herself and go, but he walked over and wrapped his arms around her waist.

"Mary, I'll be here for such a short while." He kissed her forehead, her cheek, her mouth. "You can't send me away. These hours with you are the only ones that bring me any joy."

"That can't be true," she said, yet she was so pitifully desperate to believe him!

"You make me happy, Mary. When I'm with Felicity, all

I'm focused on is how quickly evening will arrive so that I can be with you."

She was certain the statement was false. She was certain that—when they were apart—he never thought of her at all, but it was a sign of her deteriorated condition that she would latch on to it like a drowning woman clutching at a rope.

"This hurts me so much."

"How can I make it better?"

"You can't."

He kissed her again, tentatively, just a soft brush of his lips to hers, then he clasped her hand.

"Come," he said, escorting her to the bed.

She went willingly and dropped onto the mattress. They stretched out on their sides, Jordan holding her close.

"It will be all right," he claimed. "Don't worry so much."

"I can't help it."

"I'm giving you all that I can. You have to let it be enough."

"I want more from you than this."

"But *this* is all there can ever be. Shouldn't we grab for it? Can you lie here and tell me that we shouldn't seize the moment?"

"Yes, that's precisely what I'm telling you."

"We share a unique attraction. You'll never convince me to ignore it."

"We're adults; we can control our base impulses."

"If we always behaved ourselves, what fun would life be?"

She chuckled wearily. "You would say that."

"Don't fret." He eased her onto her back. "Let's build memories, instead, so we never forget what it was like."

Though it was mad and reckless, she was incapable of refusing him anything. And wasn't his attitude for the best? Wasn't it wiser to seize the moment, as he'd suggested? What was gained by restraint?

If he couldn't or wouldn't change his course, it was silly to demand more than he could give. Why deny herself his company in the present simply because she wouldn't have it in the future?

She pulled him near, acquiescing, and he smiled, which doomed her to folly.

When he gazed at her as he was, seeming to want only her and no other, it was impossible to resist him. His allure was too potent, her affection too great.

They kissed and kissed, the embrace increasing in intensity, with both of them touching and caressing everywhere. She tugged off his shirt, while he loosened the sash on her robe and opened the front.

He abandoned her mouth and nibbled a path to her breast, and he suckled her, driving her up and up the spiral of pleasure.

At his instigation, she'd become a complete voluptuary. She was consumed by her need to seek sensual arousal. Nothing else mattered. Not his other women. Not her betrayal of Felicity. Not her moral upbringing.

He left her breast and continued his trek down her abdomen to her private parts, and now that she was aware of what he planned, there was none of the embarrassment he'd engendered the first time. Eagerly, she welcomed his naughty advance, spreading her legs, providing him more access. Very swiftly, he pushed her to the cliff of desire and tossed her over.

She soared with ecstasy, and as she drifted down, he was holding her again, kissing her, laughing.

"I am so delighted with you," he said. "You have such a debauched nature. Did you realize it?"

"No."

"You're a veritable slattern, but I mean that in the most complimentary way."

"Thank you—I think."

"I'm glad you've let me corrupt you." He slid to the side and began unbuttoning his trousers. "I want to add to your dissipation."

"How?"

"I can experience carnal pleasure, too."

"Really? I was wondering if you could."

"It's all I contemplate; it's my only hobby."

"Why am I not surprised?"

"I can show you what happens. Would you like that?"

"Very much."

"It will enhance our encounters, and it will keep me from getting grouchy."

"Grouchy?"

"Yes. When you're satisfied, but I'm not, it leaves me uncomfortable."

"You poor thing."

"I've been suffering, and it's all your fault."

"I didn't know. We must put a stop to it at once."

"Yes, we must." He placed her hand on the placard of his pants. "I'm going to teach you how to touch me in a special way. Initially, it may seem a bit strange."

"I don't care. Just tell me what to do."

At the prospect of learning how to titillate him, she was thrilled, and she supposed it was further evidence of her slatternly character, but she didn't mind.

"I'm built differently than you," he explained.

"You are?"

"In my manly parts."

He guided her fingers around a sort of rod that was hidden inside his trousers. It was very large and very warm, the skin pliant and smooth. He instructed her in how to stroke across it, demonstrating the appropriate rhythm.

"What is this thing?" she asked. "What's it called?"

"It's a phallus. Or a cock."

"I want to see it."

"No."

"Jordan!"

"No," he said more adamantly.

"Why not? You've seen plenty of me, and I didn't object."

"If I remove more of my clothes, I may not be able to control myself."

"I don't want you to control yourself."

"Which is why I'm keeping my trousers on."

"What could it hurt?"

He leaned nearer and whispered, "If we're not cautious, we could make a babe."

"Oh."

She was such a ninny that the possibility hadn't occurred to her. Of course, the end result could be a babe. How could she have forgotten? The man rattled her wits!

"How does it happen?" she queried.

"You don't need to know. You just need to let me set some limits, for despite what you may have heard about me, I refuse to leave you ruined and pregnant."

"You're a cad."

"Yes, I am."

"But I find that I'm rather fond of you anyway."

"You have marvelous taste."

She started stroking him again, and he quickly reached a pinnacle where restraint was shattered. He slapped her hand away and rolled on top of her.

"I have to finish it," he said.

"I don't know what to do."

"Don't do anything."

He clasped her hips and flexed his loins, his phallus pressed to her belly. Momentarily, he uttered a soft groan, his entire body rigid, and he held himself very still as a hot liquid spewed across her abdomen.

It was the most exciting experience of her life, and she was tickled to discover that she could goad him to such a desperate conclusion.

Gradually, he relaxed, the endeavor drawing to a close, and he rested for several quiet minutes, his face buried at her nape. Then he slid away and went to the dresser, to fetch a wet cloth.

He sat on the edge of the bed and swabbed her stomach, then he tossed the cloth on the floor and grinned.

"Well, what do you think of male passion?" he inquired. "Are you about to swoon?"

She laughed. "Why? Is it common for a woman to be overcome?"

"If she's timid."

"And I'm definitely not."

"No, you're definitely not."

"Shall we try it again?"

"I thought you'd never ask."

As he lay down and stretched out, she cursed herself for ten times a fool. But she welcomed the iniquity. If she'd had a hundred years to revel with him, she would never have her fill, and when she hadn't the fortitude to extricate herself from the morass she'd created, why not dig a deeper hole?

Chapter 10

❦

"I'M warning you," Cassandra said, "as Mother never will."

"About Viscount Redvers?" Felicity asked.

"Yes."

Cassandra glanced across the room, to where Redvers, Bainbridge, and Adair were playing cards.

Victoria had invited several neighbors to supper, and the exotic trio was the center of attention. The women were trying to get Redvers and Adair to notice them, and the men were trying to peer down the front of Mrs. Bainbridge's gown.

Bainbridge leaned toward Redvers and whispered something, then she peeked over at Felicity and Redvers chuckled. Clearly, they were making fun of Felicity, and while Cassandra presumed any mockery was warranted, she detested how the Londoners thought themselves superior to the Barnes family. It galled her to be the butt of their jokes.

She glared at Felicity.

"If you wed Redvers," she advised, "he'll expect you to do all sorts of things you won't like."

"What sorts of things?" Felicity inquired.

"Marriage has a physical side that's extremely unpleasant. It's kept a huge secret because if girls knew, they would never proceed. You'll have to submit to whatever foul suggestion he makes."

"You're talking in riddles."

"You'll have to remove your clothes," Cassandra explained. "You'll have to let him look at you naked and touch you in your private parts."

"I will not," Felicity insisted.

"I'm merely sharing what I learned. I don't want you to be surprised on your wedding night."

Felicity gazed over at Redvers, where so many females were hovering. "You're just jealous because your husband was a withered old goat, but mine will be dashing and handsome."

The comment pricked at Cassandra's temper, and she should have shrugged it off, but anymore, her equanimity was in short supply.

"Do you have any idea who Mrs. Bainbridge really is?" she asked.

"What do you mean?"

"She's Redvers's consort, his mistress."

"She is not."

"She is!" Cassandra relished—in a thoroughly immature way—the chance to deliver bad news to Felicity. "She's his lover. He never goes anywhere without her."

"That's not true." Felicity studied them. At seeing how closely they were sitting, she frowned, not as sure as she had been. "If she's as loose as you claim, Mother wouldn't have let him bring her here. It would be an insult to me."

"*Mother* wouldn't? If that's what you suppose, you're a fool."

"You don't know everything."

"No, I don't, but you should ask yourself this: Are you prepared to endure a marriage where your husband has a doxy hiding around every corner? Though I must inform you that he has no intention of *hiding* her."

"What are you saying?"

"He'll live openly with Bainbridge in London while he stashes you at some obscure, rural property." Cassandra sipped her wine. "Out of sight, out of mind. That's how his kind always does it."

"You are such a liar," Felicity charged.

"Maybe I'm lying, and maybe I'm not. I guess time will tell."

Cassandra peered over at the trio again, just as Mr. Adair glanced in her direction, so that—without meaning to—she was gazing into his big brown eyes.

He was humored to catch her watching him, and he tipped his drink in acknowledgment. Mrs. Bainbridge noted the gesture, and she smirked.

"Mrs. Stewart," she called, "would you like to join us for a game of cards? Paxton mentioned that you love to play."

Adair had discussed her with Bainbridge?

At the prospect, Cassandra was furious. She shot Adair a look of such hot rage that she was surprised he didn't melt into a puddle, but she couldn't shame or cow him.

He grinned, which infuriated her even more.

"Mr. Adair was mistaken," Cassandra said. "I hate cards."

She scowled at him, visually sending the message: *And I hate you, too!*

Since the evening he'd bestowed his torrid kisses, she'd avoided him like the plague, and as he trained his wicked smile on her, every sensation rushed back.

Her cheeks heated, her breasts ached, her nipples throbbed against her corset.

Suddenly, she was entirely too warm, and she stood and left, hurrying out the rear door that led to the terrace.

The night air was crisp and fresh, and she inhaled deeply, then raced down the stairs into the garden. She wasn't certain of where she was going; she simply had to escape the insufferable drawing room chatter.

The stifling environment of her mother's home was suffo-

cating her. She was too old to be under Victoria's dominion
and control, and she couldn't abide the slow passing of days
where nothing happened and nothing changed.

If only she could move back to London! If only she had the
funds to keep her own house! But Victoria would never permit
it, and as had been proven over and over, there was no way to
fight her mother and win.

She ran down one path, then another, until she arrived at the
gazebo by the lake. It beckoned, like a secret haven, and she
hastened to it and went inside. Moonlight shone on the water,
and she sat on the cushioned bench and stared out. She was
forlorn and angry and bored out of her mind, and if her situation wasn't altered soon, she just might go mad.

His footsteps sounded long before she saw him. As if he
were a homing pigeon, he came directly toward her, not pausing to wonder where she was. He seemed to know, and as he
approached, she panicked.

What did he want? What should she do?

For some reason, when she was with him, she couldn't
maintain the cool indifference she exhibited to every other man
of her acquaintance, and she was too distressed to be sequestered with him.

He climbed the three stairs, and he leaned against the
wooden beam that marked the doorway. He'd loosened his cravat, and he was holding a decanter of liquor.

"Hello, Mrs. Stewart," he greeted.

"What are you doing here?"

"I'm following you," he brazenly admitted. "I've brought
brandy, cheroots, and cards. Which shall we try first?"

He pulled the cork from the decanter and took a swig.

In the past few days, she'd spent too much time thinking
about him. He would bring her nothing but trouble, and she
was anxious for him to leave her alone.

She rose and marched over, hoping to skirt around him and
depart, but as she neared, her senses came alive. She could
smell the starch in his clothes, the soap on his skin. There was

another scent: one that was more subtle, that she thought was his very essence.

It called to her feminine instincts, making her eager to misbehave in a fashion she'd never considered prior.

"You told Mrs. Bainbridge that we played cards!" she accused.

"Yes, I did. I lied and told her you beat me, too. She found it hilarious."

"I won't have that witch knowing my business."

"Don't worry," he said, "I didn't tell her I kissed you."

"You better not have," she threatened. "If I ever learn that you spread any gossip, I can't predict what I'll do, but it will be something you'll regret till your dying day."

He swilled more liquor, then held the bottle out to her.

"You're being a shrew," he calmly stated, "and I can't abide a surly woman. Have a drink and compose yourself."

"If you don't like how I'm acting, go back to the party. I didn't ask you to tag after me."

"I know, but I did it anyway. Doesn't it enrage you?"

"Yes. Why would you?"

"I want to kiss you again. Why would you suppose? And that necklace you're wearing is very interesting. We'll wager for it—unless you'd like to simply give it to me and save me the bother of stealing it from you?"

"You are impossible!"

She tried to shove him aside, but he was too big and wouldn't budge. He gripped her wrists and clasped her hands to his chest, and she could feel the steady beat of his heart.

They stood, tangled together, and like a magnet to metal, he drew her to him and kissed her.

For the briefest instant, she allowed the contact then, with a groan of dismay, she yanked back but didn't step away. She was conflicted about him, and he took advantage of her confusion to dip down and nibble at her nape. He hadn't shaved in many hours, so his chin was rough and scratchy, and goose bumps cascaded down her arms.

"You don't have to be afraid of me," he murmured.

"I'm not."

"I would never hurt you. Just ask any woman who's ever been with me."

"I'm sure it's a very long list."

"It is. I'm a sorry character."

He shifted away and offered her the brandy. She shook her head, declining, and he laughed.

"Don't play the modest maiden with me. I've got you figured out, remember? Have a drink; I know you want one."

She dithered, then took it, enjoying the slow burn as the liquor glided down her throat.

"That's my girl," he said as he watched her.

He linked their fingers and guided her to the bench, and she didn't protest as he sat and pulled her down, too. He arranged her over his lap, her knees on either side of him, and he eased her down so that their loins were touching.

"Relax," he coaxed.

"I shouldn't be this close to you. It's not appropriate."

"So? There's no one to see."

"I don't like it."

"You will, though."

"You are so conceited."

"I can't deny it."

She didn't know what he planned, or what *she* wanted to have happen, but he exuded no hint of menace. He wouldn't proceed against her will, and the notion was oddly liberating. It made her feel in control as she hadn't been in a very long time.

He reached into his coat and retrieved his deck of cards, with his thumb, sliding the top one toward her.

"Guess what card it is," he said.

"Why?"

"If it's higher than your choice, I win. If it's lower, you win."

"What is the prize?"

"If *I* win, I want your necklace, and if *you* win, I will do anything you ask."

"Anything?"

"Yes."

"You don't know me well enough to make such a wager."

"You'd be surprised," he contended. "Go ahead. Guess."

"Five of clubs."

"Ooh, it's a ten." He flipped it over so she could see it. "I'll have your necklace, if you please."

"I'm not giving you more of my jewelry! If I keep letting you cheat me, I won't have any left."

"If you don't wish to pay, you shouldn't play."

She snorted with derision. "Spoken like a true charlatan."

"If you won't part with your necklace, I'll have to claim another prize."

"You can't have my earrings."

"Who said anything about earrings?"

"What is it you want then?" she asked, her voice slightly breathless.

"I want to kiss you until I'm tired of it."

"No more kissing."

"Are you saying you didn't like it the last time?"

"I'm not saying that at all."

He studied her, then grinned. "Oh, I understand. You enjoyed it too much."

"I did not."

"Let's try it again—just so you're sure."

Her heart fluttered with excitement. "I don't think that's wise."

"Who cares about what is *wise*?"

He dipped under her chin again to nuzzle her nape, and he was sucking on her skin, the sensation tugging at her breasts, her womb. When he started in, she lost the ability to act rationally, and with a pitiful moan, she wrenched away.

Her chest was heaving, her pulse racing, and she was very afraid, when she couldn't fathom why. She wasn't scared of him.

"I can't. I can't," she insisted.

"I'll stop whenever you ask"—his hand was on her back,

urging her nearer—"although pride forces me to advise that, with me being so marvelous, you probably won't ask."

He captured her mouth in a torrid kiss, exhibiting none of the reserve he'd demonstrated prior, and though he was holding her, she didn't feel confined or claustrophobic. She relaxed a bit, and of course, cad that he was, he pressed his advantage.

His fingers slid into her hair, extracting the pins, so that it fell about her shoulders. He riffled through it, whispering praise, declaring her beauty, and his sweet words and tender ministrations made her feel free and wild.

She'd never previously been touched in a kind or gentle way. There'd been no hugs from her mother, no pats from a nanny, no affectionate caresses from her spouse.

She'd been ill-used, not just by her husband but by most everyone. Her body was unloved and untended, and Adair's amorous efforts were like a healing balm.

Of her own accord, she pulled him to her, deepening the embrace. He reveled in her boldness, giving her all she craved and so much more.

Gradually, he laid her down onto the bench, and they stretched out, the two of them barely fitting on the narrow space.

He draped a thigh over her, then an arm, then more of a leg. Eventually, he shifted so that his whole torso was atop hers, but amazingly, he wasn't heavy. She wasn't being crushed by him.

It was so easy to be with him, to do what came naturally to other couples, and at the realization that she could dabble with a man, that she could enjoy it, she was stunned.

He was kissing her with a great deal of relish, which made her breasts ache and throb, and she yearned to have him rub them to relieve some of the pressure, but he did nothing to increase the level of ardor, and his restraint had her frantic.

He'd aroused her until she was about to beg for more. Who would have guessed?

Much sooner than she would have liked, he drew away, and he smiled down at her, his eyes twinkling in the moonlight.

"I should win at cards more often," he murmured, chuckling.

"You said you'd keep on till you grew weary. Are you tired of me already?"

"No, I'm definitely not tired."

"Then why stop?"

"Because I need the stamina to kiss you tomorrow."

"You're awfully positive that I'll be amenable."

He rested his hand on her breast, her hard nipple poking the center of his palm. He didn't squeeze the protruding tip, but at the slight contact, her anatomy rippled with anticipation.

"I think it's safe to assume you'll do it again."

"Vain bounder."

"Yes, I am. Make no mistake."

He moved off her and sat, then tugged her up so she was sitting, too.

"Next time," he said, "we'll play cards again."

"You and your cards!"

"I want to have the chance to win your gown. Then your shoes and stockings. Then your corset."

"We've been through this before. We're not gambling over my clothes."

"Yes, we are. And I'll cheat to win them, too. I have the fondest desire to see you naked."

A rush of images swarmed in her head, of her shedding her garments piece by piece, his rigged deck guaranteeing she was bared for his prurient perusal.

"You are so wicked."

"I am." He grinned. "But so are you. You just don't know it yet. Let's get you back to the house."

It was on the tip of her tongue to say that they should linger a tad longer, but if they tarried, there'd be no way to end in any appropriate place.

He stood and urged her to her feet, and after he'd straightened her dress and hair, there wasn't any reason to dawdle. But try as she might, she couldn't make herself leave.

He was assessing her, his scrutiny particularly acute. He

seemed as if he was about to offer a pertinent remark, and she wished he would. She wished he'd explain what they were doing, what was happening, what he wanted from her.

He hugged her, then he pushed her toward the stairs.

"Get going," he said. "I'll watch to be sure you arrive safely."

"Are you coming?"

"In a few minutes."

She nodded, but didn't reply. There were so many words trying to burst out that she was afraid to open her mouth and hear what they might be.

She spun and hurried off, darting down the path. At the last second, when she would have disappeared from view, she glanced back.

He was leaned against the newel post of the gazebo, looking sexy and debonair and wonderful, as if he hadn't a care in the world, as if he'd forgotten all about her.

He gestured with his fingers, encouraging her to keep on and giving every indication that he was glad the tryst was concluded. Perhaps he *had* kissed her till he was tired of it, and if that was the case, if he decided not to dally with her again, she would be very sad, indeed.

She turned and ran.

Chapter 11

"BONJOUR, Miss Barnes."

Mary glanced up and cringed. In her trek back from the village, she'd been so distracted with thoughts of Jordan that she'd forgotten Mr. Dubois and his wagon of tonics.

Were the potions real? Or were they fake?

One of them had seemed to work and one of them had not. She marched over.

"Hello, Mr. Dubois."

"How is your amour proceeding? I trust all is well?"

"No, all is not *well*. If I had paid you, I'd demand a refund."

"But I thought your man had fallen in love with you."

"The *wrong* man. You gave me an antidote."

"Ah, yes, I do recall. And . . . ?"

"I got him to drink it, and all he did was fall asleep."

"And when he awakened? What happened?"

"Nothing. Nothing happened."

"So he hasn't fallen *out* of love with you?"

"He was never *in love* with me. He'd merely developed an

interest that was peculiar. And he's still just . . . just . . ." What was the point of the idiotic conversation? She didn't believe in his tonics! "Never mind. I simply think you should be more careful as to the claims you make. That's all."

He studied her, then took her palm and scrutinized it. She snatched it back, but not before he saw something that had him clucking his tongue.

"C'est terrible."

"What is?"

"If the antidote had no effect, we can't dampen his attraction. It is written in your hand: Fate has intervened."

The way he pronounced the word *fate* made a chill run down her spine.

"What do you mean?"

"I told you that if you swallowed the Spinster's Cure while looking at your true love, you would end up married to him. We have altered your destiny—and his. We can't change it now."

"Don't be ridiculous. He's marrying my sister."

"Is he?" he pompously mused.

Why did she listen to him? What was she hoping to achieve? Nothing could be gained by ascribing any merit to his prophesies.

"It was marvelous to see you again, Mr. Dubois," she lied. "Have a pleasant afternoon."

She started to walk on, but he had an infuriating habit of wheedling her into staying. Somehow, he maneuvered her so that she was at the back of his wagon and staring at his display of bottles and jars.

"I can give you a stronger antidote," he said. "You could slip it to him again. It might work better the second time."

"Why would I want that? I can't have him dozing off in my—"

At realizing she'd almost divulged that Jordan had been in her bed, she blanched.

"Oh no, *cherie*," he murmured in dismay. "Have things progressed so far?"

"I barely know the man in question."

"Perhaps you should speak to my sister, Clarinda."

"About what?"

He leaned nearer and whispered, "She can instruct you on how to prevent a baby."

"A . . . baby! Why would I be worried about having a baby?"

She kept her expression blank, her gaze direct and firm, as he patiently watched her. Evidently, he anticipated a sordid confession. He was a doctor of sorts, and she wondered how many females had shared tales of tragedy and woe. She wasn't about to become one of them!

"A pregnancy will not disappear," he counseled, "simply because you pray it away."

"Mr. Dubois, you overstep your bounds. I am virtuous as the day is long."

"Are you?"

"Yes."

"Then you needn't be alarmed. But just in case, Clarinda is here most of the time."

"Mr. Dubois!"

He assessed her again, and ultimately, he nodded, complicit in her litany of falsehoods. He grabbed a jar, dumped some powder in a pouch, and offered it to her.

"What now?" she asked, exasperated with him, with herself.

"If he is to marry your sister, as you insist he will, your heart will break."

"And this powder will aid me in what fashion?"

"It will cause your affection to wane. Mix it in your tea. Drink three cups."

She didn't want her affection to wane. She wanted it to burn brighter and hotter till she was consumed by the flames. Not that she could admit it.

She scoffed with derision. "You need to keep your stories straight, Mr. Dubois."

"How, *cherie*?"

"On the one hand, you tell me that your Spinster's Cure has fixed my destiny and that I'm to wed my besotted swain. On the other, you give me a remedy to ease my despair when he marries my sister. Which is it to be? Will he be mine or not?"

She'd flummoxed him, which delighted her. Obviously, a customer didn't often get the best of him, and she was tickled to have been the one.

"I don't want you to be hurt, Miss Barnes," he said very gently.

His concern seemed genuine, and she couldn't help warming to him.

She smiled and patted his arm. "I'll be fine, Mr. Dubois."

"For your sake, I hope so. I've met your grand gentleman, remember? I think he could break any woman's heart—especially yours."

"I'm sure he could."

"If my tonic has in any way been—"

"Trust me: Your tonic had nothing to do with it."

Noise sounded down the lane, and she glanced over to see Harold's carriage approaching. There was a pudgy, frumpy woman—whom Mary didn't know—sitting with him on the seat.

Mary hadn't taken that walk to his house, hadn't reminded him of the village social or Sunday church.

She'd conveniently neglected to ponder him at all, and his sudden appearance provided a much-needed dose of reality.

She could daydream and pretend to infinity, but Jordan Winthrop would never be hers, and she had to accept the fact that he was about to be Felicity's husband.

He'd been very blunt, had raised no expectations. He would be at Barnes Manor until he received Felicity's money, then he would go, and Mary would have to pick up the pieces and move on.

Harold would be where he'd always been—at the center of her world—and she couldn't forget it.

Though she didn't realize she'd exhibited any reaction,

she must have, because Mr. Dubois scowled at Harold, then at her.

"Who is this man?" he asked. "I've seen him in the village, and I do not like him. Why does he bring such a frown to your pretty face?"

"You had spoken to me about fate and destiny. Well, *he* is my destiny."

"He is your . . ." He stammered to a halt, then shook his head. "No, that can't be right."

"I'm afraid it is," she insisted.

"He is all wrong for you. I can tell from here."

"Mary," Harold called, "what are you doing?"

"I've been in the village, Harold. I'm on my way home."

"You know I don't like you to be out by yourself."

"I know. I'm sorry."

"And you've stopped to confer with a roadside peddler. Honestly, Mary. You have better sense."

Mr. Dubois snorted.

"Get in," Harold said. "I'll give you a ride to the estate."

"Thank you."

"Why I bother advising you is a mystery." He turned to the woman. "Do you see what I mean, Gertrude? She never listens to a word I say."

"Mother Talbot was correct about her," Gertrude intoned. "What type of female would refuse to be guided by a man of your maturity and wisdom?"

Mary fumed, incensed that he'd been discussing her in a derogatory manner, that he and this Gertrude person were talking as if she wasn't standing in front of them.

"Harold," she said, "who is your companion? I don't believe I've had the pleasure."

"She's my cousin, Miss Gertrude Talbot, up from Portsmouth."

"Hello, Miss Talbot."

"How do you do?"

Miss Talbot's spine was ramrod straight, and she sounded

like an insufferable snob. She and Harold would get on
famously.

"Mother is under the weather," Harold explained, "so Gertrude has come to assist." As if embarrassed by the admission,
his cheeks flushed. "Gertrude, this is Miss Mary Barnes, the
neighbor I've mentioned."

"Miss Barnes"—Gertrude's lips pursed as if she was sucking on a pickle—"I've heard a lot about you."

"I'm sure Harold has been a veritable chatterbox."

"He definitely has been."

He and Gertrude exchanged a significant look that hinted at
numerous confidences, and Mary's fury grew.

How dare he gossip to Mary's detriment!

Jordan was always kind and funny. He treated her like an
equal. He valued her opinion. He made her laugh, he made her
happy, and after spending so much time with him, Harold
seemed more fussy and pedantic than ever. She felt as if she
was choking on her future.

Mary peeked at Mr. Dubois and muttered, "If you could
give me a potion to avoid this fate, you might convince me that
you're a miracle worker."

He snorted again and spun to his shelf, then sneaked a bottle into her reticule.

"I don't have anything powerful enough to counter this disaster, but I suggest you try some of this. As needed. In liberal
amounts."

"What is it?" she asked.

"It's my Woman's Daily Remedy. It's loaded with alcohol.
Drink plenty."

He added a second item, and she raised a brow in question.

"It's another dose of Spinster's Cure," he said. "Swallow it
while staring at your fancy lord again."

"Why would I?"

"You have to find a conclusion that's better than this one."
He glowered at Harold and actually shuddered. "Good luck,
Miss Barnes."

You'll need it hovered in the air.

"Mary, are you coming or not?" Harold griped.

"Yes, Harold, I'm coming."

She walked over to the carriage, and Mr. Dubois helped her up, giving her fingers a supportive squeeze.

Harold clicked the reins, and they lumbered off. They were silent, the moment extremely awkward.

"I've been meaning to stop by"—Mary was eager to break the tension—"to inquire about the dance on Saturday night. Are we still going? I hope your mother isn't too ill that you won't be able to attend."

"Yes, we're going, and I've invited Gertrude to join us, so she can meet some of the other neighbors."

"How nice." Mary forced a smile. "I'm certain you'll enjoy yourself, Miss Talbot."

"I'm certain I will, too," Gertrude replied, and her expression could only be described as malevolent. Her dislike of Mary was blatant and unsettling.

Mary yearned to be anywhere else in the kingdom, and she peered over her shoulder, seeing Mr. Dubois in the distance. He waved, and she waved back, which brought identical scowls from Harold and Gertrude.

"Really, Mary," Harold scolded, "the company you keep. It boggles the mind."

Mary bit her tongue and blindly gazed at the side of the road, not speaking again the entire way.

"HOW long have you known Lord Redvers?"

"Oh, it's been ages."

Felicity studied Mrs. Bainbridge. "Would you consider yourself to be *close* friends?"

"Of course. Why?"

Felicity frowned. Mrs. Bainbridge was so old and so worldly. Felicity wanted to come straight out and ask her if she was Redvers's mistress, but she couldn't decide how to delve to the heart of the matter.

How did a girl probe for details about her betrothed's amours? Was there an appropriate method for discovering what she was dying to learn?

"Will you continue your acquaintance after he's wed?" Felicity queried.

"If Lord Redvers's wishes it." Mrs. Bainbridge chuckled. "And I'm positive he'll *wish* it. We're rarely separated."

Felicity's suspicions were definitely aroused.

Why would Redvers travel with Mrs. Bainbridge unless there was mischief occurring?

If Mrs. Bainbridge was a harlot, then Redvers's bringing her to Barnes Manor was an insult to Felicity.

Was she being humiliated by him without her being aware? Did everyone suspect Mrs. Bainbridge's true role? Were people snickering at Felicity behind her back?

"You seem awfully confident of his affection," Felicity dared to say.

"Don't I, though?"

"You should know that, if I become his wife, I intend to occupy all his time. I'll demand that he dote on me."

Mrs. Bainbridge laughed. "Be sure to tell him so, will you? He'll be delighted to hear that you expect him to be a devoted spouse."

She sauntered off, leaving Felicity to stew all alone on the terrace.

It was obvious that she'd failed to make her point clear. Mrs. Bainbridge had to accept that Felicity wouldn't tolerate any nonsense from Redvers. Nor would she allow Mrs. Bainbridge's association with him to tarnish Felicity.

Felicity had big dreams regarding her life in London. She would be the belle of every ball, the most sought-after guest, the most gracious hostess. She had it all planned out, and she wasn't about to have Mrs. Bainbridge interfering.

She went into the house to speak with her mother. Victoria could handle any situation, and she'd know how to handle this one, too.

Felicity found her in her sitting room, busy with correspondence.

"Mother," Felicity started, pulling up a chair, "I must ask you a question."

"What is it?"

"Yesterday, Cassandra was being particularly horrid. She said the worst things to me."

"About what?"

"She claims that Mrs. Bainbridge is Lord Redvers's . . . ah . . . his . . . his . . . mistress."

She hissed the last word, embarrassed to say it aloud, but some topics couldn't be avoided.

"She said *that*, did she?"

"Yes, and it's upset me terribly."

"I'll talk to her."

Victoria returned to her writing, effectively dismissing Felicity.

"Mother!"

Victoria glanced up. "What?"

"It can't be true." When Victoria didn't leap to agree, Felicity tentatively added, "Can it?"

"Felicity, you're very young, and you have little understanding of what matrimony actually entails."

"I'm not a child," Felicity huffed.

"No, you're not, but you don't seem to realize that the status and identity of Lord Redvers's companions is not—and never will be—any of your business."

"Was Cassandra correct? Is Redvers *involved* with Mrs. Bainbridge?"

"How can it matter if he is or he isn't?"

"Is he?" she snapped.

"If you insist on knowing—yes."

"How long have they been carrying on?"

"Several years, I'm told."

Felicity was stunned. "You knew, and you let him bring her here?"

"Why would I refuse? Mrs. Bainbridge has no bearing on your relationship with him."

"No bearing! Are you insane?" Felicity jumped up and stamped her foot, her voice rising with indignation. "I'm insulted, Mother! I'm offended to the core of my being!"

"Calm yourself," Victoria ordered. "I will not deal with you when you're acting like a spoiled toddler."

"He will be my husband," Felicity seethed, "and I will not permit him to—"

Victoria seized Felicity's wrist and yanked her down into her chair, pinching her arm hard enough to leave a bruise.

"Listen to me, and listen well," Victoria threatened. "When it comes to females, men are like beasts in the field. They wander where their interest takes them. They have no concept of loyalty or fidelity. You'll have to get used to it. Every woman does. You should consider yourself lucky."

"Lucky!"

"You'll learn this lesson early in your marriage. It won't be a painful surprise later on."

"He will not shame me," Felicity vowed.

"*He* will do whatever he pleases, and you will turn a blind eye."

"I won't!" Felicity swore. "I demand that you speak with him. I demand that he send her away. At once!"

Victoria scoffed and waved toward the door. "Go away. I can't abide such juvenile behavior."

"Fine then," Felicity said. "I'll speak with him myself."

Victoria stood and rounded the desk. She and Felicity were about the same height, but Victoria's girth made her much larger, and when her temper was roused, she was a formidable sight.

"You will say nothing to him," Victoria advised.

"I will!" Felicity persisted.

"If you breathe a word of this conversation to anyone, I will whip you to within an inch of your life."

"You wouldn't dare!"

"Wouldn't I?"

Victoria looked lethal, as if the beating might commence immediately, and Felicity reined in her fury. She'd lost the battle, but wouldn't lose the war.

While usually she'd do whatever her mother commanded, she wasn't about to submit to such humiliation. She would find a way to be shed of Mrs. Bainbridge. If her mother wouldn't help her, she'd have to resolve the situation herself.

"You haven't heard the last of this," Felicity declared, and she flounced away.

"LORD Redvers, it's dreadfully hot in here," Felicity said. "Would you stroll with me in the garden?"

Without waiting for a reply, she waltzed over to the door that led to the terrace.

Jordan glanced up from his cards and frowned. Several of Victoria's supper guests had noticed her little drama, and they were snickering.

"She's in a snit, Jordan," Lauretta murmured. "You'd better scurry over before she throws a tantrum."

"Lord Redvers!" Felicity was growing impatient.

Paxton peered over at her. "Does she think you're her pet?"

"Obviously," Lauretta retorted. "By the by, Redvers, this afternoon, she peppered me with questions about my connection to you."

"Did she?"

"Yes. Apparently, it's dawned on her that I'm not your sister."

Jordan sighed, searching for Victoria, who was nowhere to be found.

"I have a brilliant idea," he said. "Paxton, why don't you marry her instead? I'd gladly let you have her dowry."

Paxton gave a mock shudder. "I'd rather be boiled in oil."

Felicity cleared her throat, ready to call out a third time.

"You'd best see what she wants," Paxton urged. "It appears she won't calm till you obey her summons."

Jordan tossed down his cards, and he stood and went over to her.

"Let's step outside, Miss Barnes. Now!"

She spun on her dainty slipper and pranced out, but she stopped next to an open window, where everyone could eavesdrop on their quarrel. He grabbed her elbow and escorted her down the stairs and onto a lighted pathway.

He pulled her along, practically dragging her, until they were a safe distance from the other guests. Then he halted and whipped around, struggling to control his temper.

Even though she would be the worst wife imaginable, he was going to marry her no matter what, so why was he balking?

He should simply haggle over the details with Victoria, then apply for a Special License, yet he couldn't force himself to proceed.

Felicity would never be the wife he wanted or needed, and delay wouldn't change that fact. Why, oh why, couldn't sweet, amusing Mary have possessed a fortune? Why couldn't fate have shined on him just once?

"You had something you wished to say to me?" When Felicity couldn't respond, he pressed, "Get on with it."

"I . . . I . . ."

"If you're suddenly tongue-tied, it's the first time ever. Speak your piece, or let's go back to the party."

She gave herself a good shake, which yanked her from her stupor. "Yes, there is a subject I'd like to address."

"I can't wait to hear what it is."

"I don't care for your two friends, Mrs. Bainbridge and Mr. Adair."

"You don't like my friends?"

"No, I don't. They're both very rude to me—Mrs. Bainbridge in particular—and I want you to send them back to London."

The girl was either stupider than any he'd ever met, or she had more gall.

"Might I ask where you come by the temerity to instruct me as to my choice of companions?"

"I realize that it's too early to mention it, but Mother assures me that you'll propose."

"Really?"

"Yes, and since it's about to happen, we should begin as we mean to go on."

"What the devil are you trying to say? And be precise, because my patience for your nonsense is completely exhausted."

"As we're about to marry, it's perfectly fitting for me to inform you that I don't like Mrs. Bainbridge."

"No one does."

"There have been some awful rumors about the two of you, and I can't have you fraternizing. After we're wed, I absolutely won't allow the association to continue."

He was so stunned that he was at a loss as to what his reply should be.

"How old are you again?" he inquired. "I've forgotten."

"I'm eighteen."

"Does your mother know that you planned to discuss this topic with me?"

"She said I oughtn't, but the issue is important to me, so I forged ahead."

She's only eighteen, he told himself. *Only eighteen.*

He stated her age over and over, like an incantation, using it to compose himself, but it didn't work. He was angry at the world, at his father, at his destiny, and the prospect of marrying her was so ghastly that he felt as if he was about to swallow a vial of poison.

"You're very young," he started.

"I may be young, but I know what I want."

"There may be things you *want*, but you won't receive them from me, so let me be very clear: You will never interfere in my private affairs."

"I will!"

"I will come and go as I please. I will have the friends I please. I will live my life as I please. You will never—I repeat: never!—order me about."

"We'll see about that!"

"Yes, we will."

"You will do as I say," she warned, "or I won't marry you, and you won't get my money!"

"Your mother and I will decide if I should wed you or not. Your preferences are irrelevant. Now, I'm weary of your antics. Let's go back."

"We're not finished."

"Yes, we are."

He clasped her arm and marched her toward the mansion, but she was grumbling and threatening like a shrew, giving him a nauseating glimpse of what their union would be like.

"We are almost inside," he cautioned as he hauled her up the stairs to the terrace. "Cease with these theatrics, or I swear to God that I will bend you over my knee and paddle your bottom till you can't sit down for a week."

"I'll tell Mother!"

"She won't mind a whit. I'll have her full support for any discipline I inflict."

"You're a beast," she hurled, "and I hate you."

"I don't care."

He stormed into the drawing room, heedless of the stares and whispers. Victoria had reappeared and was in a chair in the corner, and he proceeded over to her, still clutching Felicity's arm.

At viewing his obvious fury, she rose and murmured, "What is it, Lord Redvers?"

"I have been insulted by your daughter, madam, and I am tired of her harangue. I ask that you deal with her, so that I don't have to."

"Felicity!" Victoria hissed.

"He won't listen to me," Felicity complained.

"I expect," Jordan said to Victoria, "that when next I cross paths with her, she will have been apprised as to how she should conduct herself in my presence, and that she will have been counseled as to the consequences should she anger me again."

"I will speak with her immediately." Rage rippled over Victoria's features.

"If you think," Jordan fumed, "that I will tolerate any amount of abuse merely to obtain her dowry, you are gravely mistaken."

He flung Felicity at her mother, then he hurried outside where he could be away from the curious and condemning attention of the guests.

Behind him, he heard Victoria say, "If you'll excuse us?"

She whisked Felicity from the room.

Jordan felt as if his world was crashing down around him, and he yearned to be anywhere but Barnes Manor. But where could he go?

If he loitered, Lauretta or Paxton would come out to commiserate, and at the moment, he couldn't bear to parlay with either one of them.

He walked down into the dark garden, swiftly putting as much distance as he could between himself and the house. He was livid and exhausted and wondering for what possible reason he would ever return.

Chapter 12

❦

"WHERE have you been? I've been waiting for hours."

"Have you?"

Jordan slipped into Mary's room and shut the door. It was very late, a single candle burning on the stand by her bed.

She was in a chair by the window, attired in a robe and nothing else. Her hair was down and brushed out, the lengthy tresses curling over her shoulders. She was wearing one wool sock, but not the other.

On seeing him enter, she rose—but too quickly—and she staggered, catching her balance on the nearby dresser.

"Oh my, I'm dizzy."

"You certainly are. What have you been doing?"

She was holding a bottle, and he took it from her, frowning, as he tried to read the label in the dim light.

"What's this?" he asked.

"It's a restorative called Woman's Daily Remedy. Monsieur Dubois gave it to me."

"And Mr. Dubois is who?"

"The peddler who's been camping outside the village."

"Ah."

Her gait was unsteady, her speech slurred, her eyes unusually bright.

"He said I should drink it in liberal doses. He thought it would be beneficial to my disposition."

"What—precisely—is wrong with your disposition?"

"My fate is de . . . depressing me."

"Your *fate*."

"Yes."

He eased her down in the chair as he peered into the bottle. Most of the contents were gone, and he sipped the remaining amount. It had a sugary, cherry taste, but behind the fruity flavoring, there was no hiding the alcohol.

"Do you drink much liquor, Mary?"

"No. Never."

"Ah," he mused again. "Did you realize that this *remedy* has liquor in it?"

"Mr. Dubois mentioned something about that."

"Well then, you can't say he didn't warn you."

He chuckled, imagining the brutal hangover she would have in the morning. She'd be wishing she'd never heard Dubois's name.

Her room was sparsely furnished. There was nowhere to sit but on the bed, so he walked over and plopped down. He faced her, feeling so much better just from being in her company.

After his quarrel with Felicity, he'd tramped around the park, exploring the unlit paths, as he reviewed the sorry state of his affairs.

How could he marry Felicity?

How could he not?

He understood that it would be a foolish blunder, yet he was bizarrely prepared to go through with it anyway. Why would he? Was he insane?

Much of his decision was being driven by anger, by pride, by his fury at his father. He and Sunderland seemed to be constantly re-fighting a battle that had begun when Jordan was a boy.

If Jordan relented and renounced Felicity, he'd never be free of Sunderland's influence and control, and Jordan couldn't bear the notion. So . . . he would bite the bullet and wed Felicity, but that didn't mean he was pleased about it.

Resigned to the outcome, he'd calmed and started back to the manor. The house had been dark and quiet, and he'd assumed he was heading for his own bedchamber. But on the stairs, when he might have turned in one direction, he went the other and ended up outside Mary's door.

He'd grown attached to her in ways he'd never intended, and he was glad she liked him more than he deserved to be liked.

"Your friend Mr. Dubois," he said, "did he have another tonic for me? Are you about to coax me into taking a sleep potion again?"

"That wasn't a sleep potion."

"It wasn't?"

"No. It was supposed to make you leave me alone."

"It didn't work."

"No, it didn't. Mr. Dubois said that it's our *fate* to be together."

"Why would he think so?"

"Because of the original tonic he gave me. Harold should have fallen in love with me, but you ruined my chance."

"I did? When?"

"One evening, out on the terrace. Mr. Dubois's instructions were to swallow the tonic while I was staring at Harold—"

"*Harold* being your besotted fiancé?"

"Yes, but you got in the way, so I was staring at you instead." She sighed dramatically. "I asked Mr. Dubois for an antidote, but it merely put you to sleep. He's certain it had no effect because our relationship was preordained. You're destined to be my husband, and we won't be able to prevent it from occurring."

"And this is why you're depressed?"

"Yes. I don't know how to make Mr. Dubois's tales come true."

He was charmed to view this side of her. She was always so straitlaced, so prim and buttoned up, and her intoxication was relaxing her tongue and inhibitions. In such a reduced condition, what might she be spurred to attempt?

"How are things going with you and Harold? I haven't seen him lately."

"I don't want to talk about Harold."

"What do you want to talk about?"

"You—and me."

She rose up off the chair, a wicked gleam in her eye, and crawled onto his lap. Her knees were on the mattress, her arms wrapped around his neck.

"What about us?" he queried.

"I've been thinking."

"And . . . ?"

"Will you marry me?" she inquired.

The question was ridiculous, and he might have laughed, but she appeared so earnest that he couldn't.

"You know I can't," he told her.

"But you seem to like me."

"I do. I like you very much."

"I'm sure I could make you happy."

"I'm sure you could, too."

"You loathe Felicity, so don't pick her. Pick me."

"I need her money, Mary. I'm sorry; I thought you understood."

"But it's *fated* that we end up together! Mr. Dubois said so."

"He's a roadside peddler, Mary. He could be wrong."

"But if you don't marry me, I'll have to marry Harold."

"I know."

"Wouldn't you care? Wouldn't you be upset?"

The prospect was tremendously galling, and it only underscored how the universe had conspired against him. Why couldn't Mary have been the one with the fortune?

"Yes, I would be very upset."

"Then don't make me do it. Save me."

She pressed her mouth to his, and her lips were soft and warm. He was overwhelmed by her heat, by her scent. The alcohol had worked wonders on her anatomy. She was all loose limbs and rubbery extremities.

The front of her robe had flopped open, giving him tantalizing glimpses of a breast, a tummy, a thigh. He slid a hand inside and laid it on her waist. Her skin was very hot, very smooth, and the sensation rattled him, making him feel strong and protective, making him feel as if he was a better man than the one he actually was.

He was anxious to watch over her, to guard her from harm, and he couldn't remember any other woman generating a similar sentiment. The realization inflamed his masculine passions as nothing else could have.

She pushed him back so that he was lying on the mattress, his legs dangling over the edge. She was hovered over him, kissing him, stroking his shoulders and chest.

He pulled her nearer, joining in with an abandon that seemed hopeless and desperate.

At that moment, he wanted her more than he'd ever wanted anything, and the knowledge that he desired her but couldn't have her was sad and infuriating.

"Do that thing to me again," she said.

"What thing?"

"Where you touch me all over. Where I feel so splendid."

She was in a hurry, dragging off his coat and cravat, and he was as eager as she to be shed of his clothes. He stood and jerked his shirt over his head so that his upper torso was bared, and she scrambled to her knees, studying him with a keen interest.

She looked wanton and delectable, her state of inebriation

making her reckless, and he was ready to travel wherever she
led. A more noble or decent fellow would have tucked her
under the covers and left. But he wasn't noble or decent, so he
was perfectly happy to take advantage when her defenses were
lowered.

She was scrutinizing him so intently that he couldn't help
asking, "Do you like what you see?"

"Yes. I didn't know that a man's body could be so . . . so . . .
stirring."

"You're *stirred*?"

"Definitely."

"What would you like me to do about it?"

"Whatever you like is fine by me."

He groaned, a dozen erotic scenes flitting through his mind.
"Ooh, you are going to be so sorry in the morning."

"Why?"

"Since you never drink hard spirits, I assume that you've
never had a hangover."

"No, I never have."

"Well, you will. And trust me: You won't like it."

"Come here," she demanded, beckoning him, but he didn't
need to be commanded or coaxed.

He flicked open a button on his trousers, then another and
another, so that they were slack around his hips, then he
swooped in, tackling her onto the mattress.

"I'm too dizzy to move that fast," she complained, giggling
as he stretched out atop her.

"Then I promise to keep you flat on your back for a good
long while." He kissed her nose, her cheek. "Tell me why you
were sitting here all alone and drinking Mr. Dubois's remedy."

"I was pondering how awful my life has been."

"It has been awful, hasn't it?"

"Yes, but you've made it better."

"I'm glad."

"I'll miss you after you're gone. That's what I was fretting
about. That's why I was drinking."

He couldn't recall anyone ever missing him before. In fact, most women grew so aggravated with him that they couldn't wait for him to go.

Only Lauretta stayed—and that was because he paid her to tolerate him.

"You're so sweet," he murmured.

"Why doesn't your father like you?" she asked in reply, the question coming out of the blue.

His breath hitched in his lungs. He never discussed Sunderland or their constant conflict, but she seemed to truly want an answer, and to his astonishment, he wanted to give her one.

"I don't know," Jordan admitted. "He never has. Not even when I was a lad in short pants."

"But there must be some reason."

"I had an older brother."

"What was his name?"

"James. We were out in a boat, and it capsized. He drowned. I tried to get him back to shore, but he was bigger than me. I couldn't do it."

Her beautiful brown eyes dug deep, immediately delving to the heart of the matter.

"And your father blames you?"

"Yes."

"How old were you?"

"Ten."

"Ten! You were a child."

"Yes."

"Your father is a bully," she huffed with disgust. "An absolute bully."

"Yes, he is."

"If he doesn't like you, I don't like *him*."

"Give him hell, my little champion."

"Aren't you the only son he has now?"

"Yes."

"Then he should be nicer to you."

"I agree. If you ever see him again, be sure and tell him."

"I will."

She gazed up at him, appearing shrewd and loyal and so very, very pretty, and his pulse made the strangest fluttering motion.

Suddenly, he was overcome by the most powerful wave of affection, and he yearned to confess what his childhood had been like. He wanted to explain about his lonely years as a boy with a deceased mother and a distant, angry father.

He wanted to describe how much he'd loved his brother, how devastated he'd been after the accident.

Because Sunderland had blamed him, there had been no solace for Jordan, no consolation, no chance to grieve. Often, he felt that he'd never recovered from what had transpired, and the bitter memories weighed him down with guilt and remorse.

Mary's interest in his past, her steadfast support, her apparent belief in him and his version of events, was like a soothing balm that he could use to heal old wounds.

Without her knowing, she'd given him a gift he would always cherish, and in the process, she made him ache to be bound to her as he'd never been with another.

He would marry Felicity, but Mary was the one he would treasure. And while he'd told himself he wouldn't ruin her, he wasn't about to ignore their physical attraction. Though it was horrid and selfish, he was desperate to join himself to her in the only way that counted.

He dropped to her breast and began sucking on her nipple, and she sighed with pleasure and arched up, offering more of herself, which he readily accepted.

She was such a sexual creature that, with minimal effort, he sent her soaring, her orgasm exhilarating and potent and as satisfying for him as it had been for her.

"You are so wonderful," she said as she floated down.

"You have to be the only person in the world who's ever thought so."

"People are idiots," she claimed. "They haven't gotten to know you as I have."

"And what is it that you *know* about me?" He was pathetically eager to hear a compliment.

"You're kind, and you're funny, and though you pretend to
be callous and cruel, you're not."

"Hmm . . ." he mumbled.

He was embarrassed by her praise, and his cheeks flushed
with chagrin. She was wrong about him, of course, and he
hoped she would never have to learn just how wrong.

He kissed her again, and as he drew away, he was too
aroused to delay the inevitable.

"I want you to do something with me," he said.

"Anything," she vowed. "I will do *anything* for you. Just
tell me what it is."

He wasn't a saint, and at her statement, he persuaded himself that she was amenable, even though she couldn't be aware
of what she was relinquishing until it was too late.

"I want to make love to you, as a husband makes love to his
wife."

"How does it happen?"

"I will join my body to yours. Here." He reached down and
slipped two fingers into her sheath.

"Really?"

"Yes."

"I was always curious."

"It's rather physical."

This was the spot where he should have been candid, where
he should have reminded her of the consequences. She might
never be able to marry her dear Harold. She might be forever
abandoning her chance for a home and family of her own, but
he was greedily silent, convinced that if he didn't follow
through, his entire life would have been meaningless.

"What does it feel like?" she inquired.

"It's difficult to explain. Let me show you."

She dithered, then laughed. "All right. Have your way
with me."

She flung her arms to the side, like a virgin preparing to be sacrificed, and on seeing her lying beneath him, so trusting and so innocently gullible, he had a peculiar attack of conscience. When he liked her so much, how could he behave so badly toward her?

But as quickly as the question arose, he shoved it away.

He wished he could change the path he'd set them on, but he'd never been a man to deny himself, and when he was so feverishly attracted to her, it was pointless to debate his choices.

Still, he found himself murmuring, "Promise me that you'll never be sorry."

"I never will be. I promise."

"Tomorrow, when you're more yourself, I couldn't bear it if you regretted what we'd done."

"Knowing you is the only thing that brings me any joy." Her smile was eloquent and wise. "I could never regret anything we did together."

"If you're sure . . ."

"I'm very, very sure."

Again, he persuaded himself that she was an adult, that she understood the risk she was taking.

He dipped to her breasts, kneading and sucking at them, driving her up and up. Swiftly, she was at the edge, and with a flick of his thumb, he pushed her into ecstasy.

She cried out, sounding merry and rapturous, and as she drifted down, he was fussing with his trousers, freeing the last of the buttons, yanking the fabric down his hips. Any restraint he might still have possessed had vanished in a fog of desire.

He clasped hold of her thighs, his torso dropping down, as he centered his cock. She was wet and enticing, and it was all he could do to keep from ramming into her like a beast.

He took several deep breaths, calming himself, gaining control. When he was more composed, he began flexing, and at the odd positioning, she tensed.

"This will hurt," he warned, "but only for a moment, and only the first time."

"It doesn't feel right."

"It will. Put your arms around me. Hug me tight."

"Like this?"

"Yes, just like that. Try to relax."

"I am trying."

"We're almost finished."

She was splayed wide, the tip of his phallus wedged against her maidenhead, and she pulled him closer, her lips tickling his ear.

"Tell me you love me," she whispered. "I know you won't mean it, but just this once, tell me so I can pretend."

At her request, a wave of lust shot through him, and he flexed with all his might.

With one forceful plunge, he entered her, and he heard himself say, "Yes, Mary, I love you."

Strangely, the words seemed to be true, and the impression was so shocking that he wondered if he should clarify or retract the declaration. He wanted to pause so he could consider his intent, but the time for rumination was over.

He was so swept up that he couldn't hold back. He thrust and thrust, being carried away by a powerful orgasm that came upon him so unexpectedly, there was no occasion for rational thought.

Without reflection, without regard to the perils, he spilled himself inside her. But try as he might, he couldn't make himself feel sorry. As the movement of his hips ground to a halt, he should have been aghast, but he couldn't find the appropriate remorse.

He felt smug and satisfied and practically silly with delight.

On the morrow, there would be plenty of opportunity to panic and fret, but while his phallus was still pulsing with his release, he was experiencing what could only be described as a profound amount of joy.

She was very quiet, very subdued, and he was curious as to her opinion of the event. He'd been very rough, when usually, he was much better at pacing himself.

"My dearest, Mary," he asked, "what do you think?"

"I'm not a virgin anymore, am I?"

"No. Are you still glad we proceeded?"

"Yes, I'm still glad."

He eased away from her, hating how she winced as their bodies separated.

"Are you sore?"

"I'll mend."

"It won't hurt the next time."

"Does that mean we get to do it again someday?"

"Oh yes, we definitely get to do it again—and again and again."

He snuggled her onto her side and spooned himself to her, tugging the blankets over them, sealing them in a warm cocoon.

"I should have been more careful with you," he said. "I should have gone slower."

"I didn't mind. It was actually rather thrilling."

He raised up and kissed her on the cheek. "You arouse me beyond my limits."

"Good."

She smiled as he rubbed a contented hand up and down her thigh.

"Could I be pregnant now?" she asked.

His heart seized with alarm, but he ignored it.

"It can't happen from just one time." He had no idea why he'd voiced the idiotic lie, but he had, and there was no withdrawing it.

"I wish I was pregnant. I wish I could have your baby."

So do I . . .

The terrifying, bizarre reply muscled its way to the fore, but he let it fade away without giving it any credence.

After his own dreadful upbringing, he hoped to never have any children. He'd had no role model to show him how fatherhood was accomplished, and he was positive he'd be awful at it.

"Don't worry about it now," he said.

She was drifting off, her torso relaxing.

"Stay with me tonight," she implored. "Will you?"

She glanced over her shoulder, her eyes droopy with sleep.

No doubt at dawn, she'd be horrified to find him nestled with her, but at that moment, wild horses couldn't have dragged him away.

"Yes, I'll stay," he promised. "For as long as you want."

Chapter 13

MARY glanced over at the window and saw that it was morning. The light seemed inordinately bright, and it hurt her eyes.

She groaned and sat up, but a pounding headache ripped through her, and she flopped down onto her pillow.

Something was different, and she tried to remember what it was.

Memory flooded in a panicked rush.

"Oh my Lord," she muttered, "what have I done?"

She lifted the quilt to verify what she'd suspected: She was naked.

Carefully, she peeked to the side, and there was Jordan, naked, too, awake and grinning. He appeared young and mischievous and born to cause trouble—which he certainly had.

"Oh my Lord," she muttered again.

She focused on her antics from the prior evening. Many were vivid in her mind. Others were hazy, while others still were lost in a black void.

One deed remained crystal clear.

Stretching her legs, she winced at how her female areas ached, how her *non*virginal body protested its new condition.

She wasn't loose, and she wasn't a doxy, and while she and Jordan had previously trysted in various ways, none of their behaviors came anywhere close to matching what they'd accomplished. She was mortified, unsure, and completely out of her element.

When she'd given herself to him, it had seemed the most natural thing in the world, but now, as sober reality crashed down, she was aghast.

Was she mad?

Her chastity had been blithely surrendered; she could never wed Harold or anyone else. If she was pregnant, and Victoria learned of it, Mary would be immediately evicted.

She'd risked everything for a night of wondrous pleasure, and while a small part of her screamed, *It was worth it,* she knew it hadn't been.

Jordan was very comfortable, as if he woke up in her bed all the time, and he was watching her, waiting to see what she'd do next.

Any bizarre act seemed likely.

"Good morning," he murmured, and he swooped in and stole a kiss. "How is your head?"

"Throbbing."

"I like you when you're drunk."

"You're a beast to mention it."

"It made you terribly easy to seduce."

"You're a cad to have taken advantage when my defenses were low."

"I don't think you should drink any more of Mr. Dubois's remedy."

"No, I don't think I ought."

"Or any hard spirits for that matter."

She frowned, recollection hammering at her. "By any chance, did I . . . I . . . propose to you?"

"Yes."

He was very smug, very humored, and she flung an arm over her eyes.

"Dear Jesus," she mumbled, "take me now."

"You shouldn't count on Him rescuing you. Haven't you heard? We fornicators are damned."

He drew her to him and gave her another kiss. For a moment, she wallowed in the embrace, but she was quickly swamped by guilt and fear. She tried to slide away, but he wouldn't release her.

"You promised you wouldn't be sorry, Mary. Remember?"

"I realize that I said I wouldn't be, but I'm . . . I'm . . ."

"It's all right. You don't need to be embarrassed."

"Oh, Jordan."

She wiggled away and stood, which only increased her mortification. Her nudity felt shameful, much as Eve's must have in the Garden once her sins were exposed.

Lurching about, she searched for her robe and found it under his trousers. Without looking at him, she jerked it on. When she turned to face him, he was sitting on the edge of the bed, the sheet covering his lap.

She scooped up his clothes and pushed them at him, but he batted them away.

"You have to get dressed," she insisted. "You have to get out of here."

"Stop it."

"No, I can't have you—"

He took hold of her hand, the simple gesture halting her comment.

"What's wrong?" he asked.

"You know what's wrong."

"We made love," he said. "So what? It doesn't change anything between us."

"Are you insane? It changes everything."

"How?"

"I can't ever get married now."

"Yes, you can. No one need ever be informed of what we did."

Tears surged and splashed down her cheeks. On seeing them, he pulled her nearer and brushed them away.

"Don't cry."

"But I've wrecked my life. And for what?"

"You're overwrought, Mary, but it's a normal reaction. Sex can be very . . . intense for a female. You're just a bit emotional, but it will pass, and you'll calm. We'll go on as we have been."

She eased away and stepped out of reach.

"You suppose I'd do this with you again?"

"Why wouldn't you?"

She gazed at him, wondering how he could be so cavalier. On her end, the incident had rocked her world, had ruined her future. On his, he looked rumbled and delectable and coolly ready to head down to breakfast.

"Could you ever imagine yourself falling in love with me?" she humiliated herself by asking.

"No," he responded in his usual blunt way, "I couldn't imagine it."

It was the answer she'd expected, but still, she staggered as if he'd struck her.

"You should go," she said. There was a tense silence, but he didn't move, and she added, "Please."

"It's not you, Mary." His expression was bleak. "I don't know how to love anyone. I never have. I don't have that sort of powerful sentiment inside me. It's not part of my makeup."

"I don't believe that."

He shrugged, but didn't continue.

"Don't marry Felicity," she pleaded, disgracing herself. "Now that you've lain with me, now that you've shown me what it's like, I'm begging you not to."

"I have to marry her."

"You could marry me, instead. I don't care if you have no fortune. I don't care if you're broke as a shard of pottery."

"I need her dowry," he obstinately asserted.

"There are more important things to consider than money."

"I can't think of any."

She stumbled to the chair and sat. They stared, separated by an impasse as vast as an ocean.

"I could make you happy," she claimed.

"Yes, you could."

"Then stop being so stubborn. Take a chance on me. Change my life! Change yours!"

"I don't have a penny to my name. A friend of mine lets me live for free in a bachelor's room above his gambling club. The bed I sleep on isn't even mine."

"If I could just be with you, I would endure any hardship."

"I couldn't support you," he said with a ringing finality.

"We could find a solution—if you really wanted to."

He sighed. "Maybe I don't want to."

She swallowed down more tears, feeling bereft, aggrieved, and so very alone.

"I see . . ."

"I don't want to get married, Mary—to anybody. I'll be an awful husband, but if I have to proceed, then I'll do it for money, but you don't have any. I'm sorry. I've tried to be so clear with you."

"I thought last night might have altered your decision."

"It didn't."

She studied him, on tenterhooks, foolishly waiting for him to say he didn't mean it, but he was stoically, intractably silent. He remained on the bed, watching her. Ultimately, he rose and walked about, tugging on his clothes.

"Would it make any difference," she asked, "if I told you I love you?"

"No, none at all."

"Then I don't. Love you, that is."

"Good, because I'm not worth it."

He went to the door, peeked into the hall, and strolled out.

"WELL?" Victoria demanded. "What have you to say for yourself?"

"I hate him," Felicity replied.

"I don't care."

Victoria was seated in the front parlor, Felicity standing before her. After pitching a full-blown tantrum, she'd been locked in her room, and Victoria had finally allowed her to be released, but she was defiant and mutinous.

"You can make me wed him," Felicity vowed, "but you can't make me like him."

"You don't have to like him. You just have to shut your mouth and do what he tells you."

"I won't live like that!"

"You will, and you'll be fine. If not, he will beat you, regularly and thoroughly. He seems to have a strong arm; I'm sure he'll get his point across quite vehemently."

Felicity turned to Cassandra, who was perched on a nearby sofa.

"Help me," Felicity implored. "Do something."

"I tried to warn you," Cassandra retorted, "but you wouldn't listen."

"He's a monster."

"All men are."

"Aren't you worried about what might happen to me?" Felicity wailed.

Cassandra scoffed. "You've been chasing this stupid dream for years, Felicity. It's become a nightmare; but then, it usually does."

"Cassandra!" Victoria snapped. "If you have nothing constructive to say, then don't say anything."

"She asked my opinion," Cassandra rebelliously sassed.

Victoria glared at her older daughter. For such a young woman, she was so jaded, so cynical, and Victoria was weary of how she moped about, lamenting her widowhood.

Victoria wanted to marry her off again, to be shed of her upkeep and dour personality, but Cassandra refused to discuss another match. The ungrateful child had actually accused Victoria of selling her the first time, of deliberately placing her in mortal jeopardy, but Victoria wasn't about to accept any blame.

She'd instructed Cassandra on how to deal with her degenerate husband, and it wasn't Victoria's fault that the unruly girl had declined to follow Victoria's advice.

"If you insist on being horrid to me," Felicity whined to Cassandra, "just go away. I have Mother sniping at me. I don't need you, too."

"I'll go," Cassandra rejoined, "as soon as Viscount Redvers arrives. I can't wait to see you grovel."

"You wicked shrew!" Felicity moaned. "Mother, make her leave. I can't bear to have her watch."

"She'll stay," Victoria declared. "If her presence shames you, so much the better. If I thought it would do any good, I'd invite the entire neighborhood."

Redvers's booted strides sounded in the hall, and the three of them straightened.

The butler knocked and announced Redvers, who was shown in. He stood with his hands clasped behind his back, his legs braced.

They rose, like a trio facing a firing squad.

"You wished to see me, Victoria?" he imperiously asked.

"Yes, Lord Redvers. I realize we had a bit of a *situation* last evening. I'm dreadfully sorry about any upset we might have caused you. I have talked to Felicity, and she has a few remarks she'd like to make."

Redvers spun toward her but didn't speak, and at viewing his angry countenance, Felicity squirmed and flushed with embarrassment.

"Lord Redvers"—Felicity gulped, then continued—"I should like to apologize for my behavior."

"And . . . ?"

"I understand that it was inappropriate of me to concern myself with your habits and your friends."

"And . . . ?"

"It won't happen again."

"And . . . ?"

"I most humbly beg your pardon."

He studied her, observing as she fidgeted. Victoria was on pins and needles, expecting him to call them a pack of provincial buffoons, then depart for London.

But he said, "Apology accepted."

"Thank you," Victoria replied. "I'm glad we can move beyond any unpleasantness, and I hope you are still planning to attend the village social with us. We would be delighted if you would deign to meet some of our neighbors."

"I will," he curtly stated.

Victoria nearly collapsed with relief. If he was willing to suffer through their paltry rural dance, then the wedding was a distinct possibility.

"Felicity has one other comment."

Felicity was doggedly silent, and Victoria's vicious scowl spurred her on.

"I would be eternally obliged if you would . . . would . . ."—she was choking on the request—"tell Mrs. Bainbridge and Mr. Adair that we are charmed by their company, and that we would like them to join us at the village social, too."

"I will extend the invitation," he said. "Mrs. Bainbridge will likely be eager to go, but I'm certain Mr. Adair would rather not."

He whirled away and left.

They were frozen in place, his footsteps fading down the hall, then Felicity whipped around to Victoria.

"I hate you," she hissed, "and I will never forgive you for this as long as I live."

"I don't care," Victoria repeated.

Felicity raced out, and though Victoria had tried to pretend great aplomb, she was shaken by the scene.

She staggered to the sideboard and poured herself a stiff brandy, downing it in one quick gulp. In the stress of the moment, she'd forgotten that Cassandra was in the room.

"That was ghastly," Cassandra chirped. "Are you happy now?"

"I'm very happy."

"Why would you do this to her?"

"She'll be a bloody countess," Victoria seethed. "Don't tell me it doesn't matter."

Cassandra gaped at Victoria as if she was insane, and Victoria barked, "What are you looking at?"

"I'm looking at you and wondering why you behave like this. What are you trying to prove? That you can make Felicity miserable all her days?"

"I don't have to explain myself to you. Get out of here."

Without further argument, Cassandra left, too, and Victoria was alone with her brandy and her fury.

"SIT, darling, sit."

They were in Jordan's bedchamber, where Lauretta had had a table set in front of the fire. She gestured to it and flashed her most seductive smile.

"All right." He sighed and plopped down in a chair.

Though she'd traveled to the country for the express purpose of entertaining him, they'd spent hardly any private time together, and she was panicked.

He had to be dabbling with a housemaid, but though she'd snooped and pried, she couldn't determine the woman's identity. If an affair was occurring, he'd been extremely furtive, and the fact that he would engage in stealth was troubling.

Why was he concealing his antics? Since he was never concerned as to what others thought of his conduct, he must have grown fond of someone who needed secrecy. But who was it?

The possible answers to that question kept her up at night, kept her fretting over the consequences both for her immediate and long-range future.

It was difficult to latch on to a nobleman like Redvers, and though he was temporarily in a financial bind, it would pass. When it did, she intended to be at the center of his life.

He had to recollect why he continued on with her, so she'd surprised him by having a special meal prepared for just the two of them.

She was attired in a red robe and negligee he'd given her the prior Christmas. The color accentuated her features, and the negligee was sewn of lace, and thus, transparent in all the pertinent spots.

For all his incorrigible ways, he was quite a romantic person, and she'd often organized similar evenings, which he'd thoroughly enjoyed. He should have enjoyed this one, too, however when he'd entered the room, he'd appeared irked, and she had to make him forget that he was displeased.

She walked behind him and massaged his shoulders.

"You're tense as granite. Let me relax you."

As she dug her thumbs into his muscles, he groaned with relief.

"That feels good."

She rubbed more vigorously. "This visit is taking its toll on you."

"Yes, it is."

"Felicity has been so horrid."

"She certainly has."

"What shall we do about her?"

"*We* shan't do anything."

"But you can't let her treat you so shabbily. Not with others watching!"

"I spoke with Victoria. She has the problem well in hand."

In the matter of his marriage, Lauretta was his constant confidante. They'd analyzed his choices at length, and he'd heeded all of Lauretta's advice. Yet suddenly, he was reluctant to confer on the topic, which was a very bad sign.

"What if Victoria isn't able to rein her in?"

"Don't worry about it, Lauretta. I'm not."

"But she—"

"Lauretta! I don't wish to talk about Felicity."

He shrugged her off and leaned forward to lift the lids on the dishes the maids had delivered. There were slices of roast beef, a thick gravy, roasted vegetables, pie, and a hunk of cheese.

He seemed bored by the selection, and she scurried around the table and grabbed his wineglass, pouring to the rim, hoping some alcohol would loosen him up.

"Shall I fill a plate for you?"

"If you'd like."

She heaped servings of everything, then did the same for herself and began to eat.

He was very distracted, and he picked at his food.

"I had the chef prepare all your favorites," she mentioned.

"Be sure to thank him for me."

"I will."

He laid the fork next to his plate and sipped at his wine, the meal ignored.

She'd known him for years, and they were actually close friends, with common hobbies and acquaintances. Conversation between them was never difficult, but for some reason, she couldn't think of a single comment.

A silence grew, then became awkward.

"What's going on with you?" she asked.

"Nothing. Why?"

"I rarely see you anymore."

"We played cards yesterday."

"That's not what I mean."

"Isn't it?"

He was being deliberately obtuse. He'd never been the type to discuss their relationship, and he was making it clear that he wasn't about to start.

"You brought me with you," she reminded him, "so that I could entertain you, but you haven't let me."

She smiled, but it fell flat. To her own ears, her remark sounded resentful and desperate, like a shrewish housewife who feels her husband's affection waning but has no idea how to reclaim it. He wouldn't tolerate jealousy or possessiveness, and she had to smooth over any misconception she might have generated.

The best way to divert him was with sexual activity, so she slithered out of her robe, her elbows on the table. The position gave him a perfect view of her breasts, but he looked at them with the same amount of interest he'd shown the roast beef.

Undeterred, she tried to slip onto his lap. But before she could, he moved away, and she plopped onto the empty seat he'd vacated.

She was seething, wanting to demand, *What the hell is wrong with you?*

But she didn't dare. He was entitled to brood, and if he kept his thoughts to himself, it wasn't her business to inquire why.

He ambled over to the window and he gazed out at the park. It was evening, dusk settling in. Something in the distance had caught his eye, and he stared at it for a long while.

Eventually, he turned to her, and her heart lurched in her chest. From his cool, detached expression, she was positive he was about to split with her.

The bastard! After all she'd done for him! After all she'd endured!

"I'm not hungry," he said.

"It's all right."

"You went to a lot of trouble."

"It was no bother."

The room was so quiet that she could hear her pulse pounding in her ears.

"I've been thinking . . ." he murmured.

"About what?"

"I'd like you to go back to London."

"But we're scheduled to be here two more weeks."

"I can resolve everything on my own. You don't need to stay with me."

"Honestly!" She chuckled, anxious to make light of his pronouncement. "As if I'd leave you in this dreary place all by yourself! You'd die of boredom without me."

"It's a definite possibility." He managed a hint of a smile.

"I'm happy to stay."

"That's decent of you, but I'd rather you went home."

The word *home* rang like a death knell, and she panicked, though she struggled not to let him see. He wouldn't put up with any hysterics, so she wouldn't give him any, but his curt edict had deeper implications than a mere request that she depart.

"Tell me what's really happening," she said. "Are you still marrying Felicity?"

"Of course."

"Then . . . why?"

"We both know what I'm going to do, and I don't need you to watch me do it."

"Has Felicity asked that you send me away? Has Victoria?"

The notion that he might have decided to grant the horrid girl a favor, that he might have decided to humor her horrid mother, was too galling to consider.

"No."

"You're not making any sense."

"I told you: I don't need you here."

"It's not a matter of *needing*. I'm here because you wanted me to be. Have you changed your mind about that?"

"I guess I have."

"Have I upset you in some fashion?"

"No."

"I must have. Please inform me of what I've done so I can apologize and fix it."

"You've done nothing. I'm just . . . torn by my choice, and I'm miserable company. You'll be happier in Town."

"You're mistaken. I'm always happier when I'm with you."

He cocked a brow, knowing she was lying, knowing she remained because she was paid to remain, but he was gracious enough not to mention it.

"I'll make arrangements for you to go tomorrow," he said.

"But tomorrow's Saturday." She flashed a credible pout. "I'd planned to attend the village social. You're aware that I was raised in London. I've never been to such a quaint, rural event. You can't send me away before I've had my fun."

"I'm not sending you away," he insisted. "I'm asking you to go."

"May I stay for the dancing?"

"I suppose, but I want you to head home the next morning."

"When will you return to London?"

"As soon as I'm wed. I expect to arrive the day after the ceremony."

"And we'll pick up where we left off?"

"Why wouldn't we?"

He assessed her in a way that had her completely unsure of his intentions, and he came over, clasped her arm, and escorted her to the door.

She glanced at the uneaten food, at the cheery fire and expensive French wine. All wasted.

"Are you certain you wouldn't like me to tarry?"

She snuggled herself to him, but he was as responsive as a block of wood.

"I'm in a foul mood. Why don't you play cards with Paxton? Perhaps I'll join you later."

"I hope you will, darling. It's so dreadfully dull without you."

She forced another smile and sauntered away. On the outside, she oozed smug confidence, but on the inside, she was teeming with fear and fury.

He'd either grown weary of her, or a fetching housemaid was keeping him occupied and he'd persuaded himself that he didn't need Lauretta anymore.

Obviously, Victoria hadn't heeded Lauretta's warning about an amour, hadn't sought out the perpetrator and gotten rid of her.

Lauretta would have to handle the problem herself.

She would not lose Jordan Winthrop. She would not give up her place in his life. Not for anyone. And she felt very sorry for the foolish female who imagined she could shove Lauretta aside.

* * *

"ARE you positive you want to proceed, Sunderland? I don't think you should."

"I don't pay you to *think*, Mr. Thumberton," Edward Winthrop, Lord Sunderland, said to his lawyer. "I pay you to act."

"I realize that, but what if you sign this, then drop dead tomorrow?"

"What if I do?"

"When you're looking down from Heaven, or up from Hell, as the case may be, I doubt you'll be glad, but you won't be able to change it."

After Edward's trek to Barnes Manor, he had redrafted his will. He'd cut off every penny, had tied up every piece of property. If he *dropped dead*, as Thumberton so darkly put it, Jordan would own a few mansions and some land that was entailed to the title, but he'd have none of the family jewelry, no furniture, no animals, no carriages, no farm equipment.

Most important, he'd have none of Edward's money. Not a single farthing would be available to keep the assets in good repair, to make them thrive. Jordan would inherit an empty shell.

He hated to leave the boy in such terrible shape, but he would not give in to Jordan's whims and misbehavior.

Edward refused to support his wicked habits, his disgusting friends, or that harlot, Lauretta Bainbridge. The Winthrop men had held the Sunderland title for twelve generations, and Edward would destroy it before he'd let Jordan fritter it away.

Over the years, Edward had tried to talk sense to Jordan, but there was no making him see reason. He'd tried bribes and gifts and threats, but Jordan simply wouldn't listen, and Edward was tired of their bickering.

Jordan's decision to wed that social-climbing ninny Felicity Barnes was the last straw.

Despite how Jordan wished it were otherwise, Edward was his father, and Edward would select Jordan's bride—

especially when the girl Jordan had chosen for himself was so inappropriate.

Edward would not be insulted or ignored. Nor would he have his heritage mocked.

Jordan would do what was proper, or he would rue it till his dying breath. If he found no benefit in the Sunderland legacy, then he could forever flounder in poverty with his lowborn companions.

So . . . the new will would go into effect, Thumberton would post a letter notifying Jordan, and that would be that.

Afterward, he'd most likely never see Jordan again. The notion was depressing and maddening, but Edward was finished worrying about Jordan or his fate.

"Look, Sunderland"—Thumberton interrupted Edward's furious reverie—"why don't you reflect for a bit? Just to be certain."

"I don't need to reflect. My mind is made up."

"Then there's no hurry, is there? You can sign it today, or you can sign it next week. The words on the page will be the same."

Edward threw up his hands. "Why do I keep doing business with you?"

"Because I give you excellent advice. Take it for once, will you?"

"No."

"Sunderland . . . Edward," Thumberton said more gently, "I've known you a long time."

"Yes, you have."

"So please listen to me: I've written many, many wills in my life. I've counseled many, many fathers. I've seen them do selfish, stupid things. Because they're angry. Because they're fed up. Because they're lonely or feeling neglected or—"

"Are you claiming I'm being . . . stupid and selfish?"

"Yes. And these irate fathers I've assisted? The ones who've disinherited their children? Who've severed all ties? They've always regretted it in the end."

Edward stared at Thumberton, a muscle ticking in his cheek. He wanted to rage at the man, wanted to walk out and never come back, but the truth was that he was sick at the idea of breaking it off with Jordan.

If he gave up on Jordan, what would he—Edward—have left? A few drafty mansions? A few aging friends who never remembered to invite him for supper?

He sighed. "What would you have me do?"

"Go to Barnes Manor. Try again."

"You know it's a waste of effort."

"I don't know that. And neither do you. He's your only remaining boy. Isn't it worth another shot?"

"No," Edward petulantly retorted, but Thumberton wouldn't relent.

"Talk to him. Don't shout. Don't threaten. Just talk. You might be surprised."

Edward fumed. He didn't want Thumberton to be correct, didn't want to admit that he was proceeding out of rage and injured pride.

Jordan was stubborn, but Edward was, too. As Jordan had said: Like father, like son.

"All right," he grumbled. "I will go to Barnes Manor and try one last time. But if he still insists on marrying that awful girl, I will be back here on Monday, and I will sign the new will. You will not dissuade me, and Jordan be damned."

Chapter 14

ॐ

CASSANDRA took a deep breath and opened the door to Mr. Adair's bedroom suite.

Everyone else was at the village dance. It was the most popular event of the year, so even the servants had gone.

She and Adair had the house to themselves.

Victoria had made a big show of trotting off with Redvers, and she'd demanded that Cassandra accompany the family, but Cassandra had refused.

The entire group had been decidedly grim, with Redvers, Bainbridge, and Felicity all fuming over various issues. How they would get through the evening without a major brawl erupting was a mystery.

Even Mary had been in an odd humor. She'd looked pale and drawn, almost as if she was ill.

Cassandra had wanted to ask her what was wrong, but there hadn't been a private moment where she might have inquired.

Harold Talbot had driven Mary to the party in his carriage,

and as she'd climbed in the vehicle, she'd seemed even more miserable. And who could blame her?

Though Mary pretended it was a secret, she had set her cap for Harold, but he would be a sorry husband. It had to be galling for Mary to be a Barnes daughter and to have such limited prospects.

Cassandra had nearly invited Mary to stay at home, too, but in the end, she'd remained silent. She'd been left alone in the big mansion. The minutes had ticked by, the sky growing darker, the house quieter.

She'd started thinking about Adair, wondering why he hadn't attended the dance, and the answer to that question had mattered more than it should.

Since the night they'd trysted in the gazebo, she'd been in a fine state, her body alive with yearnings she'd never previously experienced, and it was all his fault. He'd ignited a spark of desire she hadn't known she possessed.

She ached and pined, couldn't focus or relax, and her cravings had to be suppressed. *He* had to suppress them.

Over by the fire, he was lounged in a chair, appearing decadent and disheveled. His coat and cravat were off, and his shirt was unbuttoned down the front, the sleeves rolled back to expose his forearms.

He had a glass of liquor in one hand and a letter in the other, and he was frowning at the words that had been penned.

As she entered, he glanced up and grinned.

"What are you doing in my room, you naughty girl?"

"I'm not sure."

"Your mother would have an apoplexy."

"Will you tell her?"

He scoffed. "Not bloody likely."

"She went to the party. I didn't."

"Neither did I."

"I see that."

With her having forged ahead, she was extremely uncomfortable, but she didn't want him to know that she was.

There was a brandy decanter on a table in the corner, and she walked over and poured herself a liberal amount. She could feel him watching her, could sense his curiosity as to her purpose, when she wasn't certain of it herself.

She downed her drink, poured another, and downed it, too.

"Why didn't you go?" she asked.

"Redvers forbid me from gambling. If I was caught cheating the neighbors, he thought it might cause problems for your mother."

"How noble of him to consider her."

"Wasn't it, though?" he sarcastically replied. "So if I couldn't play cards, what was the point? Plus, I hate to dance. What about you?"

"I hate to dance, too."

"Ah . . . we have something in common."

"And I can't abide Redvers."

"Most decent women can't."

"Or Mrs. Bainbridge."

"She's a difficult person to like."

She scowled. "I've just insulted your two best friends. Aren't you offended?"

"They're both obnoxious. I admit it."

He held out his glass, gesturing with it, almost daring her to bring him the brandy. She wasn't scared of him, but she was nervous about getting too close.

He chuckled. "Are you afraid I might bite, Mrs. Stewart?"

The taunt loosened her feet. She grabbed the bottle and marched over, filling his glass to the rim.

"Thank you."

"You're welcome."

"You have such pretty manners," he said. "Obviously, your mother raised you well. You'll make some man a dutiful little wife someday."

"Shut up."

She had hoped he might reach for her, and when he didn't, she was disappointed.

He indicated a nearby chair, inviting her to sit, so she did. They were silent, drinking, pondering. He lit a cheroot, puffed at it, then handed it to her, observing as she finished it off.

"Does your mother know you have so many wicked habits?"

"No."

"Were they acquired before you left to get married or after?"

"Definitely after."

"You drank to cope with your cruel husband?"

"No. I drank to spite him."

He laughed. "You fascinate me, Mrs. Stewart."

"Do I?"

"Yes."

They were quiet again; she gazed into his beautiful brown eyes, and it dawned on her that he didn't look to be his cocky, arrogant self.

In fact, he looked weary and rather sad.

The realization stirred her to empathy. She didn't want to see this side of him, didn't want to worry about him or feel any compassion.

"Rough night, Adair?" she gently inquired.

"I've had worse."

"What's wrong?"

He gestured to the letter he'd been reading.

"I've heard from my father."

"Is that good news or bad?"

"It can be either—depending on how we're getting on."

"I'd been told that he disinherited you."

"Yes, he had. He does it every so often, after I've been particularly irresponsible."

"But he changes his mind?"

"Always. He's too fond of me. He can't stand for us to quarrel."

"He's *fond* of you."

"Shocking, isn't it?"

"Very. What did he say?"

"He's bribing me."

"Why?"

"To encourage better behavior."

"Will it work?"

"I haven't decided." He reflected, then frowned. "He's inherited a small plantation in Jamaica, and he doesn't want it, so he's offering it to me."

"As a gift?"

"Yes."

"What are the conditions?"

"None—except that I move there, run it at a profit, and stop being such a profligate mess. He's determined to make a man out of me."

She hadn't thought about the day when he would leave Barnes Manor, and the notion that he wouldn't simply return to Town, that he'd travel on to Jamaica, disturbed her in ways she didn't care to contemplate.

If he was in London, there was always a chance Cassandra might bump into him in the future, at a ball or a supper. But if he sailed off to the Caribbean, she'd never see him again.

"What would you do, Cassandra?" He used her Christian name, but she didn't scold him. It seemed a night to share confidences.

"If someone offered me a plantation in Jamaica?"

"Not just that, but anything of value that would alter your situation. If you had the means to escape your mother, to be independent, would you grab for it?"

"In an instant. It would be heaven to have my own money, my own place."

"Perhaps I should accept then."

"Perhaps you should."

He cocked a brow, his expression flirtatious. "Would you miss me?"

"No."

"Would you write?"

"No."

"My dear Mrs. Stewart, I presumed I had a lock on your affection." He clutched a mocking fist over his heart. "You wound me with your disregard."

"Not likely. You're too vain by half. I could never *wound* you."

"You might be surprised."

Suddenly, there was a new intimacy in the air. Their banter ceased, and it seemed that not a second had passed since they'd dallied in the gazebo.

He stood and extended his hand.

"Come," he said.

"To where?"

"You know where."

He glanced past her to the bedchamber. She peeked over her shoulder and could see his bed.

"No."

"Yes."

He bent down and kissed her, abruptly stirring the passion he'd previously ignited. She'd had it carefully banked, but cad that he was, he'd stoked it so it burned hotter than ever.

As he eased away, his eyes were alight with merriment and something else—something seductive and profound that she couldn't identify. It made her keen to try whatever he asked.

"Come," he said again.

"Why?" Fear had her pulse hammering.

"Because I plan to kiss you senseless, but I'm foxed and exhausted, so I need to lie down."

"I probably ought to go."

Even as she uttered the comment, a voice in her head screamed that it wasn't what she wanted at all, and he saved her from herself.

"Why? Will you sit alone in the dark and feel sorry for yourself? If you're about to get blind, stinking drunk, at least do it here with me."

He reached over to the table and retrieved a deck of cards.

"Pick a card," he suggested, "and it will help you to decide. If I draw the high card, you stay. If you draw the high card, you leave."

She pulled out a card, and he did, too. He had a king, and she had a two.

"The king takes all!" he smugly crowed. "The maiden is forced to sacrifice herself for a lousy deuce."

She snorted with disgust. "Why do I play with you?"

"Because you can't resist me. I push you to do what you secretly *want* to do."

Considering, weighing her options, she swallowed and licked her bottom lip.

"I'm afraid of what happens in there," she admitted.

"You don't have to be. Not with me. Never with me."

He rubbed her neck, soothing her, sending goose bumps down her arms. He was smiling down at her, as if he knew what she needed. As if *he* was what she needed.

He yanked her to her feet, and she went without a whimper of protest.

"PROMISE me that you won't hurt me."

"Honestly, Cassandra! Of course, I promise."

"And promise that you'll stop if I ask."

"I will," Paxton lied, intending to misbehave in every conceivable way.

Now that she was in his bedchamber, he wasn't about to let her escape without his having sex with her. On such a dreary night, when he was in such a miserable mood, he was happy to have her liven things up.

He would have to go slow, would have to beguile and entice as he never had with another woman, but the challenge would be worth it. She would take his mind off his troubles, would give him something to think about besides the grim state of his affairs.

He was thirty years old, with no money, no home, and no family—other than a father who refused to claim him most of the time.

Usually, he wasn't concerned. Usually, he was content with his pathetic lot and contemptible companions, but with the receipt of his father's letter, he was questioning his choices.

Would he always live this way? Why didn't he demand more for himself?

He wasn't a dullard. He had a natural intellect, and his father had kindly seen to it that he was educated. He was smart enough to alter his fate, so why didn't he?

His father had presented him with a viable, excellent option—practically on a silver platter—yet Paxton was too much of a coward to accept it. He'd never have made it as an explorer. He was terrified to leave England, terrified to walk away from the familiar and venture into the unknown, but he understood that his father had tossed him a lifeline.

If he didn't grab for it, what would become of him? How many more chances would his father give him? How many times would Paxton disappoint the poor man?

He was a wastrel and gambler. Would that be the epitaph on his tombstone?

His morbid thoughts were too depressing. He hated reflecting on how he'd failed at every endeavor except vice, and Cassandra Stewart provided the perfect excuse to fritter away another indolent evening.

She was staring at his bed as if it were a torture device and he was about to strap her onto it, and a strident wave of affection swept over him.

What must she have endured? How awful had it been?

He didn't want her fretting, so he clasped her around the waist and tumbled them onto the mattress. Before she could react, she was lying down with him, the worst moment over in an instant.

"Let me up," she said.

"No."

He kissed her, and for a second, she braced, ready to fight him off, when she appeared to recollect that kissing him was pleasurable. She'd done it before, and there was nothing of which to be afraid. She relaxed.

The embrace was very chaste. He didn't caress or roll on top of her. He just kissed her, then kissed her some more, and with each passing minute, she was more amenable.

Gradually, he started touching her, his fingers roaming over her torso, moving closer and closer to her breasts, until he was massaging them without objection.

As he titillated her, he was surprised to find himself delighted and charmed. Without his realizing it, the encounter had taken on a significance he hadn't intended.

He was anxious to show her how it could be between them, because he was desperate for her to like him. Gad, he wanted her to think he was a better man than the one he actually was.

Damn! he mused. Was he developing romantic sentiments? The notion didn't bear contemplating.

He pulled away and sat up.

"What are you doing?" she inquired, sounding grouchy.

"I could use a brandy."

"Now?"

"Yes."

"Why?"

"I'm enjoying this too much."

"Of course you are. You're a man. It's all you care about."

"No, I mean it. I have to take a break, so I can reassess."

"Reassess?"

"Yes."

She rested her hand on his forehead, as if checking for a fever.

"Perhaps you're coming down with something."

He suspected he might be growing ill all right; he was catching a fondness for her.

"Let me get that brandy. I need a drink."

"Lie down, you silly oaf."

"We're not in a hurry, Cassie."

"Yes, we are, and don't call me Cassie."

"Why?"

"Because . . ." She paused, struggling to concoct a reason. "Because no one ever has before, and I won't have you supposing you're entitled to any familiarity. I'm sure you'll use it to my disadvantage."

He bent over and tugged a comb from her hair, so that the lengthy tresses fell down her back.

"Why did you do that?" she griped.

"I'm not going to make love to you while you're all nice and tidy."

"And I'm not going to make love to you at all. We're simply kissing, remember? Kissing I can handle. Kissing I like. Not . . . the other."

She made a fluttering motion with her fingers, not having the salacious vocabulary to discuss sexual relations, and it occurred to him that—in many ways—she was still a virgin. She hadn't been taught the lighter side of carnality, so she wasn't aware of how satisfying it could be.

He went to the outer room, grabbed the liquor decanter, and returned to her. He drank straight from the bottle, frantic to dull the perception that he was swimming in deep waters and couldn't see the shore.

"Here," he said, offering it to her.

"I don't need any more."

"Yes, you do. There's nothing going on between us that a hearty infusion of alcohol can't fix."

She glowered, then took the decanter and downed several swallows before giving it back.

"Are you feeling better?" she asked.

"Much," he claimed, though he was fibbing again. He was a mess, overwhelmed by the sight and smell of her, fraught with unwonted yearnings and wishes.

He crawled next to her and stretched out as she studied him with some perplexity.

"What is it now?" she queried.

"You're very pretty," he murmured.

She rolled her eyes. "You don't have to flatter me. I'm already in your bed; no coaxing is necessary to keep me here."

"No, you are. Very pretty. I just want you to know my opinion." He frowned, completely out of his element for once, and he grumbled, "Oh, to hell with it."

"To hell with what?"

"I like you more than I ought," he admitted. "I have to face it and move on."

"What do you mean, you *like* me? About what are you babbling?"

"I had planned to be a cad and seduce you for sport, but instead, I find that I'm simply so glad you're here."

He shrugged, flushing with chagrin.

"Was that another compliment?"

"I believe it was."

"Then . . . what a perfectly lovely thing to say." She smiled. "I'm glad I'm here, too."

"It's more fun than dancing with Redvers and your mother."

"Definitely more fun than that."

She chuckled, then they were silent, staring, and she cradled his cheek with her palm. A powerful connection surged to life. He'd never felt anything like it, and it scared him to death.

He broke away and started in again, nuzzling at her nape, then working down. He kneaded her breasts through the fabric of her dress, and he tugged at the bodice, dipping under the edge to locate a taut, pink nipple. For an eternity, he licked and sucked at it, keeping on till she was gasping with delight and surprise. She was so distracted that she hadn't noticed how he had raised the hem of her skirt.

As he touched her between her legs for the first time, she

was pushed into an immediate and violent orgasm. She cried out with such energetic astonishment that he wondered if she'd ever previously found her pleasure, and he had a sneaking suspicion that she hadn't.

"Good Lord, Mr. Adair," she said when she could talk again, "what was that?"

"*That* was sexual satisfaction. Haven't you ever felt it before?"

"I don't think so. I'd have remembered."

"And since I have my hand up your twat, I suppose you should call me Paxton."

He slid onto her, too aroused to be tepid or gentle, but he hadn't needed to worry about her being afraid any longer. The brandy and the orgasm were taking their toll. Her limbs were loose as a ragdoll's.

"Are you going to have your way with me now?" she asked.

"Yes."

"Will it hurt?"

"Only me—if I'm not inside you in the next five seconds." She gave a throaty, lusty laugh.

"I don't want this from you," she insisted.

"I know, but you'll get over it once you discover how marvelous I can be."

"You are so vain."

"Yes, I am."

He kissed her, as he unbuttoned his trousers, as he eased himself into her. She was very wet, very relaxed, and though she tensed slightly, he entered her with no problem.

"Oh . . ." she breathed.

"Oh, indeed."

"You were correct. It didn't hurt a bit."

"No. It never will with me."

That strange wave of affection was back.

It felt so right to be joined with her, so perfect, as if he'd finally arrived exactly where he'd always belonged. The notion that he was smitten didn't sit any better than it had when it initially dawned on him.

He was aghast.

She sensed their heightened bond, too, and she didn't look any more pleased than he. She scowled, seeming as if she might complain, but he couldn't bear to listen.

"Don't say a word," he told her.

"I won't. It's just that—"

"Hush."

He laid a finger against her lips, as he began to flex, slowly at first, then more vigorously. In light of her past, he probably should have fretted over how she was weathering the ordeal, but he couldn't delay.

He suckled her breast, waiting, holding back, as her desire crested. He followed her in ecstasy, relishing a few last thrusts, then he withdrew and spilled himself on her stomach.

Neither of them spoke, and eventually, he slipped away. He went to the dresser and poured a bowl of water so he could swab her belly, so he could wipe away all traces of his seed. As he finished, he perched a hip on the mattress.

"There at the end," she said, "why did you pull out?"

"So we wouldn't make a babe."

"Oh."

"That's how it's done," he quietly explained. "The man plants his seed in the woman's womb. It can take root and grow."

She blushed. "I didn't know that. I'm a widow, and I didn't know."

To his dismay, she appeared as if she might burst into tears.

"What's wrong?" he asked.

"I had sex. It was splendid; I enjoyed it."

"Well, don't cry about it," he murmured. "Don't be sorry."

"I'm not sorry. I'm just . . . just . . . I don't know what I am, but I'm not sorry." She sat up. "I should go back to my room."

"Are you mad? We're just getting started. You can't go. Not yet."

"I need to think about this. I need to . . . to . . ."

She was never at a loss for words, and he felt he should say something to ease her discomfort, but he couldn't imagine what it would be.

He fornicated with women who were aware of what they were doing and why they were doing it. There were no fears regarding the act, no sordid history with which to deal, no ghosts of sadistic deceased husbands to vanquish.

She scrambled to the floor and stood, so he stood, too, and he dawdled like an imbecile as she straightened her clothes. There was no hope for her hair. It was down and curled around her shoulders, and she didn't try to pin it up.

"I didn't even take off my shoes," she said, smiling.

"I was too swept away to let you."

He clasped her hand and kissed her knuckles.

"It was very grand."

"Yes, it was."

She stepped away and headed out, and he hurried after her.

"Would you like me to walk you to your room?" he inquired.

"No."

"Are you sure? I don't mind."

"I'm fine. A little tipsy, but fine."

"If you're positive?"

"I am."

She was an adult and had lived in the bloody house for twenty-two years. She could certainly find her way without any assistance. He was only pestering her because—to his horror—he was pathetically eager to spend a few more minutes with her.

"Good night, Cassie." He retreated into his suite before he made an even bigger fool of himself.

"Good night, Paxton."

She sauntered away, and he closed his door and went back

to his bed, where he was delighted to discover her hair combs still scattered across his mattress.

Like a besotted swain, he stacked them on the pillow and gazed at them, as he drank brandy till dawn.

Finally, he fell over in a heap, to sleep the sleep of the dead.

Chapter 15

❦

"Miss Barnes, would you like to—"

Mary slipped off into the crowd without waiting for the entire question to be voiced, and Jordan gnashed his teeth.

From the moment the fiddler had played the first note, he'd been trying to ask her to dance, but she kept skittering away before he could.

Initially, he'd assumed it was an accident, that she simply hadn't heard his request, but the longer she continued, the clearer it became that she was avoiding him, and her behavior had him in a furious temper.

How dare she ignore him! How dare she refuse to fraternize!

He'd only attended the blasted party because he'd thought it would be an innocent way to socialize with her. Since she rarely interacted with her family, he never saw her unless he sneaked to her room in the middle of the night.

"Damned woman," he muttered to himself.

"What was that, Lord Redvers? Did you say something?"

The event was to have been held out on the village green,

but rain sprinkles had forced it into the blacksmith's barn, and the building was packed. The musicians were at one end, food tables at the other, and the dancers were marching down the center, stepping out the rhythms of the various tunes.

As the guest of honor, he was seated in a chair that gave him a good view of the festivities. Unfortunately, the more prominent neighbors were seated with him, so he'd found himself next to Harold Talbot and his homely cousin, Gertrude.

Talbot seemed to think they were chums.

"No," he replied to Talbot's inquiry. "I'm fine."

"I'm not much for dancing myself," Talbot mentioned.

"I can see that."

It was the sole benefit of the evening so far. If Jordan had had to watch Talbot parading down the floor with Mary, Jordan might have thrown himself off a cliff.

Apparently, he was . . *jealous* of Harold Talbot. The notion was too ludicrous for words.

"Don't let me keep you from joining in the fun," Talbot said.

"I won't."

Gertrude leaned across Talbot and asked, "How are you enjoying our humble village social, Lord Redvers? I'm sure it's quaint compared to what you're used to in London."

"I'm having a marvelous time."

The statement was such a lie that he was surprised he wasn't struck by lightning.

He was surrounded by people he didn't know and didn't like, and he was bored to tears. Paxton had stayed behind at Barnes Manor, and Lauretta was being obnoxious. The only person he wanted to talk to was Mary, and she wouldn't so much as glance in his direction.

She was too busy to bother. In an almost feverish frenzy, she'd partnered with every male who asked, and as she twirled by on the arm of another handsome young man, Jordan was goaded to jealousy again. The man said something, she said something back, and they both laughed.

Harold and Gertrude Talbot stiffened with affront.

"Did you see her?" Gertrude whispered to Harold, though Jordan could hear.

"Yes, I did." Harold was whispering, too.

"She is such a flirt," Gertrude charged. "I really don't know how you tolerate it, Harold. She's shameless."

"Yes, she is," Talbot agreed.

Jordan nearly guffawed aloud. Quiet, demure Mary Barnes was a brazen hussy?

He couldn't fathom why the Talbots were grousing about Mary, why they were gossiping to her detriment. He was incensed on her behalf.

Gertrude leaned over again. "Lord Redvers, how long will you be at Barnes Manor? Mother Talbot and I would be honored to invite you to supper—that is, if you have time to fit us into your schedule."

Acting like the worst snob ever, Jordan glared at her. By his haughty attitude, he made it clear that he deemed her to be very far beneath his notice.

"I don't believe I'll ever be available."

It was a hideous slight, and by their shocked expressions, she and Harold both knew it.

Jordan stood. "Now if you'll excuse me, I'm going to find Mary Barnes. I'm in the mood for a little shameless flirting."

He stomped off as Gertrude mumbled an indignant, "Well! I never!"

Hopefully, he'd offended them sufficiently that Harold would change his mind about Mary. If Jordan accomplished nothing else while visiting Barnes Manor, he would see to it that Mary's secret engagement was broken.

Jordan might not be able to marry her, but he wouldn't let Talbot marry her, either. After Jordan wed Felicity, he'd be the male head of the family, so he'd have the authority to refuse a match between Mary and Talbot.

In fact, he'd intervene in other, more substantive ways.

Once he had Felicity's money, he could use it however he

pleased. He'd move Mary to London, buy her a house, and hire her a companion. He could be with her whenever he wished, and the prospect raced through him like wildfire.

Why not? Why not? an excited voice urged. Why not make her his mistress? Why not alter her life as she'd begged him to do?

Though he couldn't wed her as she wanted, he could certainly improve her plight. He'd rescue her from Victoria, would set her up in her own home. Then he'd split with Lauretta, and he'd have Mary in her place.

The entire concept was so satisfying that he felt as if he was walking on air, and he was anxious to tell her his decision. She'd realize that he had her best interests at heart. She'd stop being angry.

He needed to speak with her immediately, and he surveyed the crowd, searching for her. To his surprise, she was over by Victoria. After skirting a few chairs, he was standing beside her. With Victoria looking on, she couldn't evade him as she had all evening.

"Hello, Miss Barnes," he said.

She peered up, and he could see how much he'd hurt her.

"Lord Redvers."

"Have you saved a dance for me?" He tried to smile, but couldn't pull it off. "May I claim the next one?"

"I'm sorry, but I just offered to fetch some punch for Victoria."

She flitted away, her insult ringing in his ears. Embarrassment reddened his cheeks.

"Mary!" Victoria scolded, but she was gone and didn't heed the admonishment.

Victoria frowned at him. "I most humbly apologize, Redvers. I have no idea what's come over her. With each passing day, she's behaving more strangely."

"She doesn't like me very much."

"That may be, but it doesn't give her the right to be discourteous. She knows better. I'll talk to her."

"Don't bother. I don't need you extolling my virtues or ordering her to be civil."

He eased away, his fury growing by the second.

The impertinent little jade! Snubbing him! Humiliating him in front of Victoria!

She would not treat him as if he didn't matter. He wouldn't allow it.

He caught up with her at the buffet, and he leaned in, trapping her against the table, while trying not to be overly blatant.

"I would speak with you," he hissed. "Outside! At once."

She didn't even glance up. "You've said everything that needs to be said, so there is no reason to converse."

She blithely grabbed a plate as if to fill it with food.

"I'm going outside as if I'm taking the night air. I will be waiting for you behind the barn. If you do not arrive in five minutes, I will come back in and cause a scene from which your reputation will never recover."

"You can bully me all you want, but it won't change anything."

He felt someone watching them, and she felt it, too. In tandem, they looked down the long table. A man was studying them, smirking, and he winked at Mary, sending Jordan's jealousy through the roof.

"Who is that?" Jordan seethed, absurdly ready to march over and pummel the man into the ground.

"He's the peddler, Mr. Dubois. He sells alcoholic tonics to desperate women, and it makes them forget themselves. But some of them remember the facts of life the next day."

"Why is he winking at you?"

"He thinks his Spinster's Cure worked. He thinks you're in love with me. But we both know that's not true, don't we?"

He glared at Dubois, then at Mary, but his glower had no effect. When had he lost the ability to intimidate?

"Five minutes," he grumbled.

He spun away, but he wasn't eager to draw attention to himself, so he slowed and ambled to the door.

The rain had kept most of the revelers inside, but a small group of men was smoking across the street. They ignored him as he strolled around the corner. Lanterns had been hung, so he made his way without any trouble.

Behind the structure, it was dark enough to hide a romantic indiscretion, and he loitered under the eaves, till he was certain she'd flaunted him.

Just when he figured that she wasn't coming, that he'd behaved like a fool, she stormed up, not stopping until they were toe-to-toe. She was in high dudgeon, as if he'd wronged her.

"What is it you want from me?" she demanded.

"I've been trying to dance with you," he said, irately but quietly. "I won't have you avoiding me."

"You brought me out here because I wouldn't dance with you?"

"Yes. I recognize that you are in a snit, but I won't tolerate it."

"You won't *tolerate* it."

"No, I won't."

"You don't own me, Lord Redvers, and you have no right to order me about."

"You are to call me Jordan when we're alone."

"Lord Redvers"—she was deliberately mocking—"we are not adolescents in the first throes of young love. You're at Barnes Manor to marry my sister, and so long as that's your plan, we won't *dance*—or anything else."

"Why do you keep throwing my marital situation in my face? From the start, I've been clear about my intentions toward Felicity."

"Yes, you've been abundantly clear."

"Then why are you acting like this?"

"Because my heart is broken."

The rawness of her remark staggered him. He felt as if he'd been slapped, and he couldn't respond.

"As I have been grievously wounded by your conduct," she continued, "I can't bear to be around you."

"Mary . . ."

He reached for her, but she held out a hand, halting him.

"I have to find a means to carry on," she said, stabbing him with her words. "I have to return to being the person I was—before you came."

"I'll only be here two more weeks."

"I don't care. Why can't you understand how difficult this is for me? Despite what I say or do, I will never be the bride you choose."

"My matrimonial decision doesn't have anything to do with you!"

"It has everything to do with me! Don't insult me by pretending otherwise." She took a deep breath, reining in her temper. "You matter to me in a manner I could never explain. You matter! But as far as you're concerned, I could simply be any loose girl who raised her skirt. I'm no one special—at all."

"That's not true. I don't feel that way about you."

"Then how do you feel?"

"I want you to come to London with me."

"As your what?"

"As my mistress. After I'm wed, I'll be set financially. I plan to buy you a house in Town and pay you an allowance. We can be together as often as you like."

"Your mistress . . ." She sagged against the wall of the barn.

"Yes."

"So I could be your next Mrs. Bainbridge."

"Well . . . yes."

When she put it like that, his proposition sounded sordid and offensive, and it didn't begin to describe his confused feelings. He thought she was amazing and unique, and he was keen to bond with her as he never had with another, yet he couldn't seem to clarify his motives, and his every comment was being misconstrued.

"Would you let Mrs. Bainbridge go," she asked, "or would you keep us both?"

"I'd let her go."

"And you'd support me for how long? Until you pick the *next* Mrs. Bainbridge after me?"

"I'm very fond of you. I imagine I'll consort with you for several years."

She buried her face in her hands. "Oh Lord, I am such an idiot."

"Why would you say that?"

"I gave you the only item I possessed that was of any value. I gave you my virginity, and my reward is that I could become your new Mrs. Bainbridge."

"There are worse things in the world than being mistress to a man like me."

"I can't think of a single one."

He wanted to be angry with her, but she looked totally bereft, and he couldn't help but be reminded that he was a callous cad.

"What's wrong?" he murmured.

"I'm ashamed that you assume I have such a low character."

"I don't believe you do."

"I'm not like the women with whom you socialize in London. I'm just me. I'm Mary Barnes, a spinster who has always lived in the country in my father's house. I'm not wild or indecent. I want a home of my own. I want a family. I want a husband who loves me, and I would never sell myself for such a small price."

"I'm sorry. I was sure the idea would make you happy."

"Then you don't know me at all."

He'd presumed that he'd found the perfect solution to their predicament. How could they have such disparate opinions as to what was an appropriate conclusion?

At her refusal, he was inordinately distressed. Why would he be? She'd just saved him an enormous amount of trouble and expense. He should be celebrating, but instead, he felt as if she'd yanked out his heart and stomped on it.

She stepped away and gazed up at him.

"I have to go back inside now. Please leave me alone."

"I can't leave you alone."

"Remember who you are, Jordan, and remember who I am. I'm begging you. I have to be able to live here after you depart."

Tears glittered in her eyes, and he couldn't bear that he'd made her so miserable.

He bent down and kissed her, and for a moment, she permitted the embrace. Then, with a wail of despair, she pulled out of his arms and raced away.

Like an imbecile, he dawdled, maudlin as a schoolboy with his first crush.

He was a fool. An impertinent, rash fool, and he deserved every ounce of her disdain. What was there to like about him?

As his father always brutally pointed out, he had no redeeming qualities. Why would he have supposed that Mary—whom he viewed as so rare and so remarkable—might bind herself to him?

He meandered out of the shadows, stopping for a minute to peer up at the sky, letting the drizzle cool his heated skin. Then he went into the barn to pretend that everything was fine.

LAURETTA was so glad she'd attended the village dance.

As the sophisticated, beautiful friend of Lord Redvers, she was the life of the party. Everyone was eager to bask in her glow, and their obvious approval was a balm for her sour mood.

She'd danced every dance, and the only way the event could have been improved was if Redvers had noticed how all the men were enthralled by her.

"Have a final sip, Mrs. B.," her current companion said.

He was a charming, courteous university student, home from Cambridge to visit his parents. So young. So cute.

He'd brought a flask of whiskey, and they'd slipped out to

have a drink. They were across the street from the festivities, under the eaves to stay out of the rain.

"Don't mind if I do," she tartly replied. She grabbed the flask and downed the remaining contents.

"I love a woman who enjoys her liquor."

"That's not all I enjoy." She raised a brow, happy to tease. Long after she'd returned to London, he'd fantasize about her.

"Are you cooled down?" he inquired. "Shall we head back and kick up our heels?"

"Let's do."

He offered her his arm, and as they would have moved off, she espied Mary Barnes hurrying from the dark yard behind the barn. She looked extremely distraught, as if she'd been crying, but at the last second, she forced a smile and swept inside.

Lauretta wouldn't have thought anything of it, but a man emerged from the exact spot where Miss Barnes had been. He appeared distraught, too.

For a brief instant, he stood in the rain, then he spun toward her, and he was clearly visible. There could be no mistake.

She was stunned, and she stumbled, her companion reaching out to steady her.

"Are you all right, Mrs. B.?"

"Yes . . . I'm fine. I just missed my step."

Redvers and Mary Barnes? Was he insane?

In a rush, desperate that he not see her, she hustled her companion along, feigning impatience to get back to the dancing.

Once she was safely inside, she rippled with fury.

Of all the horrible, despicable betrayals! He'd been ignoring Lauretta so that he could fuck Mary Barnes.

The gall! The infamy! The insult was too great to be born!

"The bastard," she muttered to herself. "The worthless, inconsiderate, philandering bastard."

Mary Barnes was going to be so bloody sorry!

Chapter 16

❦

"OPEN this door."

"No."

"Open it, right now, or I will kick it in."

"No!"

"I swear to God, Mary. I'm not joking!"

Jordan banged his fist on the wood so hard that the sound had to have wafted through the entire mansion.

It was the middle of the night, three long nights past the awful village dance where she'd had to smile and flirt and pretend that everything was fine. She'd assumed she could enter into a meaningless fling with him, but it simply wasn't in her nature to proceed with such a dangerous, unsatisfying relationship.

She wouldn't be his mistress. Nor would she watch as he finalized his courtship of Felicity, so what could she do?

Avoidance had seemed the best option.

Since she'd walked out of the barn, she hadn't seen him again, and she suspected his current fit of pique was driven by the fact that she'd told him *no*. She didn't suppose women ever refused him, so her temerity would be too much for him to abide.

"Mary!" He pounded on the wood again, the echo reverberating down the hall.

How long would it be before someone heard the ruckus and came to investigate?

If he was spotted, she wouldn't be able to deny any charge Victoria chose to level.

"All right, all right," she fumed. "Pipe down or you'll awaken the whole house."

She spun the key and stepped back, allowing him to storm inside, and it was immediately obvious that he'd been drinking. She could smell alcohol; his color was high, his hair mussed. His coat and cravat were off, his shirt unbuttoned and untucked.

He looked livid and perplexed, ready to either kiss her or strangle her, and she had no idea what behavior he would select.

She closed the door and locked it, which was pointless. They could easily be discovered, and if they were, she had no one to blame but herself. Her idiocy had landed her in her predicament, and she'd known better than to engage in such rash conduct.

For years, Victoria had been threatening to evict her. Would Redvers be the catalyst that spurred Victoria to act?

He whipped around, his blue, blue eyes freezing her in her spot.

"I give up," he snarled.

It was the last comment she'd expected. She scowled.

"What?"

"I give up! I give up!"

"What, precisely, does that mean?"

"I was going to ignore you." He started to pace. "I was never going to speak to you again. I was going to let you fuss and stew and martyr yourself on your stupid pride and maidenly offense."

He stopped and glared as if his arrival was her fault.

"I didn't ask you to come here," she insisted.

"No, you didn't, and look how that turned out."

"Not too well."

"No, not too bloody *well,* at all." He thrust out his palms, beseeching her for answers. "What do you want from me?"

"I don't want anything."

"That can't be true."

It wasn't, but she didn't know what else to say. She couldn't continue on with their affair, and they had no future she would countenance.

A complete and total separation was the only solution.

"Why are you here?" she inquired. "Why all this bother? You don't care about me, and you're acting as if you belong in an asylum."

"I do care about you!" he shouted, making her cringe at his volume.

"You have a funny way of showing it."

"What do you expect me to do?" He was pacing again. "I am not free to wed whomever I'd like. I have to marry for money, and you don't have any. I've been extremely candid, yet you behave as if I deceived you. I've explained my situation over and over—till I'm blue in the face—but you won't listen!"

He stumbled to a halt, his fury fizzling out. His shoulders slumped, and he collapsed against the wall, his back braced as if his legs could barely hold his weight.

"Why won't you listen to me?" he plaintively asked.

She'd planned to maintain her distance, to let him speak his piece, then toss him out, but his expression was so bleak that she couldn't remain detached.

The barrier she'd erected to protect herself was crumbling.

From the moment she'd met him, he'd had a lock on her emotions. He simply affected her as no other person ever had, and she couldn't disregard the tempest brewing inside him.

Had she caused it? Why would she have?

By his every word and gesture, he'd indicated that he wanted a brief liaison. Yes, he'd mentioned an arrangement as his mistress, but the position would have been temporary.

Had she mistaken his level of interest? Did he possess feelings she hadn't noted or suspected?

Perhaps he cherished her in a deep and abiding way, but being a man, he didn't know how to tell her.

The prospect—that he might love her—was arousing and dangerous. It made her eager to abandon the logical reasons she'd devised to stay away from him.

If he loved her, wasn't anything possible? If she could have him in the end, how could she send him away?

"I'm listening to you now, Jordan," she said very quietly.

"I can't give you what you want."

"You keep claiming that, but I don't think it's true."

"I'm returning to London very soon. I can't bear the thought of leaving you here, but you refuse to come with me."

"We'll figure it out. We'll find a way to be together."

"Yes, we'll find a way," he vowed. "I swear it to you."

"I can't be your mistress, though. I will only cast my lot with you if you promise to marry me. You'll have to relinquish Felicity's dowry. You'll have to cry off from any engagement."

"I realize that, and I will. I promise. I can't stand to have you so angry with me."

"I can't stand it, either."

He extended his hand, offering a truce, offering himself, and she raced over and clasped hold. He pulled her into a tight hug, then he was kissing her and kissing her until she was dizzy with the thrill of it.

"I'm sorry, I'm sorry," she kept repeating.

"I'm sorry, too."

"I love you," she admitted. "I'll always love you."

She'd taken the chance, had leapt off the cliff and confessed her feelings, but he said nothing in reply. He simply moaned and deepened the kiss.

He picked her up and carried her to the bed, and he laid her down and came down with her.

He seemed focused in a manner he hadn't been previously. He gazed at her as if he might set her ablaze, as if he was hungry for her and would never have his fill.

"Don't ever tell me," he said, "to leave you alone."

"I won't."

"It's not in me to stay away. I don't know how."

"I don't want to be separate from you. I *can't* be separate from you. It hurts too much."

Since she'd been sleeping when he'd first stormed down her hallway, she was attired in her nightgown. He gripped the front and ripped it down the center, and in an instant, she was naked. Then his hands were everywhere, on her breasts, her stomach, between her legs.

She felt as if she was drowning, as if she was plummeting to the bottom of the ocean, and he was plummeting with her. They were sinking into a hole of bliss and ecstasy from which they would never emerge.

He touched and bit and caressed, until she was writhing in agony, and when he finally clutched her thighs, when he loosened his trousers and impaled himself, it was such a relief.

She cried out with joy and hugged him close as he began to thrust.

There was none of the tempered restraint he'd shown prior. He was rough and out of control, his demons driving him to wild heights. His hips slammed into hers, like the pistons of a huge machine, his body working her across the mattress, until her head was banging into the headboard with each penetration.

As her pleasure crested, his did, too, and they ended together in a hot rush of need and elation.

As he spiraled down, as his torso relaxed onto hers, she stroked his hair, his shoulders, and arms. She yearned to confide how extraordinary it had been, how happy she was, but before she could, he drew away and promptly fell asleep. His face was buried in the pillow, alcohol and sexual lethargy rendering him incoherent.

She covered them with the blankets, and for a long while, she watched him.

When he awakened, when he was sober, they had to hash out the details of how they'd proceed. He'd sworn they would wed, and she would make any sacrifice, would endure any hardship, to guarantee that it transpired.

Eventually, she drifted off, and when she roused, the color of the sky indicated that it was midmorning or maybe even afternoon.

She frowned.

Before she'd even opened her eyes, she'd known he was gone, that he'd sneaked out without a good-bye.

There was a terrible stillness in the air, as if he'd left and was never coming back, as if she'd never see him again, which was silly.

Of course he'd come back. Of course she'd see him again. He'd *promised*.

Suddenly, the room seemed very cold, very forbidding, and she shivered.

Dread settled in the pit of her stomach, but she pushed it away and rose to face the day.

"I need to talk to you."

"Whatever it is, I'm busy, so if you'll excuse me?"

Victoria tried to sweep by Lauretta, but the woman blocked her path. They were next to an empty parlor, and Lauretta urged her in and shut the door.

"There's something you should know," Lauretta said, "but you have to swear that you'll never tell anyone where you heard it."

"Let's skip all the intrigue. Say what it is you're determined to say, and let me be about my business."

"Not until I have your word. If you're ever asked, you must pretend that a housemaid told you. No one can ever learn that you received the information from me."

"Fine. You have my word. Now what is it?"

"Do you recall when I mentioned that Redvers was dabbling with a maid?"

"Yes."

"I've found out who it is."

"And?"

"It isn't a servant."

"Who, then?" Victoria's mind raced as she tried to deduce what other female it could possibly be. She blanched. "Not Cassandra."

"No. It's . . . it's your stepdaughter, Mary Barnes."

"What is your allegation against her?"

"She and Redvers are having a sexual affair."

"If this is your idea of a joke, I find it in very bad taste."

"I saw them with my own two eyes."

"You swear this to be true?"

"Yes, I swear."

"They barely fraternize. How could it have happened?"

"He met her the day we arrived, and they had an instant connection. I discounted it, but I shouldn't have. He can be very charming, very persuasive. A plain spinster like her wouldn't stand a chance."

"Mary and . . . Redvers?"

Victoria was seething with such fury that Lauretta almost felt sorry for Mary Barnes. The poor girl had never done Lauretta any harm—save for snaring Redvers's attention—yet Lauretta had set a catastrophe in motion for her.

But as fast as Lauretta suffered the compassionate thought, she shook it off.

She knew Jordan well. He was thoroughly smitten—perhaps even in love for the very first time, and the prospect was too dangerous to consider. The spark had to be tamped out before it burned any hotter.

"I assume," Lauretta said, "that I can trust you to handle this?"

"Yes, you can trust me."

"And you'll keep my name out of it?"

"Don't worry, Mrs. Bainbridge. Your precious Redvers will never know it was you."

"Thank you."

Lauretta opened the door and slipped away.

JORDAN hurried into his bedroom suite, breathing a sigh of relief that he'd snuck in without being seen.

It was just shy of noon, the house abuzz with activity, yet he'd been rushing down the halls, without coat or shoes, his shirt buttoned wrong and untucked.

If he'd been spotted, rumors would have circulated about his behavior. Gossip would have gotten back to Victoria, causing a big ruckus to ensue.

He'd courted disaster, but had come through unscathed.

His head was pounding, his hangover debilitating, and he needed to bathe, dress, shave, and eat.

He moved to ring for a servant, when Lauretta spoke from over in the corner.

"Hello, Redvers."

She was seated in a chair by the window, drinking a brandy and smoking a cheroot.

"What are you doing here?"

"Waiting for you." She assessed his disheveled condition. "Rough night?"

"I've had better."

"You look like hell."

"I *feel* like hell."

She offered him her brandy. "Try a little hair of the dog. It will calm your worst symptoms."

He walked over, took it, and gulped down the contents, shuddering as the liquid scorched a path to his stomach. He gave her the glass, and she placed it on a nearby table.

"Where have you been?" she had the audacity to ask.

"My whereabouts have never been any of your business, and

I don't remember anything occurring that might have changed that fact."

He spun away and proceeded to the dressing room, dropping his shirt as he went. He poured water in a bowl, dipped a cloth, and stroked it across his face and chest. Behind him, he heard her enter, and he could sense her studying him, her curiosity blatant and annoying.

He glanced over his shoulder and snapped, "What is it? And I must inform you that, with the mood I'm in, you'd best not think to scold me."

"I wouldn't dream of it."

"Good. Then what is it? Please be brief. You were supposed to depart for London on Sunday. Why didn't you?"

"Is that still what you want?"

"Yes."

"You're sure?"

"Yes."

"When will you join me?"

"As soon as I'm married."

"So the wedding is on?"

"Why wouldn't it be?"

"You tell me."

He scowled. "My head is hammering like there's an anvil inside it. Don't talk in riddles."

"Victoria knows."

"Knows what?"

"About you and Mary Barnes. One of the maids saw you at the village dance."

A wave of panic surged through him, and he struggled to hide it.

If his affair with Mary was revealed, *he* would suffer no consequences, but for Mary, her life at Barnes Manor had just ended. Since he'd instigated the entire liaison, the result was completely unfair, but that was the way the world worked.

"About what are you babbling?" he said, feigning indifference.

"Victoria is in an uproar. I came to warn you."

"Well, thank you. Warning received. Now, if you don't mind, I'd like to be alone."

He glared at her, being obvious that he wished she'd leave, but she didn't budge.

"When you're back in London, what will happen to me?"

"What do you mean?"

"Will we keep on together? Or are you letting me go?"

A muscle ticked in his cheek. His temper flared.

Though much of the prior evening was a drunken blur, he faintly recalled whispering many promises to Mary. He'd thought he was eager to split with Lauretta, but in the clear light of day, everything was jumbled.

In the past few hours, he hadn't inherited a fortune. He still needed to wed Felicity, and that left him in a bind from which he didn't know how to extricate himself.

At the moment, there were too many women wanting things from him that he either wouldn't or couldn't give.

He hated discord and quarreling. If he was to break with Lauretta, it wouldn't be while he was a hung-over mess and she looked ready to kill.

"Nothing's changing," he insisted, and right that second, he was being truthful.

What might transpire in the next minute, in the next week, in the next month, he couldn't guess.

"Swear it to me," she demanded.

"I swear."

She scoffed. "As if I'd take your word for anything."

He grabbed a nearby chair and collapsed down onto it.

"What would you have me say, Lauretta?"

"Mary Barnes, Jordan? You were fucking Mary Barnes? Are you insane?"

He stared at her, not indicating by the most miniscule sign that he'd done as she'd accused.

"You're trying my patience, Lauretta, and I'm too exhausted to fight with you."

"She's Felicity's sister, for pity's sake. Do you realize the hornet's nest you've stirred? Victoria may refuse the match! We may not get Felicity's dowry."

"Then I'll find another heiress."

"I could shake you till your teeth rattle."

"You've overstepped your bounds. You're making me angry."

"After all our planning, all our preparation, you jeopardize it like this? For what? Just to slip between the thighs of some little country virgin?"

"Lauretta! You go too far."

"You're incorrigible, Jordan, but you're not stupid and you're not rash. Why did you do this? Tell me!"

There was a terrible silence, as she yearned for an answer he would never give.

Very quietly, she asked, "Are you in love with her?"

Was he in *love* with Mary?

His connection to her was unusual and thrilling. She fascinated him, and he felt better when he was in her company. He couldn't stop thinking about her, couldn't stop wanting to be with her.

Was that love? It had to be, but even if it was, he would never admit it to Lauretta.

Luckily, he was saved from replying by a knock on the door. He stood and went to the outer room. He peeked into the hall, seeing a footman.

"Yes?"

"You have a visitor, Lord Redvers."

"*I* have a visitor?"

"Yes, your father."

"Sunderland is here?"

"He awaits you in the front drawing room—at your convenience."

What the hell could he want? Could this accursed day get any worse?

"I'll be down in a few minutes."

The man left, and Jordan closed the door.

Feeling as if he'd aged ten years, as if he'd been beaten with clubs, he spun around. Lauretta was watching him.

"What is he doing here?" she inquired.

"I haven't a clue."

"You're not going to meet with him, are you?"

"I don't exactly have a choice."

He was weary of her, weary of the game her presence forced him to play.

"Go home, Lauretta. Leave for London immediately."

"I don't want to."

"Go anyway."

"If there's to be a big eruption—either with Sunderland or Victoria—you need me."

"No. Leave—and take Paxton with you."

She dawdled, rage wafting off her. He knew she wanted to scream, she wanted to shout, she wanted to pound him with her fists till he was a bloody heap on the floor.

Ultimately, she nodded, accepting defeat.

"As you wish." She swept by him. "I'll see you back in London."

Chapter 17

"WHAT do you want now, Sunderland?"

Edward gazed at his handsome, indolent, intractable son. The obstinate boy hadn't even shaved. He looked like he'd just tumbled out of bed, as if he were a criminal, or a poor person living on the street.

Why would Victoria Barnes put up with him? It was a measure of her desperation to snag a title that she'd have him in her house as a guest.

Mr. Thumberton had urged Edward to make a final attempt to speak with Jordan, but on viewing Jordan's sloppy condition, Edward's temper boiled.

He didn't understand Jordan and had never been able to forgive him for being who he was, for refusing to be more like his brother, who'd died so young and so needlessly. As a result, he and Jordan had no common ground upon which to move forward through any dispute.

Edward didn't know how to talk to Jordan, and Jordan didn't know how to listen.

"You couldn't have bothered to shave?"

He hadn't meant to snap, but he felt so ill-used, and Jordan replied precisely as Edward might have predicted.

"I didn't see any reason to clean up. It wouldn't have changed how this meeting will go. So if you traveled all this way merely to criticize my disheveled state, I'm busy. If you'll excuse me."

He turned to stomp out.

"I will not be dismissed by you!"

"And I will not be scolded as if I'm a lad in short pants. You didn't answer my question: Why are you here?"

"I came to try—one last time—to dissuade you from your folly."

"I'm perfectly happy to proceed with my *folly*—as you call it—so it's a wasted trip."

"You can't marry that girl."

"Why can't I?"

"She's flighty and immature; she'll make you miserable."

"Any woman would."

"You're behaving like a madman."

"Nothing new there."

Jordan walked to the sideboard, poured himself a whiskey, then flopped down in a chair. He gulped his liquor, appearing wretched and unkempt. He slouched in the seat, almost as if he'd like to slide to the floor and lie down.

"Tell me the truth," Edward fumed. "Why are you doing this?"

"You know why."

"Is it to spite me? To wound me?"

"Yes."

"Well, you're succeeding."

"Good. You treat me like a child, and if I have to wed Felicity to be shed of you, then that is what I shall do."

"It is a mistake you'll always regret!" Edward's voice and wrath were rising. "I can't let you make it!"

"How can you stop me?"

"I could have you committed to an insane asylum."

Jordan chortled with merriment. "By all means, please try."

"You laugh now," Edward seethed, "but after a few months spent in Bedlam, you won't think it's so funny."

"Go home, Edward. I'm sick of listening to you."

Jordan stood and went to the sideboard again. He was pouring another drink when the door opened.

Lauretta Bainbridge poked her nose into the room.

"Hello, Eddie," she said in her usual condescending manner. "What brings you to the country?"

"Mrs. Bainbridge!" Edward gasped. "What are you doing here?"

"I'm *entertaining* your son. What do you suppose? Paxton is here, too. He's cheating all the neighborhood wives out of their pin money."

Edward was so enraged by her presence that little red circles formed on the edges of his vision. He wondered if he was about to have an apoplexy.

"This is a private discussion," he shouted. "Get out!"

"Gladly, you pompous old nag. I only popped in to mention that the entire house can hear you yelling. Why don't you put us all out of our misery and drop dead?"

She made a rude gesture and sauntered away, leaving Edward so furious that he began wheezing.

He peered at Jordan, who was loitering by the liquor bottles.

"You brought her here?" Edward was stunned. "You would insult Mrs. Barnes in such a despicable way?"

"I'm just a bundle of offense."

Edward shook his head in disgust.

What was the point in trying to reason with Jordan? What was the point of hoping he would change?

He was who he was: a lazy, impetuous, vulgar knave who assumed that the world owed him a bloody favor.

"I've redrafted my will," Edward very solemnly announced.

"What took you so long? I thought you'd disinherited me years ago."

"You will not ever have a penny of my fortune to waste on that . . . harlot."

"That's all right. I'll have Felicity's." He calmly sipped his whiskey. "Will there be anything else? Are there more invectives you need to hurl? Or are you finished?"

Edward studied him, feeling quite sure it was the last occasion they'd ever see each other.

Why did it have to be like this? Why couldn't Jordan behave as was decent and proper?

"Don't call on me," Edward gravely said. "Don't write. Don't beg for cash. I am posting a notice in the *Times* that I will pay no more of your bills."

"My creditors will weep."

"I will not answer any correspondence, and I will inform the servants that you are not to be allowed onto any of my properties."

"First though, I don't imagine you'd agree to fix Redvers House."

"Never."

"Since *you* let it fall to ruin, that's not very sporting."

"If I went to the expense, you'd simply wreck it again. I won't squander another farthing on you."

"I bet you'd have repaired it if your beloved son James had asked."

"For James, yes, I would have."

"Precisely," Jordan scoffed.

Edward refused to be embarrassed over his disparate feelings for the two boys. It had never been a secret that he'd liked James best. James had possessed every trait Edward wanted in an heir, while Jordan was the complete antithesis of what was required.

"From this moment on," Edward warned, "I have no son."

"So be it."

At the crushing pronouncement, Edward felt sick with dismay. It wasn't what he'd planned to say, at all, but pride kept him from retracting the words.

He spun to depart, but as he approached the door, a woman was standing there. He'd seen her on his previous visit. She was one of the Barnes daughters—Mary or Martha or something.

"Are you fighting again?" she asked, entering the room like a petite virago.

"Leave it be, Mary," Jordan said.

"I won't. You two can't go on like this."

"You can't mend it for us," Jordan claimed.

"Miss Barnes," Edward interjected, "Jordan has been a guest here, and you've obviously formed a friendship with him, but that doesn't imply that you can—"

"Stop it!" she demanded. "Stop it right now. Both of you ought to be ashamed. My mother died when I was born, and my father died when I was a little girl. I hardly remember him."

"What has that to do with me?" Edward haughtily inquired.

"I would give anything to speak with either of them again—for even a few minutes. Jordan is all you have in the world, yet you treat him so badly."

"Mary," Jordan sharply counseled, "don't defend me to him."

"And you!" she snapped at Jordan. "Be silent! You deliberately goad him."

"I didn't—"

"Don't try to deny it. I was listening out in the hall."

"You minx," Jordan chided, smiling.

He was exhibiting an affection for her that Edward had never seen him display toward anyone.

"I know how you behave!" Miss Barnes chastised. "You provoke him on purpose. You enjoy it. Well, I say, enough! From both of you."

"Miss Barnes," Edward said, "you have some gall to lecture me."

"He is the only child you have left! How can you act as if he doesn't matter?"

"He doesn't . . . matter. Not anymore. His misdeeds have guaranteed that he is nothing to me."

"You don't mean that."

"Oh, but I do. Good day."

Edward swept by her and headed for the front door, where the butler stood ready with his hat and coat.

He put them on slowly, absurdly hoping that Jordan would rush out to apologize, but as footsteps sounded, he glanced over to see that it was Miss Barnes chasing after him.

"Don't go away angry," she said. "He's not serious. He intentionally baits you, and you fall for it every time."

If only it were so.

"He's extremely serious, Miss Barnes. He revels in discord."

"You're so wrong about him. I wish I could make you understand."

She was so loyal, so fierce in her desire to protect the slothful scalawag.

How sad that she was not the Barnes bride Jordan would marry. If she had been, he'd have selected a wife who possessed some maturity, some grit and sense.

"I've known my son much longer than you. If he's convinced you that he has any redeeming qualities, he's fooled you better than a charlatan at a fair."

He stormed out to his carriage and climbed in. As the driver clicked the reins and the vehicle pulled away, he peeked out the curtain, thinking Jordan might have relented, that he'd have come outside to wave good-bye, or that he might at least be watching from a parlor window.

But there was only Miss Barnes, hovering alone on the stoop and looking as if she'd just lost her last friend.

"LORD Redvers, may I speak with you?"

Jordan glared at Victoria, who was summoning him from down the hallway like the angel of death. He cringed, having forgotten Lauretta's warning that scandal was brewing.

Mary had run after Sunderland and disappeared, and Jordan was searching for her. He hadn't the energy to fuss with Victoria.

He was hung-over, hadn't washed, eaten, shaved, or slept, so he was in no condition to spar with her. Mary's continued residence at Barnes Manor was dependent on his comments, and in his reduced state, he couldn't do her justice.

"I'm sorry, Victoria, but I'm having the worst morning. We'll have to talk later."

"No, *I* am sorry, Redvers, but this has to be now."

"I'm feeling particularly ill. I'm going back to bed."

"If you don't attend me—this very second—you may return to London immediately." She was impossibly regal, bent on destruction.

He fumed, knowing he had to converse. It was her home. It was her daughter and stepdaughter. He was a guest, and an unpleasant one at that. He could do as she'd asked or he could leave.

He followed her into the library. She sat behind her massive oak desk and he sat across from her.

"I will come right to the point," she said, "and don't lie to me. You've exhausted my patience and abused my hospitality. I would just as soon toss you out on the road as have you as my son-in-law."

"Is this my official welcome to the family? If so, you could use a bit of work on your delivery. I found it to be a tad harsh."

"Don't be smart with me."

"I don't have to stay at Barnes Manor. If you'd rather I go, I will. I'm happy either way. There are plenty of rich girls in the world, but only a few men who will be earls. What shall it be, Victoria? Should I stay or not? Should I marry Felicity or not? The choice is yours."

He sprawled in his chair, his feet stretched out, the very picture of nonchalance.

She scowled, assessing his disrespectful posture, his sneering expression. If she thought she could intimidate him, she was sadly mistaken.

Much of his life had been spent seated across from Sunderland at a desk similar to this one. He'd endured this type of distasteful discussion a thousand times.

"I will ask this question once," she said, "and I expect the truth."

"What is it?"

"Are you having an affair with Mary?"

He had to give her credit. She was very cool, very composed, although he imagined if she'd been holding a pistol, she'd have shot him through the middle of his black heart.

Answers—all of them false—flitted in his head, and as he hesitated, she added, "Before you reply, you should know that I have a reliable witness, so it's useless to pretend to have virtue."

He let out a heavy breath, feeling as if he was perched on a cliff and about to jump off.

"All right, I don't deny it."

"Where do you come by the gall to insult me in such a fashion?"

"I won't explain myself to you. Nor will I talk about my relationship with her."

"Could she be pregnant?"

His pulse raced. "I doubt it."

"But she could be."

He merely shrugged, and she was silent, pondering, calculating the odds as to how he could be coerced.

"I heard your father shouting," she mentioned.

"We have a habit of loud discourse."

"I didn't mean to eavesdrop, but the volume ensured that I couldn't help it. I know that you've been disinherited, so your financial situation is even more dire than it was when you first arrived."

"My fiscal state has always been dire. Nothing has changed during these weeks at Barnes Manor."

"You probably haven't the coach fare to take you and your friends back to London."

"Actually, we came in my carriage, remember? Mrs. Bainbridge has been extremely adept at hiding it from my creditors. It hasn't been seized."

"That's neither here nor there. You had said that I had a choice to make, but in fact, *you* are the one with the choice. I ask that you make it immediately."

"What is it?" he inquired, though he already knew.

"You will propose to Felicity at once. Then we will send a messenger to Town to bring back a Special License. I will host a small ceremony, tomorrow morning in the front parlor. The dowry money will be transferred into your bank account tomorrow afternoon."

"Or . . . ?"

"You and your companions can depart within the hour."

"An interesting conundrum," he mused.

"You've been wasting my time."

"I certainly have."

"And you've toyed with Felicity's affections."

"I wasn't aware she had any."

She ignored the rude remark.

"You have exactly sixty seconds to decide what you will do. If you don't propose, I have several maids waiting out in the hall. They will go upstairs and pack your bags." She smiled a grim smile. "Your minute starts now."

They peered at the clock over on the mantel.

He should have been frantically reviewing his options, but all he could think about was how she'd bested him.

Yes, in his drunken stupor, he'd whispered some half-baked promises to Mary, but he couldn't keep them.

It would be lovely if the world were a perfect place, if he could snap his fingers and have the cash to purchase a house, to feed and clothe and support her. But he didn't have any cash, and he never would unless he took drastic measures.

She had an absurd fantasy where they ended up together, and it had been humorous to encourage her, but it was a pipe dream. He possessed every flaw his father bemoaned and many more besides. If she joined him in his disreputable life, she'd be miserable forever, and he couldn't do it to her.

She was the only person he'd ever known who genuinely liked him. She saw someone who didn't actually exist, but it was the man he wished he'd been. He wanted her to always envision him that way: as noble and decent and worth having.

He loved her.

He loved her because she made him laugh, because she made him happy. He loved her because she'd brought him joy and serenity. He loved her because *she* loved him, because she looked at him and saw something of value, something splendid and fine, and when he found her to be so extraordinary, he simply couldn't ruin her future by marrying her.

As he understood all too well, he would be the worst husband in history, so he had to let her go, had to relinquish any ridiculous notion she might have fostered that they could thrive in matrimony.

At the moment, she assumed she wanted to wed him, but time and distance would quell her attachment, and gradually, she'd come to her senses. She'd realize how lucky she'd been to evade a connection with him.

She'd be glad. She'd grow to comprehend that he'd done what was best for her, that he'd done the only thing he could.

While he'd been in ominous fiscal shape before Sunderland's appearance, his situation was now bleak beyond words. He would never inherit a penny from Sunderland, and he had to stop hoping for a different conclusion.

Though he'd bragged to Victoria that he'd simply pick another rich girl, it wasn't likely to happen. He'd struggled to find an heiress other than Felicity, but Jordan was a renowned scoundrel. No sane father would agree to a match.

Victoria was the sole parent he'd encountered who was greedy enough to have him in the family.

There was only one way to proceed, only one choice to be made.

The minute ticked to an end.

"What is your answer?" Victoria queried.

"Yes, I'll marry Felicity tomorrow—on one condition."

"What is it?"

"That you let Mary remain here—without penalty or reprimand—until I can make arrangements for her."

"What sort of arrangements?"

"Once Felicity's dowry is settled on me, I'll move Mary to London. I'll buy her a house and hire her a companion. You obviously detest her, so she'll be out of your hair."

"You would continue your affair?" Victoria looked as if she might faint. "After you wed Felicity?"

He hadn't really thought through what he planned. He was like a blind man, groping around in the dark. He didn't even know if Mary wanted to live in London, but he felt he had to try.

When she was apprised of his approaching nuptials, she'd be terribly hurt, and he owed her a resolution better than the one she faced.

Victoria scoffed, then shook her head.

"No, Mary will not go to London with you. I will not have Felicity disgraced."

"How would Felicity be *disgraced*?" he asked like an idiot.

"How!" Victoria gasped. "You are a notorious reprobate. People would be aware that you married one sister while dallying with the other. Felicity would be a laughingstock, and I won't have it. She will endure much in being shackled to you, but she shouldn't have to endure that."

"Then what do you suggest we do about Mary? Think what you will of me. I'm a cad; I admit it. The liaison was begun at my instigation and pursuit. I won't have her blamed, and I won't leave her here to suffer your wrath."

"I don't see that you have any other option."

"If we can't come to terms about her, then I shall bid you farewell, and there will be no wedding."

A tense standoff ensued, and eventually, she capitulated.

"You win. Mary will go to my cousin's until we learn if there is a babe."

"If there is?"

"I know of a home for unwed mothers where she can reside during her confinement. As the birth nears, I'll contact you. I can place the child up for adoption, or I can deliver it to you or your father. You can do whatever you like with it."

"And if there is no babe?"

"I will provide her with a small dowry, so she can marry and get on with her life."

"Why can't she stay at Barnes Manor?"

"I assume you and Felicity will visit occasionally. If you do, Mary cannot be here. The insult to Felicity would be too great."

It seemed as if they were bartering over a prized cow or an African slave, and she'd rattled him with her talk of finding Mary a husband.

The notion of Mary as some other man's wife was disturbing, but wasn't it for the best? She'd always wanted a husband, but Victoria had refused to dower her.

If Jordan consented to this scheme, wasn't he doing her a favor? Wasn't he making all her dreams come true?

He couldn't be so selfish as to keep her from marrying merely because he found the idea distasteful.

"Yes," he muttered, "I imagine that will work."

"Fine, then. It's agreed."

"It's agreed, but not Harold Talbot."

"What?"

"You can't foist her off on Harold Talbot. You have to select a fellow who will be kind to her, who will grow to love her. It can't be that hulking, offensive oaf."

"You're pushing your luck."

"I don't care. It's what I want. She needs a husband—a decent husband."

"I'll see to it. Now let's send for Felicity."

"Why?"

"So you can propose."

He was aghast at the prospect.

"I don't wish to propose. You're her mother. Can't you tell her what we've decided?"

"She's eighteen years old, Redvers. She's had her heart set on a grand match since she was little. I won't let you deprive her of such a wonderful part of it."

He sighed, his trepidation rising.

Could he do this? How could he not?

It's just a marriage, a tiny voice reminded him.

He didn't have to like, respect, or ever spend time with Felicity. He'd have her money, but he didn't have to have her. She could live her own life, and he would live his.

"Go fetch her," he said.

Victoria went to the hall and whispered to a maid, then she returned to her desk.

"One more thing," she stated.

"What?"

"You are not to meet with Mary privately again. I would have your word on it."

Events were happening too fast. When he'd crawled out of Mary's bed earlier in the morning, he hadn't realized that it would be their final rendezvous.

He was dejected and miserable, every inch the despicable rogue Victoria had accused him of being. Mary would never understand, would never forgive him. He needed the chance to clarify what had transpired and *why*.

When he looked as if he'd protest, she said, "You've done enough damage, Redvers. I insist you leave her alone."

"She's going to be crushed."

"I suppose you led her to believe you'd wed her instead of Felicity."

He was ashamed to admit how he'd played on Mary's sympathies and trusting nature. He simply said, "She's very fond of me."

"Typical man," Victoria spat. "You're all swine."

"I have to explain this to her."

"Then you shall do it while I am in the room as a chaperone, and I concur: She deserves to hear it from your own lying, deceitful mouth."

"You're a hard woman, Victoria."

"And Mary is a foolish romantic who will have built up all sorts of fantasies about you. I expect you to courteously dash them, so she isn't left hoping for what will never be."

He sighed again. He was bereft, troubled, contemptible beyond bearing.

"As you wish. Let's get it over with."

"We shall deal with her as soon as we're finished with Felicity."

FELICITY walked into her mother's library, taking small steps, prolonging the moment so she would recall every detail.

She had brought Jordan Winthrop to his knees!

Ha!

He had to be choking on his pride and conceit, and she was thrilled to have put him in his place. She wanted to laugh with arrogant glee. She wanted to twirl in circles and kick up her heels.

He and Victoria were over by the desk, seated across from each other, glaring.

"You asked to see me, Mother?" She acted shy and demure.

They both stood.

"Yes, Felicity. Please join us. Lord Redvers and I have been talking. He has something he would like to say to you."

Felicity bit down a grin.

She knew what was coming. Victoria had warned her to be ready, and she'd been in her room for hours, dressing to perfection.

She strolled over, but as he turned toward her, she frowned.

He looked as if he'd slept in his clothes, as if he'd been in a brawl, and there was a strong odor of alcohol hovering about his person.

Was he drunk? Had he needed to imbibe of whiskey in order to muster the courage to proceed?

Ooh . . . the wretch! He'd spoiled everything!

"He didn't even shave," she blurted out.

"Felicity!" her mother scolded. "It's not your business to comment on his condition."

"Well, he didn't. He's a mess."

Redvers grumbled an epithet. "Let's make this brief and to the point, shall we? Before I change my mind?"

"By all means," Victoria replied.

"Felicity"—Redvers was curt and cold—"will you marry me?"

Felicity's mouth dropped open in shock.

He hadn't so much as glanced at her beautiful gown or magnificently styled hair. He hadn't uttered a single compliment. He hadn't spoken a civil word.

"That's it?" she complained. "That's your proposal?"

"Yes."

"But you didn't say what you were supposed to say!"

"I believe I remembered the most important part."

"Felicity," Victoria barked, "Lord Redvers has asked you a question. You must grace him with your answer."

"But . . . but . . . he has to get down on one knee. He has to take my hand and pledge his undying love. He has to tell me that I've made him the happiest man in the world."

"Oh for pity's sake," Redvers mumbled.

Victoria growled with exasperation. "Her answer is *yes*, Lord Redvers. She would be honored to be your wife."

Felicity stamped her foot. "I want him to do it again. I want him to do it correctly."

"Are we finished?" Redvers inquired of Victoria.

"Yes, we're definitely finished." She rounded the desk and took Felicity by the arm, escorting her out. "Go find Mary and send her down. Inform her that she must attend me at once."

Felicity studied them. Redvers wasn't leaving, so it was obvious they would meet with Mary together. Why?

A frisson of concern slithered down her spine. What was happening?

"Why must you speak with Mary? Why would he sit in with you?"

"Just fetch her for me."

Victoria shoved Felicity into the hall and shut the door in her face.

Her proposal ended, her marriage set, she marched away.

Chapter 18

❦

"CASSIE! There you are!"

Cassandra whipped around to see Adair chasing her down the hall. She refused to think of him as *Paxton*, and she couldn't have him referring to her as *Cassie* right out in the open, where anyone could hear.

"What is it, Mr. Adair?"

He hurried up, skidding to a halt.

Debonair as ever, he looked handsome and elegant in a perfectly tailored suit. He'd been barbered and shaved, and he smelled very good, a hint of masculine cologne discernible beneath his clothes.

The scent tickled her senses, pricking at whatever insane itch he always goaded until she was desperate to have him scratch it.

Needing to put space between them, she took a step back. He'd expected a warm greeting and when he didn't receive it, he frowned.

"You called me Mr. Adair."

"Of course I did. We don't have a familiar acquaintance."

"You little liar. What's come over you? Why have you been hiding from me?"

"I haven't been hiding."

"Yes, you have. You've been positively dodgy."

"You're being absurd. I have no reason to avoid you."

"Don't you?"

He smiled a smile that made her knees weak, that promised iniquity, that wickedly reminded her of how she had no secrets from him.

"It's been three days since we"—he bent down and whispered—"fucked like rabbits, and I haven't seen you anywhere. If I'd had any idea of the location of your bedchamber, I'd have sneaked in every night."

"Would you be silent?"

"Call me Paxton, or I'll say it again. Very loudly."

"You wouldn't."

"I would, so call me Paxton." He glared, tapping his foot. "I'm waiting."

"No. I won't let you bully me. Go away before someone sees us."

"Why would I care if anyone sees us? Quit being such a prim shrew."

"Me! I'm not prim."

"You couldn't prove it by me. You're acting like a frightened virgin, and it annoys the hell out of me."

There was a deserted parlor next to them, and he grabbed her hand and dragged her inside. He closed the door with his toe, then shoved her back. He leaned in, trapping her against the wood.

"Have you missed me?" he asked.

"No."

"Why do you keep lying?"

His mouth covered hers in a devastating kiss. It went on and on till she was dizzy, till she managed to forget that they were in a downstairs room in her mother's house.

A servant could walk by and push his way in, and the possibility of detection added a dangerous element to their behavior. She found it oddly thrilling.

He clasped her thighs and wrapped them around his waist so that her privates were pressed to his. He was hard with desire, and she was delighted to have aroused him, experiencing none of her usual fear or revulsion. Instead, joy swept through her.

Did people really fornicate like this? Against a door? In the middle of the day? With such reckless abandon?

She was grinning, and she couldn't stop.

Like a magician, he raised her skirt and opened his trousers. In an instant, she was impaled on his masculine rod, and he was thrusting into her.

He lowered the bodice of her dress, her bare breasts hanging out, and he pinched her nipples, sending waves of lust shooting to her womb. In an instant, she exploded with pleasure, and so did he. This time, he didn't pull out, but spilled his seed far inside her, and she should have been worried, but she wasn't.

She could practically see the son they might create. He'd have Paxton's golden blond hair and her big blue eyes, and she almost wished he had planted a child.

His flexing slowed, his face buried at her nape, his eager lips hot on her skin.

"Now will you call me Paxton?" he inquired. "If you say no, I'll spank your bottom."

"Oh, Paxton . . ." she murmured. "My goodness!"

"That's more like it." He drew away, guiding her down his torso till her feet touched the floor.

They tarried, straightening their clothes, and he was studying her with the most charming expression, as if she was very dear to him.

The look unnerved her. It seemed to demand a similar look in return, but she couldn't give it to him. She didn't know how.

"What are you staring at?" She felt foolish and giddy.

He was quiet, contemplative, then he admitted, "I'm leaving."

"Leaving? Why?"

"Jordan is sick of me. He's kicked me out. Lauretta, too. She and I are heading back to London."

"When?"

"Right away."

"I see."

She'd understood that he'd be at Barnes Manor a short while, but she hadn't realized the end was so near. Panic assailed her.

"Come with me!" he urged.

"To where?"

"To London."

"London! Are you mad?"

"No. I've been thinking about us."

"There is no *us*."

"There is! Don't deny it. Something happens when we're together. It's wild and extraordinary. . . . Oh, just come with me."

"I couldn't."

"And why couldn't you? What's keeping you here?"

"It's my home."

"You hate it here. You're constantly under your mother's thumb. You trudge around as if you died at age sixteen when you were wed. Let me breathe some life back into you. Escape with me."

"To do what? You have no income. How would we live?"

"I've decided it's time for me to grow up."

"What does that mean?"

He sobered, appearing very sensible for a change.

"I'm going to tell my father *yes*, that I would like very much to take possession of his plantation in Jamaica."

"You're off to Jamaica?"

"Yes." He grinned, his excitement bubbling up. "Can't you picture me, sitting on the verandah of my grand house, gazing out at the blue sea? I'll be wearing a white suit, and I'll have a cadre of Negroes fawning over me and serving me iced rums."

She smiled, being able to absolutely visualize it, as if it was a place she'd previously resided herself. She could see the palm trees swaying in the wind, could smell the tropical flowers lining the balustrade, could feel the warm breeze drifting up off the beach sand.

"I can picture you in just that spot," she said.

"Then come with me. There's a chair on that porch for you, too."

For an insane, impetuous second, it was on the tip of her tongue to accept.

After all, what reason was there to stay at Barnes Manor?

Her mother wanted her gone, and Cassandra was desperate to depart. But in her ponderings, she'd never actually assumed it might transpire, and with Paxton offering her the chance, she was too terrified to reach for it.

She didn't know any details about him save for the fact that he was a gambler, cheat, and philanderer. How could that be the basis for a lasting relationship?

In a pinch, he wasn't the sort of fellow a woman could count upon, so she would never rashly board a ship and sail across the ocean with him. The prospect was so fantastical that he might have suggested she sprout wings and fly to the moon.

"No," she said. "I can't."

"You can!" he insisted.

"No."

He grabbed her and shook her. "Do it for me. Do it for yourself!"

"No . . . no . . ."

"I can't bear to go without you. Don't make me."

His heartfelt plea was too enticing. Her resolve was weakening, and she yearned to throw herself into his arms, to laugh and say yes, yes, yes, but she couldn't.

Despite how she complained about Victoria, Cassandra was her daughter in every way.

Although Cassandra had been wed and widowed, she

couldn't imagine marrying again without her mother's consent. Victoria would never deem Adair an appropriate spouse, would never agree to a match.

"I really couldn't, Paxton. I couldn't. I'm so sorry."

She squirmed away and opened the door, stepping into the hall without peeking first. He lunged after her, and unfortunately, her mother took that very moment to appear at the end of the corridor.

She halted and frowned, assessing the intimate scene.

"Mr. Adair, what are you doing? Unhand my daughter at once."

He moved away, and he stared at Cassandra, giving her the opportunity to tell the truth, to admit a bond, but she was a coward and always had been. She had no idea how to stand up to Victoria, and she was stubbornly silent.

He winked, taking the blame, forgiving her for her spinelessness.

"I apologize, Mrs. Barnes." He was convincingly contrite. "I didn't mean any harm."

"Lord Redvers has asked you to go," Victoria seethed, "and it can't happen soon enough for me."

"He was just flirting, Mother," Cassandra fibbed.

"In an empty parlor," Victoria charged, "with the door closed? He might have done anything to you." She glared at Paxton. "Pack your belongings, Mr. Adair, and get out of my house. Don't let me catch you sniffing around Cassandra again."

Paxton hesitated, his disappointment clear. Cassandra thought he might defend himself or beg her to be candid about their friendship, but he didn't.

He turned and left.

Cassandra and Victoria stood in place, watching him go. Then Victoria marched off without forcing Cassandra to endure a lecture on low morals.

As she dawdled in the quiet, it dawned on her that this had been her farewell to Paxton Adair. She would never talk to him again. She would never see him again.

It was the most dismal realization she'd ever had, and the lonely days without him stretched ahead like the road to Hades.

"VICTORIA," Mary said, entering the library, "Felicity told me you wanted to speak with me."

"Yes, Mary, come in."

Victoria was behind her desk, Jordan seated across from her, and Mary tamped down any indication of surprise.

Since his fight with his father, she'd been searching for him, knowing that he'd be distraught.

Why was he with Victoria?

Mary's heart pounded with anticipation. He'd sworn that they would find a way to wed. Had he already notified Victoria of his decision?

He must have!

Inside, she reeled with joy, but she couldn't let it show.

She walked over and sat next to Jordan. She was trembling, but she couldn't help it. She was so very, very glad.

"What is it?" she inquired.

"Lord Redvers has something he would like to say to you."

"All right."

Mary shifted to face him, conveying a silent, visual message of encouragement. She'd tied her hair with the red ribbon he'd bought her. She tipped her head slightly so he'd see it, so he'd remember he wasn't alone, that she was his partner and would stand by him in the pending tumult they were about to cause.

"Mary," he cautiously started, "I'm . . . I'm sorry."

She scowled, the remark confusing her.

"Sorry for what?"

"I know you heard the quarrel with my father."

"Yes, but he didn't mean what he said. I'm sure of it. You were both angry, but it will pass. You'll see."

"No, he meant it. He always means it, so my financial situation is even more dire than it's been."

He looked miserable. Dejected and sad and regretful.

She rippled with dread.

"What is it?" she asked. "Just say it."

"I have confessed our indiscretion to your stepmother."

The way he pronounced the word *indiscretion* rattled her. He made their relationship sound sordid and wrong, as if he was ashamed.

"You did?"

"Yes, and she wants me to clarify a few things for you."

"What *things*?"

"Well, from the liaison I pursued with you, I might have given you a false impression."

"About what?"

"Ah . . . you might have been hoping we'd end up together."

"Yes, I was. You were, too."

He sighed, then mumbled, "It's not going to happen."

"Why not?"

"I could never follow through, and though I knew better, I pursued you anyway."

"Mary," Victoria interjected, "you've had no experience with amour, so you aren't cognizant of what often transpires in an illicit romance. What Lord Redvers is trying to explain is that a man might whisper comments—in the heat of passion—that are a lie."

Mary's world crumbled as her faith in everything she'd ever believed was shattered. The very air in the sky had vanished. She couldn't move, couldn't breathe.

"But you promised me," she said to Jordan. "You promised!"

"Yes, I did, and for that, I most humbly apologize."

"Tell her the rest," Victoria urged. "Get it over with."

"I've decided to marry Felicity," he announced.

She couldn't have heard him correctly. She shook her head, feeling as if her ears were plugged, and she needed to clear them.

"What?"

"I've proposed to Felicity, and we're to be married tomorrow morning."

"You . . . proposed? When?"

"Just a few minutes ago."

If what he'd claimed was true, he'd sneaked out of her bed, had fought with his father, then marched into Victoria's library and arranged his wedding.

Could any man be that cruel? That shallow? That dishonest?

"You can't be serious."

"I'm sorry," he said again.

"Don't do this to me. Please! Don't do this to yourself."

"It's already finished. There's no going back."

"Last night, you told me that you wanted to change my life. You wanted to change yours. You were happy about it."

"Last night, I wasn't very sober."

If he'd stabbed her with a knife, he couldn't have wounded her any more grievously.

He and Victoria were both very calm, very composed, and she supposed she should have attempted to match them in poise and dignity, but she was devastated.

She began to weep, a flood of tears dripping down her cheeks. She couldn't hold them in, and she didn't even try.

On seeing them, he looked stricken.

"Oh, Mary, don't cry. You know I can't bear it when you're sad."

He reached out as if he might take her hand, and Victoria snapped, "Lord Redvers! You forget yourself!"

He eased away, appearing abashed, which should have provided some measure of solace, but it didn't.

She shouldn't have trusted him, and she'd never forgive herself for being so gullible. She would never forgive him for his cold disregard.

"You were going to change my life," she stupidly repeated.

Of all the sins he'd committed against her, this was the worst one. She'd naïvely assumed he would do what he'd vowed. It had never occurred to her that he wouldn't.

She'd never been more humiliated.

"You're upset now," he said, "but in the future, when you

reflect on this episode, you'll see that this was for the best. I would have been a terrible husband. I would have made you so miserable."

"No. I loved you. You could never have made me unhappy."

The remark fell into the room like a boulder dropped on gravel, a final nail in her coffin of woe.

He and Victoria stiffened—as with offense—and Victoria gestured for him to hurry.

Hadn't he said plenty? What could possibly be left?

"We have some plans in place for you," he declared.

She might have inquired as to what they were, but she couldn't speak. Mute and dumbfounded, she simply gaped at him. He had bargained with Victoria over her fate, and she thought it took some gall for them to haggle without her being aware of the stakes.

"We need to learn if there's a babe," he advised her, "so you'll stay with Victoria's cousin for a bit. Then Victoria has agreed to a marvelous resolution."

He seemed downright eager to share their news, to have her relish it, too.

"Victoria will dower you," he excitedly proclaimed, "so you can marry. She'll help you find a husband, so you'll wind up with what you've always craved: a family, a home of your own—"

"Stop it," she managed to gasp. "Stop!"

She'd wanted Jordan Winthrop as her husband. Instead, Lord Redvers was throwing her a bone, giving her a nameless, faceless spouse as a consolation prize.

It was the most spiteful, most malicious deed that had ever been done to her.

She peered at Victoria.

"Could you ask him to go?"

She would have liked to be the one to rise and stomp out, but she couldn't move.

Victoria glared at Redvers. "I'll deal with her from here on out. It's obvious she understands what's expected of her."

He rose and gazed down at Mary.

"I know you don't believe me at the moment," he said, "but I did this for you."

She didn't reply, and he paused, waiting—as if on tenterhooks—for her to thank him.

"I'll be a member of the family now," he practically boasted, "so if you ever need anything, promise me that you'll—"

"Lord Redvers!" Victoria barked. "That's enough!"

He lingered for an eternity, apparently hoping for a reaction from Mary, and when he didn't receive it, he sighed and departed.

A frightening silence descended.

Mary stared at Victoria, and Victoria stared back.

"You are not to see him privately ever again," Victoria said. "Swear to me that you will not."

When Mary couldn't respond, Victoria shouted, "Swear it to me!"

"I swear," Mary muttered.

"Of all the things you might have attempted, I would never have predicted *this*. What have you to say for yourself?"

"I'm sorry. I never meant to disrespect you. I never meant to hurt anyone."

"Really? What about Felicity? She is your sister, and he will be her husband. Yet you can sit there and tell me that you didn't mean to *hurt* anyone?"

When the affair had started, it had seemed so wonderful. She'd never looked down the road to this horrid day, to the rough conclusion where she was ruined and completely dishonored.

"I hadn't thought about Felicity."

"No, you hadn't." Victoria snorted with disgust. "Viscount Redvers presumes that I will resolve this scandal by marrying you off, but I have no intention of doing that."

The notion of Victoria picking her husband was nauseating.

"I wouldn't want you to."

"You can't remain here, though. Especially if you might be increasing. I won't have you flaunting his bastard child at Felicity."

"Are you ordering me to leave Barnes Manor?"

"Yes. Redvers is like a rutting dog, so he won't halt his pursuit of you. I can't have him visiting over the Christmas holidays, only to catch him lifting your skirt again. If he hasn't already impregnated you, he certainly could in the future. I won't court disaster."

"But . . . leave?"

"Yes."

"This was my father's home," Mary indignantly reminded her.

"Yes, it was, and if he could see how you've disgraced yourself, he would be so ashamed."

At the blunt insult, Mary blanched, but she was undeterred in her argument. "I belong here as much as Felicity or Cassandra. What right have you to throw me out?"

"I have the right, because as you mentioned this *was* your father's home, but it is mine now. I decide what is permitted under my roof. I decide who resides with me and who doesn't. You can't strut about the neighborhood with your belly swelling out to here"—she gestured rudely with her hands—"and no wedding ring on your finger. Were you imagining there would be no consequences?"

Mary wanted to complain, wanted to fight or weep, but what was the point? Her conduct guaranteed that she couldn't carry on as she had in the past, and Barnes Manor was Victoria's property. As she had always made abundantly clear, Mary stayed because Victoria allowed her to stay.

"Where shall I go?" Mary asked. "What shall I do?"

"I shall give you twenty pounds and coach fare to London. It is sufficient to pay a few months' accommodation at a boardinghouse. You'll be safe and fed while you hunt for a job. It's probably what I should have done years ago. There's never been anything for you here."

"But a boardinghouse!" Mary was sick with fury. "I am Charles Barnes's oldest daughter."

"Yes, and look where it's gotten you. You're lucky I've offered you twenty pounds. I could just kick you out on the lane to fend for yourself."

Mary was about to retort when the door flung open and Felicity hurried in. Cassandra was behind her.

"Mother," Felicity said, "we saw Lord Redvers storming up the stairs. He was extremely angry. What's happened? I'm not a child, so don't treat me like one. I demand to know what's going on."

Victoria stood, and she was very grim, as if she was a judge passing a death sentence. "Mary is leaving us today. She won't ever be back."

"What?" Cassandra gasped.

"Why?" Felicity queried. She swaggered over, approaching till she was directly in front of Mary. "It's Redvers, isn't it? She's done something awful to my fiancé."

"Yes," Victoria admitted. "I won't have you and Cassandra speculating or feeling sorry for her. Mary, rise to your feet and inform them of your treachery."

In light of how Felicity would react, it was a very cruel command. And why should Felicity be apprised? It would only hurt her, would only wreck the beginning of her marriage to Lord Redvers.

"She doesn't need to hear it," Mary insisted.

"Yes, she does. She's marrying him in the morning; she should have no illusions about him. Down the road, it will save her an enormous amount of heartache."

Victoria paused, and when Mary didn't leap up to proceed, Victoria bellowed, "Stand and tell her! At once!"

On shaky legs, Mary stumbled up, and she stared into her half sister's blue eyes. Mary saw no kindness, no cordiality, no hint of warmth.

What on earth was Mary supposed to say? How was she to confess the truth?

"During Lord Redvers's . . . ah . . . visit to Barnes Manor," Mary stammered, "he and I have . . . grown very close."

Felicity frowned. "You're talking in riddles."

When Mary couldn't explain, Victoria did it for her. "She and Redvers were having an affair. They've been doing physical things together that a man should only do with his wife, things that you will learn about on your wedding night."

"Oh no," Cassandra breathed.

Felicity's response was more potent. Her cheeks mottled with rage.

"You were dallying with my betrothed?"

"Yes."

"You deceitful, disloyal witch!"

Felicity slapped Mary as hard as she could. Mary hadn't been expecting the blow, and she staggered, lurching to regain her balance lest she fall to the floor. Felicity loomed nearer, as if she would strike Mary again, but Cassandra jumped between them.

"Felicity!" Cassandra scolded. "Stop it! Redvers isn't worth this sort of quarrel."

"Get out of my way!" Felicity seethed.

"No." Cassandra glanced over her shoulder at Mary. "Mary, are you all right?"

"Yes, I'm all right," Mary said with quiet dignity. She pulled the red ribbon from her hair and discreetly dropped it.

Victoria nodded at Mary. "Head upstairs and pack your bag. You still have time to catch the afternoon coach in the village."

"Where is she going?" Cassandra demanded to know.

"It doesn't matter," Victoria declared. "Her whereabouts are no longer any of our concern."

Mary gazed at Victoria, remembering all the difficult years she'd endured, how lonely she'd been, how unloved and unappreciated. Yet, she'd persevered, had accepted her lot, had bravely and courteously tried to fit in.

And this was her reward?

"I never hated any of you," she solemnly confided to the three women. "Despite how you always treated me, I never did."

She marched out of the room.

"Mary . . ." Cassandra said, but Mary kept walking.

Chapter 19

MARY ran through the woods, feeling as if she'd gone mad.

She should have simply proceeded to her room, packed her bag, and left as Victoria had ordered, but she couldn't obey her stepmother.

Victoria's edict seemed too unreasonable.

Mary and Redvers had participated in the affair together, yet his conclusion was marriage to Felicity and the receipt of her fortune, while Mary's conclusion was shame, eviction, and the loss of everything that was familiar.

Where was the fairness in that?

Why should Redvers escape without so much as a raised brow, while Mary was branded a harlot and kicked out on the street?

She didn't want to go to London and fend for herself. She'd never been to Town before. How was she to locate a place to live? Food to eat? A job?

With no skills or abilities, even if she'd had the vaguest

notion of how to find employment, what was she qualified to attempt?

She needed help and advice, needed someone to take her side so she might obtain a better, more equitable resolution.

Harold was the only person she could think of who might assist her. He'd always complained about Victoria's treatment of Mary. He understood Mary's plight, and hopefully, he would be able to tell her what to do.

Bursting out of the trees, she hurried across the swathed grass to the bricked drive that led to the Talbots' house.

There was a carriage parked out front, and as she neared it, the door of the residence opened.

Harold and Vicar Martin exited. Harold was dressed in his Sunday clothes, and as Mary watched, he slipped the minister a small pouch, which had to contain money.

What was occurring?

She stumbled to a halt as the minister patted Harold on the back.

"I never thought I'd see the day, Talbot," the vicar said to Harold.

"Neither did I."

"I'd given up on it ever happening."

Harold puffed up, looking pompous and pleased. "I just had to meet the right woman."

"And a fine choice you made. A very fine choice. Congratulations."

He patted Harold's back again, then climbed into the carriage.

As the vehicle moved off, Harold saw Mary, and he frowned.

"Mary, what are you doing here?"

"I had to speak with you. It's very important. May I come inside?"

"It's really not a good time."

In all the years she'd visited him and Mother Talbot, she'd never been refused entrance.

His cheeks reddened, as if he was embarrassed.

"Why isn't it a good time?" she asked. "What's going on?"

"Well . . ."

His cousin, Gertrude, peeked out the door. She was dressed in her Sunday best, too, and she had her hair braided in an elaborate coif that had flowers weaved through it.

"Harry," she fairly cooed, "Mother Talbot is ready to cut the cake."

"I'll be there in a minute, Gertie," he said.

Gertrude scowled at Mary, then went in.

Mary studied his attire, remembered the minister and the pouch of coins.

"What have you done?" she inquired.

"I've been meaning to talk to you."

"About?"

"Gertrude has been here for a few weeks, and she and Mother get on famously. You know how it is."

"No, I don't know how it *is*. Why don't you tell me?"

"Gertrude and I . . . that is . . . Mother and I were . . ."

Gertrude appeared again, and she marched toward them. In a proprietary gesture, she took Harold's arm.

"We were just married." She was smug, gloating.

"Married?"

Mary's furious gaze locked on Harold, but he was a coward and stared at the ground.

"Yes," Gertrude replied. "While he and I have been forced into such close quarters, we learned how much we have in common. It was only natural that romance blossom. Mother Talbot noticed it before we did, and she suggested the match."

"Couldn't disappoint the old girl," Harold muttered. "Keeps it all in the family, don't you see?"

Mary had never had strong emotional feelings for Harold, but for so long, he'd been her sole hope of rescue, of change. His marriage, so fast—and behind Mary's back—seemed an even bigger betrayal than the one Redvers had effected.

"I waited ten years, Harold," Mary charged. "Ten years!"

"Yes, sorry."

"You're *sorry*?" Mary gasped. "Is that all you have to say?"

"Actually," Gertrude interjected, "we're glad you stopped by."

"Why would you be?"

"It saves me the trouble of calling on you. Harold told me about your peculiar infatuation with him. He's tried to politely deflect your attentions, but to no avail, and I must insist that you leave him alone."

"Leave him alone . . ." Mary repeated like a dullard.

"He's mine now," Gertrude boasted. "If I catch you sniffing after him again, I'll have to confer with Mrs. Barnes about your behavior."

Mary glared at Harold, daring him to look at her, but he wouldn't.

"I desperately need help, Harold. I need a friend to advise me, and I came to you. Yet this is my answer?"

"Miss Barnes!" Gertrude snapped. "Honestly! Control yourself!" She dragged Harold toward the house without letting him respond. Not that the little weasel would have. The door shut without his ever glancing back.

Mary dawdled in his yard, and she stared up at the sky, wishing the Good Lord would smite her and sweep her up to Heaven.

Her heart was broken, her dreams dashed. Why carry on? Why keep trying?

Did Lord Redvers understand the full extent of the catastrophe he'd brought down on her head? If he was apprised, would he be concerned?

She had to accept that he wouldn't care.

He'd claimed that he didn't care about anything, that he had no positive qualities. She'd refused to believe him, but his conduct had proven that he was the low, despicable reprobate everyone deemed him to be.

She couldn't say he hadn't warned her. He'd been very clear; blunt, even. From the beginning, he'd intended to form no attachment, and he hadn't.

Why then, was she so shocked? So surprised? So hurt?

She started for Barnes Manor, and as she walked, a dispassionate coldness seeped through her.

She'd always been an optimist—despite how bad things appeared, there were better days on the horizon. That foolishness was over.

There was no point in hoping, in being loyal, or making an effort. There was no reward. There was no light at the end of the tunnel.

When Victoria had first explained that Mary was to be evicted, she hadn't wanted to go, but why not? Barnes Manor had never really been her home. It had once belonged to her father, but she scarcely remembered him.

What reason was there to remain? Why pursue a connection with relatives who hated her?

If she couldn't live at Barnes Manor, what did it matter where she resided? She could live in a ditch, in a hovel, in a London boardinghouse. It was all the same to her.

She felt dead inside, and as the mansion came into view, she'd ceased to worry over her plight.

Time was quickly passing, and she'd wasted too much of it. If she planned to catch the London coach in the village, she had to get moving.

She sneaked in a rear door and tiptoed up to her bedchamber. She peered around, knowing that she should have been sad or nostalgic or angry but she wasn't.

The room seemed hazy and distant, as if it was a stranger's, as if she'd never slept in it a single night.

She opened the wardrobe, hastily grabbing her few personal possessions. The only odd item was the second vial of Spinster's Cure that Mr. Dubois had given her.

He'd urged her to try another dose, but she hadn't. Nor had she thrown it away. It had humored her to have the tonic, to look at it occasionally and ponder its effect. She tossed the vial in her reticule, not wanting it, but not wanting to leave it behind where someone might find it and wonder what it was.

She had a battered portmanteau, and she packed it, buckled the strap, and strolled out.

At the landing, she nearly turned to slink out the servants' entrance. But at the last moment, she decided not to. Head high, she marched to the main staircase.

She was Charles Barnes's oldest daughter. She would depart by the front door. If Victoria didn't like it, so what?

Mary had stopped caring about Victoria's opinion. Mary had stopped caring about anything.

As she reached the foyer, Cassandra was hurrying down the hall. She noted Mary's bag, her cloak and bonnet, and she frowned.

While they'd been children, Cassandra had never been overly cordial but she hadn't been horrid, either. When she'd come home after her failed marriage, she'd been affable and supportive. Mary considered her a friend, but Mary had no parting words for her and wouldn't engage in a drawn-out farewell.

She was invisible, a ghost floating away unseen.

"Mary, there you are!" Cassandra rushed up. "I've been searching everywhere."

"Have you?"

Mary kept going.

"Mary!"

Cassandra clasped her wrist, halting her.

"What?" Mary queried.

"You're not actually leaving?"

"Yes."

"Well, don't. With the wedding and all, it's been very stressful. Wait until we're all more calm. I'll speak to Mother; I'll get her to change her mind."

"I don't want her to change her mind. I don't want to ever see her again."

"I know she's always been awful to you, and today was worse than ever, but this can't be your choice. Where will you go?"

"I'm off to London on the afternoon coach."

"To London! To do what?"

"I have no idea. I'll figure it out once I'm there."

"Oh, Mary . . ."

Cassandra studied her, her consternation great as she tried to devise an argument that would sway Mary, but there was nothing Cassandra could say.

Mary yanked away and went outside. Cassandra followed her.

"Mary, is Lord Redvers aware of what's occurring?"

"Yes."

"But he can't have thought this through. Mother said that he'd developed a *tendre* for you. Let me confer with him. He might be able to assist you."

Mary whipped around. "Don't ever talk to him about me. Don't ever mention my name."

For some inexplicable reason, Mary remembered the vial of Spinster's Cure in her reticule. She pulled it out and gave it to Cassandra.

"What's this?" Cassandra asked.

"It's a love potion. Drink it when you're staring at some man who tickles your fancy. It's supposed to make him fall in love with you. Maybe it will work better for you than it worked for me."

She walked on.

"Will you write to me, Mary? I'll be anxious to hear how you're faring."

"No."

"You can't want that."

"I do. I want it very much."

"Will you at least drop me a note when you've arrived safe and sound?"

"No."

"How about an address—after you're settled."

"Why would I let you know? If I was in trouble, what could you do?"

She continued on down the drive.

* * *

"MISS Barnes! Good day to you."

"Hello, Mr. Dubois."

He scrutinized the petite, pretty woman with whom he'd been acquainted for several weeks. She seemed different somehow: beaten down, unfocused, wary. Her distracted condition worried him.

She was attired as if for a journey, carrying a portmanteau.

"Are you leaving us?"

"Yes."

"You look upset. Has something happened?"

"Nothing more than usual."

"I see . . ."

He went over to her and clasped her elbow, subtly urging her over to the wagon.

"Would you like a cup of tea? My sister, Clarinda, is brewing a pot."

"No, thank you. I have to make the London coach. I'm late as it is."

"You're off to London? My, that's an adventure. Are you visiting family?"

"I have no family."

The pronouncement was desperately bleak, underscoring his sense that she was very distressed.

"Are you traveling alone?"

"Yes."

"Have you ever been to Town?"

"No."

"What are your plans when you arrive?"

"I suppose I'll . . . I'll . . . get a job and find a room to let. Mrs. Barnes—she's my father's second wife—gave me a few pounds. I'm sure I'll be fine."

She was such a gentle soul. The large metropolis would chew her up and spit her out. Did she have any notion of the dangers a single female could face?

"This seems rather abrupt, Miss Barnes."

"Doesn't it, though?"

"What's wrong? You can tell me."

She snorted, and she studied the shelves filled with bottles and jars. "You mentioned that your sister is with you. Might I speak with her privately?"

"Certainly."

Clarinda was over in the trees, by the stream where they had their campsite.

"Clarinda," he beckoned, "would you come here for a minute?"

Momentarily, she appeared.

"Yes?" she inquired.

"Miss Barnes has stopped by. You remember her, don't you?"

"Of course."

He flashed a curious, concerned glance at Miss Barnes. "She'd like to have a confidential chat with you."

Clarinda's eyes were wide with queries she couldn't voice. She walked around the wagon as he huddled out of Miss Barnes's sight, but remained within earshot.

"Hello, Miss Barnes," Clarinda said. "This is a pleasant surprise."

"I have a question," was Miss Barnes's reply.

"What is it?"

"Your brother once claimed you had a potion that could keep a babe from taking root."

"Well . . . yes. I do."

"Have you one that might work if the babe is already planted?"

"You mean . . . to wash it out?"

"Yes."

There was a long pause, and Clarinda shifted so that she could see Phillip. She scowled, visually asking how to proceed. Their mother had been a renowned healer, and Clarinda had learned many of her techniques.

Clarinda was an accomplished apothecary and midwife,

knowledgeable in the ways of a white witch, but she also kept some darker remedies on hand.

It was a hazardous business, meddling in pregnancies, assisting in their termination. Clarinda could wind up on the bad end of a murder charge. Yet despite the risks, she occasionally aided desperate women.

Phillip liked Miss Barnes, and he felt somewhat responsible for her predicament. After all, hadn't his tonic pushed her into the path of the wicked Lord Redvers?

He shrugged and nodded, silently granting Clarinda permission to provide the purgative.

"I have what you need," Clarinda advised.

She unlocked her box of special herbs, dumped powder into an envelope, and gave it to Miss Barnes.

"Mix it in a liquid," Clarinda instructed. "Tea or whatever. It will bring on your monthly courses and clean out your womb. Drink it right away. Don't let any more days go by."

"I won't. How much do I owe you?"

"Nothing. Just . . . promise me that you'll never admit taking it—but if you're found out, you can't ever tell anyone where you got it."

"Don't worry," Miss Barnes said, "I would never cause you any trouble."

"Thank you."

"You're welcome."

Miss Barnes turned to depart, and Phillip emerged from his hiding spot.

"Miss Barnes?" he called, and she stopped.

"What?"

"The grand gentleman up at the manor, Viscount Redvers, whatever became of him?"

"I told you: He's marrying my sister. The wedding is tomorrow."

"Oh, you poor dear."

He'd been at the village dance, and he'd seen Redvers watching her. The nobleman had been positively besotted.

Where was he in all this? Why had he allowed catastrophe to crash down on Miss Barnes? Obviously, their affair had been discovered, and she'd been kicked out of her home because of it. What sort of *gentleman* was Redvers if the exalted ass would let this be done to her? Or had he been complicit in the harsh resolution?

This was a rich snob's version of a tidy conclusion. Redvers would wed his wealthy wife, and everyone would live happily ever after—except for Miss Barnes, who was suffering all of the consequences.

If Redvers had been standing there with them, Phillip would have beaten him to a bloody pulp.

"Are you sure you should go, *cherie*?" he asked. "Are you sure this is what you should do?"

"I'm twenty-five years old, Mr. Dubois. I can fend for myself."

"But *London*, Miss Barnes."

"There's no future for me here. There's no reason to stay on."

The remark was so sorrowfully voiced, that he could barely keep from drawing her into his arms and giving her a hug.

She was such a tragic figure, with her worn cloak and hat, her tattered bag. What was the world coming to that such a sweet person could be so ill-used?

"What about your Mr. Talbot?" he suggested. "Have you spoken to him? Perhaps he could help you."

"He got married, too. Spur of the moment. I had counted on him for such a long time." She gazed off in the distance, as if she could see her life vanishing right before her eyes, then she physically shook herself back to reality. "It's pointless to fuss about it. He didn't deserve me anyway."

"No, he didn't."

She reached out to him, and he clasped hold of her hands and squeezed tight. "You were always kind to me, Mr. Dubois. I appreciate it."

"You're welcome, and don't fret. These difficulties will pass."

"I'm certain they will."

It was clear that she didn't believe it, just as he knew from experience that—once she arrived in London—things would go from bad to worse. The filthy, sprawling city would likely be the end of her.

She pulled away, ready to trek on again when a carriage rumbled toward them.

Phillip braced, afraid it might be Redvers chasing after her, but as the vehicle slowed, a beautiful, auburn-haired woman opened the door and leaned out.

"Hello, Miss Barnes."

"Mrs. Bainbridge," Miss Barnes frostily replied.

"Fancy meeting you here."

A blond man peered out, too. "Where are you off to, Miss Barnes?"

"Hello, Mr. Adair. I'm catching the afternoon coach to London."

"I didn't realize you'd left Barnes Manor," Mr. Adair said.

"It was rather sudden," Miss Barnes responded.

"Why don't you ride with us?" Mrs. Bainbridge offered. "It will save you coach fare, and you'll be much more comfortable."

Bainbridge smiled a smile that was false and amused, as if she was humored by Miss Barnes's reduced situation.

"Lauretta is correct, Miss Barnes," Mr. Adair asserted. "You must ride with us. I won't take no for an answer."

He leapt down and lowered the step, appearing gallantly eager to assist her.

Phillip studied them. Adair seemed genuinely cordial, but the woman made him shudder. No benefit could accrue to Miss Barnes from an association with her.

"Do you think you ought to, Miss Barnes?" Phillip murmured. "Maybe you'd be better off sticking with the public coach."

"It doesn't matter, Mr. Dubois. Nothing matters anymore."

He sighed. "Au revoir then, *cherie.*"

He walked her over, observing with Clarinda as Adair

guided her in, as the driver clicked the reins, and they rattled away.

"That's a dirty business," Clarinda fumed.

"Yes, it is."

"The blond fellow was friendly enough, but I didn't like the looks of that doxy."

"Neither did I."

"I feel sorry for Miss Barnes. Do you suppose she's pregnant?"

"Let's hope not."

"Have they kicked her out to avoid a scandal?"

"Apparently. The rich are so strange."

"I'd like to have a chat with that grand lord who seduced her. I'd tell him a thing or two."

"I'd like to talk to him, too—with my fists!" Phillip stared down the road, muttering, "Good luck, Miss Barnes. You're definitely going to need it."

Chapter 20

❧

"THERE now," Vicar Martin cheerily said. "I believe we're ready to start."

Prayer book in hand, he stood in front of the hearth, trying not to look impatient, but he'd been waiting forever.

Jordan was over by the window and gazing out across the park. He kept recalling his first afternoon at Barnes Manor, when Mary had marched into the trees, bent on kissing Harold Talbot. He pushed the memory away.

He had to stop thinking about her. With his wedding—*to her sister*—about to begin, it was pointless to reflect.

Felicity, Victoria, and Cassandra had finally entered the room—nearly an hour late—but Jordan couldn't complain. He'd just arrived, too. No one seemed in the mood to hurry.

He'd only been able to follow through after imbibing an ample quantity of whiskey before coming downstairs. He felt numb, as if he was watching some other man suffer through the event.

"Lord Redvers," the vicar instructed, "please stand on this side of me. And Miss Felicity, if I could have you over here?"

When they didn't move, Victoria forced a brilliant smile.

"We're all a bit unnerved this morning," she claimed. "How about if we drink a toast to the bride and groom? It might put everyone at ease."

"I suppose that would be all right," Vicar Martin said.

Victoria motioned to her butler, and they dawdled in an uncomfortable silence as he filled a tray with glasses of sherry and delivered them, which wasn't much of a chore. The only people present were the three Barnes women, Vicar Martin, and himself.

Jordan hadn't thought he'd mind the small, private service, but to his dismay, he found that he minded it very much.

Someday, he would be Earl of Sunderland. He should have been at the cathedral in London, the grand organ blaring out hymns. The church should have been packed with family and guests. His proud father should have been sitting in the front row. Sunderland House should have been open to accommodate a week of parties.

Paxton's absence was most glaring. Jordan hadn't had the foresight to ask him to stay and be best man.

If Mary could have seen the empty parlor, what would her opinion have been? She'd probably have . . .

He had to stop thinking about Mary!

He'd cruelly used her, then broken her heart and tossed her aside. After the ghastly scene in the library with Victoria, he hadn't even tried to speak with her again. He'd been too much of a coward.

What would he have said anyway? That he was a total and unrepentant ass? That every terrible thing she'd heard about him was true?

There'd been no reason to talk to her, and besides, he'd promised Victoria he wouldn't. He'd behaved badly all around, and he didn't deserve a last chance to beg her forgiveness, but still, he hated how their relationship had ended.

He'd asked Victoria how Mary was faring, but was informed that Mary had already left the property and was traveling to commence her exile at Victoria's cousin's residence.

So . . . even if he'd mustered the courage to seek her out, she was gone.

A commotion erupted in the hall, and he glanced over to see Harold Talbot strut in, his homely cousin clutching his arm.

"My dear Mrs. Barnes," Harold said, "I hope we're not late."

Victoria was disconcerted. "Actually, you're early. We're running behind, so we haven't held the ceremony yet."

"Oh, how embarrassing. I apologize."

Jordan glowered at Victoria, demanding an explanation.

"As they are our closest neighbors," she advised, "I invited them to the wedding breakfast. Is Mother Talbot with you?"

"You know she doesn't like to go out," Harold replied.

The moment was incredibly awkward. Now that the Talbots had arrived, it would be the height of rudeness to insist they tarry in the foyer while the vows were exchanged, but Jordan despised Talbot and refused to have him in the room during the service.

Victoria sensed Jordan's fury, and she averted disaster by gesturing to the butler again.

"Why don't you refill everyone's glass? And pour some for Mr. and Miss Talbot."

Harold puffed up. "Mrs. Barnes, I must make a slight correction to your mode of address."

"What do you mean, Harold?"

"I am pleased to announce that I have married Gertrude, so she is *Mrs*. Harold Talbot."

The new Mrs. Talbot giggled like a debutante, and the moment became even more awkward.

No one rushed to congratulate them. No one said a word.

"How . . . nice," Victoria finally murmured, searching for

the right tone. "Isn't this rather sudden? I didn't know you were engaged."

Jordan was delighted that Talbot had wed Gertrude instead of Mary, but he was incensed, too. Mary had pinned her hopes on Talbot, had waited an entire decade for the smarmy man to publicly reveal their understanding.

"How could you have married your cousin?" Jordan asked. "As far as I'm aware, you've been quietly betrothed to Mary Barnes for years."

At his speaking Mary's name, everybody stiffened, except the vicar, who was clueless as to the details of the unfolding drama.

Talbot blushed and stammered, "I haven't any idea where you'd have come by such a ludicrous notion."

"Haven't you? Miss Barnes admitted it to me herself. She was just about to discuss wedding plans with Mrs. Barnes."

"That's not true," Gertrude Talbot declared.

"How would you know?" Jordan snidely said. "You're not from around here. Why would you have any information as to how Mr. Talbot trifled with Mary's affections?"

"Harold told me how it was."

"*Harold* was lying." Jordan disdainfully studied them, pretending great offense. "I'll have my attorney contact you as to the amount of damages you owe Miss Barnes for breach of promise."

"You wouldn't!" Gertrude Talbot seethed.

"Wouldn't I? Your husband is a sniveling coward, who constantly took advantage of Miss Barnes's kindly nature." Jordan scowled at Victoria. "Get them out of here, and I don't want to see them back."

Victoria looked as if she might lecture him on neighbors and rural villages, but on viewing his livid expression, she herded them out.

"Well, I never!" Gertrude exclaimed as their footsteps faded.

Jordan went back to the window, so angry that he yearned to throw something.

Why was he tolerating these horrid people? Why not walk out? Was he insane?

Mary had warned him that Felicity's money wouldn't make him happy, but he . . .

Ah! If Mary rambled through his mind again, he couldn't predict what he might do.

Behind him, someone approached, and he whipped around, eager to hurl a scathing remark. On discovering that it was Cassandra Stewart, he bit it down.

He'd spent minimal time with her—or rather *she* had spent minimal time with him. She didn't like him, and she'd been clear that she didn't care to socialize.

What was she up to? If she scolded or nagged, he wouldn't be civil.

"Is there something you need?" he asked.

"Yes, there is. I'm thrilled by how you put Harold in his place. I wish I'd done it myself. I wanted to say thank you."

"Oh . . . hmm . . ." He was embarrassed by her praise. "It was easy enough. He's a horse's ass, and I loathe him."

"I'm relieved that Mary didn't end up with him. She'd have been miserable."

"I agree."

"I should probably keep my mouth shut, but Mother mentioned that you had been involved with Mary."

"Dammit!" he cursed, then flushed with chagrin. "Pardon my rough language."

"I've heard worse. I won't faint."

"Good."

"Felicity was present during the conversation, so she's aware of the affair."

"You're joking."

"No. Mother thought Felicity should know, so she wouldn't have any illusions about you. It will make for an odd beginning to your marriage, don't you imagine?"

"That's putting it mildly." He shook his head with disgust. "Is your mother crazy?"

"She can be." Mrs. Stewart hesitated, then forged on. "I'm curious about your amour with Mary. Were you fond of her?"

He might have denied a relationship, might have contended that Victoria had been incorrect, but he missed Mary, and he wasn't about to act as if the liaison hadn't occurred.

"Yes, I was. I was very fond of her."

"Then I'm glad for you *and* for her. I don't believe anyone was ever fond of her before."

He shrugged, embarrassed again by her comments. Since she'd been blatant in her aversion, he hadn't attempted to breach the distance between them, so he'd never previously seen this side of her.

He enjoyed it. She seemed to be a genuinely nice person, and she'd liked Mary.

"I have a question," she said. It was her turn to look chagrinned.

"About what?"

"I had become cordial with Mr. Adair."

"I'm not surprised; he always charms the ladies."

"Since he left, it's been positively dreary around here. We had intended to correspond, and he was supposed to provide me with his address, but he forgot. Might I impose on you to get it?"

"Yes. I'll be sure to jot it down for you."

"I appreciate it."

"If you plan to contact him, though, you'll need to write at once. He's about to sail for Jamaica."

"Yes, he told me he was."

"He was anxious to start his adventure, so he's leaving right away."

"Do you think he'll ever come back to England?"

"I hope so."

Jordan pushed down the prospect of Paxton's departure. What with all Jordan's recent troubles, he couldn't bear to consider Paxton's journey, and he was furious at Paxton's father for finally bribing his friend with an offer he couldn't refuse.

If Jordan didn't have Paxton as his companion, who would he have? No one else could stand him.

"Now I have a question for *you*," he said, determined to change the subject. "It's terribly indiscreet of me to inquire, but I'm going to anyway."

"What is it?"

"What is your opinion of your mother's cousin?"

"My mother's cousin?"

"Yes."

"My mother doesn't have a cousin."

"Yes, she does. Mary went to stay with her. I'm just wondering what sort of welcome she'll receive."

Before Mrs. Stewart could reply, Victoria returned, clapping her hands to get their attention.

"The Talbots have gone home, so let's finish this, shall we?"

"Yes, let's do," Vicar Martin said.

He smiled, expecting everyone to smile back, but no one did.

Mrs. Stewart moved to the hearth, and Jordan studied her, confused by her statement. He wanted her to clarify what she'd meant, but he didn't dare delay the ceremony to talk about his recent clandestine amour.

He walked over to the vicar, feeling as if he was gliding in slow motion.

As he stepped next to Felicity, she bristled.

"Mother told me about you and Mary," she hissed as if Martin wasn't three feet away and listening to her every word.

Jordan was grateful for Mrs. Stewart's warning. He accepted the remark with equanimity. "Really?"

"I will never forgive you."

"Why would it matter to me if I'm forgiven or not?"

Vicar Martin frowned and hastily searched for his spot in the prayer book.

"I'm only marrying you," Felicity fumed, "because I'll be a countess someday."

"Yes, you are. Had you assumed it was for some other reason?"

"If Mother wasn't making me, I'd wed a farmer before I'd have you."

The vicar snapped his book closed. They all jumped.

"Miss Barnes," he huffed, "there seems to be some disagreement between you and Lord Redvers. This is not the Middle Ages. I will not marry any woman against her will. Do you wish—of your own accord—to proceed or not?"

A lengthy silence dragged out. Felicity peered over at her mother, scowled intently, then said, "Of course I wish to proceed. I apologize for giving you the wrong impression."

"What about you, Lord Redvers?" the minister queried.

"A dowry is a dowry. Get on with it."

"I'll take that as a yes."

Martin began to recite what had to be the fastest reading of the vows ever attempted, yet Jordan didn't hear the phrases flowing by.

He kept pondering Mrs. Stewart's comment—that Victoria didn't have a cousin—and he was so rattled by the implications that he couldn't focus.

What had he done to Mary? What had Victoria done?

"Do you, Jordan Edward Addington Penrose Winthrop Viscount Redvers, take this woman to be your lawfully wedded wife?"

Had Victoria tricked him? If she had, if he'd been duped, what had happened to Mary?

Eventually, he noticed that Vicar Martin had stopped speaking. Everyone was staring.

"Ahem . . ." Martin cleared his throat. "Lord Redvers, the vows are important. You must pay attention."

"What did you ask me?" Jordan inquired.

"I *asked* if you take Miss Barnes to be your lawfully wedded wife."

Jordan gaped at Felicity as if she had two heads.

"The question isn't that difficult, Redvers," Victoria interjected. "Just say yes."

Jordan looked at Mrs. Stewart. "You were telling me something right before the ceremony started."

"About what?"

"About your mother's cousin."

"My mother doesn't have a cousin. If she told you that's where Mary is, she was lying."

"Are you certain?"

"Mary went to London—by herself."

He was dumbstruck at the news.

"But your mother and I had it all arranged."

"I talked to Mary as she was leaving. Mother had ordered her off the property, and she was traveling to London, to try to find a job."

"Cassandra!" Victoria barked. "That's enough!"

Mrs. Stewart ignored her. "I didn't think you'd want her going to London on her own, and I begged her to wait, so we could discuss it with you, but she wouldn't—"

"Where is she?" Jordan demanded, advancing on Victoria.

"I have no idea," Victoria calmly answered. "May we get back to the task at hand?"

"Where is she?" Jordan shouted.

"Lord Redvers," she stated, "you are about to marry my daughter. Is there some reason you're standing in my parlor and chatting about another woman?"

"Tell me where she is, or I'm walking out of here."

"Mother!" Felicity wailed.

"You are at the end of your wedding," Victoria continued. "You are about to make the final commitment that will bind you to Felicity forever. I insist that you concentrate on the ceremony and not your prior mistress."

"Mrs. Barnes!" the vicar scolded. "Remember yourself. Please."

"I'm sorry, Vicar Martin," she said, "but he's being foolish, and I'm weary of his antics."

Jordan stared at Felicity, at her mother. What was he doing? Why had he chosen Felicity and a lifetime of misery? He'd assumed he could go through with the match, but why would he? He'd rather live in poverty, would rather forage on the streets than face Felicity over the breakfast table every morning. All the money in the world wasn't sufficient to make it palatable.

He'd convinced himself that it was what he wanted, but it wasn't. *Mary* was what he wanted. Mary, who'd been kind to him. Mary, who'd believed he was wonderful. Mary, who had loved him when he didn't deserve to be loved.

A frisson of fear slithered down his spine.

Gad! Where could she be? How would he locate her? Anything could happen to her in London. She was insane going off like that.

"I don't want your daughter's fortune," he announced. "Give it to some other poor sap who's stupid enough to tolerate her."

He started out, and Felicity howled, "Mother, he can't do that to me, can he?"

Victoria stepped into his path, blocking his retreat.

"If you depart this room," she threatened, "the engagement is terminated. If you slink back next week or next month, we won't receive you."

"I'm relieved to hear it."

"Are you listening to me, Redvers? Felicity won't take you back. I won't let her, so the dowry will be lost to you."

She appeared very smug, presuming she had coerced him yet again. And why wouldn't she be confident?

He'd proven over and over that he would prostitute himself for cash, but in the nick of time, he'd come to his senses. He'd realized that—as Mary had always said—there were some things more important than money.

Mary was more important. A life with Mary was more important.

He picked up Victoria, setting her to the side, and he kept on.

"Redvers!" she shrieked. "You will not cry off. You will not go!"

"Mother!" Felicity howled again. "Stop him!"

"Lord Redvers," Mrs. Stewart called, the only voice in the group that could get him to halt and turn around.

"Yes, Mrs. Stewart, what is it?"

"Don't forget to leave me that address." She grinned. "And have Mary write to me, will you? As opposed to the other members of my family, I'm worried sick about her."

"I'll definitely leave that address, Mrs. Stewart, and I'll have Mary drop you a note—the moment I find her." He glared at Victoria. "You had better pray that I locate her soon and that she's all right. If she's suffered any harm, I'll take it out of your hide."

He whirled away and raced up the stairs to pack his bags.

Chapter 21

❦

"ARE you sure about this?"

"Yes. Mrs. Monroe is a friend of mine. She'll be glad to assist you."

Mary stared at Lauretta Bainbridge, knowing there was a scheme in the works but unable to figure out what it was. Mrs. Bainbridge was being extremely obliging even though she possessed no cooperative traits.

Mr. Adair had slept most of the way to London and debarked the carriage shortly after they'd arrived. When he'd left them, he'd assumed Mrs. Bainbridge was dropping Mary at the Carlyle Hotel, which he'd mentioned as an excellent spot to spend the night. But as soon as he'd gone, Mrs. Bainbridge had suggested an alternative that was less expensive.

She had a friend, a Mrs. Monroe, who rented rooms in her home, and with cost being a factor, Mary had agreed to tour the establishment. She was uncomfortable with accepting lodging from a person she'd never met, and she didn't want to impose, but Mrs. Bainbridge had insisted, and now, Mary was wondering if she shouldn't have followed Mr. Adair's original advice.

She was leery of Mrs. Bainbridge and worried that Mr. Adair might have had the better idea.

For some reason, Mrs. Bainbridge had been cordial and chatty the entire trip.

She made London sound like a grand lark, akin to a circus or an unending fair where people were happy and rich and busy and glamorous.

Mary had tried to persuade herself that she'd be fine, but as they'd approached the outskirts, then plunged into the dirty, crammed streets, she'd grown increasingly unnerved. Nothing could have prepared her for the noise, the crowds, the smells, and the general disarray.

She was very frightened, wishing she hadn't come, but what else could she have done?

She glanced out the carriage window, seeing that they were parked in front of Mrs. Monroe's house. It was three stories high, with black shutters and flower boxes. Rosebushes bloomed along the walk, and at viewing the reputable condition, Mary's fears calmed somewhat.

If Monroe was courteous and civil, the matter of finding a place to stay would be easily accomplished, and in light of all that had occurred, the prospect was soothing. However, it seemed too good to be true, and she didn't trust Mrs. Bainbridge, not being able to imagine why Mrs. Bainbridge would trouble herself on Mary's behalf.

Maybe Mrs. Bainbridge was simply humored to see Mary brought so low, or maybe she enjoyed rescuing Mary. If the situation worked out, Mary would owe Mrs. Bainbridge a huge debt of gratitude that Mrs. Bainbridge would collect in any number of ways.

"Why would Mrs. Monroe help me?" Mary asked.

"She regularly takes in women who come to London from the country. Years ago, she came herself—without a penny in her pocket. She knows how scary it can be."

"That's kind of her."

"Yes, it's very kind."

Mary glanced out again. "It looks as if she's done well for herself."

"She definitely has."

"How is she earning her income? It can't just be from collecting rent."

"She was married to a wealthy fellow, and when he passed away, she inherited the house. Now her boarders chip in. It's a beneficial arrangement for everyone." Mrs. Bainbridge smiled, appearing amiable and empathetic, but Mary refused to take her word for anything.

Mary would investigate for herself, would speak to Mrs. Monroe and see what sort of individual she was. If the circumstances weren't as Mrs. Bainbridge had claimed, Mary would simply thank Mrs. Monroe and move on.

The carriage door was opened and the step lowered. Mrs. Bainbridge climbed out and swept inside. Mary followed, relieved to be greeted by a footman, which was a sign of normalcy.

He showed them to a secluded parlor at the rear of the residence. As they strolled through, Mary noted the beautiful paintings on the walls, the luxurious rugs on the floors. The furnishings were expensive, tasteful, and clean.

She sat on a sofa while Mrs. Bainbridge went to have a private conversation with Mrs. Monroe.

After she left, it was very quiet, and Mary fidgeted. She was tired and drained, and she felt very cold, as if her blood had turned to ice. She couldn't get warm.

Mrs. Bainbridge was gone for ages, and Mary's anxiety flared. What was taking so long? What if Mrs. Monroe didn't want Mary? If that was the case, Mary would die of humiliation.

She'd just decided to give up on Mrs. Bainbridge, to leave and locate an inn for the night, when Mrs. Bainbridge entered, accompanied by a blond woman who was introduced as Mrs. Monroe.

She was older than Mary, probably thirty-five or forty. With big blue eyes and a rounded figure, she resembled Mrs. Bainbridge in sophistication and style. She was very polished, very elegant, and it was easy to understand why they were friends.

Mrs. Monroe ordered tea, then settled herself in a chair across from Mary.

"What brings you to London, Miss Barnes?" Mrs. Monroe inquired.

Mary wasn't sure what to say. She wasn't about to admit that she'd been disowned and disavowed.

"I grew up at an estate in the country."

"Yes, Mrs. Bainbridge told me about it: Barnes Manor. It must have been lovely."

"It was, but there was nothing for me there. I don't have a dowry, so I could never marry. I was living with my stepmother, and it was . . . difficult."

"Oh, I can imagine," Mrs. Monroe commiserated. She studied Mary with a keen intensity. "You have no family?"

"No."

"No one to miss you? No one to care if something should happen?"

Mary shook her head, as tears welled into her eyes. How could her life have come to such a horrid fork in the road?

"You poor dear." Mrs. Monroe reached over and consolingly patted Mary's hand. "Yours is the saddest story I've ever heard. To be all alone in the world! It doesn't bear contemplating."

A maid rolled in the tea cart, and they were silent as Mrs. Monroe poured and offered Mary a cup.

Mary drank it down, and Mrs. Monroe poured her a second serving. Mary was glad for the warmth of the beverage, for the distraction it provided. It gave her a moment to compose herself, to tamp down any maudlin sentiment.

She would not mourn her losses! She would not feel sorry for herself! What had occurred couldn't be changed, and there was no use complaining.

"Would you like to stay with me, Miss Barnes?" Mrs. Monroe asked. "I have a room available. There's no need for you to traipse about London, hunting for a place."

"You're very kind."

"I try to be helpful. I was once in dire straits—as you are. I wouldn't want anyone to suffer as I did."

"It *has* been a bit overwhelming."

"I'll be worried sick if you go off on your own."

Mary stared at her; the woman seemed sincere.

Why not? a voice whispered. It was the simplest solution.

Suddenly, she felt dizzy and overheated, and she fanned herself with her napkin.

"Is it hot in here?"

"No," Mrs. Monroe answered. "Perhaps it's stress from the journey."

"Perhaps."

Mary yawned. "I beg your pardon," she said.

"It's quite all right. Would you like more tea? If your energy is flagging, it might enliven you."

Mary gazed at Mrs. Monroe, but she looked blurry, as if she was no longer solid. Her disorientation grew more peculiar by the minute, and vaguely, she noted that Mrs. Bainbridge and Mrs. Monroe hadn't drunk any of the tea.

Only Mary had.

Mrs. Monroe filled Mary's cup again, and though Mary meant to have more, her arms must have weighed a hundred pounds. She couldn't lift them, so Mrs. Monroe leaned over and pressed Mary's cup to her mouth, holding it till Mary had swallowed down the entire amount.

Mrs. Monroe relaxed in her chair, she and Mrs. Bainbridge watching Mary.

Mary wanted to tell them that she was ill, that she didn't wish to stay after all, but she was too lethargic to speak up.

Gradually, she dozed off, her body toppling sideways onto the sofa, and as she drifted away, Mrs. Monroe said, "That was easy."

To which Mrs. Bainbridge replied, "Like taking candy from a baby."

"SHE'S so bloody gullible."

"They all are when they first arrive."

Lauretta smirked. "As if I'd actually assist her! What was she thinking? She's an idiot."

"Not everyone is like us, Lauretta," Barbara Monroe stated. "Some people *trust* other people."

"But why *me*? She knows I can't stand her. She's insane to suppose I'd be concerned about her."

Two maids had swiftly and expertly undressed Mary Barnes, stripping her of clothes and shoes and attiring her instead in a negligee and robe.

A footman entered and came over to Mary, exhibiting no surprise at finding her unconscious on Barbara's couch. He had to have seen a similar sight dozens of times over the years.

He picked up Mary and turned to Barbara.

"Where to, Mrs. Monroe?"

"I've had the blue room prepared for her."

The footman carried her out, Mary's hand dangling toward Lauretta as if she was beseeching Lauretta to stop what was happening.

Lauretta simply chuckled.

"When will the auction be?" she inquired.

"I have some gentlemen visiting tonight. I had told them to expect something especially amusing, so Miss Barnes appeared just in time."

"She was fucking Redvers. She's not a virgin."

"Yes, but we don't have to inform them. Besides, they're usually so intoxicated that they wouldn't notice a missing maidenhead if it bit them on the ass."

"And Miss Barnes will act like a virgin even if she isn't one. She's prim as the day is long."

"Wonderful. Chippingham will be thrilled."

"He's coming?"

"Yes."

Lauretta chuckled again.

Barbara ran an exclusive brothel, and her clientele was selected from the top echelons of high society. Patrons were only admitted after references were produced and backgrounds investigated.

Most of her customers were content to drink, fraternize with their companions, then enjoy a tumble with an experienced whore. But some—such as Lord Chippingham—relished a darker type of play, and Barbara was happy to supply it.

For the right price.

Lauretta hadn't lied when she'd explained how Barbara took in women who traveled to London.

Females flocked to the city in droves, anxious for jobs, but they could quickly land themselves in dangerous predicaments.

Many approached Barbara willingly, grateful to be off the streets, but a prostitute's life was difficult. Harlots perished from disease or in childbirth. They quit to get married. They became opium addicts and grew unreliable.

Barbara always needed fresh faces, and Mary Barnes would do nicely. As an added benefit—should Redvers ever cross paths with her again—he wouldn't be nearly so enthralled when he learned that she'd been sold to Chippingham.

"Thanks for your help," Lauretta said.

"And thanks for bringing her to me. She'll fetch a pretty penny."

"Let me know the details of the auction. I can't wait to hear how it goes."

"I will."

Barbara escorted Lauretta to the door and walked her out.

"I hope Chippingham wins her," Lauretta mentioned.

Barbara snorted. "You are awful."

Lauretta couldn't deny it. She wanted Mary Barnes to suffer

the worst conclusion imaginable, for though Lauretta was loathe to acknowledge it, she had a terrible jealous streak. She wasn't about to share Redvers; she wasn't about to lose him. Mary Barnes shouldn't have interfered.

As Lauretta climbed in the carriage, Barbara asked, "You're certain Redvers is finished with her?"

"Very certain."

"He isn't pining away, is he?"

"No," Lauretta scoffed. "He just wed some fussy debutante. Mary Barnes is naught but a distant memory."

"Good, because I'd hate to have him show up on my stoop, searching for her. If he found out what we'd done, I'd end up on the wrong side of his temper."

"Don't worry," Lauretta insisted, "he'll never find out."

"HE'LL come back, won't he, Mother?"

"You shouldn't count on it, Felicity."

"But I wrote letters about the wedding to everybody. The whole world will know that he jilted me!"

Victoria's lips pursed with disapproval. "How unfortunate."

"I could die!" Felicity wailed. "I could just die!"

"Be silent," Victoria griped. "All last week, you kept telling me how much you detested him. I had to drag you to the altar."

"I was going to be a viscountess. Eventually, I'd have been a countess. Now I'm nothing at all."

"There are other aristocrats. We'll snag one for you."

"When?"

"I don't know."

"Could we proceed to London immediately to start making inquiries? I want Redvers to see that I don't care a whit about him."

"Felicity! Give it a rest. Your complaints exhaust me."

"Well, he supposes that he can act however he pleases, and I—"

"Felicity! Have mercy!"

Victoria's sharp tone halted the girl's litany of grievances.

From the moment Redvers had stormed out, her harangue hadn't ceased, and Victoria was weary of listening to it.

They were huddled in her library, struggling to regroup, and they needed to decide on a plan to move forward.

Victoria had been so sure of Redvers, positive of his greed, his penury.

How could she have been so wrong? And what was she to do now?

Though she'd told Felicity that they would begin the hunt for another title, it wasn't that easy to attract a noble bachelor. Those available few were besieged with marital options.

Cassandra entered, dressed for traveling. She carried a portmanteau, which she set at her feet.

Victoria frowned.

"Where do you think you're going?"

"I'm off to London."

"No, you're not. Go upstairs and put that bag away."

"No."

"I've had nothing but sass from one daughter today. I don't need more from you. Do as I say. At once!"

"Not this time and not ever again."

Victoria stood, so angry she was shaking.

"You will not disobey me."

As if Victoria hadn't spoken, Cassandra said, "I'm taking the carriage. I'll send it back next week."

"You're being absurd. I don't grant you my permission."

"Fine then. I'll embarrass you by riding on the public coach." She whirled away as if she'd march out that very second.

"What has gotten into you?" Victoria asked. "I will not tolerate any drama."

"I'm not expecting you to. I simply stopped by to inform you that I'm leaving, and I'm not coming back."

"Not coming back? You're talking in riddles."

"Let her go, Mother," Felicity chimed in. "She's always so dreary. We don't need her moping around."

"Ah, sisterly love," Cassandra mocked. "Isn't it touching?"

"Felicity," Victoria snapped, "go to your room."

"Yes, Felicity," Cassandra echoed, "*go* to your room. You behave like a spoiled toddler; you should be treated like one."

Felicity leapt up. "Shut up, you witch."

Victoria sighed. Why had she been saddled with two such unlikable, ungrateful children?

"What will you do for money?" Victoria asked Cassandra. "If you mean to beg me for some, I won't give you any."

"I don't need any money."

"Really?" Victoria sneered. "And how, precisely, will you get on without my assistance?"

"I'm marrying again."

"You? Marrying? Don't be ridiculous."

"I'm not. Good-bye."

She sauntered out as Victoria watched, her mouth gaping in shock. Cassandra never argued, never refused to follow Victoria's commands.

What had happened to her?

Victoria shook off her stupor and huffed after Cassandra, Felicity hot on their heels. They caught up with her behind the carriage as she was checking to ensure that her trunks were safely stowed.

"Who would be crazy enough to marry you?"

"Lord Redvers's friend, Paxton Adair."

Victoria sucked in a frantic breath.

"You will not! I forbid it! I won't have that . . . that . . . slothful wretch in my family."

"I'm not asking you to. He and I are sailing for Jamaica, so you'll never have to see either one of us again."

Victoria wondered if she might faint.

"Cassandra! You're acting like a madwoman."

"No, I'm not. This is the first sane thing I've done in years." She climbed in the vehicle, and a footman closed the door. She leaned out the window. "I plan to spread rumors about Felicity in town that Redvers cried off because he learned an atrocious secret about her."

"What?" Victoria and Felicity shrieked in unison.

"We were always despicable to Mary, so I figure she deserves some revenge."

"Don't speak to me about Mary."

"Lord Redvers was fond of her, and I'm certain he's speculated as to why she never had a dowry. I've been curious, too. I'm going to request that he have Father's papers examined. I'm hoping we can sue you and win a settlement for her from Father's estate."

"You wouldn't."

"I would. You shouldn't have sent her away, Mother. It was too cruel, and your punishment shall be that no aristocrat ever offers for Felicity. I'll see to it with every bit of vicious innuendo I can devise."

"You horrid girl," Victoria charged.

"I'm ruined!" Felicity moaned.

"Don't ever return to Barnes Manor," Victoria threatened. "When you wind up broke and living on the streets, don't slither home. I won't take you in."

"Don't worry, Victoria. This was never *home*, and I will never be back."

Cassandra rapped on the roof to signal the driver. He clicked the reins, and the carriage rolled away.

PHILLIP peered down the road, observing as a horse and rider rushed toward him at full gallop.

The man was traveling dangerously fast, bent low over the saddle, the animal's hooves flying. Phillip might have ignored the demented oaf, but as he neared, Phillip realized it was Viscount Redvers.

He moved into the middle of the lane, feet braced, daring the man to canter on by.

Phillip had no idea what he was doing. An ordinary fellow such as himself never interfered with the rich and notorious. Nor was he entitled to an opinion with regard to their antics, but he was enraged over Redvers's conduct with Miss Barnes and stupidly determined to let him know.

Redvers saw Phillip and tugged on the reins, making the horse snort and rear up.

"Are you trying to kill yourself?" Redvers demanded. "Or are you trying to kill me?"

"I'd have a word with you, Your Royal Assness, before you race on by."

"Where do you come by the gall to speak to me at all, let alone in a rude manner?"

"Haul yourself down off that saddle, and I'll show you where I come by the gall."

"I'm in a hurry. I don't have time to fuss with you."

"You will fuss with me, by God." Phillip grabbed the bridle, feeling as if an insane person had assumed control of his body. "That young lady you seduced doesn't have anyone to take her side, so I damned sure will!"

At the mention of Miss Barnes, Redvers blanched, not able to pretend that he didn't know to whom Phillip referred. With the agility of a circus performer, he leapt to the ground.

"What the bloody hell are you talking about?" Redvers seethed. "And might I suggest that you be very clear and very concise."

"If Miss Barnes was my sister, you'd be standing at the altar about now, with my musket pressed between your shoulder blades to encourage a quick recitation of the vows."

Redvers stepped in so that they were toe to toe. He was taller, but Phillip was stockier. If they clashed, it would be an even match.

Would they brawl? Phillip hadn't had a fistfight in ages, and if he had to pound on an obnoxious cur, Redvers was an excellent candidate.

Redvers studied Phillip, his wagon parked on the side of the road.

"You're that peddler, aren't you? The one who sold her those tonics?"

"Yes I am, and over the past few weeks, I've gotten to know her. You have some nerve, treating her so badly."

"You seem to be laboring under the delusion that my relationship with her is your business, but I can't figure out why."

"She was lonely, and you took advantage of her! You may be a high and mighty lord, but somebody should knock some sense into you."

"And that would be you?"

"It would be my pleasure. If you'd seen her yesterday, clutching that tattered little bag! Why, if I could—"

"You saw Mary yesterday?"

"Yes, and your friends gave her a ride, but—"

Redvers grew very still. "What did you say?"

"She stopped by here, on her way to the village to catch the public coach to London, but your friends came by in a carriage. A harlot—called herself Mrs. Bainbridge—invited her to ride with them instead."

Redvers gasped. "Mary accepted? She went off with Mrs. Bainbridge?"

"Yes."

"Dammit."

"If they've harmed her, it will be on your conscience."

Redvers looked stricken, as if he might actually have cared for Miss Barnes. He spun and jumped on his horse.

"Where are you going?" Phillip inquired.

"To London, to search for her. Did she mention where she planned to stay?"

"No, but your Mrs. Bainbridge will know."

"That's what I'm afraid of." Redvers glanced over at the wagon, then at Phillip. "Don't sell that Daily Remedy of yours around here again. We're both aware that it's laced with alcohol, and I can't imagine how many women you've hurt by dispensing it."

"You're a fine one to talk about how people should act."

"You're a charlatan."

"And you're a cad and a swine."

"It sounds as if we understand each other." Redvers urged the animal into a trot as he peered back and hollered, "Thank you for worrying about Mary."

"Find her, you worthless knave."

"I will."

Then, he was gone.

Phillip dawdled, pondering Miss Barnes, then pondering Redvers's warning about his medicinal trade. He dashed over to their campsite, in the nearby trees.

As he rushed up, Clarinda asked, "What's happening? Were you arguing with someone?"

"Lord Redvers just rode by. I gave him a piece of my mind about Miss Barnes."

"You had cross words with a viscount? Are you mad?"

"Yes. But I doubt he'll have me hanged."

"How did you avoid it?"

"Apparently, he was partial to Miss Barnes, and he's off to London to locate her."

"I'm glad to hear it. She was due for some luck."

He started packing their belongings.

"We're leaving? Isn't it rather sudden?"

"I have no idea how this charade will conclude," he advised, "but I don't believe we should stick around for the finale."

"You think we'll be dragged into it?"

"These sorts of affairs never end well."

"You're right about that."

"Plus, Redvers ordered me to stop selling my Daily Remedy. If he comes back this way and sees me, he'll make trouble. I can't have him setting the magistrate on us."

"Where are we headed? To London? It's easy to get lost there."

"London? Sure. Why not?"

He threw some dishes into a trunk, then went to harness the horse.

Chapter 22

♡

"THERE'S someone here to see you, Mr. Adair."

Paxton smiled at his valet and sighed.

"Who is it this time?"

"Another young lady, sir."

"My favorite sort of guest."

"We seem to be having a flood of them," his valet said.

"Yes, we do, but a man can't ever have too many women about, can he? I don't believe it's possible."

In light of events in the country, it was odd and unsettling to be back in London, and briefly, he wondered how Miss Barnes was faring at the Carlyle Hotel. With her having just arrived in the sprawling city, she was probably more disoriented than Paxton.

Fleetingly, he imagined calling on her, asking after her condition. But he knew it would simply be a ruse to learn if there'd been any news from Barnes Manor, or if—by chance—she might be writing a letter home and could attach a note from him.

He wouldn't inquire! There was no one there with whom he cared to correspond, and if he never heard the name *Barnes Manor* again, it would be too soon.

After returning to Town, Paxton had headed straight to his father and accepted the offer of a plantation in Jamaica.

His father had been delighted, and he'd mentioned that there was a ship sailing in four days. If Paxton would like to be on it, passage could be arranged.

Why not? Paxton had thought.

There was nothing for him in London, so he'd agreed to leave right away, worried that if he didn't, his interest in the venture might wane.

Preparations had begun at once.

He and his valet were packing, but the poor fellow had to keep pausing to answer the door.

Since word had circulated that he was going, he'd been besieged with female visitors eager to wish him farewell, but there had only been one person he'd truly wanted to see— Cassandra Stewart—and she'd made her position very clear.

So to hell with her!

She could languish in the country with her horrid mother and sister. She could wither away and die of old age, living a hollow life, devoid of meaning.

"Who is here?" he asked, hoping it wasn't a certain debutante who'd been inappropriately chasing after him.

"I'm told to say it's Cassie."

"Cassie?"

He searched his memory, trying to recall an acquaintance named Cassie, but he couldn't recollect a single one.

"If the name doesn't ring a bell—"

"It doesn't."

"—I'm to inform you that it's Mrs. Cassandra Stewart."

His breath caught. "Cassandra?"

Before the man could reply, Paxton was racing down the stairs to the front parlor.

His apartment was small, with two rooms up and two down,

so it was a fast trip, and with each step, his mind whirled chaotically.

What could she want? Why had she come?

Like a besotted buffoon, he stumbled in, sliding across the floor and nearly falling in his haste.

He struggled for calm, tugged on his vest, and ran his fingers through his disheveled hair.

She was over in the corner, riffling in the sideboard that had already been emptied, and she glared at him.

"Mrs. Stewart?" he stammered. "What are you doing?"

"I'm trying to pour myself a drink. And it's *Cassie* to you."

"You want me to call you Cassie?"

"Yes. Where is your liquor?"

"All packed."

"Well, hell," she muttered, "what's a girl have to do to get a brandy around here? I could really use one. I'm a little out of my element."

"You feel spirits will help?"

"Definitely. It will give me the courage to tell you what I've come to say."

He glanced about, unable to remember into which crate the decanters had been placed. They hadn't been nailed shut yet, so he scrounged through and retrieved a bottle and a glass.

He dispensed a liberal amount and handed it to her. She gulped it back, then she grabbed him by his shirt, pulled him to her, and kissed him full on the mouth.

Though he was accustomed to brazen women, the audacious move stunned him, and he staggered away as if he'd been hit.

"What was that for, you bold hussy?" he teased.

"It's my version of an apology."

"It was a fairly good one, but what—precisely—are you apologizing *for*?"

"For loitering in the hallway at Barnes Manor, with my mother scolding us, while I pretended I didn't love you."

He cocked his head. "What did you say?"

"I said I love you, and I'm sorry."

"I heard the *sorry* part, but what's this other nonsense? You love me? Don't be absurd."

"I'm not being absurd. It's true: I love you."

He scoffed. "When did this brilliant notion occur to you?"

"When I first met you. I was just a tad slow to realize it."

He scowled, anxious to deduce what had come over her.

The last time he'd seen her, she'd been too much of a coward to admit to the slightest relationship. Now, a mere two days later, she was agog with amour.

The woman was mad as a hatter.

"I don't understand you," he complained.

"What's to understand? I'm here, and you should be glad. Stop glowering as if I were a scullery maid who broke your favorite vase."

"I'm not glad. I chased you around Barnes Manor for weeks, and you couldn't be bothered to speak to me in an open parlor. I leave, and next I know, you're beating down my door and claiming a heightened affection. Pardon me if I don't buy it."

"Oh, be silent. I'm trying to tell you something important."

"What is it?"

"You were right."

"Of course I was. I always am." He frowned. "What was I right about on this occasion?"

"I've been hiding in my mother's home, acting like a scared ninny. I've been prim and fussy and positively boring, but I don't want to live that way anymore."

"How would you like to live?"

"I want to live like you."

"Are you insane? I'm a gambler and a wastrel who doesn't have two pennies to rub together. I should take you over and introduce you to my father so he can lecture you on the wages of sin. He'd set you straight in a hurry."

"I don't care if you're a wastrel. In fact, I'm *delighted* that you're a wastrel."

"You can't be."

"Who says so?"

"I do, I guess."

He whipped away and started to pace, as he tried to figure out his motives.

He'd encouraged her to join him in indolence and vice. She'd thought about it, had decided to agree, yet he was working to dissuade her.

Was he ill? Was he growing demented?

He halted and gaped at her.

"I'm sailing for the Caribbean."

"I know."

"You'd like to come along?"

"Yes, you dunce. Isn't it obvious?"

"No, it's not *obvious*. You've spent your whole life under your mother's thumb."

"A huge mistake. I admit it."

"And now—in the blink of an eye—you're your own woman, and you're valiantly ready to cast your lot with me."

"Yes."

She opened her reticule and retrieved a vial of what looked to be red wine. She removed the cork as if to swallow down the contents.

"What is that?" he asked.

"My sister Mary gave it to me. She said it's a love potion."

"A love potion?" He gulped.

"I'm in love with you, and it's supposed to make you fall in love with me in return."

He didn't believe in magic or spells, but as she tipped the vial to her lips, he leapt toward her and tried to wrestle the thing away, but it was too late.

She'd ingested the entire amount.

His innards clenched, the strangest feeling sweeping over him, as if his fate had been sealed.

"Face it, Adair, you're doomed."

"Doomed," he murmured.

"You're going to take me to the Caribbean, and you're going to marry me. We'll live happily ever after. Since I've drunk this potion, you won't be able to resist."

"Why would you want me?"

"Why wouldn't I?"

"I'm a drunkard."

"So am I. A secret drunkard, but a drunkard nonetheless. It never seemed to bother you at Barnes Manor, so what's the problem?"

"I'm a gambler. It's how I earn my money."

"Yes, and you cheat, too. You cheat everyone, constantly. I can put up with it if you can. Just promise me that you won't let yourself be shot by some angry card player. I don't wish to be a widow again. I intend to be wed to you forever."

To a confirmed bachelor such as himself, the word *forever* sounded like a very, very long time.

"I'm a blatant fornicator."

This detail galvanized her attention. She stared at his loins.

"If you ever peek at another woman, I shall castrate you in your sleep."

At her threat, he shuddered. "You certainly make me eager to attach myself to you."

"Could you please explain to me what's happening? When you left Barnes Manor, you begged me to go with you."

"That was then," he hedged, "and this is now."

"Now? It's been forty-eight hours." Her temper sparked. "You didn't mean it, did you, you scurvy dog! You were toying with me! You didn't really want me to come along, and you asked me for some perfectly vain, *male* reason I will never comprehend. Like a fool, I believed you, and I've burned all my bridges. If I were a man, I'd kill you where you stand."

She picked up her reticule and marched for the door, which thoroughly rattled him.

"Don't go," he piteously said. "I'm glad you're here. I am."

"You have a funny way of showing it."

"You surprised me. That's all."

"Shut up!" She tried to push by him, but he grabbed her wrist and pulled her to a halt.

"Release my hand," she fumed, "or I will break your arm."

As he touched her, he was overcome by the sensation that always occurred when she was near. His heart pounded; he began to perspire. He yearned to throw her down on the sofa and dally till dawn.

There was something about her that thrilled him as no other ever had, but if he let her stay, he'd be making a commitment. Had he the wherewithal to follow through?

He was such an undependable cad, and if she bound herself to him, he'd be responsible for her the rest of his days. It wasn't as if he could tire of her and desert her in a foreign country. It wasn't as if he could grow weary of marriage and move on to some other folly.

"Let's discuss this," he said.

"There's nothing to discuss. Either you want me to go with you or you don't. What is your answer? I would hear it immediately, and if you make the wrong choice, I'll strangle you."

"I'm worried about you coming with me."

"Ha! You're worried about yourself. You might actually have to get married."

"There is that."

"You might actually have to start acting like an adult."

"Which is my worst nightmare."

She studied him, searching for an assurance he never gave to anyone. Who could rely on him? Who would risk it?

Her shoulders sagged with defeat.

"What's the matter?" she inquired. "I know you were sincere that day at Barnes Manor. Have you changed your mind? Have you decided I'm not who you want after all?"

She gazed up at him, her pretty blue eyes wide with concern. She was exquisite, and if he could make her his own, he would be so lucky.

"I'm afraid, Cassie."

"Of what?"

"Of failing you. I have no idea what it will be like there. What if it's awful? What if I can't run a plantation and we lose our shirts?"

"You'll cheat to win some ill-gotten money, and we'll buy some new shirts."

He chuckled miserably. "What if I drink myself into a stupor and die in a ditch?"

"If you perish before me, I'll kill you."

"What if I find I hate being a husband? It's completely within my mode of behavior to turn coward and abandon you." This was the crux of the affair; this was what he most feared. "Where would you be?"

She scoffed. "You've invented all these idiotic scenarios as to why I shouldn't take a chance on you. But what about *you*? What about your taking a chance on me? You think I'm such a great catch?"

"Well . . . not really. You have a few quirks that are quite disturbing."

"Damn straight. I've never done anything; I've never gone anywhere. I was raised by a crazy woman and wed to an insane man, which is the sum total of my biography."

"You're correct: You're pathetic."

"I have more problems than you can count."

"Yes, you do."

"Stop agreeing with me."

"All right."

"But"—she stepped in so that her entire torso was pressed to his all the way down—"I will always love you, and I will make you so bloody happy."

She rose up and touched her lips to his again, and he groaned with pleasure. It was simply impossible to be around her and not desire her.

There was a deck of cards on the table. She picked it up and held it out to him.

"I tell you what," she coaxed. "If you draw the high card, I go with you to Jamaica. If I draw the high card, I crawl back to my mother in disgrace."

They both knew it was a dare. He could make her select any number, so what did he want?

His life was changing fast. He was leaving England to become a prosperous gentleman in a strange land.

Was he ready to become a husband, too? Perhaps a father in a very short while? The notion of giving up his bachelor ways was terrifying.

If he wasn't a gambler and wastrel, what sort of man would be left?

"Fine," he said, accepting her challenge, and he was actually trembling. "Let's play."

He shuffled the deck, and they pulled out their cards, but as she saw them, she scowled.

"We both drew eights!" she complained.

"I can't decide what's best."

"Oh, you ass!"

She punched him in the stomach—hard—and he gave a soft grunt.

"Try again," she demanded, "and quit being such a baby. My future is hanging in the balance."

"So is mine."

He shuffled and shuffled, taking forever.

"You never lose, remember, Paxton?"

"I never do."

"I'm the biggest prize you've ever wagered over."

"I believe you might be correct."

"Are you going to let me beat you in the only contest you've ever entered that truly mattered?"

If he allowed her to win, he'd never be alone again. He wouldn't have to face the coming tribulations by himself. He would have a friend, a companion, a confidante.

She would be with him for the rest of his life.

That fact, more than any other, settled things.

He ceased his shuffling and held out the cards.

"You better have made the right choice," she warned.

"I have."

She drew a card, and he did, too. They flipped them over at the same time. Hers was a deuce, and his was a king.

She stared at them, then she started to shake, and she laughed until tears welled into her eyes.

"I knew you wouldn't send me back to my mother!"

"No man could be that cruel."

She leapt into his arms, the cards scattering, and she was kissing him and kissing him, only stopping when, behind them, the valet cleared his throat.

"You have another . . . ah . . . visitor, Mr. Adair. What should I tell her?"

"Tell her I'm otherwise engaged."

"Very good, sir."

"Then you'll have to finish the packing on your own. I'll be busy all night."

The valet grinned and tiptoed out.

"WHERE is she?"

Lauretta heard the question shouted from down in her foyer, and she frowned. It sounded like Redvers, but he wasn't due back for a week.

She was seated at the dressing table in her boudoir, wearing a robe and brushing her hair. She had plans for the evening, and she was running late.

"Mrs. Bainbridge is in her bedchamber," her butler answered.

The front door was slammed so forcefully that the windows rattled. Angry strides pounded up the stairs, then Redvers stormed in.

His clothes and boots were dusty from his journey, and he hadn't shaved in ages, so his cheeks were darkened with stubble. His color was high, and he exuded menace and danger.

Something had goaded him to a furious state, but what could it be?

For the briefest instant, she panicked, worrying that her trickery toward Mary Barnes had been discovered, but she pushed away any concern. She couldn't have been found out.

Who was there to have told him?

"Redvers? Why are you home so soon? I wasn't expecting you for several days. I hope you've come to inform me of how rich we are."

She smiled, but he didn't smile in return.

He studied her in a way he never had previously, as if he . . . he . . . *hated* her. She could barely keep from squirming.

"I will give you one chance to explain yourself," he said.

"Explain myself? What are you talking about?" She spun away, showing him her back, and she picked up her brush and began stroking her hair again. "How was the wedding? I trust it went well?"

He plucked the brush from her hand and flung it at the mirror, which shattered into a dozen pieces. "Stand up and face me," he hissed.

"What is wrong with you?" She jumped up and whirled around. "Are you mad?"

"Where is Mary Barnes?"

Lauretta carefully shielded any reaction. "Mary . . . Barnes? Victoria's stepdaughter? How would I know?"

"How many years have you known me, Lauretta?"

"Five? Six?"

"Yet you would hurt me this way? I realize there was never any affection between us, but I thought—on some level—we were friends."

"I have no idea what you're saying. You could be speaking in a foreign language."

"Who owns the carriage in which you traveled to London?"

"You do."

"Who employs the driver?"

"You do," she repeated, slowing, starting to fret.

"You didn't think I'd ask him where you took her? You didn't think he'd tell me? Could you actually suppose he is more loyal to you than to me?"

She blanched.

How had he learned that Lauretta offered a ride to the stupid wench? What were the odds that someone would have tattled?

A myriad of replies flitted by as she tried to figure out how to play it. Denial seemed best.

"Are we still discussing Miss Barnes? Because if we are, I don't—"

"Be silent!" he roared, and she lurched away, terribly afraid he would strike her. He never had before, but she'd never seen him so agitated.

"I know what you did," he seethed. "I know what you arranged for her."

"I arranged nothing."

"Be silent!" he roared again. "Your cruelty sickens me. I am aware of your penchant for malice and treachery, but to have it directed at me—after all I've done for you."

"Why are you droning on about—"

"I love her. You knew, didn't you? It's why you're so determined to harm her."

It was the admission she'd been dreading. If he loved Mary Barnes, where did that leave Lauretta?

"You *love* Miss Barnes?" Lauretta scoffed. "You're being absurd."

"Was it you who told Victoria?"

Lauretta shook her head. "Again—I haven't a clue what you're babbling on about."

He pondered, then nodded as if reaching an important conclusion. "You never were a very good liar. How did you find out? Did you see us? What?"

Her protests had fallen on deaf ears, so a different track seemed wise. She decided to brazen it out.

"Yes, I saw you. At the village dance, and I mentioned it to

Victoria." She squared her shoulders, refusing to be cowed. "You were courting disaster chasing after her."

He loomed up, crazed with rage, and he bellowed, "My private life is none of your business!"

"*Not my business?* I am your mistress. I am the only woman in the world who truly understands you. So stop shouting at me. Miss Barnes was a flirtation, and now, she is gone from our lives. You've married Felicity, and we'll carry on as planned."

"I didn't marry Felicity."

"Don't be ridiculous. Of course you did."

"No, I didn't. So you see, Mrs. Bainbridge, there is no money. There will never be any money."

She scrutinized his hard features, and she murmured, "What have you done?"

"I cried off."

Her heart pounded with alarm.

They were at the end of their financial rope. Jordan had long since abandoned his bachelor's lodgings and slept in a free room over a gambling club.

She still had the cozy house he'd purchased for her, but only because he'd staved off his most vehement creditors with promises of Felicity's dowry.

If he didn't wed Felicity, what would become of them?

She had no family and no real friends. If she lost her home, where would she go? What would she do?

"You cried off?" she scolded.

"Yes."

"Then, you'll just have to cry *on* again, won't you? We'll travel to Barnes Manor tomorrow. We'll talk to Victoria and set everything to rights."

"There is no *we*, Mrs. Bainbridge, and I never intend to speak with Victoria Barnes again."

"You can't be serious." She was growing angry and frightened. "Not after all the effort I expended in choosing Felicity!"

"You played your cards, but it was the wrong hand. If you

had left Mary alone, I'd have sent you on your way with a stipend and a fond farewell, but you didn't. You had to hurt her, and thus, you hurt me, too. Your callous behavior has guaranteed the result you are about to suffer."

"What result? What do you mean?"

"I am surrendering the house to the bank. First thing in the morning."

The announcement was so unexpected, so dire, it made her dizzy with dismay.

"But . . . but it's mine! You bought it for me! You don't have my permission to relinquish it."

"It's not up to you. I decline to continue supporting you, so I am authorizing the foreclosure. I'm sick of the fight. The house, the furniture, the carriage—it's all going. The bank's clerks will be here at ten o'clock."

"No! You will not get away with this."

A violent rage swept over her, as she thought of all the years she'd groomed him to be the man she wanted.

To have him simply change his mind! To have him fritter away property that she considered her own! And all because of a mousy, worthless spinster!

"You bastard!"

Fists flying, she charged him, managing to land a few punches before he clasped her wrists behind her back.

She was kicking at his shins, trying to butt him with her head.

"Stop it!" he ordered, but she kept on and on.

"You bastard! You bastard!"

She was weeping, her chest heaving, as she caught him with a glancing blow to the chin. He pushed her away, and she fell to her knees.

There was a terrible silence as she huddled on the floor with him towering over her. His disgust was palpable; it rolled off him in waves.

"I will return tomorrow at noon—to see how the foreclosure is proceeding. I have never hit a woman before, but I swear to God that if you are still here, I will beat you within an inch of your life. Vacate the premises by then so I don't have to prove how eager I am to follow through."

"What will happen to me?"

"Your future, Mrs. Bainbridge, matters not to me in the slightest. Just be sure that I am never forced to lay eyes on you again."

He started toward the door. She wanted to shout at him, to rail and scream, but she remained on the floor, stunned to submission.

"Where are you going?" she asked.

"I'm off to Barbara's brothel to fetch Mary, and you had best pray that she is all right."

He stomped out, and she staggered to her feet and stumbled over to the window, casting open the shutters. He was down in the street, and she watched as he leapt onto his horse, kicked it into a canter, and raced away.

"Jordan!" she wailed, reaching out as if she could make him stay simply by wishing it fervently enough. "Jordan! Jordan!"

He rounded the corner without looking back.

Chapter 23

❦

"SHE'S waking."

"Quick! Let's run and tell Miss Barbara."

The unfamiliar voices roused Mary, and she rolled onto her back. Her head pounded so hard that she winced, and she stared at the ceiling, feeling very dizzy, very confused. She gazed around the room, not recognizing her surroundings.

The entire space was decorated in shades of blue. Blue drapes, blue wallpaper, blue rugs. She was stretched out on a blue divan.

She glanced down at her torso, perplexed to find herself attired in a white negligee and robe, and she lay very still, trying to piece together what had happened.

Mrs. Bainbridge had brought her to visit Barbara Monroe. They'd chatted. Mrs. Monroe had ordered tea, and in the middle of the interview, Mary had grown very sleepy.

She didn't recollect anything after that.

How much time had passed? Who had undressed her—and why?

Obviously, treachery was planned, and she had to escape her predicament. She stood, groaning at how the sudden movement made her head throb, but she ignored her discomfort.

There was a dressing room behind her. Hoping to locate her clothes, she took several steps toward it before being halted by the bizarre realization that her ankle was shackled to the sofa.

She peered at the chain, and the sight was so strange that she wondered if she wasn't dreaming.

But no. From the aches and pains shooting through her body, she was very much awake.

She sat and studied her manacled foot, and as she fretted over it, the door opened and Mrs. Monroe entered. A burly footman followed her in.

"Hello, Miss Barnes. I'm delighted to see you've come back to us. From how long you were out, I'd begun to think you would never stir."

Mrs. Monroe pulled up a chair, and she was as calm and composed as she'd been when Mary had first met her. Yet Mary was nearly nude and chained to her sofa.

Was Mrs. Monroe insane?

"What have you done to me?" Mary asked. "I wish to leave. Where are my clothes?"

"There is a bit of a problem with them."

"What is it?"

"You can't have them—unless you pay the storage fee you've generated. Nothing here is free. I've had them laundered and pressed and hung, so you will have to reimburse me before they can be returned."

"Fine. Give me my reticule."

"Did you have a reticule when you arrived?"

"You stole it from me! You stole my money!"

"It's not stealing . . . exactly. I prefer to call it a case of finders keepers. I found it; I kept it."

"Give it back!"

Mary rose, as if she might attack Mrs. Monroe, but Mrs. Monroe wasn't intimidated, and apparently, the footman was a guard.

He stepped closer, threatening Mary with his size and demeanor, and his warning was clear: If Mary tried anything, he would deal with her. Physically.

She eased down.

"What do you want from me?" she inquired.

"It's really quite simple, Miss Barnes. You're in London, with no family or friends to help you. The city is a dangerous place for a naïve female such as yourself, so I am offering you safety and shelter."

"Why am I certain that any support would come with strings attached?"

"Of course it would. As I previously mentioned, *nothing* here is free."

"Whatever price you're demanding, I'm sure it would be much too steep."

"Not necessarily. I've assisted many others in your same position, and most of them are content with the arrangement."

"*Most* of them?"

Mrs. Monroe sighed. "It's not possible to make everyone happy."

"Where is Mrs. Bainbridge?"

"Lauretta went home after she delivered you to me. She's preparing a magnificent party to celebrate Redvers's wedding."

As Mrs. Monroe blithely referred to Lord Redvers, Mary flinched as if she'd been struck. She shouldn't have indicated an acquaintance, but hearing his name was so hurtful.

Did he know what Bainbridge had done to Mary? If Mary disappeared for good, would he ever know? Would anyone?

The pitiful fact was that she was completely alone. She could vanish, and no one would care enough to wonder what had happened to her.

Mrs. Monroe was very shrewd, and she noticed Mary's reaction.

"Lauretta told me that you were extremely fond of Redvers. How sad for you. After all that's transpired, you must realize that he wasn't worth it."

"Yes, I realize it."

"So, this is what I propose." Suddenly, Mrs. Monroe was all business. "You will work for me for two years. During that time, I will feed, clothe, and house you. You will receive a percentage of each guest's fee, and I will keep it in an account for you at my bank. After the two years, you may renew our agreement, or you may retrieve your money and move on to other ventures."

Mrs. Monroe smiled and continued. "As you might imagine, this will be very lucrative for you. Some of my girls have ended up married to a customer. Others have gone on to be mistresses of some very grand noblemen. It is a win-win situation."

Mrs. Monroe had spewed so many details that Mary couldn't absorb the information.

"Your *customers*," Mary broached, "visit you for what sort of enterprise?"

"Why, this is a brothel, Miss Barnes. Surely you've figured that out by now."

"You're asking me to be a prostitute?"

"Not a *prostitute*, precisely. You'd be a gentleman's companion."

Mary looked around at the oddly decorated room, at her scanty attire, and she began to laugh. She kept on till her disturbed merriment brought tears to her eyes.

A brothel! How fitting!

In her entire life, had any single thing ever gone right?

She'd been disowned by her kin, then duped and kidnapped and drugged inside a brothel.

What else could possibly go wrong?

"What is so funny, Miss Barnes?"

Mary just shook her head. "No. Thank you for the offer, but I never could."

"I urge you to reconsider. What you don't understand is that we intend to proceed whether you consent or not. It will be much easier for you if you're amenable."

Mary's laughter rumbled to a halt, and she glared at Mrs. Monroe.

"What are you saying?"

"You will work for me of your own volition, or you will work against your will."

"What do you mean, against my will?"

"We are about to hold an auction, where patrons will bid on you."

Mary gasped. "You're selling me?"

"Yes."

"When?"

"In a few minutes."

A vicious rage swept over Mary, and she jumped off the couch and lunged at Mrs. Monroe; she must not have been the first beleaguered woman to attack. The chain on Mary's ankle grew taut as she discovered that Mrs. Monroe was positioned just out of reach so that Mary could inflict no damage.

Still, Mary stretched and strained, trying to grab Mrs. Monroe, as Mrs. Monroe silently and unemotionally watched her failed attempts.

Ultimately, the footman approached and wrestled her onto the sofa. A towel was pressed over her nose. It smelled of chemicals, and though Mary struggled to avoid its effect, she was swiftly overcome.

She went limp and sagged onto the cushions.

The man drew away.

As she lost consciousness again, Mrs. Monroe said, "Go fetch our guests."

* * *

JORDAN leapt off his horse, his riding crop clutched in his fist, as he raced up the steps of Monroe's bordello.

Over the years, he'd been to the place many times, had partaken of the whores, had drunk and gambled, so he was aware of the routines.

A customer was supposed to politely knock, to request entrance, then speak with Mrs. Monroe so that money could change hands.

The harlots with whom Jordan fornicated had always been happy with their lot, had remained because they enjoyed the high wages and access to the upper echelons of London's male society.

He hadn't met a single one who'd been coerced into staying, but rumors about Monroe abounded. If they turned out to be true, he'd likely commit murder before the night was out.

He marched to the door, planted his boot in the middle, and kicked it open. Wood shattered, shards flying into the front parlor.

The salon was full, and at his abrupt arrival, there were shocked glances. Several men shot to their feet as others grumbled over the rude interruption.

"Where is Barbara?" he bellowed.

"Calm yourself, old boy," an acquaintance advised. "She'll be here shortly."

He gazed up the staircase and saw her hiding on the landing, peeking over the railing to assess the commotion. On espying him, she blanched with fear, indicating her complicity in Bainbridge's scheme.

As he'd hurried to her establishment, he'd been curious if Bainbridge had lied about Mary in order to garner Monroe's assistance, but there had been no deception.

Monroe had freely participated, so Jordan would show no mercy.

"Redvers?" she wheezed. "Why are you back so early? I thought you'd be gone another week."

"Is that what Bainbridge told you?"

"Yes," she admitted, sealing her fate.

"Well, Bainbridge was wrong."

He ran over, taking the stairs two at a time. He seized her by the throat and started up, dragging her along as she choked and sputtered and fought to escape.

"Where is she?" he roared, as he stomped down the corridor, slamming open each door. None of the rooms was occupied, and there was no sign of Mary.

"Redvers, let's discuss this."

"You will make no deals with me!"

He tightened his grasp, and she winced. "Redvers! Please!"

"Tell me where she is," he demanded. "You're only making it worse for yourself."

"The next floor. The blue bedchamber at the end of the hall."

He continued on, pulling her with him, wanting her to be close by when he saw what she'd allowed. He would give her no chance to slip away before he extracted his vengeance.

On the third floor, he burst into the room as an inebriated man staggered over and asked, "Barbara? Redvers? What's the meaning of this?"

Jordan knocked him aside, his grip on Monroe still very firm.

Mary was prone on a divan, and she appeared to be unconscious. There were four scoundrels present, lounging in chairs and watching her.

The degenerate reprobate, Chippingham, was leaned over Mary and lecherously ogling her.

"Move away from her," Jordan commanded, "or I will kill you where you stand."

"Redvers? Have you come to bid?" Chippingham was drunk, slurring his words. "It's not sporting of you to enter the wagering after we've already started."

Jordan stormed over and hit the man so hard that he flew back against the wall, his head banging with a dull thud. For a moment, he hovered, looking perplexed, then he slid to the rug in a dazed heap.

Jordan spun on the others, and he began flogging them with his riding crop, lashing wounds on their faces and arms.

They cowered and tried to protect themselves, but they couldn't evade his wrath.

"It's pistols at dawn, you bastards," he shouted. "I'll see each of you at Marley Field tomorrow morning."

"Redvers, stop!" one of them nagged, which provoked him to a greater frenzy.

He was herding them out, slashing and slashing until they were in the hall and running for their lives.

"I know all of you!" he warned as they reached the stairs and tumbled down. "Choose your seconds!"

A noise sounded behind him, and he whipped around. Monroe was over in the corner, agog with terror.

Jordan strode over to her.

"Has she been raped?" he hissed.

"No, no. She's asleep. She's fine."

He raised the crop and slapped Monroe across the face, rending a deep gash that would leave her scarred for life. Blood welled up and flooded down her cheek, staining her dress.

"Bring me the warmest blanket you have," he ordered.

She skittered by him and returned in a thrice. She went to the couch and carefully wrapped the quilt over Mary, easing a flap over her head to shield her features as he carried her out.

She stood, seeming ashamed and petrified, a prisoner at the gallows.

"Depart England tonight," he said, "and wherever you slither ashore, don't ever own or manage another brothel. If I discover that you are, I will hunt you down and murder you."

"Yes, Lord Redvers." She curtsied as she swiped at the dripping blood on her cheek.

"You might think I am joking. You might think you can trick or deceive me."

"No, no, I wouldn't dare."

"Be gone by first light, or I'll have you hanged."

Gently, he picked up Mary and walked out.

Chapter 24

MARY opened her eyes and stared at the ceiling, feeling very groggy; her sense of disorientation was extreme. For the second time, she'd roused while having no idea where she was.

Her head pounded, her body ached. She was lying on a bed, and furtively, she moved her foot, relieved to note that it wasn't shackled. If she was in a bad situation, she'd be able to make a run for it.

As she peeked to the side, she braced for any catastrophe, and the sight that greeted her was so bizarre she blinked and blinked to clear her vision.

"Lord Redvers?"

"Oh, Mary, I was beginning to think you'd never awaken." He sagged into his chair. "She must have used a potent drug to knock you out for so long."

She was certain she was dreaming, but as he rose and came over to her, as he eased a hip down on the mattress, his presence seemed very real.

He was disheveled, in his shirtsleeves, with his shirt partially unbuttoned. He hadn't shaved or combed his hair, and he appeared rugged and masculine and nothing like the elegant gentleman he'd been while visiting Barnes Manor.

"What time is it?" Mary asked.

"Almost dawn."

"Lord Redvers?" she said again, incredulous.

"Don't call me Redvers, and don't look so surprised."

"But I am . . . surprised."

She glanced down to find that she was still dressed, even though it was in the skimpy negligee and robe that had been placed on her by Mrs. Monroe. Thankfully, she wasn't naked.

A hideous notion occurred to her: Mrs. Monroe had claimed that men were coming to bid on her, to buy her.

Had Redvers participated in the auction? Could he be that callous? That cruel?

Suddenly afraid, she scooted to the opposite side of the bed, until she was pressed up against the wall and could go no farther.

"What do you want from me?" she snapped.

On viewing her reaction, he frowned. "I found you at Monroe's establishment, and I took you away from there. You're safe now."

"How much did you pay for me?"

"*Pay* for you? What do you mean?"

"There was to be an auction, and since you're here, I assume you were the highest bidder."

He was aghast, which made her feel a tiny bit better.

"She was holding an . . . an . . . auction? To sell you?"

"Yes."

"Someone mentioned a wager"—he let out a heavy breath—"but I was a tad overwrought. I wasn't aware of any auction."

"Then how did you know where I was?"

"As I was leaving Barnes Manor, I talked to your friend, that peddler, Mr. Dubois. He'd seen you get into my carriage with Mrs. Bainbridge, and I realized at once that you were in danger."

"Mrs. Bainbridge told me it was a boardinghouse. She said I could rent a room there, but they put something in my tea, and I—"

"Hush," he soothed. "I'm sorry. I'm very distressed about this, and at the moment, I can't bear to hear the details. Tomorrow, though, when I'm more myself, I'll have you tell me everything."

His guard was down, and he seemed very troubled, very conflicted.

"All right," Mary agreed. "I'm happy to discuss it later. It was awful, and I was very afraid."

"Don't worry: Everyone who hurt you will pay and pay dearly."

There was a grim finality to the comment that unnerved her. He sounded very aggrieved on her behalf, as if he might rashly avenge her, but she didn't want that.

With how her luck was running, if he tried to inflict punishment on Mrs. Bainbridge or Mrs. Monroe, *he* would be the one who was injured.

"You don't need to extract any revenge for me. I'm just glad to be out of there." She sat up, the blankets clutched to her chest, and she peered around, seeing a bedroom that was sparsely furnished, but clean and cozy. "Where am I?"

"We're in Paxton Adair's home." He gave a self-deprecating laugh. "I would have taken you to mine, but I don't have one."

She was very confused. It had to be his wedding night. Why was he racing around London, rescuing her from insane people?

"Where is Felicity?"

"I have no idea."

"You didn't marry her?"

"No. I couldn't."

It was a strange answer, and she watched, perplexed, as he stood and walked to the window to stare out at the starry sky. He leaned against the sill, appearing to have the weight of the world on his shoulders. She was amazed by his visible woe.

In the short while they'd been acquainted, he'd flitted through life with no qualms or cares. Nothing mattered to him, so nothing concerned him. What had happened to have him acting so out of character?

She wished it had been her predicament that rattled loose a burst of conscience, but she knew better.

He'd been very blunt: She was insignificant to him. Money was the only thing he valued, the only thing worth having.

"Why didn't you?" Curiosity was eating her alive.

"Why didn't I what?"

"Marry her."

For the longest time, he was silent, then he murmured, "Because I want to marry you."

"You . . . want to marry me?"

"Yes."

"No . . . no . . . that can't be right."

She'd been down this road with him before, when she'd begged him to abandon his quest for an heiress, but he never would, and she refused to be tricked by him ever again.

"It's true," he insisted. "I want to marry you."

"So what? The last time we spoke in an affectionate way, you said very much the same, but you've proved—most brutally—that I can't trust you. It's cruel of you to tease me."

"I'm not teasing."

"Well, I don't believe you, so can we move on to other topics? Such as, what am I to do now?"

He looked lost and bewildered, and she had to glance away.

He was such an attractive man, and she had such potent feelings for him. She hated to see him unhappy or upset. It ignited her feminine instincts, making her eager to comfort and console.

"Do you think," he queried, "that you'll ever find it in your heart to forgive me?"

"For which offense?"

He snorted, then went back to star-gazing.

It was clear that he had something important on his mind, but he couldn't spit it out. When it began to seem as if he'd stand there forever, she shifted to the edge of the bed, her feet on the floor, a quilt tugged over her shoulders and legs.

She was nauseous, and she needed to get some food in her stomach then make plans. Mr. Adair was gracious to have let Redvers bring her to his home, but how long would he allow her to stay? If he asked her to leave, where would she go?

If she'd had her clothes on, she'd have felt more competent to deal with Redvers, and she wondered if they'd been located but she didn't want to inquire. She didn't remember much of what had transpired at the brothel, and without a doubt, some of the events were best left forgotten.

"I didn't know," he said, "that Victoria had kicked you out. I thought you were sent to live with her cousin."

"She doesn't have a cousin."

"So I've been told."

"It doesn't matter."

"Yes, it does. It matters very much."

He grabbed a chair and placed it directly in front of her, so close that their feet tangled together.

She didn't like having him so near. Their prior parting had been too recent, and there had been no opportunity to grieve his loss, to mend her broken heart. On being with him again, elation swept through her, which was very dangerous.

She'd never had the willpower to resist him, and her fondness, which had had no chance to diminish, could goad her to innumerable follies.

"I'm sorry," he said, "and I'm not very good at apologizing, so I hope you won't make me grovel."

She chuckled miserably. "I won't."

"I was an idiot."

"Yes, you were."

"You repeatedly advised me I was mistaken about Felicity, that I shouldn't be so driven about her money, but I ignored you."

"You were absolutely deaf on the subject."

He glowered. "You don't have to agree with quite so much enthusiasm."

"What are you actually saying? Please skip the nonsense about marrying me, because I know you're not serious."

He clasped her hand, and while she should have scolded him and pulled away, she didn't. The past few days had been so horrid, and she received an enormous amount of solace from the simple, human contact.

"Promise you'll hear me out."

"I'm listening."

"I love you."

"Don't lie to me!" she fumed. She yanked away and fought to roll off the bed, but with their legs entwined, she couldn't escape. He pinned her down, palms on her thighs.

"I was standing in the parlor at Barnes Manor," he continued, "and the vicar was reading the vows. He came to the spot where I had to consent to have Felicity as my wife, but I couldn't do it. I made him endure the longest ceremonial pause in history as I tried to figure out why I couldn't reply."

"What did you discover?"

"I love you so much that I'm dying with it."

She inhaled sharply, disturbed by his declaration.

He seemed sincere. Could it be true? If it was, where did it leave them?

He was still broke, and she was still poor.

"You once told me," he kept on, "that you loved me, too. Tell me that I haven't squandered your affection. Tell me that you still feel the same."

His entreaty was too compelling, and tears welled into her eyes.

From the first moment she'd met him, it was as if a magic spell had been cast, and she was incapable of avoiding its heady effects.

Despite what he'd done, despite how terribly she'd suffered, she was stupidly, foolishly, naïvely in love with him.

"You could never have squandered my affection," she said and started to weep.

"Don't cry! I can't bear it when you're sad."

"I thought I would never see you again. I thought I would vanish, and you wouldn't know or care."

"My darling Mary. Forgive me, forgive me."

He pulled her onto his lap, and she nestled at his nape, her tears wetting his shirt.

For many minutes, he held her, stroking her back, whispering tender words. Then he drew away and he swiped at her cheeks with his thumbs.

"I've been thinking," he said, "and I have an idea about what we should do."

"What is it?"

"I have a tiny property north of London."

"You what?"

"I own some property. It's where I come by my title. There is a house that's in dreadful condition, as well as a small farm, but the fields are lying fallow."

"You own a house and a farm?" She gaped at him, stunned, scarcely able to believe it.

"It was my brother's, and after he died, my father was grieving, and he let it fall into disrepair. By the time I was grown and its management was vested in me, I hadn't the money to fix it, so I've never lived there. I never *wanted* to live there. It's decrepit and drafty and dilapidated, but would you wed me and help me make it our home?"

What a peculiar man he was! He actually had a rural estate where he could dwell in quiet harmony, but instead, he'd opted for the bachelor's room and London vice that had been the centerpiece of his adult years.

She'd assumed that she understood him, but what kind of person chose such an odd, unsatisfying existence? What did it imply about his character? About his wisdom and judgment?

"You've never resided there," she said, "and you obviously

view it as an unpalatable place. Why would you suddenly expect that you would be happy there?"

"Because you would be there with me."

"And that would make you happy?"

"For the rest of my days."

He kept uttering tempting declarations, and her pulse raced until she was giddy with the prospects for the future, but she was so hesitant.

He was offering marriage—again, which was a dicey proposition. He might or might not follow through. If she agreed to his scheme, but it turned out he was lying, how would she survive it? Yet if he was serious, she would have everything she'd ever craved.

The opportunity dangled between them, mesmerizing her, taunting her to reach out and grab for it.

Dare she?

"Does your country property have a name?" she asked.

"Redvers House."

With his mentioning it, the spot became real. She could practically see the sagging roof, drooping shutters, and weed-strewn flower beds. Her mind whirred with plans as to how she'd get it habitable.

Was she mad? Was he?

"*If* I said yes," she cautiously ventured, "when would we marry?"

"Tomorrow. I'll apply for a Special License. We can leave the next morning, although there are a few things I need to do first."

"What things?"

"You're not aware of this, but your sister Cassandra is here."

"In London?"

"No, *here*—in the house."

"Whatever for?"

"While I was busy seducing you, Paxton was busy, too."

"Mr. Adair and Cassandra?"

"Yes, and his father has given him a plantation in Jamaica. They're sailing on Thursday, and they're going to have the ship's captain wed them once they're out on the water."

"Mr. Adair and Cassandra? You're sure of this?"

"Yes."

She couldn't get over it, couldn't imagine it. Of all the people whom she would have predicted to never marry again, it was Cassandra. And to dashing, suave, indolent Paxton Adair! It was bizarre.

When had love blossomed for them? How had Cassandra kept it a secret?

"I was thinking that *I* have gone mad," she said, "but it seems the entire world has joined me."

"It came as a shock to me, too. So I'd like to see them off down at the harbor, then"—he paused, appearing both delighted and guilty—"I have to visit my father, so I can formally introduce you to him. After that, we'll depart for the country."

"You *want* to introduce me? Why?"

"To show him my wonderful choice in a bride." His cheeks reddened. "Perhaps he'll realize I have some redeeming qualities, after all."

"You have *many* redeeming qualities, Jordan. Ignore him when he tells you that you don't."

"My little champion," he murmured. "I nearly lost you. How could I have been such a fool?"

He slid from his chair, went down on one knee, and took her hand in his.

"What are you doing?" she inquired.

"Felicity informed me that this is how a man proposes. I want to get it right."

Her heart literally skipped a beat. If he proceeded, she didn't have the strength to refuse him, yet she would be putting her happiness, her future, her very life in his keeping.

"I have always tried," he started, "to live down to my father's low expectations."

"Yes, you have, and it makes me so angry."

"I have been belligerent and careless and lazy. It was impossible to please him, so I never exerted myself, but I don't want to be that man anymore."

"Who do you want to be?"

"I want to be the man who loves you. You look at me, and you see someone who is better than I really am. I want to be that person for you."

"Oh, Jordan . . ."

"I'm not saying it will be easy. I'm vain and proud, and I'm used to having my own way."

"You certainly are."

"We'll be poor as the dickens for a time, but we may be able to rectify our fiscal situation."

"I thought it was hopeless."

"You convinced me it wasn't."

"What is your plan?"

"There was a bit of a—let's call it a dustup—when I left Monroe's establishment with you."

The tepid description alarmed her.

"What sort of dustup?"

"You needn't worry about it, but I had intended to have a few harsh . . . ah . . . words with several gentlemen in the morning. Their representative stopped by a while ago and offered me some cash—as damages for insulting me."

"Money in lieu of fighting?"

"Yes."

"That sounds advantageous. How thoroughly did they feel you were offended?"

"To the tune of a thousand pounds."

She gasped. "A thousand?"

"Yes. So if we were very frugal, it would tide us over until we plant a crop at Redvers House. We need to get the farm earning an income again."

A spark of optimism ignited. "That's a marvelous idea."

"Cassandra had a suggestion, too."

"What is it?"

"She's been curious as to why your father didn't dower you. She was wondering if Victoria might have hidden your inheritance."

Mary frowned. "Could she have?"

"I think Victoria is capable of any bad behavior, don't you?"

"Yes."

"I'll have my attorney, Mr. Thumberton, investigate. Even if your father didn't provide for you, you might have a financial claim against the estate."

"My goodness. Such a thing had never occurred to me."

"Finally, I want to pursue a legal case against Harold Talbot."

"For what?"

"For breach of promise, for his leading you on all those years."

"You wouldn't."

"I would." He grinned. "Let me harass him. It would amuse me very much."

"You are awful."

"Does that mean I have your permission?"

In reply, she merely chuckled.

With all he'd just told her, her head was spinning.

They could marry. She'd be Lady Redvers. He would give her a home, a family. They would both find a purpose in life—that being the renovation and revitalization of Redvers House. She might ultimately learn that her father had cared for her.

She could slap back at Harold for all his criticisms and slights!

It was too much to absorb, and his comments had fanned her ember of optimism until it burned hot and bright.

How could she refuse? What did she have instead?

Nothing at all.

Wasn't he worth the risk? Shouldn't she take a chance?

Her resolve crumbled in an instant.

"What about Mrs. Bainbridge?" she inquired.

"I've already parted with her."

"She will never bother us again?"

"No, never."

"What about other women besides her? Will you have lovers? Will you support mistresses behind my back? Will I constantly be tripping over your latest paramour?"

"From this moment on, I'll have no one but you. I swear it."

"If you betrayed me, it would break my heart."

"I know, and I never would."

"Your gambling will have to end. If we can actually obtain some of this money you've mentioned, I'll kill you before I let you squander it."

"I'm tired of how I've been living. It's exhausting, being hounded by creditors. I'm thirty years old. Isn't it time I grew up and acted like it?"

"As a matter of fact, it is. I'll expect you to be a devoted husband."

"I can't wait."

"I want a dozen children."

"I hope they're all girls who look just like you."

"You'll have to stay with me in the country; you'll have to help me raise them. You couldn't decide that fatherhood is boring or tedious. You couldn't pick up and leave."

"I will never leave you. Not till I take my dying breath."

He was still on his knees, holding her hand.

He gazed at her with his beautiful blue eyes, his affection shining through.

She had never imagined this day would arrive, had never supposed that such stunning contentment would be within her grasp.

She'd never believed that he would come to his senses!

"I love you," she said.

"I love you, too," he responded with great solemnity. "Will

you have me, Mary? Will you let me give you everything you've ever wanted? Will you let me make you happy?"

She smiled and nodded. "Yes, Jordan, I will let you make me very, very happy."

"Then I am the luckiest man in the world."

❦

"ARE you nervous?"

Jordan thought for a moment, then answered, "Yes."

"Well, don't be," Mary said. "He's just like you. His bark is much worse than his bite."

"How is it that my father and I know very little about you, but *you* know so much about us?"

"You're both very simple creatures. It's not difficult to figure you out."

He frowned, unused to having a wife, especially one who understood him so completely. He'd always pictured himself to be extremely enigmatic, but apparently, he wasn't complex in the least.

He opened his father's front door and ushered her into the foyer. Despite how bitterly he and Sunderland had parted, he'd been raised in the dreary place, and he wouldn't knock as if he were a stranger.

As he helped her with her tattered cloak and old bonnet, he was disgusted with their decrepit condition. Without their requesting it, her missing clothes had been delivered to Paxton's apartment. Evidently, it had been Barbara Monroe's last, frantic act before she'd fled the city, which had been an auspicious gesture, since Mary had had nothing to wear.

"I hate this cloak," he mentioned.

She shrugged. "Beggars can't be choosers."

"Our next stop is to find some apparel for you. I insist you have a few dresses to take to the country."

"I don't need new clothes. I can wait till we're more settled."

"I'm buying you some. Don't argue with me."

"Yes, my lord husband."

He frowned again. He'd noted that she had an annoying habit of agreeing with him, when she had absolutely no intention of doing what he said.

Was this typical wifely behavior? How was a fellow to tolerate it?

Chippingham and his cohorts had coughed up a small fortune to avoid any duels, so he had some money. While he couldn't purchase garments of the highest fashion, she didn't have to go about looking like a pauper.

She was a viscountess. Her father-in-law was an earl.

"We can afford it," he declared, "and it will make me happy."

She smiled. "By all means then. Buy me some clothes."

A footman walked down the hall, and on seeing them, he gulped with dismay.

"Lord Redvers?"

"I've come to speak with Sunderland. Is he at home?"

"Yes. But . . . but . . ."

"I realize you're not supposed to let me in, but don't worry. I'll take all the blame. I'll say I overpowered you, so please tell him I seek an audience, and I've brought my bride."

The boy stiffened with amazement, and he bowed low.

"Welcome, Lady Redvers."

"Thank you," Mary said. "I'm delighted to be here."

He scurried away, and she peeked up at Jordan.

"That's the first time anyone has referred to me as Lady Redvers."

"You'll get used to it."

"I'd rather be Mrs. Jordan Winthrop."

"You can be Mrs. Winthrop when we're alone."

Shouting erupted from the direction of the library, indicating that Sunderland had been informed of Jordan's arrival and that he'd learned of Jordan's marriage.

Jordan sighed. Some things never changed.

"Shall we head him off at the pass?" Jordan asked.

"Yes," Mary said. "Let's not have him overtax himself. It's my wedding day. I wouldn't want him to ruin it by perishing from a massive display of temper."

Mary took his arm, giving it a supportive pat, and they proceeded down the hall, entering the library just as Sunderland marched toward them.

"I will not have that gold-digging mercenary under my roof!" he bellowed. "I warned you that I wouldn't—"

He saw Mary, and he stumbled to a halt.

"Hello, Sunderland," Jordan said.

Scowling vehemently, Sunderland studied Mary. "You're not Felicity Barnes."

"No, I'm not. Aren't you glad?" Mary peered over at Jordan. "Why don't you call him *Father*?"

"He ordered me not to."

Mary rolled her eyes. "You two could drive me to drink."

"Sunderland," Jordan started, but Mary interrupted.

"I don't care what he wants. Call him Father."

"He won't like it."

"It doesn't matter. Do it for me."

As he'd already discovered, he couldn't refuse her anything, and he began again.

"Father, I should like to present my wife, Mary Barnes Winthrop, Lady Redvers."

Sunderland was flummoxed, torn between insults and cordiality, and he reverted to form, rudeness being his constant companion.

"I did not give you permission to wed her," he seethed.

"No, you didn't," Jordan admitted, "but in my own defense, I am thirty years old. I ought to have been allowed some leeway to pick the woman of my dreams."

Sunderland scoffed. "Are you claiming this is some sort of . . . of . . . *love* match?"

"Yes," Mary chimed in. "We're desperately in love, and we wanted to share our happiness with you."

"I'm not happy!" Sunderland complained. "My son has disobeyed me. He has offended me with his choice."

"But I'll grow on you," Mary said. "I promise."

"Not bloody likely," Sunderland grouched.

"Watch your language, Father," Jordan scolded.

"You're not welcome in my home," Sunderland ranted. "I won't provide shelter for you as you wallow in this folly."

"Have we asked to stay with you?" Jordan countered.

"Ah . . . no. Why haven't you, you slothful wretch?"

"We're opening Redvers House. I'm sick of London, so we're moving there."

"Redvers House is a decrepit disaster," Sunderland said.

"Due to your neglect, I understand," Mary replied. "But we're fixing it up, and we'd like to invite you to join us for Christmas. It won't be near as fancy as what you're accustomed to, but we thought you might enjoy a cozy respite with your family."

"Christmas!" Sunderland huffed. "I wouldn't spend Christmas or any other holiday with you."

"December is a long way off," Mary cajoled. "If you decide you'd like to visit after all, simply send me a note. We'll have the guest room ready."

"You know where we'll be." Jordan gazed at Mary. "Shall we go?"

"Yes."

He guided her out to the foyer, and as he wrapped her in her cloak, Sunderland blustered up.

"This changes nothing," he insisted. "I've cut you out of my will. You're disinherited. What do you think of that?"

"I don't think anything of it," Jordan calmly answered. "It's irrelevant to me. I've always wanted to be free of your financial manipulation, and now I will be. I'm fully prepared for the consequences of getting by on my own."

Sunderland wasn't garnering the reactions he'd hoped, and he glared at Mary. "My son will never see a penny of my fortune, so if you planned to fleece me by marrying him, you'll be sorely disappointed."

"Actually," she retorted, "when I married him, *you* never crossed my mind."

As Jordan reached for the door, Sunderland was apoplectic.

"You expect me to believe," he gasped, "that you're leaving London for good?"

"Believe it or don't," Jordan responded. "It's all the same to me."

"You expect me to believe that you're going to settle down and become a . . . a . . . farmer?"

"Hilarious, isn't it?"

"You'll never follow through."

Mary drew away from Jordan, and she went over to Sunderland. She rose on tiptoe and kissed him on the cheek.

"Stop shouting at us," she said. "Let's be friends."

"I don't need friends like you."

"Come for Christmas," she urged, ignoring his comment.

She grabbed Jordan's hand and led him out, and at the last second, he glanced over his shoulder. Sunderland was gaping at them, and Jordan gleaned an enormous amount of satisfaction from viewing his father's stunned expression.

They climbed into the hackney they'd hired and rode away.

"He accused me of being a mercenary!" Mary fumed. "Did I sound like one?"

"No, but I like this side of you. He's such a blowhard; it's the only time I've ever seen him speechless."

"I'm betting that before the month is out we'll receive a wedding gift from him."

"You shouldn't count on it."

"He's lonely. Down deep, he wants us in his life."

"He doesn't."

"He'll show up for Christmas, too."

"He won't."

"He will. Just you wait and see."

"WRITE to me!" Cassandra called.

"Only if you promise to write back!" Mary called in reply.

She was on the dock, watching as Cassandra's ship gradually made its way out toward the center of the river. She was getting farther and farther away, her words more indistinct by the minute.

The journey to Jamaica was long and dangerous, so she would probably never see Cassandra again. Tears dripped down her cheeks, and she swiped them away.

"Keep me posted on your legal fight with Mother," Cassandra said.

"I definitely will."

"I hope you end up with all her money! Her impoverishment would be your best revenge."

Mary laughed. "Wouldn't that be grand!"

"And let me know when I'm to be an aunt!"

"I look forward to hearing the very same news from you."

Mr. Adair popped up beside Cassandra where she was leaned against the railing, and he smiled and waved.

"Take care of her, Mr. Adair," Mary yelled.

"I will."

"Make her happy!"

He said something else, but the breeze carried away his

remark. The crowd around them quieted, observing until their loved ones were tiny specks on the horizon.

"I can't believe he really went." Jordan was glum and morose.

"Do you wish you'd gone with him?"

"Maybe." There was a twinkle in his eye, and she poked him in the ribs.

"It's about time the two of you grew up and became a pair of stuffy old married men."

He stiffened with affront. "I will accept the designation of married, but not old. And never stuffy."

"No, never stuffy."

They dawdled till the ship was lost in the distance, the sails blending in among the myriad of boats that clogged the river. Then they turned and headed off to find a hackney to rent.

Their own adventure was beginning the next morning, and Mary couldn't wait.

Her own home!

She was so excited, she could barely stand it. She couldn't eat; she hadn't slept.

Jordan repeatedly described the poor condition of the buildings, trying to lower her expectations, but they couldn't be dashed. She was already enthralled with the place and knew it would be perfect. They had a lifetime to make it perfect.

They rounded the corner when, to her surprise, she saw a colorful peddler's wagon parked down the block. When she discovered that it was Mr. Dubois's, she brimmed with delight.

He had the back open, his bottles and jars neatly arranged. He was talking to a pretty auburn-haired woman, offering her one of his potions, but she wasn't interested, and she kept pushing it away.

"Look, Jordan," she said. "It's my friend, Mr. Dubois. What a coincidence! The city is so large. What are the chances we'd bump into him?"

"Yes, what are the chances?" Jordan grumbled.

Mary pulled on his arm. "Come on! Let's say hello."

She hurried over, practically dragging Jordan, who didn't seem all that enthused.

"Mr. Dubois," Mary greeted, "what are you doing in London?"

"Madamoiselle Barnes? How are you, *cherie*? I've been worried sick."

"I'm fine, and it's no longer Miss Barnes."

He frowned, studying her, then Jordan, then her again, and comprehension dawned.

"You married your grand lord?"

"Yes. Yesterday morning."

"Toutes mes felicitations!"

"You remember my husband, don't you? Viscount Redvers?"

"Yes, I remember him," Dubois muttered, and it sounded as if they didn't like each other very much.

Jordan scowled. "How come you have a French accent all of a sudden?"

"Because he's French, silly," Mary responded.

Jordan mumbled an epithet. "You're not selling any of your Daily Remedy, are you, Dubois?"

"Not a bottle in the wagon," Dubois claimed, appearing suspiciously innocent.

"Good. I wouldn't want to learn that you'd deceived any of the ladies."

Dubois's customer backed away, unnerved by Jordan's charge. Dubois shot visual daggers at Jordan, then spun to her.

"My remedies are made from premier ingredients. Lord Redvers is jesting."

Dubois leaned nearer and whispered to Mary, "You owe me some money, *cherie*."

"Money? What for?"

"Have you forgotten? I gave you my Spinster's Cure for free. You agreed to pay me double the price after you were wed."

"So I did." Mary grinned at Jordan. "Jordan, pay the man, please."

"For what?"

"I drank his Spinster's Cure, and it obviously worked some sort of magic."

"I thought," Jordan complained, "that it was supposed to snag Harold Talbot for you."

"No, it wasn't. I was supposed to marry my *true* love. That would be you."

Jordan grumbled again, but withdrew the pennies from his pocket. Dubois scooped up the coins then turned to his customer, who'd been trying to slip away without being coerced into buying anything.

"You see, Miss Hamilton, here is the very best recommendation I can provide as to the effectiveness of my tonics. Lady Redvers was all alone and *triste*—sad—like you. She was pining away for love and affection. And *voila*! She is wed to a great lord."

"Hello, Miss Hamilton," Mary said.

The poor woman dropped into a low curtsy, which embarrassed Mary. She couldn't abide the folderol that went along with being a nobleman's wife, and she didn't imagine she'd ever grow accustomed to it.

"Miss Hamilton"—Mary reached out and encouraged the woman to rise—"I'm only recently married. Don't make a fuss."

"Thank you, milady."

"We needn't stand on ceremony," Mary advised. "Just plain Mary will do."

"Thank you . . . Mary. I'm Helen Hamilton."

"This is my husband, Lord Redvers. You may fuss over him if you like. He enjoys it."

Hamilton dropped into another curtsy.

"Hello, Lord Redvers."

"Miss Hamilton. Be wary of this fellow's medicines."

"I am, sir."

"His tonics can be a bit . . . invigorating."

Dubois glowered at Jordan, then he retrieved a vial and held it out to Miss Hamilton.

"I've been telling Miss Hamilton," he explained, "that she should try my Spinster's Cure. It is very powerful, *non*?"

"*Non*. I mean *yes*," Mary concurred. "Very powerful, indeed."

"Madamoiselle Barnes drank it, and she was wed in four weeks, as promised."

"Five weeks," Mary said, "but why quibble?"

Jordan harrumphed.

Mary took the vial from Dubois and handed it to Miss Hamilton.

"Have a dose," Mary offered, "with my compliments."

"Oh, I couldn't," Miss Hamilton protested.

"I insist. I hope it works as successfully for you as it did for me."

Miss Hamilton was disconcerted by the gesture, but too polite to argue with a viscountess. She stuck the vial into her reticule and hurried away.

As she vanished, Jordan asked, "Are you matchmaking now, Lady Redvers?"

"I guess I am."

"I've often heard that the newly wedded think everyone should join them in the matrimonial state."

"Why not? I want the entire world to be as content as I am." She gazed at Dubois. "I understand, Mr. Dubois, that you rendered some assistance to Lord Redvers on my behalf."

"I merely told him about that shrew who invited you to ride to London in her carriage."

"It was a timely warning. I experienced a spot of trouble when I arrived, so your intervention was deeply appreciated. Thank you for helping me."

"You're welcome, *mon amie*."

"Take care, and say hello to your sister for me."

"I will."

She and Jordan started off, as Dubois called after them.

"Hey, Redvers!"

Jordan glanced around. "What?"

"I have a manly tonic that will keep you fit in the . . . well . . . in the husbandly arena . . . if you know what I mean. Would you like to try a sample?"

"I needed your magic to win her," Jordan replied. "I don't need it to keep her. She's all mine."

"Forevermore," Mary agreed.

"No potions necessary," Jordan added.

They smiled and walked on down the street.

"MICHAEL! What are you doing?"

Captain Tristan Odell glared down the hall at his younger half brother, Michael Seymour.

"Tristan," Michael casually replied, "I didn't realize you were home."

"Obviously."

Michael—the recently installed Earl of Hastings—had his arms wrapped around a very fetching housemaid, his lean, lanky torso pressing her against the wall. Not that she appeared to mind.

She was buxom and plump, her abundant breasts scarcely constrained by corset and gown, and thus, the exact sort of female Michael relished.

A love bite was plainly visible on the girl's neck, so mischief had been brewing. If Tristan hadn't walked by, Michael would have lured her into an empty parlor, would have had her skirt thrown up and her drawers tugged down in a fast attempt to lose his virginity.

It was hell, trying to keep the eighteen-year-old boy in line. With his golden blond hair and big blue eyes, his broad shoulders and six foot frame, he could have been an angel painted on a church ceiling. Women took one look at him and promptly forgot every lesson they'd ever been taught about decency and decorum.

"What's your name, lass?" Tristan asked the maid.

"Lydia, Captain Odell."

"Be about your duties, Lydia, and I don't want you to sneak off with the earl ever again."

She glanced at Michael, expecting him to counter the edict, but Michael merely grinned, a shameless, unrepentant rogue.

"Yes, Captain Odell," she sullenly mumbled.

"I don't care what he promises you," Tristan warned. "I don't care if he offers you money or plies you with gifts. You are to refuse. Do I make myself clear?"

"Yes, sir."

"If he pesters you, and you can't dissuade him, come to me at once."

"I will."

"For if I stumble on another tryst, you'll be fired immediately. I won't give you a chance to explain. You'll simply be turned out without a reference."

The threat of termination got her attention. She curtsied and left, but she was mutinous, and Tristan knew it was only a matter of time before she'd be searching for other employment.

"You!" Tristan pointed an admonishing finger at Michael. "In the library!"

Tristan spun and marched off as Michael complained. "You're such a scold. You never let me have any fun."

"This isn't *my* fault."

"The way you carry on, one would think you were my mother."

"Don't bring your poor mother into it. If she hadn't died when you were little, she wouldn't last long now, watching you. Your antics would be the death of her."

"My mother would have loved me," Michael confidently claimed. "She would have thought I was marvelous. All women do."

Tristan rolled his eyes and plopped down into his chair behind the massive oak desk. Though Michael was the earl, he slouched into the chair across—like the recalcitrant adolescent he was.

The prior earl, their philandering father, Charles Seymour, had passed away six months earlier, orphaning Michael and his twelve-year-old sister, Rose.

There were several relatives who could have stepped in as guardian for the two children, but Charles—for reasons Tristan couldn't fathom—had named Tristan.

Tristan was Charles's oldest, but illegitimate, son, the product of an illicit romance between Charles and Tristan's Scottish mother, Meg. Charles had owned a hunting lodge near Tristan's village and had visited every autumn. As a wealthy, urbane aristocrat, Charles had possessed the same charisma as Michael, and pretty, foolish Meg hadn't stood a chance.

She'd died when Tristan was a baby, so she'd been unavailable to insist on continuing contact with his father. Tristan had only seen Charles a few times, and he'd been given scant fiscal support.

Tristan had made his own way in the world, had embraced his love of sailing and the sea. He owned a small shipping company and sailed as captain of his own merchant vessel. He was never happier than when he was out on the water and flying over the waves, so it had come as an enormous surprise to learn that he'd been roped in by Charles, cast as mentor and protector to his half siblings whom he'd never met.

At age thirty, Tristan had never been married and had no children of his own, so he knew nothing about parenting. He was floundering like a blind man, groping about in the dark.

Yet he wasn't eager to be compared to his negligent father, so he took his responsibilities seriously. When he'd received the letter advising him of his guardianship of Michael and Rose, he'd grudgingly traveled to London to assume his duties.

Michael and Rose weren't overly distraught at Charles's demise. Nor did they seem to miss him. Apparently, Charles had been as absent in their lives as he'd been in Tristan's. They viewed his loss as one might the passing of a distant friend of the family.

"Well"—Tristan struggled to look fatherly—"what have you to say for yourself?"

"She's very fetching? She's loose with her favors? You're a stick in the mud?"

Tristan snorted with disgust. "You're hopeless. I have no idea why I lecture you."

"Neither do I. It's a waste of breath."

"It certainly is, but you must heed me: You don't want to gain a reputation as a fellow who tumbles his servants. Those kinds of men are regarded as swine."

"I don't feel like *swine*. I feel randy as the dickens."

"You have an obligation to your employees. You can't frivolously ruin them—even if they beg you to."

Tristan glowered, stupidly expecting to elicit some evidence of remorse, or at least a hint that Michael recognized his behavior to be rash and wrong. He was a peer of the realm, so he should set an example, but as Tristan had quickly learned, Michael would act however he pleased.

He'd been raised by nannies and governesses—pushovers all—who'd been dazzled by his delightful smile and charming manners. With his being eighteen and horridly spoiled, there wasn't much Tristan could do but peck like a hen, while keeping a tight rein on Michael's fortune, a staggering array of money and property that he wouldn't completely control until he was twenty-five.

"I've enlightened you as to girls"—Tristan's cheeks flushed with embarrassment—"and the urges we men suffer because of them. You have to be cautious."

"It was just a kiss," Michael contended.

"Kissing can swiftly lead to more, and trust me, a low-born doxy like Lydia is a mercenary. If you impregnated her, you'd end up supporting her for the rest of your life."

Bored with the topic, Michael yawned. "Quit nagging. I like you, Tristan, but honestly, you can be positively tedious."

Michael flashed an imperious glare, filled with youthful disdain. Tristan had sailed around the globe, had whored and debauched in cities from Bombay to Shanghai, so he was in no position to chastise, but he felt compelled to guide Michael in his carnal conduct.

Michael was an *earl*. There were standards to be maintained, as their father had pointed out in a letter he'd written to Tristan on his deathbed.

Watch over Michael and Rose, Charles had penned. *Be kind to Rose. Dote on her as I never did. Be stern with Michael. Teach him the lessons I never bothered to impart . . .*

The words were powerfully binding. Tristan was desperate to do right by Michael and Rose, desperate to make his father proud—a situation to which he'd never aspired when the man had still been alive.

"I've explained the mechanics of sexual activity," Tristan reminded him, "and I hope you've paid attention."

"Oh, yes"—Michael grinned wickedly—"and I can't understand why you're working so hard to prevent me from practicing what you described. It can't be healthy to be so physically frustrated."

"You have to wait until you're married."

Tristan nearly choked. Had that sentence come from his own mouth?

"Ha! I don't know why you're so determined to keep me in the dark."

"It's not the *dark* I'm worried about. It's the baby that arrives nine months later."

At all costs, Tristan would thwart Michael from siring any bastard children. Being a bastard himself, it was a sore subject for Tristan, but he couldn't get Michael to grasp why it mattered.

"I wish you'd take me to a brothel," Michael blurted out.

"A brothel?"

"Yes. If I could dabble with whores occasionally, I'd be—"

Tristan was saved from the conversation by a knock on the door. Michael's cousin, Maud Seymour, poked her nose in. She was a few years older than Tristan, a fussy, unremarkable widow with mousy brown hair and unmemorable gray eyes.

For over a decade, she'd resided in the mansion, with her sixteen-year-old daughter, Miriam. She'd served as the earl's hostess, as well as a detached mother-figure for Michael and Rose.

She was the ultimate hanger-on, the dreaded poor relative who'd come for a visit, ingratiated herself, and never left.

She was used to running the household, having had no supervision from Tristan's father over the accounts or servants, and she'd been furious over Tristan's barging in and seizing control. Tristan tried to be cordial, anxious to build a rapport rather than fight over territory.

He didn't care about the house or servants. He cared about Michael and Rose and ensuring that their futures and fortunes were secure.

"Yes, Maud, what is it?" he asked.

"An applicant is here to interview for the position of Rose's governess. A Miss Helen Hamilton."

Tristan bit down a curse. He'd forgotten about the interview. Rose had been without a governess for almost two years, and while she insisted she didn't need one, Tristan insisted she did.

He'd immersed himself in the search, but he couldn't find the exact person he wanted.

Rose was a lonely, sweet girl, and so far, the candidates had seemed too old or too grumpy or too lazy to be allowed to watch over her. Maud claimed he was finicky, and he probably was, but he had to keep stopping himself from asking why—when she'd been in charge for so long—the post had remained unfilled.

Finances weren't a problem, and Tristan suspected that

Maud didn't like Rose enough to trouble herself with hiring someone.

"You don't have to bother with it," Maud told him. "I'm happy to talk to her for you."

"I don't mind meeting with her," he stated. "It's my duty to Rose."

"You're so conscientious," Maud simpered, flattering him. She was practically batting her lashes. "It's so refreshing to have a man about the place who enjoys being in command."

"What am I, Cousin Maud?" Michael inquired. "Chopped liver?"

"You," Tristan needled, "are an arrogant boy who's barely out of short pants."

"You think I'm a boy," Michael retorted, "but if you gave me half a chance with the ladies, I'd show you that I can—"

"Michael was just leaving." Tristan cut him off, terrified of what risqué comment he might make in front of Maud.

"Yes, Maud," Michael agreed, "I'm leaving. The maids are having tea down in the kitchen. I promised I'd join them."

"He's not going to the kitchen to chat with the maids," Tristan said. "He's going to his bedchamber to contemplate his many deplorable character traits."

"I don't have any deplorable traits," Michael boasted. "I'm flawlessly wonderful. Ask anyone."

Tristan rolled his eyes again. "Maud, escort him out, then send the applicant down to speak with me."

Maud and Michael departed, and Tristan sat, listening as their footsteps faded.

"A brothel, indeed," he muttered to the silent room.

If Michael started frequenting whores, his name would be permanently sullied, which Tristan couldn't permit.

His father's deathbed letter had contained the request that Tristan arrange brilliant marriages for Michael and Rose, to partners befitting their station. If Michael developed a reputation as a philanderer, who had bastard children scattered hither and yon, no sane father would have him as a son-in-law.

More footsteps sounded in the hall. They were dainty and hesitant, and before he could fully shift his thoughts from Michael and his budding sexuality, the interviewee entered.

On seeing her, he frowned.

She was very pretty, petite, slender, and willowy, with a gorgeous head of auburn hair and big green eyes. Her skin was creamy smooth, her cheeks rosy with good health, her lips red and lush as a ripe cherry.

Her manner was pleasant, her dress neat and trim. She seemed to glide rather than walk, providing evidence of education and breeding.

No doubt she'd be perfect, a cheery, competent, and interesting person whom Rose would adore, and he detested her on sight.

He'd specifically informed Mrs. Ford at the employment agency that he wouldn't consider any attractive, young females. Not with Michael in a constant state of lust. Was Mrs. Ford blind?

"Is this the library?" She peered around at the walls and walls of books that stretched from floor to ceiling, and she chuckled. "Of course it is. That was a silly question, wasn't it?"

She focused those beautiful green eyes on him, and he felt as if he'd been hit with a bolt of lightning. She seemed to know things about him that she had no reason to know, seemed to understand what drove him, what he wanted, what he needed, and the sensation was so bizarre and so alarming that he actually shuddered.

"May I help you?" he queried.

"I'm looking for Captain Odell."

"You've found him." He stood, certain he appeared persnickety and overbearing. "And you are . . . ?"

"Miss Helen Hamilton. I've been sent by Mrs. Ford at the Ford Employment Agency to—"

"Yes, yes, I'm aware of why you're here." He gestured to the chair that Michael had just vacated. "Sit."

At his sharp tone, she faltered, then forced a smile and

came over, carefully balancing on the edge of the seat, her skirt demurely arrayed, her fingers clasped in her lap.

They stared as if they were quarreling, but she didn't cower as he wished she would. He was eager to expose a chink in her armor so that he would feel justified in rejecting her.

"Well?" he asked.

"Well what?"

"Where are your references?"

"Oh, those." She waved an elegant hand as if a prior endorsement was of no consequence. "I didn't bring any."

He breathed a sigh of relief. No references. No job.

"Then we needn't continue this discussion. I can't imagine what Mrs. Ford was thinking."

"Would you hear me out?"

"No."

As if he hadn't declined to listen, she began extolling her virtues. "I could have penned some fake letters, but I didn't because I'm too honest."

"Are you?"

"Yes. You see, I've never been a governess before. However, I've had excellent schooling. My studies included languages, art, science—both biological and geological—history, penmanship, and I'm also trained in the finer graces such as dancing, painting, and—"

He held up a hand, stopping her. "Thank you for coming."

He pointed to the door, indicating she should leave, but she didn't. Her gaze brimmed with hurt, and perhaps a flash of desperation, and he felt as if he'd kicked a puppy.

"I speak French, Italian, Latin, and a bit of Spanish."

"No."

"I sing like an angel."

"No."

"I can play pieces by Mr. Mozart on the pianoforte."

"No."

"Please?"

"Good day, Miss Hamilton."

"Mrs. Ford said I was exactly who you were looking for."

"Mrs. Ford was wrong."

She scrutinized him, her head tipped to the side as if he were a curious bug she was examining.

"Why are you acting like this?" she stunned him by asking.

"What did you say?"

"Have I offended you?"

"No."

"That's not true. From the moment I arrived, your dislike was palpable. Tell me what I've done so that I can apologize, then we'll move on and conduct ourselves like rational adults."

"I have no desire to continue."

"But . . . why?"

"My reasons, Miss Hamilton, are none of your business."

His comment fell into the room with a heavy thud, his discourtesy blatant and mortifying. Despite his low antecedents, he was a gentleman, and he hated upsetting her, but he wanted her to go away.

She seemed to deflate, appearing vulnerable and defenseless, a tragic figure who could benefit from a steady male influence, and he was irked to find himself wondering what it would be like to be the man who supplied it.

"May I be frank, Captain Odell?"

"No, you may not."

Once again, she blathered on without permission. "Mrs. Ford urged me not to mention it, but my father was Captain Harry Hamilton of the Forty-seventh Dragoons."

Tristan recalled a scandal that even he—being far out to sea and away from England—had heard about: a torrid affair, a duke's mistress, a duel in which the dashing Captain Hamilton had recklessly perished.

"If Harry Hamilton was your father, then you most especially would not be appropriate for this position. I wouldn't want you within a hundred yards of my ward."

"I'm twenty-four years old, Captain Odell. I have two sisters. Jane is eighteen, and Amelia is only twelve—the same age as Lady Rose. We're all alone in the world, and I can't provide for them. I need this job."

"I'm sorry, but no."

"I'll work for free, for a whole month. Give me a chance to prove myself."

"It wouldn't do any good."

"Weren't you in the navy when you were younger?"

"I was."

"Then I'm begging you, as a favor to my father, a fellow soldier who served his country honorably for decades. Help me save my sisters."

She reached out to him, trembling, beseeching him, and Tristan was too moved to reply. He simply shook his head.

To his horror, tears welled into her eyes, and he nearly leapt over the desk and shielded her face so he wouldn't see them.

Though he was a tough, swashbuckling sailor, he was a sap for a woman's tears, and he couldn't bear to know that she was so unhappy. Her woe made him want to assist her, to watch over and shelter her and her destitute siblings, and he bit down on all the comforting words that were fighting to burst out.

"Go now," he said very quietly.

Rudely, he grabbed a stack of correspondence and pretended to read it, effectively dismissing her.

He could sense her studying him, her probing attention wretched and intense.

Ultimately, she sighed and left, and he collapsed into his chair, feeling like a cad and a heel. He wasn't generally so callous, and he was chagrined that he'd been cruel to her, but London was a brutal place, and there were too many poverty-stricken females. He couldn't save any of them, and he wasn't about to try.

It dawned on him, though, that he could have slipped her a few pounds to ease her immediate plight.

Eager to catch up with her, he hurried out to the hall and proceeded to the foyer when—to his disgust—he ran into Michael and Miss Hamilton.

Michael's arm was around her waist, and she was pressed to the wall, much as Tristan had witnessed earlier with the housemaid Lydia.

So . . . Miss Hamilton was not only the daughter of a notorious scoundrel, but she was loose and indecent, too. Had she come specifically hoping to bump into Michael? He was definitely rich enough to solve her problems. Had seduction been her scheme all along?

"Michael!" he snapped. "Unhand her at once."

Michael chuckled and stepped away, while Miss Hamilton stumbled, struggling to right herself.

"She tells me," Michael said, "that you didn't feel she was suitable to be Rose's governess. She must be joking. *I* think she'd be spectacular."

Michael's naughty gaze roamed down her torso, and she blushed furiously.

"Weren't you going to your room?" Tristan asked him.

"Why yes, I was."

Michael strolled away, as Miss Hamilton peered at Tristan, her expression unreadable. He couldn't decide if she was embarrassed at being molested or at being discovered.

For the briefest moment, it looked as if she might explain or defend her behavior, but instead, she spun and stomped out.